an UNEQUAL harmony...

I0615846

an UNEQUAL
harmony...

... the discordant melodies of love, life and faith

SOUVIK GUPTA

Srishti
PUBLISHERS & DISTRIBUTORS

SRISHTI PUBLISHERS & DISTRIBUTORS
N-16, C. R. Park
New Delhi 110 019
editorial@srishtipublishers.com

First published by
Srishti Publishers & Distributors in 2013

Typeset by Eshu Graphic

Dedicated to
My Grandparents
(for lending an ear to every tale I narrated)

Acknowledgement

When a piece of art comes out, there is never just one person responsible for it. And when the first work releases, it needs a lot more support from others than possibly the work of a seasoned player. So, hereby I thank a whole lot of people who made this book happen by contributing in diverse ways.

Let me start by thanking the entire team at Srishti Publishers for believing in this book and rendering support at every stage. The editorial team did a fabulous job of in rectifying errors in the manuscript and giving valuable insights.

The next person who deserves the maximum acknowledgement and credit for the book is a dear friend who read a short story of mine and asked me to write a novel on the same. Well, he is also the one who designed the cover for the book. Dada (Soumen Dutta) – this book wouldn't have existed had it not been for that one comment you wrote on my blog saying "this short story needs justice as a novel".

There are two souls whom I have constantly badgered with my manuscript and pestered them to comment and criticise. They are always among the first people I send whenever I write something. Piu (Sanchari Chakraborty) and Mongo (Argha Narayan De) – I wonder if I would have been a writer without your support and encouragement.

Then, there are people without whom I would have been incomplete as a person – friends, motivators, guides – who render a meaning to my life by being present. Arka Sinha – you are my biggest confidant and I learn something from you every time we talk. Manoj Bharathi – I hate you immensely because you are the most unsocial person I know. But I cannot deny that you are a gem of a person and in some ways, my alter ego. What do I say about Praveen Dhawan and Saswat Kumar Sahu? Would I have been another aimless corporate guy had the two of you not urged me to follow my dreams? Absolutely! I don't know what makes the two of you believe in me so much, but I hope I live up to that faith. Nachiket Chitre – I got a friend in you when I needed one the most. You have been like a hero figure to me, someone I not just adore but look up to as well. If this book works, then my next book will be a tribute to the five of you – Arka, Manoj, PD, Sahu & NC.

"An Unequal Harmony..." is a piece of fiction but it is definitely coloured by the interaction with different women I encountered at different stages of my life. All of you have been so impactful and influential in my life that my perceptions and views have evolved because of you. Maybe this is not the platform to name everyone – but whether you taught me History or you were my team leader in a TV project, whether we were best friends who later fell in love or we chatted long hours on Google talk, whether you were a boss who scolded me on one hand and called me a kid on the other or you were a colleague whom I called 'Mummy', whether we constantly flirted during our MBA days or you held the camera for my short films – you all are brilliant. Reva is a bit of each one of you.

Of course, like every individual, I would be forever indebted to my entire family for the love and faith they have bestowed me with. Maa & Baba – for giving me everything that I needed, Papai Dada & Junnie Didi – for believing in me when few people did, Buai & Buamashai – for showering me with such warmth and love – I cannot ever thank you enough.

Last, but not the least, let me thank the three people who agreed to give their photographs to be used on the cover page and made it look attractive with their gorgeous faces on it. Tanya Chopra, Jitin Gulati & Aksshat (Raj) Saluja – I am so grateful.

Prologue

DAY 1
3:18 a.m.

She released the brake and gently pressed her stiletto on the accelerator. The speedometer moved from the 55 kmph mark to that of 70 as she firmly steered the black sedan through the dimly lit Worli Sea Face. The watch on her right arm showed the minute hand just overtaking the hour hand and moving towards four. The radio channel was playing one of her all time favourite songs – "Meri jaan… mujhe jaan na kaho meri jaan" – the legendary Geeta Dutt's last recorded song, picturised beautifully on the ethereal Tanuja and her father's favourite actor Sanjeev Kumar. The purple sari rolled down her arms as she pulled it over her shoulder, around the black blouse. Through the windshield, her eyes caught the deserted stretch of the Rajiv Gandhi Sea Link – lit up by fluorescent cable wires.

He was in the next seat, wearing a crimson shirt teamed with black trousers and black boots. There was something impregnable about the silence that had ruled their conversation through the last twelve hours, with unspoken pangs of grief relegated behind the facade of smiles. If only he didn't love her so much, maybe things would have been much simpler.

She downed the windows and a sudden gust of breeze filled the car. The day had been warm and the nation had been praying that, contrary to certain predictions, it wouldn't rain at the big event scheduled in a few hours' time.

'Eight years later, we are at the same spot,' one of the RJs said, *'will we repeat what we did eighteen years ago? Will Dhoni be the one to realise Sachin's incomplete dream?'*

She turned the headlights on full blast and ran her fingers fondly through his curly hair. *Such a baby,* she wanted to say but decided against it. He looked up, smiled affectionately, held her arm and turned around.

'Leave my hand,' she giggled like a teenager. He always brought out this aspect of hers. 'I am driving sweetheart.

'You can drive with one hand,' Siddharth cajoled, 'this is my side pillow now.'

She laughed out, when a sudden shriek caught them by surprise. Almost in a flash, four cars zoomed past them. Filled with youngsters hooting and cat-calling at the other cars, they relentlessly chased each other, neglectful of the speed limit.

'Bastards,' Siddharth spoke from the adjacent seat.

'Come on,' Reva hated curse words, 'they are young guys. They are entitled to this much fun.'

He shook his head and looked outside the window. Reva held the steering wheel and took a left turn as the car cruised up the incline of the Sea Link. The three and a half mile bridge looked resplendent in the series of lights as Siddharth gazed at the serene Arabian Sea, with its faint ripples illuminated by streaks of golden and blue. *It knows everything,* he felt, *the sea knows everything about all of us yet it is quiet. Is it a confidant or a secretive old man who doesn't share secrets with others? But then there are people who say that the sea returns everything – is it because the sea is vindictive or is it too generous to appropriate without donating in return?*

'Hey,' she looked at him, 'what are you thinking?' Reva softly touched his cheek.

She knew what he had been pondering over – for not just that day, but the previous few weeks as well. Both of them knew what his reply would be. In a way, it was good that she had broached the topic. *Some things have to come to an end,* he thought, *and maybe we should have thought of it earlier.* Maybe they had; maybe they were just too naive to prognosticate the implications of the very feeling that they had sequestered behind the walls of formalities and conventions; or maybe they had just feigned ignorance of the same, expecting the reality to never beckon them out of their reverie. He was about to respond when a crashing sound alarmed them.

Reva promptly grabbed the steering wheel – her fists clenching into the cover, her eyes dilating in shock. Trying to overtake a rival, one of the cars carrying the youngsters banged into the divider. The driver seemed desperately attempting to rein his car but the SUV spun at an indomitable speed across the lane, and suddenly a young girl was thrown out of the right rear door.

'Look out,' he shrieked.

But it was too late. Their car was barely 200 metres away and the girl was scarily close to the wheels. Reva knew that even if she were to pull the brakes, the car would stop only after running over the girl. With all her might, she swerved the car. Siddharth shot up and held the wheels with her, as the SX4 screeched across the breadth of the bridge and crashed into the left railing; not being able to control the motion, it toppled rightwards.

Reva's head struck the horn and the sound permeated through the silence of the night as Siddharth struggled to open the seatbelt and put his hand under her blood-soaked eyes.

***

DAY 1 –
10:05 a.m.

'Shucks', Anshuman frowned. His beard looked oddly unkempt. And one of the most important presentation of his advertising career was scheduled in less than an hour's time. His team had spent a sleepless week over this. Plus, the previous night, he had received the biggest offer of his life from one of the most sought-after celebrities in the country. Life was great, only if…

Even a stubble needs maintenance, he shook his head disapprovingly, *a scruffy look is never fashionable.* The overnight stay at office had left dark patches under his eyes, and his knee-long denim kurta was crumpled from the night on the couch. The light atop the mirror highlighted the contours of his face as Anshuman Mehra stood in the restroom and yawned. The cell phone display revealed meager battery backup, but no new calls or messages. He had a feeling she wouldn't call. He just knew.

The frigid water seemed to breeze in some energy into his skin as he stood by the large round glass basin and splashed it on his face. *It's going to work,* Anshuman assured himself, *you have come up with an idea they can't turn down.* A couple of knocks on the door alerted him. Sophie's alarm! He was taking too long. It was time to get ready for the meeting. But not before calling Reva…

The phone kept ringing. Anshuman looked at his watch as he opened the door and stepped into his cabin. *It is past ten and she is still asleep?*

*

At a posh nursing home in Bandra, Reva's mobile phone kept emanating an old romantic song – Lata Mangeshkar's "Aaj kal paon zameen par nahi padte mere". A woman in her early thirties, dressed in her service uniform, walked into the doctor's chamber and heard the phone ringing. She had joined the hospital just a few days ago; was barely a known face around. The job meant a lot to her and she knew that one wrong step would bring crashing down all those hopes that the new job had piled in her heart. But something in her said that she needed to take the call. The silvery Curve vibrated on the doctor's table as Mrs Gaitonde walked sceptically towards it and picked it up. 'Jaan' the name flashed on the screen.

She pressed the green button and held the phone to her ear. 'Hello.'

'Who is this?' Anshuman looked at his phone's display. He had not dialled a wrong number.

'Who are you, sir?' the lady questioned back.

'This is my wife's number,' Anshuman sounded confounded. 'Has she left it with you?'

'Well, no,' Mrs Gaitonde cleared her throat. 'I am Ms Reva's attendant at Apollo. She is admitted here, sir.'

'Now, who is that?' Anshuman chuckled. He was sure it was one of Reva's journalist friends playing a prank on him. 'It's not a very good joke.'

'No, sir,' Swarnalata said awkwardly. 'I am indeed her attendant.'

'Okay,' Anshuman sounded incredulous, 'then why didn't you call me if Reva is indeed admitted in your hospital? You have a patient and you didn't even bother to find who her relatives are?'

For a moment, the question unnerved Swarnalata. The man's words contravened all that she and her colleagues had assumed for the past few hours. If the caller was truthful, then the man they had addressed as the patient's spouse was an impostor. But then, Siddharth Kashyap had not even allowed anyone tend to his wounds before Reva was operated on. All the nurses had their hearts gone out for the injured man who loved his wife so deeply that even the sedatives couldn't bring sleep to his eyes before she recuperated. And now, the caller was saying that Siddharth Kashyap was never the husband. Indeed, the caller's name was stored as "Jaan" in the patient's cell phone. And she could make out from the caller's voice that he wasn't prevaricating. Swarnalata was stuck on the horn of a dilemma – whom could she believe, the man she had admired or the man she couldn't distrust?

'Actually,' Swarnalata Gaitonde swallowed and paused to prepare an answer, 'we thought we have her husband here.'

One

Anshuman Mehra

'"*Thanks*" isn't as simple a word as we make it out to be; in fact, it's a rather complicated one. We say it so many times every day that we finally lose contact with its essence. How many times do we feel that our lives would be incomplete without the person we are thanking? We are too busy, too self-occupied, too conscious, too vainglorious to accept that we all are incomplete beings and that only half of what we are, is actually because of us – the rest is the contribution of others.'

Dean Prabhakaran stood at the centre of dais, holding the microphone with his left hand. The blood red robe neatly draped over his corpulent frame, as he spoke to the graduating batch.

'Long journeys are always intimidating, because you stand a chance of losing your comfort zone. And when you commence the journey, sceptical of reaching the destination, you have had it.'

Except for a couple of yawns and few drowsy faces, the entire audience listened to the speaker with rapt attention as their chief mentor delivered the valedictory speech.

'When I joined this institute ten years ago, I was unsure in which direction it would take me. Leaving a comfortable job, joining the education industry, taking accountability of each department – there has been more than one occasion when I doubted my intentions and possibilities to succeed. And I truly believe that had it not been for you guys and your seniors, my stint wouldn't have been what it is today. So, on your graduation and my tenth anniversary in this institute, I would like to take the opportunity to share a bit of wisdom – three years late but better than never.'

The students broke into chuckles, and the concentration towards the speech increased.

'I have often found one common trait among many guys graduating from this institute – conceit. The vanity of being an alumnus of India's best creative institute often makes you overly indulgent with your own thought process. It's good to have your own views but let other ideas permeate as well. At times, it's better to keep the "I" away and let "We" play a bigger role. Just the way you enjoyed working with your friends on projects and presentations, you must show equal respect to your partner both in the boardroom and the bedroom.'

A murmur of appreciation waved through the hundred and fifty strong batch. A mention of bedroom always garnered more response than one of boardroom.

'Learn to accept when you are wrong and your colleague is right. And learn to apologise whenever your views don't match with your wife's.'

The murmur turned into a roar of laughter. Even the girls joined in.

'Well, I'm sure the three married guys in your batch will be able to tell you better – especially the one who got married in the midst of a semester!'

The Dean looked at Tirthankar Bhardwaj, one of the students of the batch, who had surprised everyone by announcing his wedding in the middle of a semester. The laughter continued along with some hoots from various corners of the room.

'But, above all, I want you guys to do one thing – go out there and kill the competition. Show everyone that you are the best.

Show the world that anyone who passes out from this institute is the best in the business. Make me proud, make your alma mater proud, make your family proud, and above all make yourself proud of your own achievements. My heartiest wishes are with all of you. Have a wonderful life!'

The hall erupted into thundering applause.

Anshuman Mehra sat in the second row, marking every word of his favourite professor. Anshuman was scheduled to join work in another fortnight, and there was something he surely wanted to do – be successful! Proving Papa wrong was vital; and more than Papa, it was his condescending attitude that Anshuman wanted to defeat. Half of this ambition had already been achieved – Anshuman had got through his dream company at the campus recruitment; and in two weeks, his life would change forever.

***

'So, you want to make ads and films?' his father looked at him.

'I am not going to direct ads or films,' Anshuman explained indifferently. 'I will be the creative brain behind it – the one who gives ideas.'

'How are you going to give ideas?' his father spoke in the archetypal patronising tone. 'What do you know about ads?'

'More than what you know about this home,' Anshuman shot back.

'Anshu...' Maa shrieked, 'is that the way to talk to Papa?'

Anshuman looked at his mother for a while, and stormed into his room.

'This is the kind of learning he has imbibed from you,' he could hear his father screaming at his mom.

He had grown up listening to all of this, being repeated over and over again. There was always a guideline set for him, a designated path he was supposed to traverse and make others happy. Hence it was expected of him to ace his class in school – and he reinstated the belief every time he emerged the valedictorian, almost nonpareil in competency in mathematics and science. And everyone in his or her palace of cards was happy until Anshuman decided to abjure the chance to complete M.Tech from IIT Kanpur and took up a course in Communications Management.

'He is academically inclined,' his father would infer. 'He isn't cut out for creative field.'

'Why don't you finish your M.Tech first and then do what you want?' his mother and some peace-loving relatives would intervene.

'And why am I supposed to do everything double?' He would shout back, 'just because I am good at it?'

'Your horoscope tells me clearly,' the response was anticipated. 'All astrologers have said the same. You are destined to be a hard-working official in a technical field and not in a creative one.'

'Oh really?' this explanation would unfailingly throw him off. 'I am supposed to be something because I was born at a wrong moment. What kind of explanation is that?'

'That is the truth destined for you,' his father would smirk. 'You accept it or take your life to the gutter.'

How could his father say that? Even if he didn't want to support his son, at least he could have refrained from demoralising him. He hated the comment; he hated the smile even more.

'So what does your horoscope say?' Anshuman would make his tone overtly sarcastic, 'That you are destined to be this "middle class loser government banker" all your life?'

'Anshu...' his mother would shout, as shocked relatives would insist he apologise.

'Had this been another nation,' a self-imposed advocate of Dad explained in a condescending tone, 'your father would have thrown you out of the house, because you are already eighteen.'

'Had this been another nation,' Anshuman shot back, 'my parents wouldn't have burdened me with their expectations as a return of the favour for bringing me to this world.'

'This isn't about the return of a favour,' his mother burst out emotionally. 'How could you make such a comment? We are saying all of this just because we want you to be happy; so that you don't have to go through a crisis like we had to.'

'I will be happy, Maa,' Anshuman threw his hands in the air to convince his mother. 'And I will be successful. All you've got to do is give me a chance and some time.'

After weeks of incessant debates and arguments, the senior Mehras finally yielded. And Anshuman joined his dream institute to pursue the course he had aspired for.

**

In another fifteen hours, the train was scheduled to leave for Mumbai.

Anshuman was busy checking his bags, matching the list to ensure he hadn't missed anything. The quarter dozen suitcases lay piled on one side of the floor while he scrutinised the contents of the kit bag. He always had a habit of carrying superfluous items, later blaming himself for all unwarranted luggage.

'Will you be able to carry all of this alone?' Maa spoke from behind and startled him.

Anshuman looked around and gathered himself.

'Who is going to help me?' he smiled sheepishly. 'It's okay. I will get a porter at the station.'

'How will you shift your entire luggage from the guest house?' Maa was concerned as always.

'Don't worry,' Anshuman gave his mother a half hug and went back to his bags, 'there will be a carrier.'

'I have something to give you,' Maa spoke in a sceptical tone making it evident that the "something" was related to his father.

She came forward, brought out an envelope from underneath her sari, and handed it over to him. Anshuman looked at it for a while and then took it. It had twenty-five hundred rupee notes folded together.

'I won't need so much money,' Anshuman defended his pride. 'The company is going to bear all my expenses till I get my first salary.'

'Still,' she tried to persist, 'your dad wants to ensure you don't have any problem.'

'Ask him to stop his charity in that case,' Anshuman turned back to put his loafers in the kit bag. 'I am already burdened by it, isn't it so?'

'Don't be cynical, Anshu,' Maa chided, 'and you two should not expect me to be the mediator all the time.'

'I don't expect that, Maa,' Anshuman didn't look back. 'You don't have to, as there's never going to be peace between that man and me.'

'Don't refer to him as "*that man*",' Maa shouted. 'He is your father.'

'Why are we having this discussion?' Anshuman finally turned back, 'I know he has done a lot for me. But he has never missed out on any opportunity to make that evident. And I can't spend my life feeling thankful to him.'

'You finally did what you wanted to,' Maa said as tears slowly streamed from her eyes. 'He couldn't stop you, could he?' She paused and added. 'You know what the problem is, Anshu? You two are too alike.'

'I am not,' Anshuman could feel the goose bumps on his feet as he turned around and zipped the bag. 'I am not. I am not.'

***

Mumbai was nothing like either Lucknow or Ahmadabad – the city where he had grown up or the city where he spent the most important years of his learning.

It was this vast ocean which gulped every little stream that flowed into it. And given the pace at which life worked here, one wouldn't realise how time flew by. Perhaps it had something to do with the sea breeze that armoured the denizens of the metropolis with such relentless vigour that they never seemed out of breath. Even at one in the night, a Mumbai road looked like an evening street of Lucknow. *Guess that has something to do with the size of their apartments,* Anshuman used to initially mock, *they are out on the streets because their homes are too small to live in.* The cramped apartments could make any resident of the Nawabi city claustrophobic. An entire flat in Mumbai had the same area as that of the Mehra backyard, and the price was five times higher than any apartment could ever fetch in his hometown. If that wasn't enough, all he could possibly eat on the streets were vada pav, pav bhaji or franky! To add to that, he had to waste two hours travelling everyday in packed trains and buses, which were perennially under terrorist threats.

But all these faded as problems as the days passed.

Slowly, Anshuman started falling in love with the city. *You can do what you want without any fear of prying eyes, earn enough to dance with unknown girls at posh discos, defy norms of living practices without having to hear about them, and above all – dream big!* He told himself that he couldn't have been in a better place. *After all, you are in the city of the Shah Rukh-s, the Sachin-s and the Ambani-s! Glamour, fun and money – Mumbai is the capital of all.*

**

'Welcome to the city that wakes up before it goes to sleep,' Bala Sir welcomed him on the first day of work. 'I hope you get accustomed to it sooner than to the work.'

Anshuman smiled. He was yet to know how apt Bala Sir was.

'You get everything here,' Bala gestured to him to sit, 'except time.'

'I was bored of excess leisure,' Anshuman replied confidently. 'Perhaps I will be able to compensate for it here.'

'I like that zest,' Bala nodded and offered his new protégé a cigarette.

'I don't smoke,' Anshuman shook his head.

'Can people be creative without cigarettes, alcohol and sex?' Bala laughed naughtily.

Anshuman felt embarrassed. 'I hope I don't need any of them to find my own sense of aesthetics.'

'I hope so too,' Bala pursed his lips in appreciation of the young man. 'There's a spark in you that I saw during the interview. I hope that doesn't fizzle out – not only for you, but also for the company and me. Our growth rates are all directly proportional.'

'It won't wither away, sir,' Anshuman sat up straight, 'especially with you around to guide me.'

'Welcome to the Genesis family,' Bala shook the hand of the management trainee.

Genesis had always been a dream for Anshuman and he utilised every bit of this opportunity to ensure the days were as beautiful as the dreams he saw every night. True to the prediction of Bala, Anshuman proved to be a gem – a solitaire which shone brighter with the friction of each passing day. Anshuman garnered the respect of his juniors, the trust of his clients and the dependence of his bosses. Within three years, he built a reputability for himself in the industry, something his bosses had acquired over a larger part of a decade. With a track record that left all his contemporaries envious, Anshuman scaled past them with such giant strides that the only comparison he faced was with the stalwarts of the profession. Everything Anshuman Mehra touched turned into gold. Rising from the post of an account manager to the creative head took him the least time in the history of the company. And when the Airfone campaign fell into his lap, things were only destined to get better.

Two

Present Time

DAY 1
11:56 a.m.

The conversation with the Apollo help-desk had only smoked up a cloud of questions.

'Is Reva admitted there?' he panted over the phone.

'I beg your pardon' the operator responded.

'I am sorry,' Anshuman felt inane for overreacting. 'Is Mrs Reva Mehra admitted in your hospital?'

'Give me a minute, sir,' the lady said.

After an almost unending minute, she came back on the line.

'We have Mrs. Reva Kashyap here,' she said. 'That's how her name has been registered, if both of them are same that is.'

They were the same. He knew it. It couldn't have been a coincidence with same name and phone number. But Kashyap? Someone had registered Reva in the hospital using a different surname. Who could that be? None of their common friends would do that. It must be one of her friends. But why would that person submit this name? And why did that friend not call him up, when her phone was working?

'Can you tell me what happened to her?' Anshuman felt a sudden debilitating pain in his legs.

'Sorry, Sir,' the lady explained, 'all I know is that she was in a car accident.'

The journey from his Goregaon office to Apollo had been the most disquieting hour of his life. Anshuman drove his silver German car, while his misty eyes looked out for explanations amidst the melee of the crowded city streets. He could see a host of hovering faces, each with its share of panic and exuberance but none with an answer to his queries. Anshuman felt stranded in the midst of a maze, blindfolded, without a helping hand to edify him. It was a jigsaw puzzle he wanted to solve but had no clue where to begin.

As the car pushed into the hospital parking lot, Anshuman could feel his feet tremble on the brake. Beleaguered by questions that shrouded everything he could see ahead, Anshuman sat within the car pondering over possibilities which could well profane the sanctity of his connubial life. As eagerly as he wanted to decrypt the mysteries, the fear of knowing something discomfiting started getting on his nerves. He scratched his nails on the steering wheel. Everything was in chaos. Who could that person be? And how did Reva have an accident? Anshuman wanted the answers, but what crippled him was the fear of uncovering a truth that could shatter the most precious part of his existence. Anshuman Mehra rested his head on the seat and exhaled.

**

'ICU on the fourth floor,' the representative at the enquiry-counter informed him.

Anshuman took the stairs. He needed to buy some more time. But tougher than anything he had presumed was walking up to the ICU. *What if I arrive and am told that Reva is dead?* Every time he wanted to speed up the stairs, the fear slackened him. When he finally reached, what awaited him was news better than he had anticipated.

Reva had survived the accident but wasn't fully fit.

'I want to go in,' Anshuman told the nurse. 'I need to see my wife.'

'I am sorry, Sir,' Swarnalata replied. 'I can't allow you without the doctor's permission.'

'Who is in charge of her?' Anshuman enquired.

***

Dr Fariza Ahmed, one of the leading neurosurgeons of Mumbai and the busiest at Apollo, sat at her office desk. Her pink salwar suit matched her fair complexion, while the pair of pearl ear-studs fitted as the only accessories. She was ostensibly a few years elder to Anshuman, but the glow on her face seemed to defy her age and the demands of her job.

'Come in,' Fariza replied with an inquisitive look on her face. Anshuman slid the door open.

'I am the husband of your patient,' Anshuman could see her frown. 'Reva is my wife.'

The room was deftly done, almost like any other hospital room, yet maintained a touch of differential elegance. A watercolour version of Albrecht Durer's self-portrait hung on one of the walls of the window-less chamber, the painting's dark colours contrasting the pallor of the walls. The wrought iron table lamp lit the stapled bunch of papers on her desk as she searched for some information on the internet.

'You are Reva Kashyap's husband?' she looked surprised.

'She is Mrs Reva Mehra,' Anshuman shook his head. 'She is not Kashyap. She was never Kashyap.'

Anshuman opened his wallet and passed it over the table. Dr Ahmed took it and saw the photograph under the transparent pocket. The man in it was sitting in front of her, and the woman was the one she had operated on just a while ago.

'Then... how come...?' Fariza could observe the same doubt in the man's eyes.

'I am not sure,' Anshuman answered, predicting the question in advance. 'Even I want the answer to the same question.'

Dr Ahmed handed over the wallet to him. Swarnalata had faintly mentioned about the phone call but she assumed that the novice was mistaken. As a doctor she had never been in a similar situation – absolutely clueless of what to say.

'I want to see her once,' Anshuman spoke feebly.

There was something about this man that made her trust him. Perhaps, there was some other reason behind the faith, but all of it only worked in favour of Anshuman.

'Fine,' the doctor sighed and got up. 'But if she is your wife, you have to be strong. She may not look the way you would expect her to.'

Almost immediately at the remark, the ad-man could feel his eyes well up. It was tough for him to visualise Reva in any way other than her gorgeous self.

**

Today, she looked awfully different.

Leaving his shoes behind, Anshuman Mehra tiptoed into the ICU with Dr Ahmed by his side. When he finally saw Reva, a mixed reaction of horror, shock and relief rushed through his veins. He knew he should have expected this but couldn't come to terms with it at that moment. Reva's face was wrapped with a thick white bandage, her left cheek blotted by a pad of wool and her body covered by a spotless white cloth. Her hair was rolled into a cap, while her right arm rested by her side, attached to a host of syringes and wires. She lay pseudo-lifeless and her breathing was barely palpable. For a while, the only sounds audible in the unit were that of the breathing of the three onlookers and of the cardiac machine showing that the patient was still alive.

'Can you put some balm on her lips?' Anshuman could hear himself say.

Reva's lips were chapped, while her closed eyes looked dull, not bordered by kohl as she always preferred them to be.

Fariza looked at the patient and smiled faintly.

'On the outer border,' Anshuman insisted. 'She looks too morbid like this.'

'I said you should get a grip over yourself,' Dr Ahmed looked straight at him. 'You cannot expect her to look lively. She is in the ICU.'

Anshuman breathed heavily, while the nurse, Mrs Gaitonde, wiped a teardrop rolling down her cheek.

'Actually, I can't remember a moment when she didn't look vibrant,' he suppressed the pain in his voice and looked at the doctor. 'She has always looked pretty, ever since the first day I saw her.'

Three

Anshuman Meets Reva

The drenched July winds splashed against the sliding window of the fifteenth floor apartment. Anshuman had been living in the rented Thakur Village flat for the last three and a half years. He unlatched the lock of the twelve feet wide glass pane and pushed it open, and in a moment the rain soaked his face and the turquoise-blue knee-long kurta. Anshuman stood there, savouring the whisky and the rain. Mumbai had made him fall in love with the monsoons.

The next day could very well prove to be the biggest turning point of his professional life. Airfone's "Pigeon Campaign" was due for release in less than 24 hours. The response so far had been exhilarating.

'We are spending a fortune on this campaign,' the VAS Manager of Airfone had confided in him, 'and if this falls flat, I'm dead.' Anshuman sipped the masala tea and looked at his biggest client. 'Losing my job will just be a formality,' Banerjee laughed.

The glass filled with a large peg of bourbon clinked with the sounds of ice cubes. From somewhere in the giant hall of his flat, Kishore Kumar sang one of his most cherished tracks – "Badi sooni sooni hai, zindagi ae zindagi". Anshuman's relationship with his parents had ameliorated over the last few years but not to the state where he could divulge his insecurities and anxieties to

14

them. After all, despite the alternate day calls, he had continually turned down Maa's requests to come home. It took Gayatri Mehra a year to realise that her son didn't intend to return to her house, and soon she stopped pestering him, consoled by the fact that at least Anshuman responded to her phone calls and even called her voluntarily on Sundays. Anshuman, on his behalf, had suggested that his mother should visit him once in Mumbai and had even offered to send flight tickets, but the plan never got materialised. In his own discreet manner, Anshuman had made the offer only to his mother and Gayatri Mehra knew that she couldn't leave her husband behind.

The room was getting cooler in the rains when the doorbell rang and shook him out of the reverie. He turned to look at the clock. *11:30,* he thought to himself, *who's here so late?*

Anshuman traipsed towards the door, his legs swaying in casual non-liner motion, the ice cubes tinkling against the glass. He turned the lock and pulled open the door. The late night visitor was someone who appeared even more worried than the host. Shubhanshu Banerjee stood at the door, smiling sheepishly at his friend cum business associate.

'Hey, Banerjee,' Anshuman sounded pleasantly surprised. 'Come in.'

Around five inches shorter than his 6'1" friend, Shubhanshu looked weary in a white kurta-pyjama set and black thick-rimmed glasses. He was around a decade older than Anshuman, but looked even older in his attire.

'You look like you've just jumped out of bed and standing at my door,' Anshuman grinned.

'That sounds real horny, AM,' Shubhanshu stepped in.

Anshuman laughed out. 'I have no interest in men nine years elder to me,' Anshuman moved aside to let his guest come in. 'Look at you! You look like a grandfather.'

'Don't be under the illusion that you are going to escape getting old,' Shubhanshu fell on the bean bag. 'By the way, I hope I didn't disturb you.'

'Thanks for asking,' Anshuman closed the door and moved back towards the drawing room. 'No, you only ended my loneliness.'

'So that's good or bad?' Shubhanshu looked at him.

'Very good,' Anshuman confirmed and sat down on the sofa. 'I am tired of it now. Solitude seems good at times but not always, definitely not before a big day.'

'It will be fine,' Banerjee smiled. 'The reviews have been pretty positive till now. The response is going to be good.'

'Hope so,' Anshuman exhaled. 'Oh, what would you like to drink?'

'Nothing,' the visitor sat up. 'Pass me a cigarette.'

'So, what brings you here?' Anshuman passed the cigarette case. 'Don't tell me it's pre-release jitters!'

Shubhanshu lit the cigarette and inhaled deeply.

'No,' he shook his head and let out a whirl of smoke. 'I just wanted to be away from home for some time. Just the way you hate your loneliness, I detest the silence at home.'

Anshuman nodded. He knew what Banerjee meant.

'It has been around three years since we have stopped talking,' Shubhanshu rested his head on the bag and continued, 'three bloody long years. For the first couple of years, it was like *"Dinner's ready"* or *"I am off to work"* or perhaps *"There's a call for you."* But all of that has stopped. And now the medium is either a servant or an sms. People think we are a happy couple who don't fight or quarrel. What they don't realise is that we don't even speak to each other, so there isn't much scope to quarrel.'

Anshuman looked at his guest intently. He realised that Shubhanshu must have had a bad day at home. There was a hint of suppressed anguish, mixed with ineffable complaint.

'I dread being home on weekends,' Shubhanshu went on. 'I dread being at home actually. Our family has stopped residing there, overtaken by silence which stays throughout the day, only to increase when we return in the evening.'

'Leave it,' Anshuman interrupted, hearing a sob. 'Just take it slowly. Time heals everything.'

'We have used up all our time, young man,' Shubhanshu tried to hit a jovial tone, 'and haven't gotten anywhere.'

'Hmm...' Anshuman emptied his glass and got up. 'I need another drink now.'

'What you need now, AM,' Shubhanshu became his usual self and looked at his host as the latter moved towards the bar, 'is a girl. Drinking alone in a deserted flat on a rainy night isn't going to help your case.'

'How come a Bong is telling me to get married?' Anshuman poured another peg of the bourbon in his glass. 'Don't you guys marry later than anyone else in India?'

'Stop pretending to be that young, dude,' Shubhanshu sat up. 'You are 28. That's a decent age to get married.'

'Get me a sexy Bengali lass,' Anshuman smiled and walked back to the sofa, 'like Bipasha or Koena.'

'You are neither John nor Fardeen,' Shubhanshu winked. 'So, be modest and don't dream beyond what you are worth.'

Anshuman laughed out.

For an hour, the two men chatted about their personal lives and their dream campaign for which they had poured their hearts out. It was around two hours past midnight when they decided to call it a night.

'I have to drive back all the way to Santacruz,' Shubhanshu stood up, held his waist arched backwards. 'Got to be back now. Monday blues start in eight hours.'

'Drive safely,' Anshuman followed Banerjee to the door. 'Now that you are sure your job is safe.'

Shubhanshu chuckled.

'Yeah,' he stepped outside the door and looked back. 'Best wishes to us.'

Anshuman nodded and raised his glass. 'Cheers.'

***

Chand Pias became a national singing sensation almost overnight. Airfone's Pigeon campaign better known as "Kabootar Line Maare" turned into a rage, and Chand's song of the same title was on everyone's lips. The man behind the success was basking in the glory, loving every bit of the attention. But the sudden importance also brought in attention and intrusion, which got increasingly officious to handle.

'Is this Mr Anshuman Mehra?' the lady on the phone asked.

Anshuman rummaged through the papers on his desk, searching for an invoice from one of his vendors. He looked around, dressed in a white linen shirt and denims, while the loudspeaker emanated the lady's voice.

'Are you sure of the number you have dialled?' Anshuman said disgruntled.

'Yeah...' the woman said confused.

'Then, it has to be me,' Anshuman's disgust echoed clearly in his voice, 'isn't it?'

'Did I call you at an inopportune time?' the woman sounded apologetic.

Anshuman finally came across the sheet bundled within a wrong folder.

'I am sorry,' he realised the unwarranted impertinence. 'The overdose of work is really getting on my nerves.'

'I understand,' a chuckle was audible on the other end. 'By the way, I am Reva Gokhale from Daily Times.'

'Okay,' Anshuman handed over the paper to the peon and signalled him to photocopy it. 'So, you want another interview?'

'Yeah,' Reva Gokhale laughed out, 'I do want an interview. But you can trust me on the fact that it will be different. I am not going to focus on your "Kabootar Line Maare" campaign.'

'Hmm,' Anshuman pondered, 'then what are you interested in?'

'I am interested in you,' Reva said and corrected herself instantly, 'I mean... umm... my interview will be focused on you rather than your work.'

'Okay,' Anshuman cleared his throat. 'Sounds interesting!'

'So, when shall it be?' the journalist stepped into the next gear. 'Can we schedule it for the first half tomorrow?'

'Not tomorrow,' Anshuman almost exhaled in shock. 'Tomorrow is Wednesday, right? Make it Friday, five in the evening.'

'Friday?' Reva sighed, 'Okay.'

'Thanks,' Anshuman smiled, 'I've got to push off now. Just send me a reminder two hours before the scheduled time.'

'Perfect,' Reva replied. 'Take care, Mr Mehra. See you on Friday.'

'You too...' Anshuman disconnected the line.

**

Chand strummed the guitar and smoked a joint stuffed with an ample dose of marijuana and a comparably insubstantial amount of tobacco. Even at twenty four, the popular jingle composer and singer loved the collegiate hippie look with his thick curly hair, long goatee and funky attire. He wore a deep v-necked magenta t-shirt paired with dark blue jeans, accessorized by a giant thumb ring and a big golden cross hanging from his neck.

'You should make a Hindi masala movie, dude,' Chand let out a cloud of smoke. 'How did you ever guess this tune would be a hit?'

Anshuman winked at him through his rimless glasses. He was dressed in a white self-embroidered kurta and blue jeans – the quintessential "Anshuman" attire. The watch with his initials emblazoned shone on his wrist, as he responded to one of the mails on his laptop.

'I might make a masala movie one day,' the ad-man grinned. 'But you'll make your Bollywood debut much before that.'

'Really?' Chand seemed pleasantly surprised by the prediction. 'Let's hope so. But my voice won't suit the trademark romantic songs. It's too raspy for that.'

'There's always scope for something unique,' Anshuman assured, 'and raspy...'

The landline telephone rang and interrupted the conversation.

'Excuse me,' Anshuman pressed the loudspeaker button. 'Yes?'

'There's a journalist to meet you, Sir,' the receptionist said, 'Ms Reva Gokhale from Daily Times.'

'Yes, yes. Send her in two minutes.'

'Coolio,' Chand picked his cue and packed his guitar. 'You carry on with your interview with Ms Gokhale; I'll catch up later.'

'Wait, wait,' Anshuman pressed the "Send/Receive" button on Outlook Express to ensure his mail was delivered. 'Let me introduce the both of you; not that I know her myself.'

'Are you nuts?' Chand laughed. 'Why will she meet me?'

A knock on the door caught their attention as the door slid open and a lady peeped in.

'Please come in,' Anshuman called out from his seat

The door parted open and he saw her for the first time.

She was fair and slim, around 5'4" tall, wearing a glossy ocean-blue kurti with white pyjamas crumpled near the ankle, white stilettos and a silver anklet adorning her right leg. She wore matching blue and white oversized earrings that sneaked through her permed hair; her face was minimally made up with a glossy natural shaded lipstick and a single line of kohl outlining her dark brown eyes. Holding a white self-designed leather purse in her left hand along with a mobile phone, she extended her right arm towards the interviewee.

'Reva Gokhale,' the journalist spoke.

'Aaaaa... Anshuman Mehra,' he shook her hand.

'Yeah,' she smiled awkwardly, 'of course!'

Anshuman looked at Chand and introduced the guest to him.

'This is Chand Pias,' he spoke, 'the man who made our campaign a sensation.'

'Oh, really?' Reva moved ahead and gave her hand. 'You are on almost everyone's cell phone these days – half the junta I call seem to have the same caller tune.'

The singer blushed and shook the journalist's hand. 'Thanks,' Chand looked up at Anshuman. 'It's all because of this man.'

'How did you find each other?' Reva looked at them. 'I don't know if that's the right way of putting it.'

The men chuckled.

'He approached me after watching a performance of mine at Pop,' Chand narrated. 'I was sceptical but he thought it would work. And the rest is history.'

'And history it has made,' Reva spoke jubilantly. 'Awesome! It's a pity people don't appreciate singers in our country until they sing for Bollywood or as they say – the Indian Film Industry.'

Chand pursed his lips and nodded at the statement. 'I gotta go now,' he tugged at the guitar-case and hung it on the right shoulder. 'You guys carry on with the interview. See you later.'

'Sure,' Reva spoke as Chand made his way out of the room.

'Excuse me for a minute,' Anshuman looked at Reva, 'I'll be right back.'

'Absolutely,' she sat on the sofa, 'no problem.'

Anshuman followed Chand out of the room to see him off.

'Think of a song for that chocolate thing,' he patted the singer's back. 'See you next week then. You have more time than you possibly require.'

'Yes, boss,' Chand winked as they shook hands, 'but control your emotions inside the room.'

'What?' the remark caught Anshuman off guard.

'Control your eyes,' Chand smiled impishly, 'or else she'll see right through them.'

***

'So, you believe in the adage that the consumer is your wife and not a moron,' Reva pressed the record button on her dictaphone and put forward the first question of the interview, 'or you make independent rules for yourself?'

'Aahh...' Anshuman moved back on the sofa, 'actually I have seen my dad fooling my mom for quite some time. Not that he cheated on her or something, but he had perennially kept her under the illusion that we were perfectly happy, which was never the scenario.'

Reva listened to the answer keenly.

'But somehow Maa could never sense a way out for herself,' Anshuman went on. 'Perhaps she had become addicted to the 1000 square feet of security. She was too fettered to nurture an independent goal and realise that a perfect life means much more than a home and a family. So the "wife" adage doesn't really work for me.'

'More than concern for society or security at home,' Reva pointed out after her interviewee was done with his take, 'it's the fear of being alone. We all are so afraid of being alone, aren't we? And perhaps it's this fear, which makes us sceptical of changing the existing. Status quo – isn't that what we all want?'

'Perhaps,' Anshuman replied absent-mindedly as his mind raced with a new set of questions wondering whether his mother had given up on everything for the security as he had surmised or the yearning for status quo as the journalist opined. 'So I would rather say the consumer is your child whom you can't fool because he has the same DNA,' Anshuman lit a cigarette.

'You mince your words well,' she smiled in appreciation.

'That's what we are paid for, ma'am,' he smirked. 'You do it through columns and I through ads. Our media are different but the objective is same.'

Reva smiled and nodded.

'So, how did advertising happen to you?' she shot her next question. 'Did you kind of always know it was your calling?'

'Not at all,' the response was contrary to what she had expected. 'I was pursuing engineering at NIT Surat when I realised my calling was elsewhere. I got a chance to complete my masters from IIT Kanpur but decided against it. From there on, a long journey started and it is going on till date. Convincing my folks that I want to pursue something which they had never even considered as an option was tough. But I guess I was too stubborn to relinquish my dreams.'

The interview carried on for a couple of hours. They went on chatting and laughing at each other's comments. Mutual respect grew as they discovered the other's knowledge about their professions. She knew Piyush Pandey's works and how Prasoon Joshi fared in comparison. He knew why Prannoy Roy was still such a big name in the world of news.

'Last question,' Reva ticked off the last point from her planner. 'Is it true that every creative man has a muse? Let us know who inspires Anshuman Mehra!'

'I don't have a muse yet,' Anshuman pursed his lips. 'Guess that's why I am making ads on pigeons.'

Reva laughed out aloud. Anshuman joined her.

'My client Shubhanshu Banerjee says I should now get a girl for myself,' Anshuman remarked. 'He says that at 28, I am already running behind time.'

'Trust me you're not,' Reva assured.

Anshuman looked outwards, almost as a futile attempt to dissemble the uncharacteristic blush on his cheeks. It was getting darker yet not dark enough for the busy city. The watch showed ten minutes past seven as he stole a glance at it.

'I have taken a lot of time off your schedule,' Reva exhaled and closed the diary. 'Thank you so much! Rarely do I get a chance of having such a discussion and not a mundane question-answer session. I hope you enjoyed it as much as I did.'

'A bit more than that,' Anshuman blinked.

'Take care, Mr Mehra,' Reva stood up.

'Anshuman.'

She smiled, 'Reva.' She turned around and went off towards the cabin door. For a moment, he pondered and just as she was about to exit, he called out to her.

'Reva.'

'Yes?' she turned back.

'Will you meet me tomorrow, Leopold, 8 p.m.?'

They met the next evening. And two years later, Reva became *Mrs Reva Anshuman Mehra.*

Four

Present Time

DAY 1
1:55 p.m.

The injuries were serious and an internal haemorrhage was gradually pushing Reva into a state of non-recovery. *She could slip into a coma any moment*, the doctor informed Anshuman, *I am surprised that she hasn't. She must be a really strong woman.*

He agreed. He had always found something very strong about her mind – ever since they met for the first time during the interview. He was besotted with her intelligence and charm, and despite their differences, he had never failed in appreciating her wit or stopped being in awe of her persona.

Dr Fariza Ahmed handed a glass of water to Anshuman.

'Get your friends over here if you can,' Dr Ahmed suggested, 'the longer you stay alone, the more will the pain invigorate.'

'I can't share my grief with everyone,' Anshuman shook his head. 'I have always been like this. An introvert!'

'In that case,' Dr Ahmed cleared her throat, 'get someone from your family out here.'

'Can you tell me how this happened?' Anshuman looked at the doctor curiously. 'How did Reva meet with the accident?'

'I think the details are with the sub-inspector, who made the report,' Dr Ahmed frowned. 'Let me check.'

She leaned over and dialled the extension on the intercom.

'Ask Lata to bring a copy of the police report,' she paused. 'Yeah, yeah, the accident patient... Mrs Kashyap.'

Anshuman looked up at her. He realised that was Reva's identity in the hospital even now.

'I am sorry we have to address her by that name,' Dr Ahmed said to Anshuman. 'It would be great if you could provide any identity proof of hers. Mrs Gaitonde will bring the police report.'

Anshuman sat in the doctor's chamber as Reva's personal attendant appeared, carrying the police report. It was issued by a Sub Inspector Mane. The hospital form was countersigned by S. Kashyap, with a tick on 'spouse' as the form of relation. The report mentioned that the victim was driving a black SX4 on the Bandra-Worli Sea Link around half past three the very morning, and had hit the railing in an attempt to save a young girl.

'This isn't making any sense to me,' Anshuman looked at the doctor. 'Reva was driving a black SX4 on the Sea Link? That's not possible. We don't own such a car. How could she be driving one, that too at 3:30 in the morning?'

'That was the information we were given,' the doctor pursed her lips. 'I think only Mr Kashyap will be able to furnish the details.'

'Who is he?' Anshuman nodded in recognition of the name from the report.

'We have no idea,' Fariza shook her head. 'Actually he was the one who brought her to the hospital. Haven't you heard of him ever?'

Anshuman shook his head sceptically.

'S. Kashyap,' Anshuman pondered. 'I don't know of anyone by that name; he might be her friend. I don't know all of them. But....' Anshuman looked at the report again, 'He signed as her husband.'

'I shouldn't be saying this,' the doctor cleared her throat. 'But people at times do so to avoid further complications or delay before an operation.'

Anshuman nodded acceptingly. He knew she was right.

'But how does he know her?' the question still haunted him. 'And why didn't he call me after getting her admitted? Can you keep this discreet till I meet the man?'

'Sure,' the doctor nodded.

'Where is he?'

'Room number 305,' the doctor said. 'Let me take you.'

'Is he also admitted here?' Anshuman sounded surprised.

'Yeah,' Dr Ahmed spoke in a matter-of-fact tone. 'He was with her in the car. His injuries are less severe, but he has fractured his right arm and has a couple of stitches on the forehead.'

'He was with her in the car!' the growing suspicion was evident in Anshuman's voice.

'The car belongs to him,' Dr Ahmed informed.

'It is his car,' Anshuman could feel his entire body enervated at the thought of the impending revelation, 'and she was driving it at 3 a.m.'

'All your answers are with him,' Fariza Ahmed seemed as worried as Anshuman.

'I want to meet him alone,' Anshuman stood up.

***

Anshuman walked out of the doctor's chamber. In hasty steps, he moved down the stairs to the third floor. *Take a right once you reach third floor,* Dr Ahmed's instruction reverberated in his ears, *and you will find the room on the second to your left.* Room 305. He pushed open the door and saw a young man lying on the bed. A nurse was changing the bandage on the man's head as Anshuman stepped inside. The man seemed to be in his late twenties and was of the same height as him. But the man was fairer and could boast of a physical structure Anshuman never could. *He is younger than we are*, Anshuman told himself, *Reva and he cannot be friends.* There were minor injuries beneath the man's eye while the plastered right arm hung from the neck and rested on his abdomen.

'Mr Kashyap,' Anshuman called him.

The nurse turned around and saw the intruder in the room.

'Excuse me,' she frowned, 'you are not supposed to be here.'

'I want to meet Mr Kashyap,' Anshuman spoke. 'I know he is unwell. I just want to speak to him for a moment.'

The patient looked up drowsily. He had seen the man standing in his room. They hadn't been introduced formally, but he had seen his picture on more than one occasion and heard about him almost every day.

'Please wait for the visiting hours,' the nurse sounded disgruntled.

'It's alright,' Siddharth spoke and tried to get up.

'Please, sir,' the nurse spoke alarmed. 'You are still under the effect of tranquilisers.'

'Roll up my bed,' her patient instructed. 'I need to talk to him.'

The nurse thought of declining the offer but the patient seemed resolute. She put her arm on the lever and rolled up the bed.

'Please excuse us, sister,' Kashyap spoke. 'Our conversation is personal.'

Anshuman realised that the man had identified him. But how did he do that? Anshuman had never heard of him, leave alone meeting him, and this man seemed perfectly cognizant of his identity and purpose of visit. He had even read what Anshuman was going through.

Our conversation is personal, the suspicion grew every moment, *is he really who I think he is?*

The nurse walked out of the room.

'Are you alright?' Anshuman moved towards the bed.

'Better,' the man smiled, waiting for the other to continue.

'I didn't get your full name,' Anshuman looked at him.

'Siddharth,' the man answered. 'Siddharth Kashyap.'

'I am her husband,' confidence was slowly oozing out of Anshuman's voice.

'Anshuman Mehra,' Siddharth said. 'I know.'

'You know me?' Anshuman sounded curious.

'Yes, of course,' Siddharth nodded pragmatically.

'Then why did you register her by the name of Reva Kashyap,' the inquisitiveness was now getting the better of Anshuman. 'The doctor told me it could be because you wanted to save time for the operation, but I want to know it from you.'

'That was a reason but not the main one,' the man smirked at him.

'Then?'

'Because that's what I think of her,' Siddharth tried to sit up. 'That's what she means to me.'

'I don't get you,' Anshuman shook his head at the indistinct response. 'How do you know her? How do you know each other?'

Siddharth looked straight into Anshuman's eyes, unapologetically and unabashedly.

'Reva and I are in love.'

Five

Siddharth Kashyap

The morning rays had just dawned on Mumbai as the Aravali Express stopped at the Chhatrapati Shivaji Terminus. Two nights in the cramped second-class compartment had left Siddharth dreary, when he finally stepped down on the platform with a rucksack and a suitcase. A porter approached him and tugged at his suitcase. Almost alarmed at the uncalled help, Siddharth looked up.

'What?'

'Tell me where you want to go,' the porter grinned. 'You won't be able to carry it alone.'

'Will you do it for free?' Siddharth spoke sarcastically. 'I don't have money to pay you.'

'Free?' the porter dropped the suitcase. 'You came to a new city without money.'

'I said I don't have money to pay you,' Siddharth raised the handle of the suitcase and pulled it behind. 'There are few things I can afford to spend money on now.' The second part of the sentence was almost inaudible as it was directed more at himself than at the stranger.

Fashion Street hadn't started its busy schedule when Siddharth walked along it towards Churchgate Railway Station. Often a taxi slowed by his side to see if he was interested in a ride. The thirty minute walk told Siddharth that his next days would be a far cry from the undemanding flippant days of Ajmer, his hometown, which had everything for himself except opportunities to pursue his dream – photography.

**

'What if you get lost in such a big city?' his mother had feared. She had never been out of the town. Her fears were way different from those of her husband's.

'He is too old to get lost,' Siddharth's father chided his ignorant wife. 'My fear is how he will make a living.'

Siddharth's mother held the end of her pallu by her face and looked at the two men. She knew she would never be able to suggest things her husband could. She was illiterate, backward, and all she knew was managing the household – which she hardly considered as portentous as her husband's job. He knew the world.

'Mumbai is a costly place,' the 49-year old man smoked the hookah and looked at his son. 'We don't have enough money to support you for long.'

Siddharth knew his father's fears were well-founded. All his life, Shankarlal Kashyap had been in Rajasthan. His honesty had garnered a lot of respect but failed to bring in the money. And Mumbai was indeed far more expensive than his town.

'I will manage, Bapusa,' Siddharth sat at his father's feet and held his knees. 'You don't need to worry. There are a lot of jobs in Mumbai. I am a graduate and good-looking, I will surely get something. All I need from you and Maasa are your blessings.'

'That's always there with you,' the senior Kashyap placed his right hand on his son's head. 'Your mother and I never had a second child because we wanted to get the best for you. We might not be rich but we tried earnestly and you have been brought up in the finest of ways. What makes me scared now is whether you will be able to adjust to a place where almost everyone is better off than you.'

'That won't be for long,' Siddharth promised his father. 'I will soon be as affluent as the others.'

For all he knew, he had to keep this promise.

**

The Churchgate-Virar local dropped him off at Mira Road. As instructed by Mrs Patil over the phone, Siddharth took a rickshaw and reached his destination.

Mrs Patil, the owner of the paying guest facility, welcomed the new guest with her special cardamom tea and laid down all the guidelines in front of him.

'Don't bring non-veg food, alcohol and girls into my house,' she spoke candidly. 'With your looks you will get the fast Mumbai girls pretty soon but don't you dare bring them here.'

'I am not fast myself,' Siddharth said sheepishly and his landlady laughed contentedly.

'You will have another guy sharing the room with you,' Mrs Patil spoke as they walked towards Siddharth's first abode in the new city. 'He is a bit weird but overall a nice chap. He might bore you with his music at times but sings well. If you don't like him, just tell him to stay away and he won't trouble you. He is a nice guy, I already said right?'

Siddharth nodded. 'Yes, ma'am.'

'Call me Patil aunty,' the lady corrected as they climbed the broken staircase and turned into the thin corridor that took them towards Siddharth's room. 'That's what everyone calls me here. I have been running this place for twenty years now.'

Siddharth looked around as they walked through the aisle, bordered by a decrepit iron railing and hanging pots containing wild flowers and creepers. As he stood there, Siddharth saw a muddy field that stretched around the corner of the lane on which Mrs Patil's house stood. A host of young kids had gathered in the ground to play football. For a moment, Siddharth felt a pang in his heart as he realised that he would never go back to the same old days where every evening meant a raucous get-together of friends and fighting over goals or wickets.

'The way I have handled this business is atypical of Marathi women of our neighbourhood. People here call me Patil Aunty PG Waali!' Mrs Patil laughed and blabbered on. 'Even my husband calls me aunty at times. Worthless fellow doesn't do anything but drinks like a fish every night and falls asleep with his dhoti undone.'

Siddharth let the last statement pass without commenting, very much like the others, as Mrs Patil knocked on a door.

'These guys, I tell you,' she banged at it again and looked at Siddharth. 'They have forgotten that getting up early is good for health. Everyone seems to be nocturnal these days. What all do you guys do so late? Don't tell me, I know what you do!'

Siddharth smiled at the statement. He found it wiser not to say that he was a late riser himself. After a couple of loud knocks, a young guy opened the door. His long curly hair was ruffled; he had a Hindu mythological tattoo on his throat which had a cross hanging from it. He wore more ornaments than most women Siddharth had seen in his town. The guy looked at both the visitors drowsily and let out a giant yawn.

'This is your new room-mate,' Mrs Patil moved past the guy into the room and signalled at Siddharth. 'He has come from Ajmer and is not interested in music.'

'I don't have a problem with music,' Siddharth chuckled. 'I am horrible at it myself though.'

'Cool,' the guy gave his hand.

Siddharth shook it, 'I am Siddharth Kashyap.'

The guy nodded and smiled, 'Chand Pias.'

***

The offer from the call centre came within a week. But the daily exertion and low salary left with neither time nor enough money.

His passion was reduced to safeguarding the DSLR camera his father had bought for him a day before he left from Ajmer. On his weekly days off, Siddharth wandered into the neighbourhood to take photographs. Often a perfect picture would take hours – *I have to wait for the right moment for the expression I want,* he would tell himself. And when he was impressed with any of them, he showed it to Chand who always heaped him with plaudits.

Friday nights were scheduled for party in the guest house - when Mrs Patil would travel to Nerul to stay with her sister, and both alcohol and non-veg would find their way into the room. Often Mr Patil would join the younger men and entertain them with his amusing anecdotes and views of life.

'A house runs best when the woman is strong,' he guzzled the entire drink in one go and shook his head with pleasure. 'Men need strength in only one part of their body.'

As much as Siddharth hated Mr Patil for his laziness and ludicrous jokes, he liked the man for honest confessions about his failures and dependence on his wife.

'I like this man, you know,' Siddharth said as they lay on the roof. 'He can dare to laugh at himself.'

'That's because he has made a laughing stock of himself,' Chand never cared for the fact that the man was their landlord or he was sleeping around five metres away. 'You gotta be successful man. There isn't any alternative to success. Hardly anything in this world is more fulfilling than living your own dream.'

'And what's your dream?' Siddharth turned and rested his body on the elbow.

'I can visualise myself playing in "Pop on the Rocks",' Chand stood up. 'It's heaven man. It's the best place in the country for a live performance.'

'And I want to capture the best faces of the country,' Siddharth lay on his back and looked at his friend, 'the most popular models and the biggest stars. Show them and the world that few people know the art of presenting a face the way Siddharth Kashyap can.'

'With your looks, man,' Chand smiled, 'you should be a model. Look at yourself. You are above six feet tall, you have a sculpted physique, you're fair and have firm jaw lines – you will burn the ramp.'

'I am more comfortable behind the camera,' Siddharth got up and pushed his body backwards to the low boundary wall of the roof, 'than in front of it.'

'Can I tell you something, Sid,' Chand spoke almost spontaneously as Siddharth turned, with his back facing Chand and legs swaying over the boundary wall. 'Can you promise me you won't start judging me because of it?'

'What?' Siddharth looked back and smiled. 'You are gay?'

Chand saw the grin on Siddharth's face and realised he was joking. He walked up hastily to Siddharth and sat down beside him on the parapet.

'No, I'm not,' Chand spoke and turned to check if Mr Patil was still asleep, 'but I am bisexual.'

Siddharth laughed casually but the expression on Chand's face said that he did not say it in jest. Siddharth's smile faded away and he looked at Chand with a confounded frown.

'Are you serious?' Siddharth looked suspiciously. 'Why are you telling me this? You don't fancy me, do you?'

'No, not at all,' Chand spoke in alarm. 'You're not my type. But I needed to tell somebody. It's tough to keep it within, man. And you are my best friend. I thought you would understand. I do feel attracted towards some guys. But obviously I will not feel whole and complete with every man I meet on all levels of my physical and spiritual being, the way you wouldn't choose just about any girl and hope to be happy with her. But thankfully, I find women attractive as well, and I know I can have a steady lifelong relationship with a woman as well – both sexually and romantically.'

Siddharth listened intently. At the end of it, he heard himself say, 'That was profound.' Siddharth wondered whether he actually meant the expression or it was an unintended joke that Chand thankfully didn't catch. He looked on, without saying anything else, as if waiting for Chand to calm down.

'I have tried to suppress this feeling all my life,' Chand continued while his voice grew increasingly sombre with every word, 'and I feel guilty about it. I am being unfair to myself as well. And so, I needed to vent it out. I had rehearsed this a zillion times but never said anything. I knew I would spit it out one day, without thinking of the consequences. But I needed to tell someone who wouldn't be judgmental and would just accept me the way I am. My parents can never do that, so the next person whom I could offload myself to was you.'

The tears expressed how desperately Chand wanted his room-mate and best friend to be convinced. Siddharth knew how crucial his acceptance was to Chand. He gently held Chand's face in his hands. The usually flippant musician looked up, his friend's hint of support draining out his long-standing contained emotions.

'I won't be judgmental, I promise,' Siddharth wiped the tears from his friend's face. 'You will always be my dearest friend.'

'Thanks,' Chand spoke under his breath and held Sid's arms.

'But tell me one thing,' Siddharth spoke curiously while Chand looked at him keenly. 'You have never fancied me?'

'No...' Chand spoke without hesitation.

'Okay,' Siddharth pursed his lips and nodded apprehensively. 'Then I am surely not as good looking as you say I am.'

Under the cloudless night sky, the two friends roared in laughter and hugged each other.

***

The last thing to be on someone's wish list during a lazy summer afternoon is a power failure. It was his weekly day off and Siddharth sat in his room, wearing a pair of shorts, a wet cloth on his back, and reading an article on photography published in the Mumbai Mirror. A series of loud knocks on the door alerted him. Siddharth put on his vest and rushed to open the door, anticipating Mrs Patil to break some bad news about the electricity. But his room-mate stood there, instead of the landlady, flaunting a broad grin flashier than his latest bling.

'I have finally got what I wanted,' Chand Pias shrieked and hugged his room-mate, 'Finally!'

'What are you saying?' Siddharth knew what his best friend wanted. 'You will be performing at...'

'Pop On The Rocks,' Chand jumped in the air.

'I deserve a treat now,' Siddharth spoke animatedly. 'And it better be a lavish spread.'

'We should dutch it, dude,' Chand winked back at his friend.

'Why?' Siddharth looked baffled.

'Guess what!' Chand walked into the room, 'I showed your CD to the manager and he has offered you a project.'

Siddharth felt his heart skip a beat as he stared at his friend, without responding.

'He wants you to do a total folio of their centre,' Chand spoke all at once and waited to catch the expression on Siddharth's face. 'He wants it to be the gallery collection for their website.'

Siddharth's reaction surprised both of them as he burst into tears and hugged Chand tightly.

'You know I am bisexual, right?' Chand teased and embraced his room-mate, 'I am not used to handsome guys hugging me like this. I might get horny.'

Siddharth slapped his back and held him tighter.

***

Chand started performing regularly at the popular club in Parel. His Tuesday and Friday performances turned out to be major attraction for the audiences. With his unique sense of fashion and interactions with crowd, Chand became increasingly popular among the teenage audience. In fact, it was his burgeoning fame at the POTR that resulted in huge footfalls in the other clubs where Chand performed on the remaining days.

On the other hand, the gallery design for POTR ushered in other campaigns for Siddharth. None of them was worthy enough to be a landmark in his career, but money started flowing in. In fact, when Siddharth displayed his photographs at the Nariman Art Gallery, all of them sold over the weekend – something almost unheard for first-timers. And, much to the grief of Mrs Patil, the two friends shifted out of Mira Road to their new pad in Andheri.

***

'What you need now, Sid,' Chand spoke over a drink, 'is a great folio with a good model.'

'Yeah,' Siddharth sipped the drink. 'I have been thinking over it for some time now.'

'You have made quite a few contacts,' Chand looked intently. 'Just tell them that you are open to doing portfolios as well. I am sure you will get plenty of them.'

'I did get quite a few offers,' Siddharth spoke, 'but I am a bit sceptical. It gets boring after a certain point of time.'

'There's a lot of money, man,' Chand raised his brows. 'And you have to start with smaller assignments. You can't expect Hrithik Roshan to approach you for a shoot.'

'Yeah...' Siddharth sighed and got up to fetch a beer from the fridge. 'I guess I should start with the offers I got.'

'Cool,' Chand liked it when someone accepted his suggestion. 'Aaaahhhh.... I forgot to tell you something. There's one thing that you can try.'

'What?' Siddharth turned to look at his friend.

'Maya Bose is scheduled to come to Pop next week to judge the War of DJ-s, a competition Pop will be hosting,' Chand patted himself on the back for remembering the right thing at the right moment. 'I can arrange to get some of your photos taken to her.'

'What are you saying?' Siddharth couldn't believe Maya Bose might take a look at his work.

'She encourages new guys,' Chand nodded. 'But then, the diva that she is, I am sure there are hundreds of photographers across the country queuing up to take her snaps. So, you've got to present her something that no one else does.'

Maya Bose. The name in itself was good enough to make the entire country sit up and take notice. He had been enamoured with the lady ever since she won the Miss India crown. Siddharth was in high school when Maya had won the pageant. When he went into college, he maintained a secret scrapbook which was kept at the bottom of the trunk that carried all his study materials. The multicoloured scrapbook contained pictures of Maya from all walks of her life – available in every newspaper and magazine that Siddharth could get his hands on. Be it her shows, movies or any programme, he was always the first one to watch them or read about them. All his friends back in Ajmer teased him saying *"Maya ka saiyya"* but he loved that. It only reinforced his fascination with her.

'Don't worry,' Siddharth knew what he would gift her. 'She is going to love this one.'

***

Amidst media glare and fanfare, Maya Bose stepped inside *Pop on the Rocks* to judge its prestigious annual event – War of the DJs. Her rise from a supermodel to one of Bollywood's most sought after faces had been anticipated and supported by fans. Her portrayal of strong feminine roles on celluloid with élan had dumbfounded all critics who panned models as poor actors. And when she grabbed the National Award for her maiden Bengali film "Draupadi" - even her harshest detractors found themselves turning into sycophants.

Maya looked exquisite in a black backless gown accessorised with a diamond necklace and large earrings, as she sat between the two other judges. Her smile and enthusiastic nod of the head showed how much she enjoyed each performance. The host announced a break after the fourth performance, when a boy carrying a box wrapped in silver paper and a red ribbon approached Maya Bose. She took it with a curious smile and unwrapped the present.

The contents were amusing. Maya Bose saw her life, framed in photographs and presented in a bouquet of memory. A fan had almost sketched a biography with her snaps right from her modelling days to her last film – some from newspapers, and some from movie stills. But what lay underneath all these pictures was the most heart-rending. It was a picture she hadn't seen herself. *Surprising! When did someone take it?* Maya saw herself wearing a black tracksuit, her hair arranged into a tight ponytail and knotted high up. She realised it was one of her early morning workouts in the previous week. She was just out from the gym when a little kid had approached her for an autograph. As she signed on the paper, the kid handed her a bunch of lilies and ran away. She smelled them and smiled merrily. Someone had captured that emotion of hers. *Wow!* Maya hadn't seen herself like that for years. It was the irreverent Mayurakshi Bose from college days who did things for her own pleasure. Things had changed ever since she took up modelling; it was always the others she wanted to please. A barrage of memories inundated Mayurakshi as she wondered whether she would ever regain the same carefree effervescence. *Possibly never,* her heart responded, *you have sold your soul to the spotlight.* She feigned a smarting in the left eye and quickly turned her chair to wipe the drop of tear that was about to betray the shackle of her restraint. As she turned the frame, her eyes caught a note taped on the inside of the top cover. *"Isn't she more natural and more beautiful than the others? Let me prove to the world that they haven't seen the prettiest Maya yet."* – Siddharth Kashyap.

Maya Bose looked up, certain that the sender must be around. And from the balcony of the second floor – a young man bent over the railing and looked pleadingly at her. Maya smiled and nodded appreciatively.

Siddharth's stage was set and his dream was turning true.

Maya Bose's portfolio was almost on everyone's lips in the industry. She had personally recommended him to whole lot of editors. And when one of Maya's pictures taken by Siddharth made its way to the cover of DIVA, India's leading fashion magazine, Sid Kashyap was immediately touted as the new entrant in the elite league of fashion photographers. He was all around, and the city of dreams seemed to have stopped to get captured in his lens. Siddharth kept on doing tons of magazine work after that but what brought him real money were the advertisement offers that started pouring in. The commercials not only brought him closer to the industry, but turned out to be the perfect source to fund everything he wanted.

However, the next turning point in his life came exactly half a year later, when the country's most flamboyant industrialist approached him to shoot the beauty calendar for his company. The twelve-pager, featuring the world's most prominent models, became one of the first calendars to gain popularity and become a huge success all over the country.

Six

Present Time

DAY 1
2:40 p.m.

'Love?'

He had come to thank the man for bringing his wife to hospital on time. And the man just made his marriage look like a farce. There had been questions lingering in his mind, ever since he spoke to the nurse on the phone, but Anshuman couldn't convince himself that the man he was going to meet was involved with Reva in an illicit liaison! Perhaps, he should have. Wasn't it obvious?

'You are in love with Reva?' Anshuman sat on a chair facing Siddharth Kashyap's bed.

'She is in love with me as well,' Siddharth replied. 'It's not just one-sided.'

Anshuman could feel his fist tightening into a grip. He wanted to punch the man on his face. Siddharth Kashyap was claiming that Reva loved him, and the bloatedness with which he spoke alluded he was right.

'Why else would she be driving my car at three in the morning?'

The smirk almost triggered him to react. But Anshuman controlled himself and got up.

'I don't know what to do,' Anshuman stared at the other man in his wife's life. 'Should I hit you for what you are or thank you for bringing her here?'

'Neither,' Siddharth looked back straight at him. 'Your feelings were never a part of our relationship.'

'Quite understandably,' Anshuman nodded his head and smiled dryly. 'Your relationship was never worth it; because had you been me, I wouldn't have ever been you.'

'You couldn't have been me,' Siddharth smiled sarcastically.

Anshuman pondered over a response but decided against it and darted towards the door. However, as he pulled it open, Anshuman realised he couldn't just let this argument die and accept defeat.

'You know what, Mr Kashyap,' Anshuman turned and looked at the man. 'I felt sorry for you when I saw you lying here, in this state.'

He pointed at Siddharth's bandages and fractured arm.

'But now I don't,' Anshuman went on. 'You brought this upon yourself. I guess you deserve it. And so does she. The irony is that I can't just walk away.'

'You can walk away if you want to,' Siddharth looked on firmly. 'I am here to ensure that Reva is fine.'

'You surely did ensure that she is fine,' Anshuman pursed his lips in contempt. 'That's why my wife is lying in the ICU – looking lifeless like never before. She never even had an injury when she was with me. You brought this upon her. And so the last thing I can do is to depend on you to ensure that she is fine.'

Anshuman had just insinuated that Siddharth deserved the blame for Reva's critical condition. Siddharth's guilty conscience had been killing him for the last twelve hours and Anshuman Mehra was definitely not the person to censure him. Siddharth fumed in anger, but before he could say anything, a knock caught their attention.

Anshuman turned as the door sneaked open and Swarnalata Gaitonde entered the room. She carried a black vanity bag in her right hand, and looked sheepishly at the man standing in front.

'This is her bag,' Mrs Gaitonde said. 'Your wife's bag I mean. Dr Ahmed asked me to hand it over to you.'

Anshuman took the bag. The stitching had come off in the bottom right corner, while one of the straps was missing. He looked at the bag and smiled feebly at the nurse. 'Thanks.'

'You can check if the contents are fine,' Mrs Gaitonde said. 'I hope nothing has been misplaced.'

'It's alright,' Anshuman felt embarrassed by the statement. 'I am sure everything is fine.'

'Oh...' Mrs Gaitonde searched the pockets of her hospital uniform and brought out a cell phone. 'This is her phone. There are a couple of messages and a few missed calls.'

For a moment, he thought of reading the messages. But something just struck him the moment he held the phone. *I don't even want to know who called her.* Without even checking anything, Anshuman took the phone and switched it off.

'Thanks for keeping faith in us,' Mrs Gaitonde smiled and paused before adding. 'Do you think she would have any identity proof in her bag?'

The suggestion struck Anshuman like a bolt of surprise. Mrs Gaitonde was right. How could he have not thought about it? Reva always carried her driving licence along.

'Absolutely,' Anshuman zipped open the bag, 'her driving licence must be in the bag. Just a minute.'

Anshuman darted towards the sofa and emptied the contents of the bag on the sparkling white leather. Almost at once, all of Reva's belongings – her cosmetics, reading glasses, pens, her planner, a small mirror, few visiting cards and a wallet – everything lay strewn on the couch. But there was no trace of the driving licence. Anshuman checked the other pockets but the document he needed was conspicuously absent.

'Where is her driving license?' Anshuman looked at Siddharth, breathing heavily.

'I don't know,' Siddharth shook his head. 'It may be in the dashboard.'

'Where is your car?' Anshuman stood up straight.

Siddharth bent over to his left and brought out a bunch of keys from the drawer adjacent to his bed. He stretched out his arm and handed over the bunch to Anshuman.

'Downstairs.'

***

The elevator stopped at the parking lot in the basement. Anshuman stepped out, his eyes searching for a black SX4. As much as he hated the thought of getting into the car belonging to that man, he needed the documents to prove Reva's identity. And perhaps more than her identity, it was the fact that Reva belonged to him, which he wanted to tell everyone.

It wasn't very tough to locate the only damaged car among the host of unscathed ones. The entire right side of the car was vandalised in the accident – the windows were shattered, the bonnet was cracked and the rear door bent inwards. Anshuman stood there, looking at the car with compassion and apathy mixed in equal amounts.

She was in this car when the accident happened, a part of his heart said while the other argued, *she was with another man.*

Suppressing his anguish, Anshuman walked towards it and opened the central lock. The yellow lights flashed with a beep and Anshuman pulled open the driver's door. Everything inside seemed plundered, as if someone had mercilessly smashed everything that lay inside. Anshuman slowly got into the driver's seat. As if compelled by an unseen force, Anshuman sat there and closed the door. The steering wheel was smudged with blood and fingerprints. *They must belong to both her and the man*, Anshuman thought and looked around, *but the blood must be hers, she was driving when the car....* He looked around and saw a few other traces of his wife lying around. Her shoes were lying on the floor, an ear-ring on the side seat. *She must have been sitting there while the man drove to the hospital.* The crumpled seat cover was stained with blood. Anshuman softly ran his fingers on the seat and leaned backwards to catch a breath. However hard he tried, it was tough to restrain the tears that were flooding his eyes.

Her driving licence must be in the dashboard, he reminded himself and sat up, *I am here to collect it and prove that she isn't Mrs Reva Kashyap but Mrs Reva Anshuman Mehra.*

Wiping his eyes, Anshuman pulled open the dashboard. Siddharth Kashyap was right. Not only her driving licence, but her passport was also there. Anshuman pulled out the two and scanned them carefully. The DL photo was taken a year after she shifted to Mumbai while the passport was made after they got married and decided to tour Germany for honeymoon. There was, however, one similarity in both the pictures. Reva looked equally pretty in both of them. *How can you possibly look this beautiful in your passport picture,* Anshuman recollected comparing their passport photographs and telling Reva, *look at my photo, one can very well enlist me on India's most wanted list.* She had laughed out loud and hit him on the arm. *What crap,* she had blushed.

Anshuman ran his fingers to wipe the tears that rolled down his eyes onto the passport, and looked at his wife. *Reva is mine. She couldn't be anyone else's.* He loved her a lot, and he knew she loved him as well. Minor disputes and a young chap couldn't part them. Anshuman smiled affectionately and assured his wife's photograph that everything would be sorted. *We'll be fine, baby.*

He leaned back to see if there was any other document in the compartment. He put his hand in and felt a plastic bag. It was a blue bag carrying the car's registration papers. Anshuman exhaled and put the bag back, when he realised something else had fallen out. He bent down and ran his fingers under the seat to take it out, when his phone started ringing. Anshuman pulled out the mobile phone from his pocket, while his other hand still scanned the floor underneath the seat. He looked at the screen. 'Papa' the name flashed. He slid the green bar when his other hand struck a packet and he brought it out.

'Hello,' Anshuman could faintly hear his father's voice, when he saw the small rectangular box lying on his palm. Suddenly, all the compassion that had been grown in his heart for Reva gave way for disgust and contempt. He stared at the packet of condoms in his hand, while his father's voice was still audible faintly on the other end. 'Anshu....'

Anshuman cancelled the call and threw the packet away. Failing to control himself, he started oscillating back and forth on the seat while his hands gripped the steering wheel tightly. As if not defeated already, he had to see this. His jaws gritted in fury while his eyes melted into tears. In the deserted car-park, Anshuman Mehra held the steering wheel and burst out crying – howling in pain and anger.

***

Siddharth lay on his bed, trying to fight the effect of tranquilisers. *It had been quite a while since Mr Mehra had left with the car-keys,* Siddharth looked at the clock, *and he should have been back by now.* Sister Gaitonde stood in his room, looking away.

'Why don't you sit down?' Siddharth looked at the lady.

'I am fine, sir,' Mrs Gaitonde shook her head. 'Please don't bother.'

Siddharth was about to speak again when Anshuman entered. He walked silently towards the bed and handed over the keys, the sudden change in his expression being overtly prominent.

Siddharth looked at the man and realised that Anshuman's eyes seemed swollen and more placid than they were forty minutes ago.

'Is everything alright?' Siddharth spoke sceptically.

'Yeah,' Anshuman nodded and turned towards the nurse. 'Here's her passport. It has her identity. Please take them to Dr Ahmed and get Reva's name changed in your register.'

'Sure,' Mrs Gaitonde took the two things and nodded firmly. 'I will take it to Fariza Ma'am right away.'

Anshuman looked vaguely as Mrs Gaitonde walked out of the room.

'How long has this been going on?' Anshuman said and turned to Siddharth. 'How long have you been involved?'

'Around six months now,' Siddharth replied indifferently. 'Why do you care all of a sudden?'

'Because I want to know,' Anshuman sounded desperate. 'Don't you think I need to know? I deserve to know everything because for whatever happened between the two of you, my life was also at stake.'

'Let her come back to senses, Mr Mehra,' Siddharth tried to look away and reclined on the pillow. 'She is the best person to tell you everything.'

'I can't wait...' Anshuman seethed in anger.

'For another day,' Siddharth spoke calmly. 'It's better for you not to hear it from me. She will explain things I can't.'

The two men sat silently, a few feet apart in the same room, when Dr Ahmed barged in.

'Mr Mehra,' she called.

Anshuman almost jumped up in alarm.

'Yes, Doc,' he spoke as Siddharth sat up hurriedly. 'Is Reva alright?'

'Well she is,' Dr Ahmed hesitated.

'Then?' Siddharth spoke suspiciously. 'Any bad news?'

Fariza Ahmed was one of the most prestigious neurosurgeons in town and her anxious face couldn't signal something favourable.

'I do have some bad news to share,' she looked at Anshuman.

'What?' Anshuman felt his heart miss a beat.

'We just realised she was pregnant,' the doctor explained with moist eyes. 'Tough luck!'

Fariza looked on as Anshuman exhaled and tried desperately to muster enough courage to continue the conversation. Unnoticed by the doctor or the other man in the room, Siddharth pressed his head tightly into the pillow, unable to withstand the implications of the statement.

'For how long?' Anshuman finally brought himself to say it.

'More than a month,' Fariza Ahmed sighed.

'That's quite long, isn't it?' Anshuman spoke suspiciously. 'Do you think she knew that she was,' he paused for a moment before adding, 'expectant?'

'Can't say,' Fariza Ahmed spoke. 'She might have guessed it.'

'Anything else?' Anshuman looked at the doctor, every passing moment incapacitating him.

'You got to take care of yourself,' Dr Ahmed patted his left arm. 'Be strong. There might be tougher moments ahead.'

Anshuman nodded.

'I will be in my cabin,' Dr Ahmed concluded and left the room.

'When did you meet her for the first time?' Anshuman turned towards Siddharth as soon as the door closed behind Dr Fariza Ahmed.

Seven

Siddharth Meets Reva

'It seems we had our fortunes written simultaneously, doesn't it?' Chand parked the car in the garage. Siddharth sat beside him with a huge carton of clothes on his lap.

'Yup,' Sid smiled, 'and will you be kind enough to move out and open the door for me?'

**

A month after Siddharth's picture of Maya Bose made it to the cover of DIVA, Airfone's "Pigeon" campaign hit the market.

If Maya's mud-idol Durga pose left people wanting for more, everyone in buses and trains was humming "Kabootar line maare". While singing jingles became almost a weekly routine for Chand, offers began to pour upon Siddharth from all corners.

It was during this time that Siddharth conducted his first major individual exhibition at Bandra. Contrary to what people expected, he didn't have one popular face in his gallery of faces. Maya Bose inaugurated the event where Sid Kashyap displayed his gamut of unexplored faces. The collection of 51 black and white photographs had a melange of urban, suburban and rural women, including Patil Aunty, caught exquisitely during one of her daily chores.

The star-studded week-long festival received critical acclaim from the media and the fashion circuit unequivocally. But no one expected the kind of commercial success Siddharth received. And perhaps it wouldn't have been so had Rajvardhan Bhalla not dropped in on the penultimate day of the show.

One of the most glamorous industrialists of India and the owner of the nation's most celebrated fashion magazine, DIVA, Rajvardhan had garnered a name for his fetish for art, women and antiques. Bedazzled by the 14 pictures remaining, Bhalla decided to buy the entire collection of 51 for a mammoth sum of 1.2 crores. He ordered Siddharth to make a new copy of all the pictures. And Siddharth was just too happy to oblige.

Almost simultaneously, Chand made his way into mainstream Bollywood. After a series of super-successful jingles like "We on the Butterfly", "Drowned in your jadoo", and a three minute track for the "Amazing India" campaign comprising 16 different styles of music, Chand Pias' expertise became known to everyone in the film industry. His first composition featured as his only song amidst an entire album by a popular trio of music directors. But his neo romantic thumri touched all hearts and became the most successful track of the film. And the R.D. Burman award for new talent that year was the icing on the cake.

Chand's second Bollywood album comprised 18 tracks – each song distinctly unique from the rest. From folk Punjabi, old school jazz, acoustic rock to an Indian wedding song – Chand put all of them together with a Midas touch. And the twin-CD collection became the highest-selling album of the year. To add to his luck, the film went on to achieve cult status – giving the music a massive followership as well.

When Chand and Siddharth decided to shift out of their Andheri flat, they chalked out plans to stay close. And the simplest way was to buy flats on consecutive floors in the same building. However, despite shifting to Yari Road, the two friends felt reluctant to leave the place that had been witness to their biggest achievements and chose to turn the pad into a joint studio – each taking half of it.

**

The lock turned in flat number 501 and Siddharth entered his new 2BHK apartment. Avneesh Sikandar had done the interiors for him, keeping in mind Siddharth's personality and sense of style. Avneesh had been a close friend and had done the art for most of Siddharth's shoots. So, when Sid started scouting for his new apartment, he had to promise that the interiors would be done only by Avneesh.

The flat had glossy and bright colours with well-matched wrought iron and glass furniture to render a modern and lively ambience. The mixed palette on the walls had portrait photographs from Sid's personal collection, highlighted by contrasting lampshades and large animal printed ceramic vases.

His parents were supposed to arrive a week later for the official inauguration of the flat. So Siddharth made a low key entry with few rituals his mother had asked him to follow and a dinner with his old flat-mate cum new neighbour.

***

DIVA, in association with Rajvardhan Bhalla, brought back its prestigious Fashion Week in the beginning of fall of 2008. The event, one of the most anticipated ones in the glamour world, was one of the pioneering episodes in the circuit, redefining how the world looked at the Indian fashion scenario.

Attended by the most prestigious designers and models, the DIVA Fashion Week almost determined the trends for the following year. The designers went out all out to claim spot at the finale of the week, while models and their PR machineries ensured that they garnered the maximum spotlight. *If you are in the good books of Rajvardhan Bhalla,* they all knew, *your career in the industry is secure.*

Siddharth kept those seven days in his calendar booked for the event. He could vividly recall the first instant when he had stepped out on the red carpet along with Chand and Avneesh. He had felt his heart throbbing exuberantly, his face unable to guile the emotions bubbling in his stomach. That was the third year for him but the excitement hadn't reduced, because every year brought in a new surprise.

And 2008 was going to change his life forever...

**

Siddharth looked dapper in the velvet jacket teamed with contrasting sequined t-shirt and jeans, complemented effectively by his newly grown stubble. Rohit had convinced Siddharth to wear the jacket for the finale. Not to anyone's surprise, Rohit Chhabra had bagged the finale at DFW. After the praise he had garnered in the last two seasons across all the Indian fashion fiestas, and the plaudits that were showered on him at Paris Fashion Week, it was almost guaranteed that Rohit would seize the most coveted spot in DFW.

Siddharth was introduced to Rohit the year before by Bhalla himself. And even before they knew, the two ex-Ajmerites had struck a chord. 2008 was even more special for Sid, because Chand was featuring twice on the final day – composing the musical arrangement for Rohit's show and performing with his troupe in the closing ceremony.

'All eyes and ears are going to be on this show,' Rohit said as Chand made a scratch composition in the studio and Siddharth sat there to encourage them.

'You two are going to rock,' Siddharth patted Rohit. 'You are my friends.'

Siddharth had introduced Rohit and Chand, without knowing that they would hit off so well. And if all of it wasn't enough, Maya Bose was the showstopper for Rohit.

'What an evening it's going to be!' Siddharth started his car ignition.

***

The crowd roared from their seats when the anchor announced the start of Rohit Chhabra's collection. Rohit took the ramp, and with a pensive tone from Chand's cello playing in the background, he started the show with a two minute long speech on life, death and afterlife. The show 'Parijat Ensemble', christened after the flower 'Parijat', represented 'afterlife' – life beyond death. Rohit moved back slowly until he faded into the smoky background, from which emerged his first two models, as the cello faded into the main track.

The show began with a thundering applause.

Rohit used ample of grey, black and white colours in his collection of chiffon drapes – with well rehearsed expressions and deftly matched make-up along with a unique collection of headgear. Chand had matched the apparels and expressions excellently with powerful strokes of the Spanish guitar and Theremin, with his own voice raspy voice rendering an eerie feel to the show. Finally, when Maya Bose took the stage in a spotless white chiffon gown flowing behind her, everyone erupted in appreciation and amazement.

In the end, Rohit appeared with Maya, while the cheer from the crowd made it evident that the show was a success. Siddharth clapped with glee for all his three friends who had stolen DFW from everyone else and made the night such a grand one.

**

Samaira Khan hugged her favourite photographer. She wore a bright red and peacock blue crepe sari with a haltered neck blouse which flaunted her cleavage generously. She kissed Siddharth on the cheeks and looked at him with a grin.

'Someone's looking irresistible,' Samaira gushed. 'I wish I were ten years younger.'

'Well, I don't mind the age gap,' Siddharth winked and looked at Samaira from head to toe, 'especially when someone looks this stunning.'

'Naughty boy,' Samaira slapped Siddharth lightly on the arm and adjusted her sari to give a broader view of her cleavage. 'Wait, I will introduce you to someone.'

Samaira walked away while Siddharth turned to greet another guest. They discussed the show and expressed admiration for the collection when Samaira patted him on the back. Siddharth turned while the guest excused himself and walked off.

'This is Reva,' Samaira introduced, 'one of the most gorgeous journalists of the nation. She should have been a model, right?'

Siddharth was attuned to Samaira's exaggeration. But the lady standing in front of him was someone who had finally justified the adjective. Without a doubt, Reva was the most exquisitely dressed guest at the party that night. Her off-white zardosi sari was pinned on the narrow strap of the same coloured blouse, and flowed over her body. Her make-up was subtly done, eyes made prominent with the right amount of kohl, cheek bones highlighted with a faded rust tinge and lips glossed in a natural colour. Siddharth couldn't help smiling in admiration. Of all the people present in the party who made extra efforts to attract shutterbugs, this lady had preferred keeping it simple and yet looked far more elegant than others. Siddharth loved women who knew what made them look good.

He nodded. 'Very true.'

'And this is Siddharth,' Samaira spoke and rolled her hand through his upper arm, 'one of the most popular fashion photographers around. Getting a compliment from him is a big thing girl. You shouldn't have got married so early.'

'Trust me, it changes life for the better,' Reva smiled at her friend and looked at Siddharth. 'And especially when you are married to the right man.'

'Well I can't deny that,' Samaira agreed, 'Anshuman Mehra is quite a catch himself.'

'So, you are married to the advertising wizard,' Siddharth sipped from his glass of Macintosh.

'Yup,' Reva seemed pleased that Siddharth knew her husband.

'And she does the Page 3 for Daily Times,' Samaira intervened. 'So, behave well if you want to see yourself in the papers.'

'A socialite reporter, huh?' Siddharth smirked.

'Yes,' she smiled mischievously. 'My duty is to ensure your attending parties isn't futile.'

Siddharth looked down and chuckled. *She is quick witted as well.*

'I'll be right back,' Samaira excused herself as she was beckoned from another corner of the floor. 'You two carry on with your conversation.'

'Sure,' Siddharth smiled.

'So, you are a fashion photographer?' Reva looked at him. 'I haven't seen you around in parties.'

'I am not too fond of parties,' Siddharth chuckled. 'I prefer keeping a low profile. Since when have you been in Page 3?'

'Four or five months,' Reva lifted her hand and waved at someone. 'I got tired of business.'

'Oh,' the new revelation surprised Siddharth. 'You were a business reporter prior to it?'

'Yeah,' Reva lifted a glass of Virgin Mary from one of the waiters roaming around. 'That's how I met the *advertising wizard*.'

Siddharth pursed his lips and nodded.

'Do you know Anshuman?' Reva sipped from her glass.

'Not really,' Siddharth shook his head. 'I have only heard of him from my best friend.'

Suddenly, a loud cheer grabbed their attention.

Chand Pias took the centre stage with his guitar. He was clad in a black self-embroidered knee long kurta, black pyjama and black Kashmiri styled waist coat. He was accompanied by three other musicians – one on the keyboard, one on the bass guitar and the third on the drums.

'That's the guy I was talking about,' Siddharth pointed at Chand. 'He is my ex room-mate.'

'Chand Pias,' Reva looked pleased, 'I know him. He is a close friend of Anshuman's too. He was there at our wedding reception as well.'

Siddharth nodded, expressing that he knew about his friend's long-standing association with Anshuman.

Chand crooned five songs back to back – a Bryan Adams solo, a popular A.R. Rahman number and three original compositions.

'Excuse me,' Reva said after Chand ended the first song, 'will catch up with you later.'

As she turned and walked towards another guest, Siddharth stared at her in amazement. Her blouse knotted behind revealed her shapely back which had the right curves leading down to her hips, with the sari wrapped around it neatly. *No wonder Hussain paints his ladies in saris.*

'Ms Reva,' he shouted to draw her attention amidst the chaos.

She turned, looking quizzically at him.

'Will you do a photo session with me?'

She shook her head and went off. 'Cameras hate me,' she replied before turning away.

***

Chand came down and gave Siddharth a hug.

'Was it nice?' he enquired and pulled his kurta.

'What do you think?' Siddharth teased. 'Excellent!'

Rajvardhan Bhalla finally took the microphone after the closing ceremony performance. Clad in his trademark striking off-white achkan, designed by Rohit himself, which went well with his salt and pepper hair and thick framed black glasses – the fifty year old owner of DIVA exhumed an aura, unmatched by anyone at the party.

'The past week had been one of the most humbling experiences of my life,' he looked at the crowd and spoke. 'The kind of love you shower on DFW every year is beyond any expression of gratitude. But I would still say "thanks".'

Everyone smiled and looked at the mesmerising host.

'I was waiting to share some good news with you for quite some time,' he smiled playfully, 'but then I thought that nothing would beat this to be the ideal moment.'

Samaira Khan ambled across the room and stood by Siddharth. She circled her arm through his and winked at the young photographer, listening to the anchor with rapt attention.

'DIVA is doing its first full on international project,' Raj announced, 'its first international calendar, in association with Revlon and Prada. It will feature 12 of the top 15 contestants from this year's Miss Universe and will be shot at three places – Havana, Miami and Copacabana.'

The shock on Siddharth's face pretty much conveyed what everyone else in the auditorium felt. However, as he turned and saw Samaira, the smirk on her lips told him that there was more to follow. She signalled him to look back towards the stage.

'Plus, DIVA will be inaugurating its first international show,' Bhalla looked at the quietly murmuring crowd, 'the Spring Collection in Venice in three months time.'

The murmur of shock was now a roar of disbelief and, a moment later, everyone started applauding.

'My favourite Rohit will be working with Prada for the Calendar collection,' Raj Bhalla spoke, 'and Siddharth Kashyap will be in charge of the creative designing and photography.'

'Fuck,' Siddharth could hear himself say as he turned to look at Samaira again. 'You knew it!'

'You deserve it, sweetheart,' Samaira winked and kissed him on the cheek.

'I am yet to believe this,' Siddharth said when Bhalla beckoned him to come to the stage.

Rohit and Siddharth took the stage and hugged Rajvardhan Bhalla, as the crowd cheered them on. As Siddharth looked at the crowd, his eyes met Reva's and she held up her glass and lipped "Congrats". He nodded in acknowledgement.

**

Half an hour later, Siddharth met Reva on his way out. She was busy talking to a guest when he went up to her.

'Hi,' Siddharth said from behind and she turned back.

The guest congratulated Siddharth and went away.

'So what do you think of the photo shoot now?' Siddharth smiled.

Reva laughed out. 'I didn't say *no* because I distrusted your skill or whatever,' she raised her eyebrows. 'I just don't like the idea of posing for cameras. I have always been like this.'

'And why's that?' Siddharth frowned.

'Never been photogenic you see.'

'Oh come on, you are kidding me now.'

'Not exactly, I just don't like it. Sorry but...'

'Okay.'

'All the best for the calendar though.'

'Thanks.'

They shook hands and Reva walked away again, unaware that their next meeting would mark the beginning of a relationship that would defy all norms, and change their lives forever. Siddharth looked at her, feeling like a silly hero from some soppy romantic drama, hoping that she would turn to look back at the right moment. But she didn't.

'There's always a next time,' he smiled to himself and whistled to his car.

Eight

Present Time

DAY 1
4:05 p.m.

'She did photo shoots with you?' Anshuman looked inquisitive.
'Thrice,' Siddharth nodded. 'She was better than any other woman I have captured in my camera – a complete natural!'

'She has always been confident,' Anshuman sighed, 'but there was no reason for hiding this from me. I wouldn't have objected.'

'It was her personal space, Mr Mehra,' Siddharth replied. 'It was not because she wanted to hide something from you. She just wanted to do something which didn't pertain to her daily chores.'

'And why couldn't have I been a part of that?' Anshuman frowned.

'You are an overpowering man, Mr Mehra,' Siddharth smiled wryly.

'Overpowering?' Anshuman spoke astounded when the sound of a phone ringing startled both of them.

Anshuman took out his cell phone from the trouser pocket. Bala Sir was calling.

'Hi Bala,' Anshuman answered the call and walked out of the room.

'I heard about your wife from Sophie,' Bala said. 'I feel really bad. I hope she is better now.'

'Thanks for the concern,' Anshuman closed the door. 'She is still in the ICU.'

'Don't worry, she will be fine,' Bala comforted. 'Let me know if you need any help.'

'Sure,' Anshuman smiled weakly.

'How did it happen?' Bala sounded curious, 'I heard she had an accident.'

'A car crash,' Anshuman paused. 'She was returning home when the car ran out of control and hit a truck.'

'Oh lord,' Bala gushed, 'I hope she's not badly hurt.'

'The injuries are serious,' Anshuman sat on the corridor seat, 'but she should be okay. I guess it will take some time.'

'Just be strong and stand by her,' Bala suggested. 'That's the only way to help your wife out.'

'I'll be there as long as she wants me to,' Anshuman exhaled. 'I will call you in some time, Bala. The doctor wants to see me.'

'Sure,' Bala agreed.

Anshuman cancelled the call and held the armrest of the seat. He had just made an excuse to avoid more uncomfortable questions. In the day's panic, he had forgotten that this situation was bound to bring up a lot of questions about Reva – sooner or later. He hadn't prepared the answers yet. This was the first time he lied about what had happened to Reva. Surely, it wouldn't be the last time either. Bala was someone he considered a friend. Bala had lent him a helping hand during his journey to success. He was the guide Anshuman had looked up to in times of crisis. Yet, the fear of revealing the truth behind Reva's accident to him seemed scary. Despite the close relation they shared, Anshuman knew that such stories often brought out the inquisitive bugs even in the most genuine of friends. And news like this spreads the fastest. *But how long will I be able to suppress what has happened?* Anshuman thought. *It is bound to come out. What if it comes out the ugly way – in some way that goes beyond my control?*

The effort to hide the news would be fruitless. Yet, he wanted to save Reva and himself from the moment of truth; at least, till she woke up and was in a state to answer all the lingering questions. Perhaps things weren't as bad as Siddharth Kashyap made them out to be. There must be another version of the tale which wouldn't be as acerbic as the one this man was putting forth. He needed her to be fine; just to get up and clarify everything and say that she was still very much in love with him.

But what if Reva woke up and said that the man was correct? What if she decided to bring her new relationship out of the closet and end their marriage? Perhaps she had been trying to allude to the fact that she wanted to get away, but he had never realised it. Was it really so? Did she on any occasion ever mention that she would prefer terminating this marriage rather than continuing it? No... not that he could ever think of.

Yes, they had their share of differences. They fought at times but they did make up, didn't they? He cared for her. Didn't he come down all the way to be with her on her birthday? He fought with his parents to marry her. He admired her for her intellect and praised her ability to defy norms. Above all, she was everything to him. His entire personal life revolved around her. She was the only person who had instilled in him the love for home – the place he had detested. It was only after marrying her that a desire to come back home every evening grew in his heart. He couldn't let that feeling die. She couldn't just leave and shatter all the dreams he had been nurturing for so long.

In six months time, he would be turning 35. It was time to start a family. He had told her about it but never imposed himself upon her. All he did was to put forth his argument and then validate it. Did he go overboard in his persuasion and hurt her sentiments? Is it this aspect of his personality which Siddharth referred to as overpowering? Reva never said such a thing. She would have surely mentioned it had he been overly dominant in their relationship. Didn't he comply with her arguments whenever he felt she was right? Even at times when he thought her arguments weren't justified, he had agreed with her.

The deluge of thoughts was driving him crazy. He had turned numb – the noises around him had died out. He sat on the chair, his mind restlessly wandering through the past four years to find out which was the moment that could have instigated her to step out of their marriage. *Your marriage is as strong as the weakest moment it faces,* his father had once advised him. Wasn't he a part of those weaker times too – wasn't he equally depressed when they fought and stayed apart? Couldn't he have been adulterous when arguments with Reva forced him to stay at office or made him travel for 48 hours across the globe fruitlessly? But such a thought didn't even cross his mind. He couldn't even imagine cheating on his wife; and it was equally impossible to think that she could have done that to him.

'Mr Mehra,' someone pushed his arm.

Anshuman looked up. He felt the touch but the voice reached him feebly. The lady seemed to be in her early twenties and was dressed in a nurse's uniform. She looked at him intently.

'Mr Mehra,' she spoke again, 'are you alright?'

This time Anshuman heard her. He nodded weakly.

'Dr Ahmed wants you to come up immediately,' she said. 'Your wife is not responding to medication. There has been a sudden decline in her health.'

'Something is wrong with her?' Anshuman couldn't get up on his feet. 'Is she dying?'

'I can't tell you that,' the nurse spoke. 'I just want you to come up with me. Dr Ahmed wants to meet you. She has something important to discuss.'

Anshuman held the chair firmly and stood up. For a moment he felt his limbs numb. His breathing was heavy. He shook his head and finally decided that the weakness would grasp him as quickly as he would let it do so. And like a wounded king granted the last wish to save his kingdom, Anshuman broke the shackles of fear and hesitation, and ran across the hospital corridor. His legs ably supported his determination as he darted up the stairs and hurried to the ICU.

*

Dr Fariza Ahmed was informed about Anshuman's arrival and she scurried out of the Intensive Care Unit.

'We need to operate on her right away,' Dr Ahmed spoke. 'There's been a sudden deterioration.'

'What's the matter?' Anshuman panted.

'There's a clot in her upper neck,' Dr Fariza explained. 'We need to rush into surgery. Any delay might be fatal.'

'Go ahead,' Anshuman assented even before the doctor had illustrated the details. 'You have my consent.'

'Great,' Dr Ahmed replied in a matter-of-fact way. 'You need to sign certain papers. She will guide you.' Fariza pointed to the nurse who had broken the news to Anshuman. 'And I guess the reception will ask you to make an interim payment.'

'I'll do that,' Anshuman nodded. 'You get her to the OT.'

'Perfect,' Dr Ahmed looked at a nurse standing behind her. 'Get her out.'

Reva was struggling in pain as the ward boys pushed the stretcher out of the ICU. The sound of her breathing turned louder as she her body wriggled from one side to another. Two nurses held her firmly to the bed as they all rushed towards the operation theatre. Reva's teeth gritted as she moaned in pain. The sight debilitated Anshuman as he ran along in horror. The OT doors opened and the attendants pulled her inside. He turned to see Dr Ahmed running out of her chamber to the operation room. Anshuman looked at her, his eyes speaking silently of his fear.

'We'll try our best,' Dr Ahmed patted his upper arm. 'She will be alright.'

'I will wrap up the formalities,' Anshuman attempted to gather some strength. 'Please ensure nothing happens to her.'

Dr Ahmed went in. Anshuman stared at the room as the door closed and the red light turned on. The nurse came out soon and looked at him.

'Shall we go, sir?'

Anshuman waited for a long moment before finally turning towards her.

'Let's go,' he finally said and turned around to see someone he didn't expect.

Siddharth Kashyap was standing a few metres behind them, looking pale. His right arm hung from the neck while a crutch supported his left underarm, buttressing as well as debilitating his movements. Anshuman noticed that Siddharth's right ankle was injured and he could barely place it on the ground. Yet, the man looked on, unflinchingly ignoring the pain. For a split second, Anshuman could feel a streak of admiration for the man.

'How come you are here?'

'I... I don't know,' Siddharth stammered. 'I just felt something was wrong with her.'

'They have found a clot in her neck,' Anshuman informed. 'Dr Ahmed is operating on it.'

'Shall I wait for you at the reception?' the nurse looked at Anshuman, 'I will get the papers ready while you come.'

Anshuman nodded. The nurse walked away.

'What papers?' Siddharth sounded concerned.

'Some bond I suppose,' Anshuman replied. 'Plus they want the interim payment to be made.'

'I will make the payment,' Siddharth cut short the last statement. 'She was with me when it happened. So, she is my responsibility until she is fine.'

'She is still my wife, Mr Kashyap,' Anshuman looked straight at the younger guy. 'For all that you share with her, I am still her guardian.'

Anshuman walked past Siddharth when the latter interrupted.

'I am not denying that you are legally bound to her,' he spoke.

'Don't mock my relation with her,' Anshuman blurted out. 'It's not just about legalities or formalities. We love each other.' He paused and added, 'At least I love her a lot.'

'I am not trying to insult you or your marriage,' Siddharth slowly turned with the support of the crutch. 'All I am saying is that paying for her treatment will make me feel less guilty.'

'Pray to god that your company doesn't prove to be fatal for her,' Anshuman looked at him with moist eyes. 'If she pulls through, there will be no guilt. But she is far from fine now.' Anshuman paused and sighed. 'Trust me, if Reva doesn't survive, I won't let you live to feel any burden of guilt.'

Anshuman turned and walked along the corridor. Siddharth stared as Anshuman turned at the head of stairs and skipped down. The doors of the OT were firmly shut, while the fate of all the three lives unfolded within. *Reva has to get up – she has to be fine and she has to clarify everything.* It was not about sharing the guilt; it was about unveiling the truth before everyone.

***

The phone rang at the Nagpur residence. It was 5:30 p.m. by the clock and the residents of the Gokhale home were busy in their respective chores.

Milind was sitting on the sofa, with his right leg lifted in the "lucky" position, as the Indian bowlers desperately tried to retain the Sri Lankan team to an attainable target. Mahela Jayawardene seemed to be in tremendous form, and if his onslaught were to continue, India's chances of winning would appear bleak. He heard the phone ringing but he couldn't afford to disturb the "lucky" position, lest the next ball disappeared over the boundary line.

'Aai, can't you take the call?' he shouted at his mother who was busy making the evening snack. 'The phone has been ringing for quite some time now.'

'Can't I say the same thing to you?' she shouted back. 'Don't tell me you are studying.'

Now, that was the only area where she attacked him every time. He didn't have an answer, especially after what happened two days ago. He shrugged off the comment and walked across the drawing room to pick up the call.

'Milind?' Anshuman spoke on the other end.

'Jiju,' Milind almost jumped at Anshuman's voice. 'What a pleasant surprise!' Perhaps it was the first time his brother-in-law was calling them. It was always his sister who would call up while his Jiju would join in to say a "hi" at the very end of the conversation.

'Is uncle home?' Anshuman asked curtly. Reva used to hate it whenever he referred to her father as "Uncle". *It's too formal,* she complained, *if I can call your parents "Maa" and "Papa", why can't you do the same to my parents?* But Anshuman could never bring himself to calling his parents-in-law 'Maa or "Baba". It didn't come naturally to him.

'Baba?' Milind could feel the grimness in Anshuman's tone. 'Not yet. Is everything alright? Taai is fine, isn't she?'

'I don't have his mobile number,' Anshuman went on. 'Can you ask him to call me as soon as he reaches home?'

'Is there anything wrong with Reva?' Milind sounded worried.

Milind's mother heard the last sentence and rushed out of the kitchen. Her glasses were covered with steam as she looked at her son.

'What happened?' she appealed. 'Is Reva fine?'

Milind lifted his arm and signalled to her to wait.

'You don't sound okay,' Milind held the phone, while his mother tugged at it.

'Give it to me,' she was already in tears. 'My heart felt something is wrong with my daughter. Let me talk to Anshuman.'

Milind hushed his mother and stared angrily at her.

'Stop crying and stop pulling the receiver,' he chided. 'Let me talk to him.'

Milind's mother stared at her son when the doorbell rang. She knew that it was her husband. It was the same time when he returned from school every day. She ran towards the door and, as expected, found her husband waiting. He smiled at her but her tears drained the joy on his face.

'There's something wrong with Reva,' she sobbed. 'Anshuman has called up but he is not saying anything. He wants to speak to you.'

Reva's father dropped his bag and ran inside.

'I asked Milind to let me speak,' Milind's mother complained about her son, 'but he didn't.'

'Jiju,' Milind saw his father coming. 'Baba is here. I am giving the phone to him.'

'Anshuman,' Reva's father spoke as soon as he held the receiver. 'Is something wrong with her? Where are you right now?'

'I am at Apollo,' Anshuman tried desperately to control his emotions, 'Reva is admitted...'

'She is admitted at Apollo?' Reva's father managed to say while the other members in his family gasped in shock. 'What happened?'

'She suffered a car accident last night,' Anshuman informed. 'She's critical, Uncle.'

The middle-aged school principal could feel his limbs tremble, hearing the frail voice of his son-in-law. He had always known

Anshuman for his stoicism and reserved expression of emotions. And hearing Anshuman's broken voice, Mohanlal could say that things were going out of hand.

'Is she dead?' he mumbled while his wife clutched his sleeve tightly and his son looked in horror. 'Are you hiding anything from me?'

'No,' Anshuman collected himself. 'She isn't dead. But she is undergoing a critical surgery. It's very difficult. Even one of Mumbai's topmost neurosurgeons is sceptical. I can't handle this all alone, Uncle. Can you please come down?'

'Sure, sure,' Anshuman's father-in-law said. 'I will be there by tomorrow afternoon. Do we have that much time?'

'I hope so,' Anshuman rubbed his nails. 'Try to come as fast as you can.'

'Are you alone over there?'

He wasn't alone. Neither could he say "yes".

'There's a friend,' he finally said. 'Please try to come as fast as possible.'

Anshuman ended the call. He wanted his father-in-law to be there. He had revered the man for his strength of mind and principles. Ever since Anshuman became a part of the Gokhale family, his father-in-law had never differentiated among Reva, him and Milind. Mohanlal's presence would provide the solace Anshuman had been searching for ever since his arrival at the hospital. But would it be right to introduce Siddharth Kashyap to his father-in-law? Will the man be able to handle the shock of the revelation?

I won't tell him anything, Anshuman told himself, *but I need him here. Perhaps he will have to face the truth, but not before Reva wakes up and tells it to him herself.*

It had been almost five years ever since he first met Mohanlal Gokhale at their Nagpur residence. A really long time ago but the memory was indelible in his mind...

Nine

Marriage

The table clock showed 10:30 a.m. when the intercom rang in Anshuman Mehra's office. He pushed the papers aside to find the phone and lifted the receiver.

'Sir, the trainee has arrived,' the receptionist said. 'Shall I send her in?'

'Just give me five minutes to clear my desk,' Anshuman laughed.

'Sure.'

Anshuman piled the papers and clipped them into their respective files. He pulled open the drawers and was putting the files in, when the trainee knocked on the door.

'Come in,' Anshuman called out and closed the drawers.

The door opened and a twenty-four year old girl peeped inside.

'May I come in, sir?' she asked nervously.

'Please do,' Anshuman said looking into his laptop.

The girl entered the room. She wore a white full-sleeved shirt and black trousers, matched with black stilettos and a black over-sized bag dangling from her right forearm. She was the girl Anshuman had chosen a month and half ago from one of the top MBA colleges. Despite no prior experience in advertising, it was the promise of her positive attitude during the interview that eventually convinced her interviewer.

'Good morning, Sophie,' Anshuman smiled sarcastically as Sophie D'Costa pulled a chair.

'Really sorry, sir,' she was alerted by the tone in her boss' voice, 'I messed it up today morning. Boarded a Virar bound fast train which went from Borivali to Andheri directly. So, I had to catch a slow train backwards and reach Goregaon station.'

'You are in an industry where excuses don't work,' Anshuman signalled at the chair and asked her to sit down. 'One mistake can cost your client crores, and you your job.'

'I understand, sir,' Sophie sat down timidly and placed the bag on her lap.

'So where is your guest house?'

'Mira Road.'

'It's okay, you will get used to all of this. Mumbai absorbs everyone. It took me time as well. But then the city starts growing on you, and you start growing with it.'

Sophie smiled. She liked the positive vibe she got from her mentor. Ever since she landed in Mumbai from Trivandrum, the city instilled a fear with its heat, pace and nonchalance. Her two years of MBA at Kozhikode had painted a different picture about the world, which got demolished almost overnight at the nation's busiest metropolis.

'I won't be looking after your training,' Anshuman lit a cigarette and walked up to the glass window overlooking the congested Western Express Highway, 'but you will be reporting to me. And if you successfully complete the project assigned, maybe we will have the good fortune to work together.'

'I will look forward to that day, sir,' Sophie spoke elated. 'You can vouch for the fact that I won't disappoint you.'

'Great,' Anshuman gave his hand, 'all the best then.'

Sophie walked up to her mentor and shook his hand.

'Thank you so much, sir.'

***

Back in Lucknow, the September sky was always clear without a cloud in sight. But in what way was Mumbai ever similar to his hometown. A light drizzle settled in, with the evening sky still effulgent enough for the streets at 6 p.m. The good thing about the drizzle was the cool wind which blew along with it; the bad part however was the congestion on streets. Not that Mumbai's traffic wasn't infamous, the rains just made it worse! The fact that a major part of the city depended on a highway only added to the woes. However, complaining wasn't going to help his case. So, Anshuman Mehra decided to enjoy the moist Friday winds with old Kishore Kumar songs all the way from Goregaon to Chembur.

Reva was staying with one of her senior colleagues due to the latter's ill health. Dipanwita Banerjee had been the pillar of support for Reva at their office, and it was time to return the favour.

'How is she now?' Anshuman opened his shoes and walked into the drawing room. 'Has the temperature gone down?'

'Better than before,' Reva spoke from the kitchen as she poured a glass of water for Anshuman, '99 degrees. But she's still pretty weak. Guess it's the antibiotics.'

Anshuman watched his girlfriend as she deftly managed things at her colleague's home. *Perhaps adjusting to new environments comes naturally to women,* he thought, *and almost as quickly, they start getting a hold of the place.* Wearing a mono-coloured loose overflowing kurta teamed with printed Patiala leggings and dupatta of the same design, Reva looked beautiful in her simplicity. The firmly tied ponytail tossed from one side of her back to another as she spoke and walked back to hand over the glass.

'Go in and meet her,' Reva spoke in an animated tone. 'She will feel nice. Meanwhile I will make some tea for you.'

Anshuman nodded. He wasn't a stranger to Dipanwita, and neither being Reva's colleague was the only relation she shared with him.

'Wait,' Reva said as he turned. She stepped quickly towards Anshuman and hugged him tightly. Anshuman circled his arms around her as she planted a kiss on his chin and gave him another tight hug.

'Go in,' she moved away, 'and try not to discuss Shubhanshu.'

Anshuman had been a witness to one of the worst phases in Shubhanshu and Dipanwita's life, when they decided to move apart and stay separately, without probing legal complications. He had tried to make peace, and so did many. But the middle-aged Bengali couple had resolved to separate and give each other the much required space they felt was necessary.

'Staying under one roof and not talking to each other isn't doing wonders to our marriage,' Shubhanshu had justified his stance. *'Perhaps we would feel the need only in times of absence. Perhaps we will start talking to our own souls.'*

The memory struck Anshuman as he stepped inside Dipanwita's room and saw her lying on the bed. Surprisingly, her relation with Shubhanshu had improved over the last 18 months. They had started talking occasionally to enquire about each other's well-being. However, the betterment in the relationship had no ostensible impact on their physical appearance. Shubhanshu had started looking much older than he actually was, and Dipanwita's frail health stood testimony to the negligence for her own health.

'Come in, ad guru,' Dipanwita joked at the hesitant steps of her guest. 'My god, you have put on so much weight!'

'And you are looking fabulous,' Anshuman stepped inside and sat on the sofa, 'I love dark circles.'

'Hilarious,' Dipa frowned. 'Sit down and crack some more jokes. I am amused.'

'Why not?' Anshuman smirked. 'Finally something's amused you.'

'You still blame me for the separation, don't you?' the Associate Editor-in-Chief of Daily Times turned sombre. 'You think I spoilt Shubho's life.'

'I don't blame you for anything,' Anshuman shook his head. 'I just wish you had stayed together and not waited for the distance to creep in.'

'When your dreams gradually move out of your reach,' Dipa replied, 'it's better to let them live peacefully without hankering after them and ruining the remnant peace.'

'Does Banerjee know you are ill?'

'No,' Dipanwita sounded alarmed, 'and do me a favour by not telling him.'

'Don't you think you should give your marriage another chance?' Anshuman looked solemnly at Dipanwita, feeling helpless that he could do nothing to ameliorate the relation of a pair as affable as Shubho and Dipa.

'The distance has worked favourably for us,' Dipanwita removed the coaster and sipped from her glass of water, 'I don't want to stretch my luck and destroy all that I have gained in the last one and half years.'

'And you don't want to get divorced either?'

'Nope,' she put the glass back at its place. 'I have become too used to calling myself Dipanwita Banerjee. A new surname would sound odd.'

Both of them laughed at the response; they both knew that was barely the reason.

'Perhaps it's the feeling of being still married to Shubhanshu that instils a lot of strength in me,' she confided. 'He remains a part of me even in his absence.'

'But you still blame him for what happened.'

'Perhaps,' Dipanwita exhaled and smiled feebly, 'and so does he.'

'Strangely neither of you found out that the one to blame was fate and not each other.'

'Whom have you chosen, Reva?' Dipanwita pointed towards her colleague entering the room. 'He is a boring professor.'

'My dad is a professor as well,' Reva handed the tea-cup to Anshuman. 'Perhaps that explains my choice.'

'You two are going to make me fall ill out of embarrassment,' Dipanwita held the cushion over her face and looked at them sheepishly.

Reva laughed and sat on the bed to hold Dipanwita's hand. 'As much as I hate discussing this topic, I would be lying if I say I don't agree with him.'

Dipanwita rolled her hand to clasp Reva's fingers softly. 'I will be fine,' she smiled feebly and looked at Anshuman. 'So, what's the surprise in store? Any special place you want to take her to.'

Anshuman looked shyly at Reva and realised she had divulged the news to her colleague. 'Well....' he searched for an answer, 'it's...'

Dipanwita laughed out at the innocuousness of the ad-man's expression.

'Don't bother,' she chuckled. 'I hate when others get the surprises and not me.'

Reva hugged her boss as they bade farewell.

'I will be back tomorrow afternoon,' Reva took her purse. 'Call me if you feel ill.'

'Enjoy your night,' Dipanwita winked at her friend.

***

The car steered through the Lokhandwala lanes and stopped outside a newly constructed building. Evident from its name, built by one of the top builders in Mumbai, the 27-storeyed tower looked stunningly posh and attractive. A giant marble facade led to the main entrance that circled behind and overlooked the car park situated inside the basement.

'Now, what's the surprise?' Reva looked confused as she stepped outside the car and looked at the building.

'Well... you see the surprise before your eyes,' Anshuman bit his tongue mischievously.

'What the f...' Reva's eyes dilated in surprise, 'you want to say that....'

Even before she could finish her line, a key-ring flew over the car. She caught it hesitantly.

'27C – top floor,' Anshuman winked. 'It's all yours.'

Reva could hear herself shrieking at the top of her voice. The surprise had caught her off-guard and she clasped her mouth with both her hands. Anshuman laughed as she ran around the car and hugged him tightly.

'I can't believe this,' her body floated in the air as Anshuman held her by the waist. 'You bought a flat here?'

Anshuman held her face in his hands. 'It's ours.'

*****

Reva pushed open the door and walked inside. Anshuman had decorated the flat just the way she would have. With a beige base, the drawing room exuded an old-world charm with the teakwood furniture, brass clocks, life-size historic paintings and minimal furnishings. Anshuman had laid out the perfect home in front of her. She looked around in amazement, swallowing every minute detail with her eyes, and loving every bit of it.

'How is it?' Anshuman put his arms around her. 'Do you like it?'

'I hate it...' she turned in glee and hugged him yet again.

'This is where we'll live after getting married,' Anshuman winked.

Reva successfully controlled her chuckle at the audacious remark. She brought her face closer to his and looked at him in mock arrogance. Anshuman had never broached the topic of marriage. It was the first time he had mentioned it, and he did it in his distinctive style.

'Should I consider this as a proposal?' she teased as her nose rubbed against his.

'Consider this as information,' he smiled as his nose touched hers and his eyes shifted down from her face to her lips. The embrace tightened around their backs as they both looked at each other seductively.

'What if I am in no mood to marry you?' she looked up from his lips to his eyes. 'You never said how much you love me.'

'I hate speaking redundantly,' his arms pulled her closer as they breathed close to each other. 'I let my actions do all the talking.'

'Yeah right,' she could now feel his warm breath on her face and throat. The smell of cigarettes was strong and she loved it. She slowly stepped on his feet and reached up.

'What's the next step you are planning?' she hardly finished her line when he replied.

The kiss was warm, long and passionate.

She was gentle, shapely and feminine. He was rough, strong and masculine. He rolled his body over hers as their souls brushed across each other on the canvas of love. His hair rubbed against her soft bare skin, as both of them drowned the other in a whirlpool of desire. He licked her navel and slowly moved up. She wanted him more; he desired her no less. His lips moved up her throat as her fingers ran down his back. His chest pressed against her breasts as his fingertips rubbed against her face. For a moment, they gazed into each other's eyes before he slipped his tongue into her mouth, and lingered on. Her body convulsed upwards in pleasure, as his fingers made way through her cascading hair and stroked her back. His hand held her back and moved down her thigh. She breathed heavily as a drop of tear rolled down her eyes and he kissed it. It tasted of love.

It was the first time Anshuman and Reva had made love. Like all first encounters, it was long awaited and delightfully cherished. As they lay together on the bed, wrapped in each other's arms, he kissed her nose and said, 'Let's meet your parents.'

***

Exactly a week later, the early morning flight ferried Reva and Anshuman from Mumbai to Nagpur. It was the first trip for them to discuss marriage with parents. Reva had called her father beforehand to inform him about their arrival and the purpose of their visit. The drive from Dr Babasaheb Ambedkar International Airport to the Gokhale residence gave them time for the final moments of preparation.

'Don't smoke anywhere in our house,' Reva looked nervous as she passed on a peppermint to Anshuman. 'And don't try that pseudo Punjabi machismo avatar of yours. Dad is going to hate that.'

'Anything else, ma'am?' Anshuman winked. He had been apprised of the guidelines thrice before that conversation. But even he was nervous. 'Don't worry,' he held her hand smiled. 'I won't do anything to hurt them.'

After twenty minutes on the highway, the car finally turned towards Civil Lines. The avenue marked prominently with trees had some of the poshest bungalows in town – from those of dignitaries to the ones belonging to top government officials. The car stopped in front of a two-storeyed bungalow.

'Ground floor,' Reva puffed and put the goggles in her bag. 'Calm down.'

'I am okay,' Anshuman chuckled and put his arm around her shoulder.

She immediately shrugged it away and shot him an angry look. He bit his tongue and opened the iron-gate leading onto the path towards the ground floor.

The maid arrived with lemonade and sweets for everyone. Anshuman took his glass and smiled sceptically at his prospective in-laws. He had never been half as nervous during any of his corporate presentations or for that matter even during his campus placement interview. But it didn't take him much time to realise that the people he was dealing with were quieter and less intimidating than his own family.

'So, you are an ad filmmaker,' Milind sounded excited. 'That sounds super cool.'

Milind Gokhale was six years younger than his sister and contrary to her publicly reserved personality, he was energetic and lively. One could look into his large black eyes and see the inquisitiveness in them. His thick curly hair reminded Anshuman of Chand. And Reva had already intimated him of Milind's passion for playing the guitar.

'Not exactly,' Anshuman smiled sincerely enough to mask his irritation at the question. There had been innumerable people who asked him this. And by now, he was tired of explaining the difference. 'I conceptualise advertisements. I do not direct them. But I am present sometimes on the production floor.'

'You remember the ad of the couple with colourful dupattas?' Reva looked at his mother. 'His was the brain behind that.'

Mrs Krutika Gokhale seemed in her late forties, with big eyes resembling her son's, dressed in her best attire and seemingly in awe of her daughter's choice. Pretty much like Anshuman's mother, her world revolved around her family. She had prioritised her family over her stable government job and, pretty much like all mothers, mastered the art of managing the household with unmatched dexterity. With grown up children and lesser workload, her companionship with the idiot box had increased over the years. And she was well informed about the daily soaps and the advertisements in between them.

'The chocolate ad?' her eyes bulged in excitement. 'You made that one?'

'He created the idea for that,' Reva rectified and realised her choice had struck instant chord with her mother. It had been Krutika's favourite advertisement over the years and to see the man who had come out with the idea – she couldn't have asked for more.

Reva loved the fact that Anshuman had been able to bond effortlessly with her entire family on their very first meeting. It was his charm and magic with words which had enchanted her and he had won her family over with the same flair. But in the entire conversation, her father acted like a silent spectator – smiling and speaking occasionally. Contrary to her expectation, Anshuman had observed the same. Despite the undivided attention that he received ever since his arrival, Anshuman could notice the pragmatic look on Reva's father's face. The man seemed hardly impressed with his experience or achievements; on the contrary, scepticism marked the contours of his face. It was only after dinner that Mohanlal began a conversation with the new man in his daughter's life.

**

Anshuman stood in the veranda with Milind, discussing their choice of music.

'I am a jazzoholic,' Milind laughed, 'I just love it.'

'I am not that fond of jazz myself,' Anshuman smiled, 'but there's a friend of mine who knows a lot about jazz. Chand Pias. I don't know if you have heard of him.'

'He recently composed the music for a movie right?' Milind looked animated. 'But that was hard rock.'

'Yeah...' Anshuman smiled, 'but he plays jazz equally well. You should hear him perform sometime. Why don't...'

Before Anshuman could complete, Mohanlal Gokhale called out for his son.

'Milind,' he walked into the veranda. 'Go and help Reva make the beds. Your mother is making arrangements for tomorrow's breakfast.'

'Okay,' the young guy nodded and excused himself. He pranced towards the room, while his father walked into the veranda.

Anshuman looked on anxiously as the elder man walked ahead, with his hands locked behind his back. Anshuman was not as comfortable with him as he was with the other members in the family. Somewhere in his heart, a pang of discomfort teased Anshuman that Reva's father had not approved of him.

'You liked the food?' Mohanlal spoke cordially. 'It must be different from the food you generally have.'

'Absolutely,' Anshuman spoke almost immediately at the first question and stopped to let Mohanlal continue with the second.

'It is a bit different from the North Indian food I have grown up eating,' Anshuman went on, 'but I am quite used to all kinds of food, and pretty much divulge myself in any variant that tastes good. Hostel and bachelor life do that to you.'

'True,' Mohanlal smiled. 'I did my masters from Calcutta University and PhD from there as well. So for a long time, I was alone and depended solely on street food and the bare minimum that I could prepare. The cook I hired seemed to cook only Bengali dishes and whenever I tried to make something, the food seemed to burn in protest. Or else, it would just remain uncooked.'

Anshuman laughed out. He could relate to every bit of the experience.

'Except for maintaining my vegetarian sanctity,' Mohanlal went on, 'there was hardly anything I didn't eat. You must be eating meat yourself, right?'

'Yes,' Anshuman wished he could skip the question, 'but I've stayed in Ahmadabad for two years and I am pretty used to a vegetarian diet.'

'Anshuman,' Mohanlal spoke, 'I am addressing you by first name if it's okay...'

'Of course,' Anshuman spoke embarrassed.

'There are things I want to discuss with you before you two decide to take the plunge,' Mohanlal's tone turned serious. 'I hope you are not very sleepy or else we can talk tomorrow morning.'

'Not at all,' Anshuman tried his best to get informal. 'I sleep pretty late.'

'Let's sit,' Mohanlal pointed at the cane chair set at the end of the veranda.

Mohanlal Mehra had passed his doctorate with distinction, and had been in academics ever since. He joined one of Nagpur's leading engineering colleges as lecturer in Mathematics but later shifted to a graduation college as a Professor. With few years remaining in his career, he decided to take up the post of the principal of a renowned private high school. Throughout his life, he had advocated against the idea of school and college teachers taking up tuition classes to supplement their salaries. Despite the conservative earnings, he had always given his children the life they wanted and fulfilled whatever little his wife wanted. Though he was hesitant at Krutika's decision to leave her job, he welcomed it and remained thankful to his wife for the sacrifice she made to raise their kids.

'Reva might look like me,' Mohanlal spoke, 'but she is very much like her mother at heart. She has always been fiercely independent in whatever she wanted to do. She knew exactly what she wanted in life. Reva's mother used to earn more than I did when she decided to quit her job and concentrate on bringing up Reva and Milind. Not many would have the courage to do so. Women have that strength of making sacrifices without any penitence. We don't. But even then, not many women have that strong will to take their own calls and stick to them without needing a man confirming the same. Like her mother, Reva had always known what her heart was set out for and what she could renounce. She gave up dancing so that Milind could take up music. At that time, we couldn't afford lessons for both of them.

But Reva never felt sorry for herself; on the contrary, she felt it was her life and she had taken a call. She had given up something for her brother.'

Mohanlal took a deep breath and went on.

'As parents, we appreciated this aspect of hers. We like the fact that our daughter has such strength of character. So, there was hardly any conflict of opinions or priorities between her and us. But that's not going to be the case when you start staying together. Your relationship will be a totally different ball game altogether. For you, it won't be possible to abide by all her decisions. At times, you might feel she is doing something you don't subscribe to. We as parents might let her be; you won't be able to do so. Because your life would depend much more on her than ours ever did. You got to have ideas in mind and tricks at hand how to resolve such issues.'

Anshuman sighed. He had never thought of marriage with such seriousness. Yes, he had seen Reva's fiercely independent facet but he had loved it. He had never assumed a scenario where her decisions would hinder anything in his life.

'What do you suggest?' he exhaled.

'Be patient,' Mohanlal spoke instantaneously as if he expected the question coming. 'Don't rush into anything. The more you get impatient with her, the more obstinate she becomes. On the contrary, if you can keep your cool you might be able to make her go back on her words. I hope she will change once she is married but it's a safe trick to learn.'

Anshuman chuckled. He hadn't arrived at the Gokhale residence thinking that Reva's father would give him tips about managing his daughter's temperament. The man he had felt sceptical to interact all this while, told him what he needed to learn the most about his marriage.

'We often use the adage that women bind a home together,' Mohanlal smiled at his would be son-in-law. 'But my thirty years of nuptial life has taught me that men can play almost as important a role in building a family successfully. And in today's time, their role is getting more significant than before. The best thing you can do is to do only what you are supposed to, and leave all the decision making to the woman. This has helped me a lot.'

Anshuman wanted laughed out but resorted to just a grin.

'I will surely keep it in mind,' Anshuman tried to control the outburst of his emotions. 'In fact I am not good at managing the house. So, I would completely surrender that to her.'

Mohanlal looked at his watch and took a deep breath. 'It's quite late now,' he leaned back to flex his muscles and let out a sigh. 'Go and rest.'

Both the men stood up and walked back towards the door, as Mohanlal kept his hand around Anshuman's shoulder, welcoming him into the family.

'Have you spoken to your parents?' he said as they turned around the door and entered the drawing room, 'Are they okay with everything?'

'Next week, I'll be off to Lucknow,' Anshuman informed. 'There's no reason for any objection from their side. But they don't know anything about it yet.'

***

Anshuman boarded the next Friday morning flight to his hometown. After a spirited encounter with his in-laws the previous week, it was time for the tougher deal. He knew his parents and their orthodox approach towards such issues. All he hoped was that his improved relation with them over the past few years would make the proceedings easier.

The half an hour drive from the airport landed him outside his home – the same building which had been a witness to his childhood and adolescent memories. But ever since he joined his engineering course, the days spent at home became limited. And it was almost six years since he had left home for Mumbai. His only medium of contact with his family was the phone. The frequency of calls varied from time to time; but despite his mother's requests, he had never returned to meet them. And when he was finally home, they had no clue of his visit.

A young girl opened the door for Anshuman. She wore a floral printed kurta with matching patialas and dupatta pinned neatly on the shoulders. Her brows frowned at the sight of the stranger at the door. She had never seen him earlier.

'May I help you?' she looked at him curiously.

'And who are you?' Anshuman looked at him with a surprised look.

'How does it matter to you?' she charged in return. 'You are the one at the door. You should be answering me.'

'Really?' Anshuman pursed his lips in admiration. 'Great. Call your madam then.'

'Who is it, Parminder?' a voice called out from the kitchen.

Gayatri Mehra walked out, wearing a light golden salwar-kameez suit, and stopped at the sight of her son. Her eyes were fixed on him while her mouth opened up to scream.

'Anshu...' she cried out aloud as tears filled her eyes.

She rushed ahead to hug him and when Anshuman held his mother tightly, he could feel her body shiver from the shock. He held her head against his shirt as she continued crying and embraced him tightly. She had waited for this moment for years and knew her son would eventually come back.

'I knew this,' she was hiccupping from the sobs, 'I knew Waheguru couldn't punish me like this. I have prayed for this moment for years.'

Anshuman knew how she had borne the brunt of disputes between his father and him. She was the referee who could just listen but could not take sides. She looked up, held her son's face in her arms and kissed it all over. Anshuman could feel the warmth of her tears against his skin and she held his cheek against hers and cried. He knew his mother would be surprised to see him but hadn't fathomed the intensity of her grief. For a moment, he felt extremely selfish at having made a scapegoat out of a person who loved him more than everything.

'Come on,' he finally spoke and held her face in his hands. 'Don't cry so much. You will fall ill. I am perfectly fine and am with you now. So, stop crying.'

As expected, Akashdeep Mehra reacted with much more stolidity when he saw his son later in the evening. He walked into the house and, as if for a moment, he couldn't recognise Anshuman. The mutual bitterness had subsided and with growing age and a long period of separation, they had also matured to accept the coldness in their relation with more grace. And when Anshuman went up to hug his father, Gayatri Mehra felt that her fragmented home was finally coming back together.

'What brings you here?' Akashdeep Mehra spoke at dinner. 'You haven't come here to see how your parents are, have you?'

Gayatri looked at her son as he glanced up from the plate and stared at his parents.

'Have you married someone already,' Papa went on, 'or are you getting married?'

Anshuman had never thought his father would read his intentions so clearly. How he hated for sharing the same genes which made him more vulnerable and transparent to the man.

'I am getting married,' he sighed.

'What are you saying?' Gayatri sounded alarmed. 'You didn't tell me all day.'

'I was waiting to share the news with both you and dad together,' Anshuman could feel his toes stiffen. 'I would have told you after dinner.'

'What does she do?' Akashdeep Mehra cut short his son's explanation.

'What's her name?' Gayatri looked at her husband and then at her son, suggesting that it was a more important question.

'Her name is Reva and she is a journalist,' Anshuman looked at both his parents.

'Reva what?' Akashdeep looked straight at his son.

'Gokhale,' Anshuman answered.

'Marathi?' Gayatri frowned sceptically. 'You haven't chosen a Punjabi girl for yourself?'

'And where is she from?' Dad took hands off the plate and stared at him. 'What's her hometown?'

'Nagpur,' this interview was tougher than the one he had experienced last week, 'but she works in Mumbai. Her parents are in Nagpur. How does it matter if she is Punjabi or Marathi? I know her for around a year and half now. She is a great girl.'

'Do you think a Marathi family will accept an UPite Punjabi guy as a suitor for their daughter?' Akashdeep quizzed. 'I hear they are pretty conservative people.'

'They are okay with it,' Anshuman looked confident as he had crossed that hurdle beforehand. 'They like me and have consented to the marriage.'

'So, you have already met them before asking your parents?' Akashdeep went on while his wife looked at him and their son like an umpire refereeing a tennis match rally. 'Basically, you are not asking us but you have come here to invite us for your wedding.'

'I am not going around the country inviting everyone for my marriage,' Anshuman paused and took breath before continuing with the second part of his explanation. 'I met them because they came over to Mumbai to meet us.'

He knew the lie was a small price to pay for peace. After all these years, he hadn't returned home with the intention of getting into an argument with his father. Reva had strictly instructed him to be polite and explain the scenario as gently as he could.

'How do we meet the girl now?' Gayatri held her son's hand. 'Can she come down?'

'It'll be a bit difficult,' Anshuman pursed his lips. 'She just took a long leave sometime ago. I can make her talk to you and you can see her as well.'

'Okay,' Gayatri looked unsure but she looked pleadingly at her husband requesting him not to argue. 'Will she be able to see us as well?'

'Absolutely,' Anshuman smiled zealously.

**

That night, Anshuman Mehra had enough reasons to throw a party for anyone who worked at Skype. For the next forty minutes, mummy Gayatri chatted and giggled with her would-be daughter-in-law Reva over the messenger while daddy Akashdeep dropped in for a brief and sceptical introduction.

Anshuman looked on amazed at the unexpected camaraderie between the two women in his life. They exchanged all that they knew about Anshuman who felt like a victim for loving both of them. So, as his past and present were shared and laughed at over the net, Anshuman realised his marriage was now safe on the cards.

**

The 8th of February, the very next year, the Gokhale residence was the busiest abode in the locality. The guests stayed at a half an hour's distance from the house, while the Mehras were put up at a relative's vacant flat on the same lane.

Around half a kilometre away, Rani Kothi lawns were decorated lavishly for the occasion, as Mohanlal Gokhale looked after the arrangements himself and ensured that everything was in apple pie order. A few of his cousins and nephews made sure that nothing went amiss that evening. Their son-in-law and his relatives were all Punjabis. Hence, it was imperative that they shouldn't be offended by anything. Mohanlal had even planned to arrange a special counter for non-vegetarians, but put it off at Anshuman's insistence.

Akashdeep Mehra walked into the venue with a couple of Anshuman's close mates in tow to have a look at the arrangements and help the bride's party. Mohanlal saw Akashdeep Mehra and hurried over to meet him. This was the second time the two parties were coming together, the first one being a formal introduction cum engagement ceremony the previous November.

'Good morning, Mr Mehra,' Mohanlal Gokhale shook his hand. 'Why did you trouble yourself by coming here?'

'You have been working for so long,' Akashdeep smiled. 'I just came over to see if you need any help.'

'What are you saying?' Mohanlal shook his head. 'Do you think I will take help from my daughter's father-in-law? No way... You are our guests here. Please get some rest. I am extremely happy doing this.'

Akashdeep grinned and shook Mohanlal's hand again.

'I hope I can do as much whenever you come down to Lucknow,' he said.

'Don't embarrass me like this,' the bride's father smiled. 'We have got Anshuman for our daughter. We don't need anything else.'

Akashdeep smiled. Despite the differences with his son, he always enjoyed the attention and praise Anshuman's achievements had brought in. And this time around, he was equally proud of the girl his son had chosen. Despite the brief interaction with Reva, Akashdeep could see that even he couldn't have found someone more eligible and apt for their son. He was about to say so when Milind hugged his father from behind.

'Baba is a great fan of Jiju,' Milind complained. 'I am already scared about my status in the family in the future.'

Akashdeep laughed as Mohanlal stroked his son's head.

'The more you get to know Anshuman,' Akashdeep Mehra said proudly, 'the more you like him. That's the best part about him.'

'That's even more frightening,' Milind laughed, 'because Jiju impressed Baba in their first meeting. And if this affection grows, then I am going to have tough time ahead. They chatted for two hours when Taai and Jiju came home for the first time. What an impression in the first meeting! Taai and Jiju are tough examples for me to follow.'

'Anshu came here before?' the smile on Akashdeep's face vanished almost instantaneously. 'You met him when he came here?'

'Reva and Anshuman came here a week before he went off to meet you in Lucknow,' Mohanlal looked concerned at the sudden change in Akashdeep's reaction.

'Okay,' Akashdeep could feel his head spin in anger. 'I was not aware of that.' He exhaled and tried to fake a smile, 'I will just go and check all our relatives are fine.'

'Sure,' Mohanlal looked sceptically. 'I will arrange for everyone's breakfast.'

By now, Akashdeep's breath had started inflating. When Anshuman saw his father enter the guesthouse, he knew something was wrong. But he was surrounded by relatives readying for the turmeric ceremony. Anshuman sat on a stool, as the women stood around waiting for their chance to smear turmeric on the groom. Gayatri's mother was the first to get the opportunity. The old lady was Anshuman's only surviving grandparent and had come down from Lucknow to be with her little boyfriend on his special day. Gayatri was next in line, as the women giggled and looked at the groom sitting diffidently in his vest and shorts.

Akashdeep walked in for a brief moment and looked at his son and wife. 'Meet me when you guys are done.'

Gayatri looked at her son and he pursed his lips to express that he had no idea why they were wanted. An hour later, Anshuman walked along the corridor with his mother to his father's room. A marigold got stuck under his right foot as he stepped into his father's room, trying to remove the flower.

'When did you meet them for the first time,' Akashdeep gritted, 'your in-laws?'

The question was enough for Anshuman to realise what had happened. He had feared the question creeping up in their earlier meetings and had made sure that it hadn't. At times, he had pondered over telling Reva to warn her family, but decided against it. She wouldn't have understood his reason for lying and neither would her folks. However, by then, he had stopped thinking about it, almost sure that the matter was dead and buried. Bu as luck would be, it turned out otherwise.

'Why did you lie to us?' Gayatri looked at her son. 'You could have told us.'

'This thing would have happened even then,' Anshuman looked at her.

Gayatri knew that her son was being honest. 'You could have told me,' she held her son's hand. 'I would have tried to make your Papa understand your perspective.'

'Brilliant,' Akashdeep Mehra threw his hands in air. 'That's where he has learnt all of this.'

'Papa, please,' Anshuman hated how his father dragged Maa in their conversation and blamed her, 'let's keep this between the two of us.'

'I am going home,' Akashdeep Mehra ended the discussion.

'Listen to me,' Gayatri rushed to her husband. 'I know you are angry with him. And your anger is absolutely justified. But it's such a special day for him and us as well. You can scold him later on. Let's not spoil everything today.'

'Make any excuse you want,' her husband was in no mood to relent, 'but I can't stay here today. I am not asking you to come with me. You can stay here and take care of the rituals.'

'But it will look so weird,' she insisted. 'Just wait for a day. Let the wedding go off peacefully. You can go home tomorrow.'

'It was more important for him to take permission from the girl's family than from us,' Akashdeep could feel his voice turning gruff and loud. 'We might have as well as given birth to a girl in that case. What's the benefit of having a son?'

'We didn't come to take permission,' Anshuman defended his stance. 'We wanted to share the news and take their suggestions. And don't treat me like a catch. This son-daughter thing...'

'Look what they have done to him,' the senior Mehra screamed at his wife. 'They have moulded him to make us his second priority.'

'Stop!' Anshuman could hear himself shout in disgust. 'Stop dragging others into our argument. I didn't do this intentionally to hurt you. I just wanted to avoid you feeling betrayed and that's exactly why I lied then. But, if you want to make that an issue and leave, I won't stop you.'

'Anshu...' Gayatri looked pleadingly at her son.

But by then, Anshuman had already turned and walked towards the door. As he pulled the door open and stepped out, he saw Krutika Gokhale standing there. The middle-aged lady, carrying a plate of sweets and snacks for her daughter's in-laws, didn't expect this sudden chaos hours before her daughter's wedding. She looked shaken as Anshuman stormed angrily into the corridor. With all her courage, she smiled feebly at her would be son-in-law. Anshuman looked back, as if wanting his mother-in-law to understand the situation by herself. She nodded and patted his cheek.

**

Akashdeep Mehra left for airport within an hour while Gayatri stayed back with the relatives, trying her best to distract others from the absence of her husband. But there was no perfect excuse, especially after they had seen his livid expression. Anshuman saved his mother from further embarrassment by not revealing that her counterpart knew everything.

Reva and Anshuman finally got married.

On the 11th of February 2007, the two held their reception in Mumbai. The Banerjees appeared together, surprising the new Mehras, and all the invitees turned up to wish the couple a happy conjugal life. The Mehras made everyone comfortable as guests kept pouring in at the Trident Banquet Hall. Chand performed his latest chartbusters and made sure the guests remained busy on their feet throughout.

A week later, Anshuman and Reva flew off to Frankfurt.

Ten

Present Time

DAY 1
6:20 p.m.

Anshuman produced the health insurance card at the reception. The service executive smiled at him and tallied the card details with the database. As her client looked outside blankly, she turned to speak to her colleague sitting on the adjacent chair.

'I am sorry, sir,' the lady called.

'Excuse me,' Anshuman looked back at her.

'This card won't be valid here,' she said.

'It has a cashless facility,' Anshuman tried to justify, 'and my insurance company has a tie-up with you. We have about eight lakh rupees of coverage and the due date is still far away.'

'You are absolutely right, sir,' the lady smiled back, 'and all your details are accurate as well. But we can hold this entire thing, I mean the policy, valid when we have the report of an accident against her name.'

'That's what you have, right?' Anshuman frowned. 'You have her accident report from some sub-inspector. Dr Ahmed told me so.'

'The police report is in the name of Mrs Reva Kashyap,' the receptionist explained. 'We need a police report in the name of Mrs Reva Mehra stating that it was an accident.'

'But they are the same person,' Anshuman sighed disgusted. 'How does it matter?'

'I won't be able to explain this to your insurance company,' she answered. 'I need to have the documents in place. Why don't you have a talk with your agent?'

'Hmmm,' Anshuman shook his head and went back.

The insurance agent's number kept ringing as Anshuman held the receiver. The call ended without response, as Siddharth Kashyap held a nurse's hand and crutched ahead towards the reception.

'Why are you roaming around?' Anshuman looked perturbed at Siddharth. 'You are not in a state to do that. And I don't want two liabilities together.'

'Why can't you just let me pay the money?' Siddharth breathed heavily from the exertion. 'You can solve your insurance problem and pay me back. We shouldn't delay the payment.'

'I have a credit card as well,' Anshuman replied curtly. 'So, that is not an issue.'

'Still...' Siddharth was about to put forward his counter-argument when Anshuman's phone rang up. Anshuman lifted his index finger and excused himself to attend the call. The insurance agent had called back. The name "Pankaj Bhatia" flashed on the screen.

'Mr Bhatia,' Anshuman walked out of the door, 'I need some help from you.'

'Well,' Bhatia replied after he heard the entire thing, 'you know, Mr Mehra, I am at Wankhede today. So, I won't be able to give you the options. But I guess you should get a new police report in this case. That will kind of simplify things. Still, it will be difficult today since everyone's watching the match and tomorrow is a Sunday.'

'You said such minor issues won't cause any problems,' Anshuman retorted. 'My wife is in hospital and you want me to go around police stations to revise FIR documents?'

'I am just helping you to ease out the process,' Bhatia consoled him. 'The BSG department is definitely going to raise some concern over that. She can't claim the policy if she is not your wife.'

'So, what you told me doesn't hold true and was just pure sales talk,' the anger in Anshuman's voice was evident. 'Thanks for all the help.'

Scoundrel!

***

The blue of the twilight had faded and a faint grey stepped in to colour the sky. It was gradually turning darker. Anshuman looked at his watch, as the dials showed 7:25 p.m. The Indian team seemed to have lost a couple of crucial wickets; or at least that's what the moans from the cafeteria suggested. Shubhanshu was supposed to call back half an hour earlier but there had been no response till now. As much as Anshuman hated insurance companies and their sales strategies, he had no option but to abide by their rules. He needed a new report from the sub-inspector with Reva's original name on the paper, but the cop wouldn't oblige without permission from the higher ups.

Shubhanshu had messaged that he knew a cop who could help him out. But the ACP was a tough catch and Banerjee himself was in Scotland. So, Anshuman had no option but to wait till he could get through to the cop and book an appointment. The advertising wizard strolled restively around the lobby, checking his phone every minute to ensure he hadn't missed the call, while Siddharth sat on a sofa and spoke to his own contacts.

'Shall I ask Mr Bhalla?' Siddharth looked up sceptically.

'Who's Mr Bhalla?' Anshuman stopped and looked at Siddharth.

'Raj Bhalla,' Siddharth knew it was not the most apt suggestion. But still, Rajvardhan Bhalla knew the most powerful people in town and had the ability to solve problem with much greater ease than anyone else.

'Whoa! Rajvardhan Bhalla,' Anshuman scoffed at the naivety of the proposal. 'You want the entire media to flock here? I am trying to keep this under wraps.'

'I won't ask him to come here,' Siddharth defended, 'but at least he can give us some lead.'

'Thanks,' Anshuman turned and started walking again, when Shubhanshu called.

'Finally,' the desperation was evident in his voice. 'When can the guy meet us?'

'Eleven is very late, Banerjee,' Anshuman's urgency was palpable as he held the phone and listened to his friend's response. 'But are you sure that the guy will be able to help us out with that?'

'He'll be at the Bandra police station right?

'No, this hospital comes under that. So, the report has to come from there, right?'

'Fair enough, I am going by your words. I'll be there at eleven.'

'Thanks.'

After a long time, a smile of relief marked Anshuman's face. It was a temporary accomplishment but a long awaited respite. At 11pm, even the police would corroborate that Reva was his wife.

'Great,' Siddharth spoke in a congratulatory tone, 'so you finally found a way out.'

'Yup,' Anshuman nodded and almost immediately it struck him that Reva was still in the operation theatre. A lightning of remorse struck him as he realised what he had ignored in the entire rigmarole of finding a way to prove himself right. Maybe at times, he was indeed as selfish as Reva said. He turned around and looked at Siddharth.

'Let's go to the OT.'

***

The operation lasted for approximately four hours. There was no clue whether the person who had kept the two men entangled in empathy and bitterness was going to survive the major surgery. Dr Ahmed had confessed that it was going to be critical but then, she was also the best. She hardly had any record of a failure. And now, she was the only one who stood between Reva and death.

Anshuman and Siddharth sat in the lobby, waiting for someone to come out of the room and disseminate the news about Reva's health. However, there was no trace of anyone coming out of the operation theatre. A deluge of thoughts flooded Anshuman's mind yet again as he pondered over the implications of what lay ahead. Mohanlal Gokhale was due to arrive in a few hours. At times, he thought he would give up everything and pass on the responsibility to his father-in-law. But it only brought in a sense of penitence as he felt like an apostate trying to run away from his duty. At the same time, the prying eyes he had circumvented till then were bound to gain cognizance of the scenario, and ogle at it while the realities crystallised.

Siddharth, on the other hand, had no option but to keep the armour of self-defence on, at least till Reva could wake up to hold his shield. The man standing in front of him had already claimed that he was the culprit behind her state. He didn't want the world to blame him for killing her. He loved Reva more than her husband; and only she could convince the world. Their love couldn't be so futile that he would be relegated to being a trespasser in someone's marriage.

Finally, as nurse Gaitonde came out of the room, Anshuman sprang up and walked hastily towards her.

'Her heartbeat was fluctuating,' she tried to put on an encouraging smile. 'That's why it took us so long. She is fine now.'

For a moment, Anshuman could feel his entire weight deaden

his knees, as he bent down and exhaled. 'Thank God!' a drop of tear rolled down his lashes as he closed his eyes and felt the lump is his throat dissolve.

Siddharth gripped the base of his seat and slowly leaned back on the wall. His breathing was finally relaxed. He closed his eyes and muttered a small prayer. Slowly, he held his crutch and limped up.

'Thanks a lot, sister,' Siddharth smiled gratefully at her.

She nodded at him and went away.

'I knew it couldn't be that bad,' Siddharth looked at Anshuman.

'At least some of your guilt is absolved,' Anshuman spoke dryly and paused. It was an unnecessary statement. 'Sorry,' he looked up and sighed. 'Let's have some tea. Come.'

'I don't like tea,' Siddharth shook his head.

'You can have coffee then,' Anshuman shrugged. 'I don't drink coffee, that's why I said tea.'

'You know,' Siddharth smiled. 'She makes the best coffee I have ever had.'

'Reva?' Anshuman looked amazed. 'But she never has coffee at home. She prefers tea.'

'Reva doesn't like tea,' Siddharth frowned. 'She drinks coffee with me. And she loves it.'

They looked at each other for a while. For a moment, both men wondered what could be the best way to explain the scenario.

'I am sure there are many such things where her choices varied like this,' Siddharth looked away in disbelief. 'We never knew her, did we?'

'Perhaps we never tried to,' Anshuman sighed. 'We just interpreted her the way we wanted to, and fell in love with our own interpretations.'

***

'It's a part of the post nascent crisis,' Anshuman sat in the cafeteria. 'All marriages go through this when the fluorescence of the early period slowly fades away. Things seem rosy the first year or two before you start pointing out the vices in your partners more often than the virtues.'

Siddharth nodded in agreement.

'I knew my marriage was not perfect,' Anshuman went on, 'and neither were we.'

'You doubted her?' Siddharth said.

'No, no,' Anshuman blurted out, 'I never did. In fact, I always thought my marriage was faring pretty well. I was proud of its success, until I saw you and realised how much I had failed.'

'The problem is with expectations,' Siddharth tried to infer. 'You treated her way you wanted her to be, but she could never do the same because you never moulded yourself to her wishes the way she could fit into your daily routine. Men and women, you see.'

Anshuman pursed his lips.

'The same is true for me as well,' Siddharth justified, 'or else she would have left you and come to me. Her intelligence mattered to you, her beauty to me. So, we both loved a part of her and she loved us back in parts.'

Anshuman looked at his teacup and ran his fingers around its rim.

'What do you think,' Anshuman questioned, 'made her cling on to you?'

'I made her feel beautiful,' Siddharth smiled, 'and she liked that feeling.'

'Do you really think it was love?' Anshuman said, 'Or was it just lust that kept you together?'

'There's lust as often as there is love,' Siddharth sipped his coffee. 'So, neither of them is unnatural. We were not guilty of that.'

'Then what were you guilty of?' Anshuman looked puzzled.

'Feigning to be mere acquaintances in public,' Siddharth looked up. 'We were guilty of pretensions.'

Anshuman chuckled at his opponent's misplaced sense of guilt.

'It's an art to pretend in public,' he looked at Siddharth. 'It's not her fault. Marriage teaches this lesson to everyone.'

Eleven

Reva

'It is going to be far tougher than it sounds,' Mohanlal sat at the dining table facing his daughter. 'Hunting for news in big cities with unknown people around you is going to be difficult.'

'When did I ever say it's going to be easy?' Reva savoured the curry, while her mother served the others. 'But then, there is more news in Mumbai than there is here.'

'Don't make that sound,' Krutika slapped the head of her son who chewed his food noisily. 'At least let them hear each other.'

'I am not eating that loud,' Milind scowled.

'Eat quietly,' Mohanlal looked at his son. 'It's about personal etiquette.'

'Can we please come back to what we were discussing?' Reva intervened to save her brother.

'Don't spoil him,' Krutika dropped the spoon into the bowl. 'He is too old to learn manners now.'

'Then it's not going to help anyway,' the siblings winked at each other.

'Coming back to Mumbai,' Mohanlal shook his head.

'Thanks,' Milind munched his food again.

'I am sure, Baba,' Reva smiled reassuringly at her father, 'like always. I wouldn't have taken this step had I not been absolutely certain.'

'Trust me, she will get a Punjabi guy for herself,' Milind laughed.

'You are seeing someone?' Krutika Gokhale spoke astounded.

'When did you start taking him seriously?' Reva looked at her brother angrily, 'And from where did this come up?'

'She will be in Mumbai – the big jungle,' Milind tried to justify his statement. 'Obviously she will find those hunks from the north far more attractive than our local lot.' He looked around and continued. 'Let's accept this. These Punjabi and Muslim guys are ruling Bollywood because they are handsome, and we localites can't compete with them because we aren't. Of course there are exceptions.'

'Yeah,' Reva looked firmly at him, 'and you are an exception. Eat your food.'

***

Reva was right. The new city was far more eventful than her hometown 860 kilometres away. And she experienced something new that she had never done before in Nagpur – competition. There were tons of reporters and journalists who jumped at the slightest opportunity to break the smallest of news; something that made her life quite miserable. Unlike most of her rivals, she hated the idea of taking little pieces of information and then blowing them out of proportion, just for the sake of sensationalism.

A month after she had joined, Reva was introduced to her boss and the regional head – Dipanwita Banerjee. When Reva walked into her cabin for the first time, the middle-aged senior correspondent was talking to someone over phone.

'Yes, Rahul,' she spoke and signalled at Reva to sit.

'I don't want to know your personal obligations, sweetheart,' Dipanwita went on while Reva looked at her intently.

A very traditional Bengali sense of dressing, she thought as she studied the rich cotton sari with a matching blouse, the red and white bangles on the wrist, the big red bindi on the forehead, and the rimless reading glasses hanging from the spectacle chain. There was a composed gracefulness about Dipanwita Banerjee's persona – something very striking and attractive.

'The tapes should reach me by today evening, Rahul,' Dipanwita raised her index finger indicating her junior to wait for a minute. 'I can't afford to delay it any further. See I am very lenient because I know that all of you are under a lot of pressure. But I can't let you take me for granted.'

Reva felt her toes tremble at her new boss' tone. She knew she would soon be at the receiving end herself.

'You please sort out the differences with your girlfriend and concentrate on your work,' Dipanwita covered the mouth of the receiver and asked her visitor if she wanted tea. 'You know what Prabhat does to me. I abide by my deadlines and I expect you guys to do the same.'

Reva shook her head and sighed.

'No problem! Just let her be and get back to office. Women sulk when you pay them too much attention. She will be okay when left alone.' Dipanwita laughed over the phone. 'See you.'

'So do you like the new place?' Reva's new boss sipped from her glass of water, 'Bombay – the city of adulterated dreams!'

Reva smiled at the comment. 'Too noisy,' she confided, 'and too much of travelling.'

'And a tough place to save money,' Dipanwita added with a smirk.

Reva smiled.

'Sorry we couldn't meet earlier as I have been away on an extended tour,' Dipanwita opened the uppermost drawer of her desk. 'I have heard nice things about you but the honeymoon period is almost over.'

'I know,' Reva looked on.

'You like business, right?' Dipanwita opened a folder and scanned through her new junior's resume once again. 'I feel you will do well with business related news.'

'I like... umm...' Reva searched for words at the unexpected proposal, 'not sure how good...'

'Don't worry, it's not the *Wall Street Journal*,' Dipanwita winked at her. 'After all we are the *Daily Times*. We are known for gossip and scandals, aren't we?'

Reva looked at her boss, without a clue how to respond.

'What you will primarily do is meet up with men from the corporate sectors,' Dipanwita paused and pondered for a while, 'and try to get interviews with popular guys in the business circuit. I am sure they won't refuse you.'

Reva blushed.

'Just don't be shy,' Dipanwita warned. 'I know you are a smart girl. I want you to be humorous. Not that you can be humorous if that's not your strength, but try to put in comments that will amuse them and make you look intelligent, because people are tired of dumb microphone carriers.'

Reva chuckled yet again.

'Trust me,' Dipanwita added in a more matter-of-fact tone. 'Your boss, Jennifer, is a bimbette herself. She would have been better off having kids at home, but she fetches a lot of interviews with her clothes. I want you to bring me more content on board.'

'I will do my best,' Reva tried to sound her sincere best.

'I am sure you will,' Dipanwita tied her folder and placed it back in the drawer. 'Now, get back to work.'

Reva stood up and walked back towards the door when Dipanwita called her again.

'You will be reporting directly to me,' the information came. 'I have a feeling you will not disappoint me.'

Reva exhaled. 'Okay.'

'But that doesn't mean I'm promoting you,' Dipanwita smiled mischievously, 'or raising your salary.'

Reva smiled and left the room.

***

During the next three years, Reva grew close to her boss. Dipanwita proved to be not only an able senior but also a mentor who helped her up the corporate ladder. The relation grew beyond a professional bond to personal dependence. While the senior colleague proved a support during times of distress and ethical dilemmas at work, the junior saw her through during an elongated phase of personal crisis. Despite her inexperience with complexities in marital relations, Reva turned out to be the rock Dipanwita needed when she decided to move out of her home.

**

'Jennifer,' Dipanwita Banerjee shouted from the door of her cabin.

Almost immediately, the boisterous Daily Times office turned quiet. Reva had just walked into her office after an interview when the yell caught her by surprise.

Jennifer Masceranas, once Reva's senior but now in the same position, ran across the office towards Dipanwita's cabin. But before she could reach the door, a bunch of stapled papers flew out and hit her face. Everyone looked at each other in shock as Jennifer bent down to pick the papers.

'Did I want a business interview or details of his sex life?' Dipanwita shouted loud enough for everyone to hear.

'I didn't ask him anything about his...' Jennifer mumbled her answer halfway when she was stopped.

'When did you meet your wife for the first time?' Dipanwita read aloud from a sheet she held in her hand. 'You went there to ask him about his new business campaign. The next question you perhaps wanted to ask was whether he prefers a missionary position or a dog shot.'

'Oh my god', Reva heard a colleague mutter as all eyes dilated in disbelief.

Jennifer weakened into tears, realising that the entire office was witnessing her deprecation.

'I have no interest in seeing you cry,' Dipanwita Banerjee said sternly. 'Just get lost until you learn how to conduct an interview.'

Jennifer rubbed her tears which had already smudged the eye-liner, 'I am sorry.'

**

'It's not her fault,' Reva stood in Dipanwita's cabin and looked straight at her. 'She didn't break up your home.'

'Don't,' Dipanwita raised her hand but the young girl standing in front of her was in no mood to relent.

'The first day I stepped into your cabin,' Reva went on, 'I heard you instructing Rahul to keep his professional and personal lives separate. But I don't see you doing that. Jennifer didn't ask any question she shouldn't have. We are not *Wall Street Journal,* remember? Our readers love reading about love and sex lives. We don't sell pure business.'

Dipanwita looked up, still breathing fast.

'You owe her an apology,' Reva was surprised by the courage she was displaying.

Fifteen minutes later, Dipanwita Banerjee stepped out of her cabin and walked straight to Jennifer's cubicle, where the latter was writing a story on the interview. The sight of her boss coming towards her seat was a scary sight for Jenny.

'Ma'am,' she stood up immediately.

'I am sorry, Jennifer,' Dipanwita kept her hand on the junior's shoulder.

'No, ma'am,' Jenny could feel her uneasiness.

'I shouted at you in front of everyone,' Dipanwita looked around. 'I am here to admit my fault before the others as well. I over-reacted. A bit too much! I am really sorry.'

As Reva looked on and smiled, Jennifer Masceranas burst out crying and hugged her boss, while the latter put her arms around the junior.

**

'How was yesterday's interview?' Dipanwita asked over lunch as they sat at in the office cafeteria.

'He is very knowledgeable,' Reva munched on the sandwich and added, 'and smart too.'

'I know,' Dipanwita nodded in acknowledgement of the fact. 'I have known him for a long time.'

'Really?' Reva was taken aback by the statement, 'How? You didn't tell me.' Before her boss could reply, she had guessed the connection. 'Your husband is with Airfone, right?'

Dipanwita nodded.

For a while, they ate quietly. Reva knew how much it hurt her senior talking about her husband or her marriage. Reva had tried to convince Dipa that things could improve with time, and that moving out would be a bad option. But somewhere in her heart, she realised she was too young and inexperienced to understand the complexities of her senior's marriage.

'So, what else did you guys discuss?' Dipanwita broke the ice. 'Did you find him good enough?' There was a teasing tone in her voice. 'Is he the right guy?'

'Actually,' Reva paused and raised her eyebrows.

'What?' Dipanwita sat up at the unexpected coyness in the response.

'Anshuman asked me out for a date,' Reva smiled sheepishly.

'He did?' Dipanwita realised she had spoken louder than what she expected of herself. 'What did you say? Don't tell me you turned him down.'

'We are meeting today at Leopold Cafe,' Reva broke the news, and found her boss laughing in glee. '8 p.m.'

'Amazing!'

***

Anshuman was quite formally dressed for the date. Reva chuckled at the sight of the black pinstriped suit but couldn't help appreciating the panache with which he carried it off even in the informal ambience. Anshuman, on the other hand, was bowled over by her purple evening dress and the way it draped around her.

'This is my first date in Bombay,' Anshuman confessed as they walked along Marine Drive after the meal. 'I feel quite odd.'

Reva laughed at the confession. 'Guess that's why you were wearing a suit,' she teased.

'You bet,' he replied with a tinge of awkwardness. 'It's been quite some time since I wore a fancy t-shirt.'

'But you should,' she insisted. 'You must be around twenty-eight but you don't look so.'

'Really?' he blushed. 'Thanks.'

'By the way,' it was time for her to admit. 'It's my first date here as well.'

After a moment's pause, they laughed out together. He laid down his handkerchief and sat by the road. She smiled to herself and sat down beside him.

'Were you in a relationship before?' she asked him during the conversation.

'It sounds weird,' he tried to control the embarrassment, 'but I have never been in love.'

'Nothing's weird about that,' she assured him. 'There's always a right time.'

'You have a boyfriend?' he garnered some courage and asked her.

'I had one,' she looked at the sea and turned at him. 'I wouldn't have been here if that wasn't *past tense.*'

He smiled at the remark. 'What happened then?'

'Nothing! Basically it was never meant to be. He was just not my type.'

'And what's your type?'

She laughed. 'Actually it was usual college romance – mushy, inexperienced, and immature!'

They looked at each other for a while and then turned to gaze at the sea. The cool night breeze with the fully lit up Queen' Necklace is one of the most resplendent sights of the city.

That night, when Anshuman dropped Reva home, both of them had inkling in their hearts that it might just be the beginning of a relationship they were both looking for. The courtship lasted for a year and half before Anshuman broached the topic of marriage. Though she had thought of the same, Reva had resolved not to be the first one to talk about it. And when he asked her, there was no way she could have turned him down. Her family was a bit conservative by nature, but she was confident her choice would win them over with his honesty, just the way he had enamoured her. It was his family that concerned her more. She knew Anshuman didn't share a good rapport with his parents, especially his father. He hadn't been home in six years, he had told her once. But when he assured her that things would fall into place, she believed him like every other time.

**

'Didn't I tell you she would marry a Punjabi guy?' Milind taunted his sister while helping his mother make the beds after dinner.

'Were you seeing him while in Nagpur?' his mother looked at her inquisitively.

'No, Aai,' she threw the pillow straight at her brother's face. 'I met him quite a while after reaching Mumbai. We know each other for a year and half now.'

Her mother still wore a puzzled look while Milind laughed.

'That was a fluke,' she assured her mother before the latter could pose another question. 'By the way what's Dad talking to Anshuman about?'

She had hardly finished the question when she saw the two men entering through the veranda door, with her father's hand over Anshuman's shoulder. She pointed the same to her mother and smiled elatedly.

***

The first time Reva physically met her in-laws was during the engagement. As mutually decided, they kept it a very low profile ceremony with only the family members around.

She had spoken to her mother-in-law before, once through a video-chat and once over the telephone. It took her no time to realise why Anshuman was so fond of her. With Gayatri's friendly disposition and caring nature, it was rather surprising that Anshuman could stay away from meeting his mother for a good part of a decade. And even more surprisingly, Gayatri Mehra had no complaints against her son. She seemed to love him unconditionally. Her father-in-law, on the other hand, was a man who remained to himself. She hardly saw him smile during the engagement ceremony. Though Anshuman had assured her that his family had no problems with the marriage, she found it difficult to infer the reason behind the stoicism of the man on the occasion. Neither could she understand why the man left his son's wedding and went away citing some inexplicable urgency, till Anshu told her the reason. Though at times, she could feel a soft corner in Akashdeep's heart for his son, their mutual coldness had discomfited the entire Gokhale family. But her mother-in-law made up for all the uneasiness they had felt. With her warm gestures and hospitality in Mumbai, Gayatri left a deep mark in their lives.

A week after their reception at Mumbai, Anshuman and Reva flew off for their honeymoon to their chosen destination – Germany.

As all the direct flights were full, the couple decided to reach Frankfurt via Zurich. It was the best option; moreover, it also provided them with six hours to check out the celebrated Swiss city. However, the wait to catch the connecting Lufthansa was enough for Reva to realise her folly choosing the destination. She cursed the fact that she had avoided Switzerland, purely to escape the clichéd honeymoon destination. But every moment of hers in Zurich reinstated what Dipanwita had suggested: Zurich should have been their destination, not the stopover.

With ample time in hand, Reva and Anshuman planned to go around the city before boarding the next flight. They cruised along the river Limmat for around half an hour before reaching Lake Zurich – one of the famous city spots. Extending to the southeast of the town of Zurich, the crystal-clear lake was ethereal with its serene beauty. *It is one of the rare lakes in the world*, Anshuman informed her, *that forms a source for potable water for the people in the city. You can drink it without any kind of purification.*

Their next stop was the popular food joint beside the Opera – Titbits. With an exquisite spread of vegetarian food, it proved to be the best choice. While Anshuman gorged on the vast spread at the vegetarian buffet, Reva ordered a sandwich and the item that looked the most delicious on the list – Mango Lassi.

'Try something else,' Anshuman spoke disappointed. 'You don't need to drink something just because it says lassi.'

'Well, I can go back and tell others I had lassi in Switzerland,' she winked. They both laughed at the silliness of the entire thing.

Reva loved the location of the restaurant. It was a minimally designed street-side joint with the Alps in the background; people sat at their tables and quietly ate their food, talking to each other in low-pitched voices as a beautiful young girl stood across the street and played the *Scent of a Woman* tune on her violin. It was a place where she could have lunch every afternoon. As Reva walked over to drop a franc she had exchanged at the airport, her heart sank in the whirlpool of thoughts.

Why do we rush so much every day, she told Anshuman. *Look at these people. They are so much at peace with themselves, not bothering about the next train to catch or the travails of having a low-paying job.*

However, it was the last stop that turned out to be the icing on the cake – the Lindenhof.

It is the oldest part of the city, with settlement traces dating to pre-Roman eras, and conserved as a recreational space – a green oasis and automobile free public space of the old historic city centre. Situated on the Lindenhof hill, to the left of the Limmat and the much celebrated romantic quarters of Schipfe – the place charmed the newlyweds with its beauty and old world charm. As Reva roamed around the site of the Roman castle, she felt she could spend an entire week there, without doing anything. And finally when they reached the zenith, she could feel her heart skip a beat. The entire city was laid out in front of her. With the giant Grossmunster Cathedral towers, the Bahnhofstrasse Street, the Limmat River flowing through the city and an endless count of houses and rooftops with the Alps in background horizon, the city looked pristine. *Beautiful,* she could hear her heart say, *I wish I hadn't planned on going somewhere else.* As people moved around, some made notes in their diaries and some drew sketches, she lamented the thought of leaving the place in such a hurry. Anshuman held her hand to signal it was time to make the return journey to airport – shattering her dreams and bringing her back to reality.

'Can't we just cancel Frankfurt,' she looked with pleading eyes, 'and stay here?'

'We have everything chalked out, baby,' he said. 'I have already paid the advance.'

She knew he was right.

Perhaps it was the hangover of her feelings for Zurich that soured the rest of her journey. Once they were on the short flight from Zurich to Frankfurt, all Reva could see were snow-capped mountains with small huts and lush green grass. It was a sight she had never cherished before –something so mesmerising that she wanted to hold on to it forever. And after half an hour, she woke up to the plane descending among thousands of skyscrapers. All she could see were buildings and cars. There was no way to distinguish this place from New York, Hong Kong, Singapore. This was Frankfurt! It was almost like Mumbai sans the crowd, pollution and smiling faces. The city seemed to be in a rush – with no one, absolutely no one in a mood to rejoice.

She had been so upbeat at the thought of hiring a BMW 7-series and driving down the Autobahn when she had made the plan. But after the experience she had savoured at her previous destination, everything seemed to fade in comparison. Anshuman and Reva had surmised that the unusual choice will enamour them with all the things Germany is known best for - luxury brand of automobiles, no speed-limit highways and unlimited beer - the three reasons to let go of romantic Paris and splendour Switzerland in favour of this highly urbanised Deutschland. Yet, as they travelled to the neighbouring cities and drove to Cologne and Bonn via the exquisite highway, the only sight she could hang on to was that of the Zurich city laid out before her from the top of Lindenhof. On the sixth day, they visited Nurburgring – just 80 kilometres from Cologne. Home to the one of the best Formula 1 racing tracks where one gets to drive a car around the track at racing speeds, the place had excited both of them for its sheer prospect of fun and common love for racing. But as Anshuman utilised every moment and drank more beer than water, Reva realised that the first difference in choices had surfaced in their new life. She wanted to dismiss it and move on, but something in her heart did not permit her to.

***

As many friends had told her, the first year of marriage was an elongated honeymoon. Life seemed like a bed of roses for the couple who overlooked all the differences and vices in the partner for the sake of love. They accepted the other just the way they were without any demands of adjustment. It was only the beginning of the second year that differences between the couple started creeping in. The first major reason was that Reva decided to shift from the business section.

'But you are good at it,' Anshuman opined. 'Why do you want to change?'

He was seated at the dining table while she brought in the food from the kitchen.

'Because I am bored,' Reva explained. 'It has been too long in the same section."

'It's your domain,' Anshuman expressed his disagreement clearly. 'I am doing the same thing every day. We can't just leave what we're competent in for the sake of excitement. We don't belong to that age.'

'That may be true for you,' Reva walked towards the table with the bowl of rice and went back to fetch the dal. 'My area of competency is journalism, not business. Like you are passionate about advertisements, I am good at presenting news.'

'Can you please wait and finish the discussion?' Anshuman felt irate at her walking in and out of the kitchen. 'This is so annoying.'

She laughed out. Anshuman was very strict about manners and etiquette. 'Okay,' she placed the dal on the table.

'What do you want to do?' he took a deep breath and asked.

'Crime,' she sat on the chair like an excited teenager sharing career plans with her parents, 'something that will give me goose bumps.'

'Are you mad?' Anshuman rubbished her idea with a smirk. 'No way are you shifting to Crime.'

'I have planned it for a long time, Anshu,' she was taken aback at the refusal, 'I mean...'

'You are not doing it,' he placed his foot down. 'I am not going to let you do it.'

'There's no danger, sweetheart,' she knew he was concerned. 'Nothing happens to journalists.'

'I don't need any justification, Reva,' he waived off the argument. 'You are not getting into the Crime section. Apart from the danger bit, you are not cut out for it. Your USP is the way you carry yourself – capitalise on that. Do Entertainment if you want, but not Crime!'

'Anshu, please,' somehow he seemed so aggressive that she felt unnerved. 'I have been thinking of doing it...'

'End of the discussion,' he interrupted her for the second time during the conversation and started serving the rice on his plate. 'I don't want to talk about it anymore.'

'I serve the dinner every night,' she stood up. 'I could have done it today as well.'

As Anshuman poured the dal in a bowl, she went back into the kitchen.

**

The next day, Reva broached the topic before Dipanwita. As they sat across the lunch table and opened their lunch boxes, she narrated how Anshuman firmly refused to let her do Crime. Surprisingly, her boss reiterated almost exactly what her husband had said at the dining table the previous night.

'I think he's right,' Dipanwita scooped a spoonful of the salad and chewed it. 'I don't feel you are right for that department.'

'You think I won't be able to do it?' Reva was surprised at the comment. She had always thought that her senior found her capable of anything.

'Frankly,' she paused and pondered over how she should frame the second part, 'I don't. What do you want to do in Crime? Why waste your looks in a field that doesn't deserve it? If you want to do something else, try Entertainment or Page 3 for that matter.'

Reva hated the first option, not because she disliked the section but it was the same option Anshuman had suggested during their argument the previous night.

'You think I will be good in Page 3?' she looked up sceptically.

'It might not utilise your talents fully,' Dipanwita munched the sandwich and smiled, 'but you are going to kill the competition.'

***

It was known to everyone that Samaria Khan was the mistress of the much married Rajvardhan Bhalla. Besides being a former model and associated with brand DIVA, Samaira was also the favourite of the shutterbugs. A complete party freak, heedless to the reaction that her relation with Bhalla fetched, Samaira basked in the glory the industrialist's company brought her. Though Rajvardhan had never come out before the media and accepted their relation, it was his silence that affirmed everything. His wife, on the other hand, had never made any acerbic statements about the other woman in her husband's life, and was surprisingly cordial with Samaira.

'Welcome to the party, my love,' Samaira kissed Reva on the cheek. 'You look stunning.'

'Not as gorgeous as you,' Reva returned the compliment. 'Look at you. You seem to get sexier with each passing day.'

'Come, I'll introduce you to someone,' Samaira tugged at her guest's arm. 'He'll decide who looks better.'

'Who?' Reva laughed and walked along with her host.

Samaira walked along the hall, holding Reva's arm. They stopped behind a man whose back was towards them. Samaira patted his back and he turned around to look at them.

'This is Reva,' Samaira introduced, 'one of the most gorgeous journalists of the nation. She should have been a model, right?'

Reva felt embarrassed at the unexpected introduction. She looked at the man and realised that he had noticed her reaction. He seemed around four or five years younger than her. In a velvet jacket with contrasting sequined t-shirt and jeans, he looked trendy and smart. *Must be a model,* Reva thought to herself.

The man smiled and nodded appreciatively. 'Very true!'

'And this is Siddharth,' Samaira spoke and rolled her hand through his upper arm, 'one of the most popular fashion photographers around. Getting a compliment from him is a big thing girl. You shouldn't have got married so early.'

Siddharth Kashyap. She had heard a lot about him lately. His DIVA edition with Maya Bose followed by the enormous amount Bhalla paid for his photographs at his exhibition had been making waves in the circuit. And she soon realised that the maverick photographer was an equally impressive speaker. The fame and regular interaction with media had moulded him at a young age. There was a certain panache with which he carried himself.

The party was more eventful than it was anticipated to be. The principal reason could be ascribed to Rajvardhan Bhalla's announcement of his expansion plans. He was taking DIVA to a global level, and as expected, the connoisseur of glamour was doing it with style. For the rest of the evening, everyone found that one topic to hush and gush about. And Reva knew that the rest of the country would do the same for the next few days.

'Coming here has paid off well for you,' a guest told Reva. He was another party regular, who loved the very sight of Reva.

'Absolutely,' she laughed. 'This is big news. The buzz will start tomorrow morning.'

'You will make sure it does,' the man winked and Reva laughed out again.

'Hi,' someone spoke from back.

Reva turned in surprise and saw Siddharth standing there.

'Hey,' she acknowledged, 'Congrats.'

'Congratulations,' the man looked at Siddharth.

The latter acknowledged the wishes from the unknown person and turned to Reva again.

'I'll take your leave, Reva,' the guest excused himself. 'See you again.'

'Goodbye,' Reva smiled at him and then turned to look at Siddharth.

'So what do you think of the photo shoot now?'

Reva laughed. The idea of being persisted for a shoot by someone of Siddharth's calibre and fame was indeed humbling and exciting. Which girl wouldn't like to be captured by someone who knows how to make her look beautiful? A part of her wanted to jump at the proposal. But then, she had never been too keen on posing for cameras. Though a few people had suggested that she could take up modelling, none as popular and adroit as him had ever approached her. It felt bad turning him down, but she knew Anshuman wouldn't be pleased with the idea. Even if he didn't ask her to turn it down, the idea of modelling wouldn't go down well with him. She had to say "no".

'I didn't say *no* because I distrusted your skill or whatever,' she raised her eyebrows. 'I just don't like the idea of posing for cameras. Have always been like this.'

'And why's that?' Siddharth frowned.

She thought of a reason but came out with a poor one. 'Never been photogenic you see.'

'Oh come on, you are kidding me now.' Siddharth rubbished the explanation. After all the compliments she had received that evening, it was surely tough to make someone believe she was not photogenic; and definitely not the man who knew the camera better than most.

'Not exactly, I just don't like it.' Reva just wanted to escape without further discussion on the same. 'Sorry but...'

'Okay,' Siddharth sighed. He had realised she wouldn't tell him the actual reason, but would not agree to the shoot either.

'All the best for the calendar though,' there was an apologetic tone in her voice. There was a part of her that still wanted to accept the offer, but she had decided against it.

'Thanks,' Siddharth gave her his hand and she shook it.

Twelve

Present Time

DAY 1
9:15 p.m.

The two men were still seated in the cafeteria, engaged in their conversation. They never realised when the enmity between them had subsided, giving way to empathy for each other. It was their concern for Reva that kept them together throughout the day.

'It's still easier for us,' Siddharth broke the silence, 'to introspect and analyse what went wrong.'

Anshuman looked at him.

'But we both concentrated on our individual lives,' Siddharth went on, 'whereas for her, the focus was divided into three parts – you, me and herself – and the third part we never knew.'

'Don't make her sound like a victim, Siddharth,' Anshuman refuted. 'I can understand what she must have gone through but nothing justifies what she did.'

Anshuman saw Siddharth's expression of disapproval as he spoke.

'Trust me,' Anshuman went on, 'you would have said the same had you been me. My relation with her had all the strings knotted, none of which tied the two of you. I was never bad to her, I gave her everything and neither was I incapable in any way to make her happy.'

'You are right, Mr Mehra,' Siddharth nodded finally, 'and your feelings are right at their place. But love is very strange. It often blossoms where it's not meant to grow.'

Anshuman was about to comment how cheesy the line sounded when Siddharth's phone started ringing. *How could Reva like someone who sounded so cheesy!*

'Tell me,' Siddharth answered, 'yeah... cafeteria... third floor.'

'You got a visitor?' Anshuman asked.

'Chand is here.'

The entire crowd in the cafeteria burst out into a moan of anguish. Anshuman and Siddharth looked at the television set at the corner, with a multitude of eyes ogling into it, anxiously awaiting the culmination of their long-standing dream. And the same seemed to have come crushing down as Gautam Gambhir rushed down the track and went for the slog, only to let the ball crash into the mid-wicket and send the bales flying. There was a gasp of disappointment but almost immediately the crowd in the cafeteria applauded the departing batsman in unison with the audience at the stadium.

***

Chand was in the midst of a recording when Sid had called.

The electronic timer on his recording machine's taskbar showed 3:15 p.m. when an assistant rushed in and handed over the phone to him. The apprentice knew Chand hated being disturbed during any recording, but it was one of those exceptions his boss always allowed.

'*Sir, it's your friend, Siddharth,*' *the boy informed Chand.* '*He says it's urgent.*'

'*Come whenever you can,*' *his friend said as the ground underneath him seemed to give away.*

'*I will come right away,*' *Chand said, his voice shaking.*

'*Finish the song,*' *Siddharth told him,* '*I am fine.*'

'*Are you sure?*'

'Yes.'

'Okay. I will make it ASAP.'

'Chand, there's something else.'

'Tell me,' the musician spoke earnestly. *'You want me to get something?'*

'There's someone here you might feel awkward meeting.'

'I would feel awkward? Who?'

'Anshuman Mehra!'

'Anshuman?' the surprise in Chand's voice was palpable. *'Why is he there?'*

'She was his wife.'

For a while, Chand was dumbfounded. So, that was the girl Siddharth was involved with! Chand knew that Siddharth was dating someone, and wanted to wait for the right moment to share the details with Chand. Siddharth knew the kind of relation Chand shared with Anshuman and his family. Yet, he had been going through all of this behind his back.

'I was your best friend, Sid.'

'You still are.'

'And you never felt you needed to tell me this. Anshuman Mehra's wife!'

'Chand... I know...'

'Dude, you know how much I respect Anshuman Mehra. He is the one who made me what I am today.'

Siddharth had never heard his best friend this angry and hurt. There had been trying times when Chand was passing through a rough patch – but he had never lost his temper. Keeping his cool was one of his biggest strengths, something Siddharth had always admired about him.

'I understand, Chand.'

'What I don't understand now, Sid, is how I am going to face that man?' Siddharth could feel the genuine pang of worry in Chand's voice, *'What's going to happen when he comes to know of it?'*

'He knows. I told you he is here.'

'Yeah, of course,' Chand seemed to struggle for words. 'Is he in front of you?'

'No,' Siddharth looked at the nurse standing in his room. 'He has gone downstairs to fetch Reva's driving licence from my car.'

'I will be there in some time.' Chand hung up.

The thought of facing Anshuman with this burdening sense of guilt was debilitating Chand from within. Breaking the trust of the man who had given him the first big break made him feel miserable. On the other hand, it was also about his best friend and biggest confidant. The friend who had been his biggest pillar of support through the toughest of times, the friend who had accepted him unconditionally – Siddharth was someone whom Chand could never think of betraying. All he could wish for at that point of time was to take a stand that could appease both men. *Why didn't Sid tell me whom he was seeing,* he cribbed, *I wouldn't have let this happen!*

As Chand stepped into the cafeteria, he caught a glimpse of Anshuman and Siddharth sitting at a corner table. Even before he could look apologetically at his mentor, his best friend's injuries caught his attention. Siddharth's head was bandaged, his right arm was plastered and a crutch stood by his side – Chand could feel the tears fill his eyes at the plight of his ex-room mate. He brushed the tears away and walked towards the table. Anshuman was the first to notice him. Siddharth caught the glance turned around.

'Hi,' Chand looked at Anshuman, at which the latter nodded.

'Hey, man,' Siddharth gave his left hand. 'Sit.'

'You look miserable, Sid,' Chand gushed as he sat on the adjacent chair. 'You didn't tell me it was so serious. I would have come earlier.'

'I am alright, dude,' Siddharth smiled. 'Don't worry about me.'

'So, you knew all about this?' Anshuman interrupted their conversation, 'Chand Pias?'

The musician had been dreading this question and hadn't been able to come up with a convincing answer.

'He didn't,' Siddharth replied on his friend's behalf. 'He had no clue about the girl I was dating.'

'How is it possible, Chand?' Anshuman still stared at the new entrant. 'Your best friend was seeing someone for six months, and you didn't want to know who it was?'

'He asked me,' Siddharth replied once again. 'I told him to wait for the right moment.'

'I am sorry, Mr Mehra,' Chand turned to look at Anshuman. 'I know you can think that I kept you in the dark.'

'No, he doesn't,' Siddharth interrupted before the other man could reply. 'Your relation with him is professional, Mr Mehra. And even if he knew, he doesn't owe you an explanation for keeping his best friend's personal life secret.'

'But that friend's personal life also included mine,' Anshuman could feel his teeth gritting in anger. Chand's presence was making the anger resurface.

'I had no clue,' Chand spoke. 'So, there was no way I could have stopped all of this.'

'Your life is your problem, Mr Mehra,' Siddharth replied firmly, 'not his. Don't drag him into something he is not involved in.'

'How could you be so ungrateful, Chand?' Siddharth's outburst convinced Anshuman that Chand was party to it.

'You gave him a break,' Siddharth protested, 'and he gave a super hit jingle for your ad. He's not obliged to you.'

'I want to talk to you alone,' Anshuman got up and walked off towards the door.

'You don't need to go,' Siddharth told Chand. 'You don't need to make yourself feel guilty about it.'

'It's better that I talk to him,' Chand got up.

Siddharth felt choleric at dragging the innocent guy into the matter.

'Chand, wait,' he got up and turned. But before he could control his movement, his left foot slipped and he tilted backwards, while his hands reached out for support. As one of the ward boys standing at the cafeteria reception ran ahead to catch him, Siddharth's fingers just managed to touch the side of the table and within a split second, the photographer came crashing down. His right elbow collapsed on the chair and the wooden seat flipped over to hit his head.

'Shit,' Chand ran to him but by then his friend had hurt his already fractured arm. Blood started streaming out of the right side of his temple while Siddharth wreathed in pain.

***

'How could you all be so careless?' Siddharth's nurse shouted at them. 'Even if he is desperate himself, you should have seen to it that he was careful.'

'I am sorry, sister,' Anshuman knew that he was indirectly responsible for this.

'Thank goodness the arm is okay,' the nurse looked disgusted at the two men. 'But he has hurt his head again. Whatever the issue is, can't it wait till he gets well?'

The stitches on Siddharth's head had come open and had to be redone. It could have been far more serious than it was. Anshuman knew this was not warranted. But the looming question was whether he could wait. Every passing moment was not healing his wound, rather aggravating the pain. He had calmed himself down but Chand's arrival sorely increased the sense of betrayal.

'It can,' he looked at the nurse. 'Surely it can.'

'It would be better if you could let him rest now,' she looked at both of them, making it evident that it was time for them to leave the room.

**

Anshuman stood beside the giant glass wall of the waiting room. A streak of fluorescent lights had illuminated the giant bridge, which was hailed by the Indian media as an architectural marvel. He had always loved the Rajiv Gandhi Sea Link.

'I seriously had no idea what was going on,' Chand spoke from behind, his reflection prominent on the glass beside Anshuman's.

The man spoken to was quiet. In some corner in his heart, Anshuman Mehra knew that Chand was saying the truth. Their relation had gone beyond a professional partnership, and the musician had gone through an acid test of honesty. He knew it would be unfair to ignore all that Chand said because of his anger at Reva and that man.

Yet, another part of him wondered how Pias could have not known anything about his best friend's romantic escapade. He had heard tales from Chand about his best friend who was once his room-mate, then a flat-mate and now a neighbour. With such a long and close association, it was almost implausible that Chand was oblivious of such a major phase in his mate's life.

'Does she know you are here?' Anshuman finally spoke.

'Yeah,' Chand exhaled. 'She'll be here soon.'

'She is coming here?' Anshuman turned to look at Chand.

'Yeah,' the musician nodded, 'she was a bit hesitant but I think it's time we take everything out of the closet. Why feign ignorance when everything is out in the open?'

'Perhaps,' Anshuman turned back to look at the city through the glass, 'the night can't hide as many secrets as we expect her to.'

**

Sophie D'Costa had always held her boss in high reverence and there had been no other man in her life she had looked up to. Anshuman's stature was higher than anyone else she knew of.

The very morning when Anshuman rushed out of the office without a thought about impending meeting, she knew something was amiss. An hour later, he sent her an sms saying that his wife had been in an accident. She was shocked and informed Bala Sir about it, but couldn't gather courage to call up Anshuman herself and talk to him.

Sophie had known Reva for a long time, right from the time she had joined Genesis. The woman had an enviable charm; beyond the curtain of beauty, she was an extremely strong woman. No wonder a man like Anshuman Mehra had fallen for her. There had been instances when she felt uncomfortable with Reva's overpowering presence in her boss' life. Sophie had seen Anshuman browned off after family disputes which had become quite frequent at one point of time. However, things seemed to improve and Sophie realised, her boss' marriage had survived its crisis.

Chand's phone call came like a bolt from the blue. She had met Siddharth a couple of times at Chand's place. Though they had barely interacted, she liked the guy as he was Chand's best friend. When she heard that Siddharth was having an affair with Anshuman's wife and that they had been in the accident together, the world around her started to spin. She was not part of their lives, yet connected to them intimately.

When Chand wanted to ask her out, he had conveyed the message through Anshuman. Closely associated with the musician, her boss not only conveyed the message but also passed a note of acceptance for the man. Like many young girls, Sophie also had a liking for the young fashionable singer-composer. But going out with him was something she had neither envisaged nor desired. She had met Chand a few times at the Genesis office but they had hardly interacted. So, the invite took her by surprise. But with Anshuman's approval, she decided it was worth a try. And it turned out for the best. Underneath the artistic avatar, Chand was like any other normal guy who believed in simplicity, friendship and having fun.

'Executive waiting room, third floor,' Chand told her over the phone. 'Come up.'

**

'Do you think I would have let him keep this from you?' Sophie assured her boss, 'Siddharth hardly ever shared any secrets with him.'

Anshuman nodded. After all these years, he had come to trust her completely. More than anything, a strong conviction always marked his belief – Sophie would never lie to him.

'I guess I just reacted at the spur of the moment,' Anshuman admitted. 'I trust both of you. It's just that for the last 12 hours I am having a tough time believing everything I've been told.'

Sophie and Chand sat together on the sofa, facing Anshuman who sat on a single sofa on the opposite wall.

'It was really nice of you guys to come down,' the ad-man smiled. 'I don't have many friends whom I could call.'

'I thought Mr Banerjee would be here,' Sophie expressed surprise at not seeing Anshuman's closest friend present at the hospital.

'He is in Glasgow,' Anshuman explained, 'but his wife will be here soon.'

'Mrs Mehra's boss?' Reva confirmed.

'Yup,' Anshuman smiled, acknowledging that his junior knew every detail about his family.

'You can surely tell us if you need help,' Chand offered, sensing the man's loneliness.

'Absolutely,' Sophie joined in. 'You know we are always there.'

'I know,' Anshuman smiled affectionately at the young pair and added after a pause. 'So… is everything set for the d-day?'

'Yes,' Chand nodded.

'Nothing,' Sophie negated her fiancé's statement. 'We are absolutely clueless about what's going to happen.' She looked at Chand with a smile and affirmed. 'No clue at all.'

Chand winked and smiled mischievously.

'There are only two weeks left, right?' Anshuman veered the discussion from himself, 'By now, all the preparations should have been finalised.'

'You are talking of the ideal case scenario, sir,' Sophie looked at Chand. The latter tried to hold her hand but she shrugged it off. 'Someone here doesn't even know what he's going to wear for his wedding.'

'How long does it take to buy a tuxedo?' Chand looked at Anshuman for support. 'Why do you need to buy it a month ahead?' He looked at his fiancée, 'have you ordered your gown?'

'I already have,' Sophie shot back. 'Don't compare yourself with me.'

'Don't fight guys,' Anshuman tried in vain to be the peacemaker.

'He hasn't even spoken to the church,' Sophie complained to his boss. 'I don't know how he is going to get a booking.'

'Why haven't you got it done?' Anshuman said, catching his junior by surprise with the question.

Chand laughed out at the remark. He clapped and looked at Sophie. 'Why haven't you? You now owe him an answer because I didn't ask the question.'

'You are supporting him?' Sophie looked in disgust at her boss. 'Why should I get the booking done?'

'Why not?' Chand and Sophie got into an argument even without caring for the third person there. 'We are in this together.'

'You have been in Mumbai for years,' Sophie justified her claim, 'I came much later.'

'How many years do you require to get a booking done for a wedding?' Chand challenged the claim, 'And that too your own.'

'Fine, I'll do it,' Sophie accepted the defeat. 'This is the best way to pass the buck by making someone else feel responsible for it.'

'I am really surprised that a couple can fight as much as you guys do,' Anshuman interrupted, 'and still get married.'

'We are getting into the habit,' Chand smiled and held Sophie's hand, 'so that it doesn't feel awkward after the wedding.'

Unknowingly, Chand ended up making an inapt statement. Sophie tightened the grip on Chand's fist, to make him realise that the remark was uncalled for. Chand immediately realised his folly and tried to change the topic.

'Actually, she....' he started speaking when Anshuman interrupted.

'You are right, Chand,' the ad-wizard spoke. 'Perhaps we should have had some practice as well. Then, things might have not become as ugly as they have.'

Sophie threw an angry glance at her fiancé. Chand bit his tongue. He realised the mistake was done and it was beyond repair now. Fortunately for him, a nurse walked into the room and looked at the musician.

'Are you Mr Chand Pias?' she asked even though she knew who he was.

In a flash, the entire attention of the room shifted towards the nurse.

'Yes...' Chand stood up surprised and anxious at the same time. 'Is anything wrong?'

'Nothing,' she smiled at the frown on the man's face, 'Mr Kashyap wants to talk to you. Don't worry, he's fine.'

'Okay,' Chand nodded.

The nurse left.

'I'll be back,' Chand turned to others in the room.

'It's alright,' Anshuman cut him short. 'Go and talk to him.'

Sophie looked at him stolidly, without any mark of either approval or otherwise. Chand turned and walked towards the door.

'Chand,' Anshuman called him before he exited.

Chand looked back.

'Tell him I feel bad,' Anshuman sighed, 'for what I did to him.'

Chand smiled and nodded.

**

'What do you think of me now?' Siddharth spoke as his best friend sat beside him.

'Does it really matter to you?' Chand looked pragmatically.

'So, *you* blame me as well?' Siddharth could find his wall of defence stiffening at the question of his friend. Chand was the last person who he thought would accuse him. Even if everyone else's opinion belied his love, Siddharth felt that Chand would stand by him.

'Whom do I stand by at this point – the friend who loves her or the man she is married to?' Chand knew that the predicament had shattered his own set of priorities. He could have fought the world for these two men, but judging a duel between Siddharth and Anshuman was his toughest job ever.

'You knew the woman I was dating is married.'

'I thought it was a joke.'

'You didn't think so. I never made it sound like a joke.' Siddharth dispelled Chand's ingenuous attempt of covering up.

'Perhaps I didn't take you seriously.' Chand sighed in exasperation.

'That's your problem.'

'Is this why you have called me here?' Chand had never been so agitated with Siddharth, 'To argue with me and defend your position?'

'No,' Siddharth chuckled at the question, 'I just wanted to say sorry. I have spoilt your last two weeks of bachelorhood.'

'You are still not sorry for getting yourself into such a mess. You were wrong to have got into this relationship,' Chand looked befuddled at his friend's obstinate behaviour.

'Neither do I consider that wrong nor will I ever be sorry.'

'You didn't keep your promise either, did you?'

'You mean your challenge?' Siddharth had kind of forgotten about it. 'No, I thought I would,' he groped for an answer, 'but couldn't.'

'I told you I am braver than you are.' Chand chuckled. Such was their friendship that it could waver effortlessly between ridicule and flippant banter. He wished it had stayed like that and they wouldn't have landed at this difficult juncture.

'Oh come on! I was just waiting for the right time.'

'You were waiting for a right time to tell me that you were sleeping with Anshuman Mehra's wife?'

'Don't make it sound so crude.' Siddharth immediately shot back.

'Didn't you make fun of me when I said I wanted to marry Sophie?' Chand couldn't forget Siddharth's sardonic reply on hearing about his betrothal to Sophie.

'Dude, you were in love at that time. I made fun because you were letting go of your relationship just because you wanted some social security.'

'And why did you come to that conclusion? You think I don't love her?'

'Are you sure you're over Rohit?'

For a moment, Chand felt stumped by the question. He would have emphatically said *yes* had the questioner not been someone who could see through him.

Chand and Rohit had struck a deep friendship while working for the DFW finale. A couple of months after the show, while Siddharth suddenly went off to Manali, they decided to visit Khandala for the weekend. An inebriated night brought them much closer and the two realised how passionately they had craved for the other as they made love in the hotel room. Chand returned to Mumbai and confided in his best friend about the new turn of events in his life.

'Will you spend the rest of your life together?' Siddharth looked amused.

'I am not sure,' Chand shrugged. 'Who cares about what the future has in store for us?'

Siddharth nodded.

'We are together at this point of time,' Chand went on confidently. 'That's what matters.'

'Hope so,' Siddharth pursed his lips. 'Wouldn't it affect your career?'

'I am not going around telling people about this,' Chand got up frustrated. 'This is personal.'

Sadly for him, Chand couldn't live with this secret for long. Not that he faked his love for Sophie, but he realised that this relationship was more acceptable than the one with Rohit Chhabra.

'Does she know that she still has a risk of losing you to him?' Siddharth smiled at his friend.

'Sophie is marrying me because she knows she doesn't have that risk,' Chand got up. 'You are yet to realise the value of faith, Siddharth.'

'Faith? Are you trying to be funny?' Siddharth scoffed, 'How can she trust a guy who could never be fully satisfied with her?'

'Was Reva Mehra with you because she was not satisfied?' Chand looked at him.

'I don't know, but your case is different, dude,' Siddharth shrugged his shoulders arrogantly. 'Her body will only crave for men, but you will desire both. Tell me, Chand, can you be faithful to her all your life? Isn't she cherishing an illusion?'

'You know what, Siddharth, I sometimes feel you only pretend to be my friend but you have never accepted me completely.' Chand felt his voice weaken with the reply.

'Being a friend does not mean that I will turn a blind eye to a fact.' Siddharth looked at his friend as coldly as he could.

'You don't need to do that. You only need to take it as it is,' Chand said almost pleadingly, 'but you have never done so. Every time you tease me about it, I feel it even more strongly. Your pseudo masculine complex always gets in the way.'

'If our friendship had really meant that much to you, Chand,' Siddharth knew that his hostility had stemmed from his vulnerability, 'you would have stood by me today!'

'Are you trying to make me feel guilty to absolve yourself of your own guilty feelings?' Chand looked at him with bloodshot eyes. 'You always need to prove that you are right.'

'I am right,' Siddharth gritted his teeth. 'I don't need to prove this to anyone. And I thought at least you would agree with me.'

Chand shook his head in exasperation.

'I am going home,' he said. 'Call me if you need any help.'

He walked towards the door, expecting his friend to apologise. But the sorry didn't come.

'By the way I forgot to tell you,' Chand turned to find his friend looking eagerly at him. 'Anshuman Mehra says he is sorry. Maybe not to me, but I guess you owe him an apology.'

Chand darted out of the room. As he walked along the corridor, the musician could feel his limbs enervate from the encounter with his best friend. He briskly wiped away the tears rolling down his eyes and as he reached the top of the staircase, he held the railing and took a deep breath, letting the grief subside lest Anshuman and Sophie should see him in such a state. For all the differences, Siddharth was still his best friend; and none in the world would be privy to their squabble – not even his fiancée.

Alone in his room, Siddharth turned around, looking away from the door. His eyes welled up with tears for the first time in the day. He had just lost his biggest support system. But he couldn't show others how weak he felt.

Thirteen

The Beginning of a Friendship

A nshuman was touring Bangkok for an ad shoot, when Reva joined him midway. It was the launch of an international brand of sports gear in the Indian market and two of the hottest selling names of the nation were endorsing them, one of them being Maya Bose. But, like most other women of the country, Reva was more curious to meet the new cricketing sensation who also starred in the advertisement.

'I have met Maya many a time,' Reva told him clearly over the phone, 'and she is a lovely lady. But I am dying to meet Robin Soni.'

'Okay, ma'am,' Anshuman laughed.

The next day, the creative director of the campaign introduced his wife to her favourite sportsman.

'Robin,' Anshuman introduced, 'this is my wife, Reva.'

'Hi,' the cricketer courteously gave his hand, 'Robin.'

'Obviously,' Reva shook it. 'I am a huge fan.'

'Really?' the cricketer blushed as if it were the first time a girl had said that. 'It's great to know that women are watching cricket as well.'

'I don't know about the game,' the journalist smiled, 'but I definitely watch you.'

Robin looked down embarrassed while Anshuman struggled to find an apt rejoinder. Seeing the two men turn red, Reva burst out laughing.

'Superb,' Maya Bose said as everyone turned around to look at her. 'One woman can stump two men at one go.' Maya looked at Robin and added with a tease, 'And I thought you were a wicket-keeper.'

'Hey Maya,' Reva went ahead and gave her a hug. 'Long time no see.'

'People like your husband keep me away from the fun parties,' she teased. 'What can I do?'

'At least I keep you away from people, who don't deserve your company,' it was Anshuman's turn to flirt. 'You should thank me for bringing you here.'

'Oh I am so grateful, sweetheart,' Maya Bose held his hand as Anshuman winked at his wife.

'Don't try to make the lady jealous, Anshuman,' Robin joined the conversation. 'She will be my date tonight, won't she?'

'Without a doubt,' Reva put her hand in the cricketer's. 'My pleasure.'

'Amazing,' Maya Bose announced. 'So it's dinner tonight after pack up. We will dance with our respective dates and hope the married ones won't chicken out.'

'We won't,' the Mehras spoke in unison.

***

The party continued for a couple of days more before the shoot was completed. Anshuman and Reva decided to travel together to the tranquil Siem Reap after the loud and bustling Bangkok. It was however more of the wife's idea but the husband didn't oppose it, because of two reasons. One, he remembered how morose she felt during the Frankfurt trip and two, she was a far more pronounced traveller than he was.

Reva had heard a lot about Cambodia and its serenity. She had seen Baraka and fallen in love with the country. However, if there was one thing that enamoured her the most, it was the world's largest religious building – Angkor Vat and its magnificence.

The Bangkok Airways flight took just an hour, and the couple was at the immigration check counter of Siem Reap Angkor International airport. It was a newly-built one but already popular among the tourists.

'You want a Coke or something?' Anshuman asked his wife while she stood by the conveyor belt. 'I am very thirsty.'

'Nothing,' she replied. 'You go and have something.'

'You can take the bag, right?' Anshuman asked.

'Yeah,' Reva smiled. 'It's just one small bag. Your one is with you in any case.'

'Okay,' he turned and skipped away as she turned to check her luggage.

After half an hour, Anshuman returned, without a bottle of Coke in his hand but a mark of thorough ire on his face. His frown was visible over the rim of his glasses and Reva realised that something was amiss; and most probably it had something to do with the beverage her husband was searching for.

'What took you so long?' Reva looked worried.

'There isn't one shop that sells Coke,' he handed her the water bottle. 'What sort of a country is this?'

The anger in his voice was palpable. She smiled and decided to divert his attention.

'Come on,' she put her arm in his. 'Let's go.'

The taxi that took them to the hotel was highly overpriced for the distance that it covered and it didn't do anything to alleviate Anshuman's anger. But what eventually placated him was the hotel in Angkor Thorn lane which they had booked. For the luxurious suite, the hotel charged them a meagre twenty five dollars per day. Almost instantly, the anger on Anshuman's face turned into a smile because by then, he had realised that Cambodia was by far less expensive than Bangkok. Reva hated that smirk but she was happy that things didn't turn out so bad.

The next thing they enjoyed was the Khmer cuisine. Besides being highly affordable, what attracted Anshuman the most was the resemblance with his two favourite food styles – Indian and Chinese. While Reva savoured the vegetarian Ban Haow noodles, he devoured the delicious Cha Knyey to his heart's content.

'This is amazing,' he spoke elated. 'How can you not have meat?'

'How can you have some other animal's flesh?' She retorted, 'You are killing something for your food!'

'Aren't you ending a plant's life by uprooting it?' he teased her. 'Just because it doesn't move, its life is less precious?'

'Oh, shut up,' Reva rubbished the argument. 'Plants are never going to be extinct. You can plant another tree. But you cannot grow another animal you eat up.'

'So it's about the resources of your consumption,' Anshuman chuckled, 'not about the animal or the plant's life!'

Reva rolled her eyes and let the argument pass.

The next morning, they awoke to the aroma of jasmine tea, a speciality at the hotel, served just before the breakfast comprising rice porridge with salted eggs, pickled vegetables and dried fish. The food definitely did enough to make up for the airport fiasco the day before.

'How can a man not like a place where the food is so awesome?' Anshuman's smile showed his satisfaction.

Reva grinned. Cambodia had offered her the recipe to amend her husband's mood.

As planned, they boarded a local tuk tuk to buy tickets for a one-day Angkor Wat sightseeing. They were cheap too, worth $10 each. She glanced again to see whether he had that funny smile on his face, but it had long faded away. Instead, there was a smile of affection for the place. She breathed a sigh of relief. And then they finally reached Angkor, the city of the temple, lying to the north of the more modern Siem Reap. The place that was famous for the one temple which finds its place even on the national flag of Cambodia – the Angkor Wat.

For Reva, it was a long-cherished dream coming true. She had been besotted with the world's largest Hindu temple for a long time. And now, it was before her – the Vishnu temple chequered with Buddhist idols – the graven images of temple dancers seemed alive on the walls of the Angkor Wat. She traipsed along the premises, spellbound by each of the intricate carvings around the site. They hopped from rock to rock in silence, trying to decipher the mystery of the temple, which with the magnificent reception, enthrals all its guests. Anshuman struggled through the tourist manual and tried to speak Khmer to the local toddlers; some of whom even managed to cajole him to buy souvenirs. However, for Reva, it was rediscovering the lost path to the Khmer kingdom. They managed to go atop the bull temple and the view just melted her heart.

The past has its fine imprints on the sands of time and the silence has its impregnable mark on the dust-clad quondam fields, Reva wrote in her diary.

Siem Reap is indeed colourful and vibrant with tourists in search of their tastes. We settled for the Indian cuisine at the fine restaurant named "Kamasutra" on the main street. After a few rounds of haggling over the prices of souvenirs at the pawn shop, we were back in our hotel room.

The day after, we travelled to a cottage near the Siem Reap river, away from the din and bustle of the city. It was a cosy place and we lazed there for a while, enjoying every bit of the occasional drizzle. They say rain gods are generous to the visitors in Cambodia. I wish I had lived in the past, devoid of tourists and surrounded only by nature. Stones, they say, have truly preserved the time in them, have seen it all and are testimony to the fact that once a vibrant kingdom flourished here and boasted of the best architects of their time.

While I was star-gazing in the afternoon, Anshuman reminded me of our evening flight back home. I packed my bags, gathered my souvenirs and rushed to the cab. As I was heading back to the airport, I could see a past left behind, untouched by civilisation. And as we bid adieu, the stones readied to greet more tourists.

The stones talked to me and the petrichor is still fresh in my lungs. And I come back carrying those "memories" back home. I am a traveller.

**

The landline rang loudly. Reva walked through the drawing room and picked up the cordless receiver.

'Hello,' she rubbed her right hand on the kitchen apron.

'Reva?' her mother-in-law's voice came from the other end.

'Maa,' she replied gleefully. 'How are you?'

'I am fine,' she replied. 'So, how tough is life with my son?'

Reva laughed, 'Pretty good.'

'He can a bit tough at times,' Gayatri Mehra spoke, 'can't he?'

'Yes,' the daughter-in-law agreed, 'especially if you argue and don't agree to his point of view.'

Gayatri chuckled. 'He just likes winning arguments,' she added, 'and loves having the last word.'

Reva chuckled. 'You really know him well,' she couldn't help but agree.

'Nobody will ever know him better than you or me,' Gayatri assured her.

'You think I will ever be able to know him as much as you do?' Reva sounded sceptical.

'I am sure you will,' the senior Mrs Mehra was more confident than her younger counterpart. 'I know him as my son. You will know him as your husband.'

Reva smiled at the answer.

'His relation with you is much more symbiotic,' Gayatri analysed. 'That's when you really know a person.'

'You are so fair, Maa,' Reva acknowledged. 'No wonder Anshu swears by every word you say.'

'Mothers have to be fair,' Gayatri replied nonchalantly. 'You will understand it when the time comes.'

'You don't think we should have a baby now?' Reva sounded surprised at the remark. 'My mother keeps telling me I should.'

'I know you want to focus on your work right now,' Gayatri understood. 'It has just been two years since you guys got married. So, there shouldn't be any hurry. You should enjoy the freedom now.'

'You are so sweet, Maa,' Reva couldn't believe someone of her mother's generation could be so progressive in her thoughts.

'Don't wait for too long though,' Gayatri drew the line casually. 'But then if Farah Khan can have three babies after 40, you have a lot of time left.'

Reva cracked up at the unexpected remark. 'You sure know all the news from Bollywood,' she sounded surprised.

'I have my fun before your Papa gets home,' Gayatri replied in a matter-of-fact tone.

Reva laughed out aloud. Almost at the same instant, the door-latch turned and Anshuman entered the room.

'He is here,' Reva turned and looked at her husband, 'Maa.'

Anshuman pointed his index finger and asked her to wait for a moment before he could take the call.

'He will be here in a moment,' Reva told her mother-in-law.

'He needs to wash his hands before touching the receiver,' came the reply.

Reva chuckled. 'I guess he got the gift of gab from you,' Reva was amazed by the old woman's wit. 'Wish he had a sense of humour like you as well.'

'He got some qualities from his father as well,' Gayatri Mehra replied.

This time, the younger woman almost went rolling off the sofa. Anshuman tapped on her shoulder and she turned back.

'What are you laughing about?' Anshuman snatched the receiver. 'It must be about me.'

'You know you are a laughing stock,' Reva shot back and hit him on the arm. 'We were discussing Farah Khan if you want to know.'

'Off all things,' he looked with a frown and replied to his mother, 'you were laughing over Farah Khan?'

'We were discussing her kids,' Gayatri laughed. 'She has three lovely children.'

'Yes she does.' Anshuman stretched out on the sofa, 'So you want us to have kids?'

'She says we have time,' Reva called out from behind.

Gayatri confirmed the same over the phone. 'I am in no hurry,' she said. 'Take your time.'

'Thank you,' Anshuman picked a cigarette from the case and lit it.

'Don't smoke,' Gayatri promptly said.

'I am not smoking,' Anshuman said in a shocked tone and looked at his wife laughing at him being caught.

'When do you plan to come over, Maa,' he diverted the topic. 'You promised you would come and stay with us for some time.'

Reva shook her head acknowledging that Anshuman wouldn't be able to deceive the woman who perhaps knew him much more than she did.

**

'I just don't belong here,' Anshuman stepped out of the car. 'These parties make me...'

'Oh come on, Anshu,' Reva walked over to him and brushed the collar of his coat with her fingers. 'This is just a regular party. You'll be absolutely fine.'

'But what do I talk about?' Anshuman looked up and she tightened the knot of his tie. 'I don't know most of them and they are all so fake.'

'Don't be so biased,' she rubbished his claim. 'They are just a bit dramatic. We don't come here every week. It's just a one-off event. Samaira specially requested that I bring you over. It's her party.'

'Ok,' he exhaled, 'but you promised we won't stay too long.'

'We won't,' she smiled and put her arm into his as they walked inside.

Samaira Khan was known for her lavish parties. Though infamous for her relationship with Rajvardhan Bhalla, she could always manage to gather the most celebrated socialites in the city to attend every bash she threw. Dressed in a Persian blue gown that flaunted her figure at the right places, she hosted the evening with an aplomb that was characteristic to her persona.

'Whom do I see?' Samaira walked ahead and greeted the guests. 'Look at you, such a gorgeous couple.'

'Thank you,' Reva smiled, looking resplendent in her red zardosi sari that contrasted with Anshuman's black three piece suit.

'I am so happy you could take time out and come,' Samaira gave her hand to Anshuman. 'I really wanted to meet you.'

'My pleasure,' Anshuman held the lady's hand softly and shook it. 'Why don't you come over to our place some time?'

'I would love to,' the host nodded appreciatively at the invitation as Reva smiled at her husband's chivalry.

'Please make yourselves at home,' Samaira walked them to the centre of the party. 'I really hope you have a nice time.'

'Come on, Sam,' Reva held her friend's hand. 'We will take care of ourselves. Don't worry about us.'

'The bar is over there,' Samaira pointed at the most congested corner of the venue. 'Help yourselves with whatever you like to drink. I'll be back shortly.'

'Absolutely,' the Mehra couple said together.

As the night flowed by, Reva gradually dissolved into the party. To Anshuman's pleasant surprise, everyone at the gathering paid her a lot of attention and she basked in the glory. However, he soon started feeling discomfited by the sheer cluelessness with which he roamed around, smiling courteously at people he didn't know or listening to guffaws over topics he couldn't comprehend. The cacophony of such bashes made him quite uncomfortable, and with Reva mingling and moving around, the disquiet sank in more and more.

'I will be back in some time,' he tapped her on the arm.

'But where are you going?' she held his arm and cajoled, 'Stay here...'

'I am outside,' he assured, 'I will be back after a smoke.'

Anshuman promised to return after a cigarette but never complied to the same. From time to time, Reva found herself stealing a glance at the entrance, but Anshuman was nowhere to be seen. She strolled around, getting caught in a conversation with almost everyone at the venue. Despite the anxiety in her heart, she put on an exuberant facade as they complimented her on her looks and latest articles or enquired about Anshuman's whereabouts. One of the guests was the photographer she had met earlier at DFW.

'Mrs Mehra,' Siddharth approached her. 'It's nice to see you.'

'Siddharth Kashyap,' Reva managed her glass of wine and shook his hand. 'Same here. So, how's work?'

'Good,' he smiled, 'but sadly, I couldn't manage to get my best photograph.'

'Really?' she looked inquisitive. 'Why?'

'Because the model I approached thought she doesn't look good in pictures,' he pursed his lips and nodded sheepishly.

'That's bad,' she said before it struck her whom Siddharth was referring to. 'Oh!'

She burst out laughing, amazed that the photographer hadn't forgotten her fixation.

'You still remember that?' she smiled. 'I am sorry I can't get out of that... phobia if you can call it that.'

'If women like you have such phobias,' he smiled, 'we will be out of jobs.'

Reva looked down, blushing at the earnestness of the compliment, when Samaira Khan joined the two.

'So you guys didn't need an introduction this time,' she popped in, 'but I need to spoil that by stealing the man away.'

'Your guest,' Reva looked at the two. 'I will find my man somewhere outside.'

'Absolutely,' Samaira tagged her arm into Siddharth's. 'He just disappeared, right?'

'Mr Mehra is here?' Siddharth looked surprised, 'I would love to meet him.'

'Sure,' Reva smiled. 'Let me find him first.'

'Bring him back,' Samaira chuckled as she went back into the party with Siddharth.

Reva dialled her husband's number yet again. This was her tenth attempt, and the response was still the same. Her call was on wait as Anshuman was busy talking to someone else. She handed over her glass to the waiter and walked out of the hall. He was nowhere around. She scanned the entire venue before being directed by the security guard towards the parking area where the latter had seen Anshuman. When she finally reached the car, Anshuman was sitting in it and working on his laptop, talking to someone over the phone. For a moment, she was filled with rage. She gathered herself and knocked on the window. He looked up and rolled the glass down.

'You are done?' Anshuman smiled, startling her.

'I have been trying to call you for the past one hour,' she controlled her anger. 'You said you would be back after a smoke.'

'I was on a call,' he justified his stand. 'It was urgent...'

'Didn't you see my calls waiting?' her patience was running out of steam but she didn't want to create a scene at the party. 'Couldn't you just tell me that you were here?'

'I needed to log on...' Before Anshuman could complete his sentence, Reva snatched the phone from his hand.

'Hello,' she said as Anshuman looked stunned.

'Hello, ma'am,' Sophie had heard the conversation between the Mehras.

'Sophie,' Reva's anger was evident in her voice, 'can your discussion be kept on hold till tomorrow morning?'

'Yes, ma'am,' Sophie's voice was quivering. 'I will meet sir in the office tomorrow.'

'Great,' Reva was almost cruelly pragmatic. 'Please don't call when we are at a party.'

'I had called her,' Anshuman protested and came out of the car.

'And I thought you got a call about some urgent work,' Reva was sneering now.

'It was urgent,' Anshuman protested, 'but I had...'

Before he could complete his sentence, she handed back the phone and prepared to walk back.

'Bring the car to the exit,' Reva said almost with the turn. 'I will be there.'

Anshuman stood perplexed as she darted towards the banquet, seething in anger.

Reva walked up to Samaira and tried her best look calm though she failed to mask her anger. The host looked at her in surprise. She had never seen the journalist with such a livid look on her face.

'I need to go home right away,' Reva informed her. 'I am really sorry.'

'Is everything alright?' Samaira looked tensed and held her friend's arm. 'Are you alright?'

Reva nodded impatiently. 'I will call you tomorrow,' she walked away.

Samaira looked at the journalist with unease, as the latter walked towards the door, the end of her sari dragging behind her on the floor and her lean frame forming a picturesque silhouette against the flood lights beaming into the room from atop the gigantic entrance door.

'Trouble in paradise,' Siddharth looked at the host and whistled, as the latter hit him on the arm.

'She is just stuck in the wrong relationship,' Samaira opined.

'And I thought you were fond of Mr Mehra,' he sipped his rum.

'Great men never make great husbands,' she surmised. 'They are too much into themselves.'

'Am I great?' he winked.

'You are a dog,' she laughed. He joined her.

**

The drive back home was quiet. Anshuman didn't know how to explain his situation. That's how he liked ending all his arguments – an explanation to illustrate how he was right but interpreted wrongly. But for the first time he was clueless.

'I didn't ask you to leave the party,' he said as they walked up the stairs.

'You think it was a kids' party?' she screamed as if waiting for the instigation to do so. 'And no one would notice that you were gone.'

'It is not my cup of tea,' he tried to justify himself.

'For one night, Anshuman,' Reva burst out. 'For one night, I wanted you to come along with me to the party. I wanted you to be a part of my world. Was it such a big thing to ask for?'

'I had no one to talk to.'

'Haven't I been to your parties where I knew nobody? I just followed you, nodding at every god-knows-what topic you discussed. I have never asked you to be a part of my world. This was the first time because Samaira had especially asked me to bring you along.'

'I wanted to stay, but they were all so fake.'

Anshuman knew this was his weak point. He couldn't sustain an argument without making strong remarks about others. Objectivity during a quarrel was not his forte. Alas, this time around, it was the worst mistake to commit.

'Fake!' Reva threw her hands in the air with disgust. 'Yeah right!' Isn't that your favourite word for anything and everything that you don't like? And you assume that everyone I meet at your parties is perfectly natural. At least, the people here were much more cordial.'

'But it's part of my work.'

'And this is work for me too. You are not the only one who works in this house. I might not earn as much as you but it's enough for myself at least. I don't sit at home and depend on you.'

Both of them were losing their composure now. Reva was already agitated; Anshuman too was turning red with rage. He had never liked being accused unnecessarily, especially not during an argument.

'I have never said that. Don't put words in my mouth.'

'Isn't that what you feel about everything in this house?'

'No, I don't. Perhaps someone else in my position would have. But I have always been gracious enough not to mention such things. And as far as my parties or my world are concerned, I had never forced you to be a part of those. You came because you liked them or because you had other motive.'

'I had a motive?' Reva was shocked.

'Didn't you come to Bangkok because you wanted to meet Robin?'

'Is that what you really think?' Reva screamed. 'Someday or the other, you would have come out with this. Basically I am an unsolicited part of your world – someone who just got plain lucky and managed to impress you! That's what you think, right? Thank you for making me realise that today, Mr Anshuman Mehra.'

At times, things cross a certain line from where there is no return. This was their first argument which had gone beyond what either of them wanted it to. Reva turned down the stairs and darted out of the house. Anshuman called her a couple of times but didn't make an earnest effort to stop his wife from leaving the house, half an hour before midnight. Apologising had never been his strong point and tonight, he failed to say "sorry" yet again. His mother would say it was a trait he inherited from his father. As much as he hated that, his inflated ego at that point of time wouldn't allow him to surrender.

**

'Stop here,' she said.

The auto-rickshaw driver stopped by the side of the road. Reva paid him and got down.

She had contemplated going to Chembur, but troubling Dipanwita was hardly a wise thing to do. When alone, this was the best place to be – Juhu Beach. The vast expanse of the sea lay before her. Though she loved its gurgling sound, she was in no mood to walk on the beach. The sea would make her feel even lonelier. A couple of cafeterias were still open. But, sitting in restaurants and cafeterias was something she didn't want to do either. She just walked along the road by the beach. The salty smell filled the air, as a few auto rickshaws and taxis slowed to check if she wanted to hire one. There were few people, and some of them looked at her suspiciously.

The mobile phone rang in her purse. She took it out. "Jaan" it flashed. Anshuman was finally calling, half an hour after she had left. She cancelled the call and kept walking. It was getting late and she realised it was not a wise thing to be alone, even in Mumbai, a city that never went to sleep. There was a message. It was him again. *Please come back, it's very late. Not safe.* Still not a *sorry* for the humiliation he had made her face. He would never admit his mistake but would only justify his actions. It was just the way he was. She knew this well but she couldn't excuse him that night.

All of a sudden, a car stopped next to her.

'Reva,' someone called out and took her by surprise. For a moment, she thought Anshuman had found her; but it turned out to be someone she least expected.

Siddharth Kashyap was calling her from his car. Of all things, that man had to find her in that state in the middle of the night.

'Mrs Mehra,' he called her again.

She pondered over a response but then started walking again. She didn't want to face him again that night. He was too young and frivolous to understand what she was going through.

'You don't have to tell me everything,' Siddharth came running behind, 'but at least we can talk.'

For a split moment, the statement shocked her. Could he gauge what she felt? Or was it a plain coincidence?

'I don't want to talk right now,' she frowned at him.

'Ok,' he smiled. 'You want to walk. Let's walk.'

He didn't wait for her answer. He started walking. But it was only after he had walked ahead a bit that he realised Reva hadn't moved.

'Walk,' he shrugged his shoulders.

'Why are you doing this?' she looked straight at him.

'I love walking by the beach at night,' he said in a matter-of-fact tone. 'It's very soothing.'

'Alright,' she turned and started walking in the opposite direction.

'Mrs Mehra,' Siddharth ran after her. 'Wait.'

'Why are you doing this, Mr Kashyap?' she turned to look at him.

'Shouldn't I be asking you that?' he retorted. 'Why are you walking alone on this street at this time of the night?'

'How does it matter to you?' she sounded exasperated. 'How much do you know me that you can question me like that?'

'Are you trying to be nasty so that I go away?' he raised his brows and looked at her with a smile. 'It won't work with me. I am not leaving.'

'I am not in a state to talk normally right now.'

'I don't mind if you behave a bit abnormal,' he grinned.

'What's the matter with you?' Reva sighed and gave up hope of shooing him away, 'Why are you trying to be this Good Samaritan for no reason?'

'Well,' he walked a bit closer, 'it's just not safe to be out here alone.'

'Did I ask for your advice?'

'No, I am not advising you. I am just informing you. There are many other women who walk or travel by auto at this time of the night, especially on this road.'

'So?'

"Someone might mistake you for one of them.'

'What?'

Siddharth didn't explain. He smiled naughtily and looked around. For a moment, Reva failed to understand what he meant. Then she understood what he was trying to say and though angered by the comment, she couldn't help giggle at the thought.

'I guess I am a better-dressed one,' she tried to control the embarrassment.

'Most of them are these days,' Siddharth added almost nonchalantly, 'except the she-males.'

'You know a lot about them,' she teased, almost forgetting her sombre mood, 'don't you?'

'Now, that is your usual sarcastic self,' Siddharth laughed, 'not the oh-I-am-so-lost look.'

'Yeah right,' she nodded, 'so, my actual self is sarcastic.'

Siddharth smiled at the reply. 'Come on,' he said. 'Let's go somewhere. Have a coffee and then I'll drop you home.'

'I don't want to go home right now.' Reva surprised Siddharth by the acerbic response.

'I kind of realised that when you walked out of the party,' Siddharth said seriously lest she got offended. 'But that's where you should be right now.'

Reva looked at him and then turned away.

'I know,' he stammered, 'I know that you don't need any advice. Well, in that case, you can come home with me.'

Reva turned and frowned at him. 'Go home with you?'

'I mean, not in that way. We can go to my studio. It's close by. You can see my photographs.'

Reva pondered for a moment. 'Okay.'

**

The Andheri west flat off S.V. Road was the professional hub of the two friends. Though they didn't frequent it together, Siddharth and Chand ensured that the den was well maintained even in their absence – not only their individual areas, but also the other half.

'Not bad, yaar,' Reva entered the apartment and looked around. She noticed the photographs hanging on the wall.

Almost the entire flat was decorated with photographs from Siddharth's favourite collection. He was known for his portrait pictures and the glossy walls bore testimony to his expertise. The man not only knew how to capture expressions well, but there was also a love that oozed from every frame. He loved his object and treated it with utmost affection, as if with a tenderness so as to preserve the innocence in them.

'Is that Maya?' Reva pointed at a picture in the middle of the room.

'Yeah,' Siddharth laughed.

'Is she without make-up?' the reporter sounded surprised. 'Not many have seen her this way.'

'This picture kind of marked the beginning of my career,' Siddharth confided, 'and Maya had no idea she was being photographed.'

Siddharth narrated the entire event that led him to his first major portfolio. She laughed and applauded at the risk he had taken.

The music studio was equally well-arranged, with all the instruments neatly a kept in a row. While Siddharth was busy making coffee for both of them, Reva walked around the other half when a small poem written on the wall caught her attention.

I need to go away,
Before you ask me to stay...
Else I'll forsake all,
And in your love would enthral...

I need to go away,
Before you unveil my way...
Else you'll get to learn,
How in your absence I yearn...

I need to go away,
Before you go astray...
Just to be able to opine,
That being in love is divine...

Reva read it twice. She had loved Chand's compositions and liked the use of words even in his jingles. But she hadn't heard these words before. There was a poignant feel in the romance of the verses. The lover wanted to run away before the counterpart did the same, only to infer how beautiful it was to be in love. Betrayal was the way out chosen only to escape being betrayed. Wow! She was immersed in the thought when her host entered with two mugs of coffee.

'Madame,' Siddharth interrupted her reverie. 'Coffee with Siddharth?'

Reva took her mug from him. 'Are you always so horrible?' she pressed her lips. 'I mean your jokes.'

'I am sure you meant me as well,' he shook his head.

'No no,' Reva laughed, 'I didn't.'

Siddharth looked at her radiant embarrassed face and smiled.

'I was just going through this poem,' Reva pointed at the wall. 'It's so nice – short but meaningful. It's kind of stark and unconventional, yet so honest.'

'Thanks,' Siddharth bowed.

'It was for Chand,' Reva teased him. 'I have never heard it in any of his jingles.'

'Thanks on behalf of Chand,' Siddharth clarified. 'And as you said, it's a bit unconventional for commercials.'

'I seem to befriend men, who are artistic,' she looked at him and smiled cajolingly, 'and all I can contribute is writing articles about them.'

He looked at her, as she bit her lips and shot him an enticing smile. She looked stunning. He just wanted to grab his camera and capture that smile in his lens. Shit! Most women would die to get photographed by him, but this woman just kept refusing him.

He decided to hold that thought. And it proved quite beneficial. They discussed a billion things about each other's professions. At times, when she traipsed around the house, eyeing different stuff, he took his camera and took her snaps. Since he had turned off the flash, she didn't realise that she was being photographed.

The night passed by quickly. Reva had rubbished the photographer as a young nouveau riche brat, who never missed an opportunity to charm her. But the six hour long chat changed her perception of the younger guy. He surely lacked the sophistication of Anshuman but there was a spirit which kind of rekindled her college days. Though she hated every time he cracked a silly joke, they never failed to amuse her.

'So, when did you develop this passion for photography?' she asked in her usual journalistic tone. 'Or did it happen by chance?'

'No, no,' he sipped from the second cup of coffee and shook his head. 'My fascination with photos started way back in school.'

'Okay,' she nodded. 'What class were you in when you took your first picture?'

'Lower middle class,' he said instantly and with a straight face.

For a moment, she was stumped.

'I meant which standard...' she tried to rectify her question but he had already started laughing by then.

'Idiot!'

She cursed him and giggled at the same time.

**

The next morning, Siddharth dropped her at the Lokhandwala residence.

'I am really thankful,' Reva said before getting out of the black SX4, 'but I really don't know how to return the favour.'

'Well, you know how you can!' he looked mischievously.

'You won't let it go, will you?' she looked amazed at the man's persistence. Why on earth did the man want to take her pictures when he had the opportunity to shoot with the world's most ravishing models at dream locales?

'Wait,' he said and promptly picked up the camera from the back seat. With equal alacrity, he displayed the last pictures he had taken, and handed it over to her. Reva held the camera and saw her pictures.

'Gosh!' she screamed. 'When did you do this?'

'That's what I do best,' he shrugged his shoulders. 'See, I proved your phobia wrong.'

'Okay,' she handed back the device to him, 'if you say so.'

She had agreed. He couldn't believe the same method worked for her as it had done for Maya Bose.

'Wow!' he was ecstatic. 'It's a deal then. You won't turn me down.'

'I won't. Goodbye,' she opened the door and walked out.

'Bye,' he replied as he watched her go.

**

Anshuman and Reva eventually made up after a couple of days. He didn't say sorry but promised to be more encouraging in future.

Reva finally accepted it, and life as they knew it went back on track. Siddharth called her a week after and insisted on fixing a date for the photo shoot. After some deliberation, she finalised a time in the following week. There were moments when she contemplated telling Anshuman about it. *But it's just one day,* she reasoned with herself. *And not that these pictures are going to be published in magazines or whatever.* However it was when Siddharth asked her to join his ongoing shoot at Manali that she felt uncomfortable.

'Are you mad?' she shrieked over the phone. 'I can't go there.'

'Your travel and expenses are on me,' he insisted. 'I will pick you up personally from the Delhi airport!'

'That's not the point,' she said. 'I can't come.'

'Come over the weekend,' he went on. 'I'm sure you are free then.'

'And what do I tell my husband?'

'Chand told me that Mr Mehra is going off for a shoot to Poland.'

'Are you spying on my life?'

He laughed. 'No. I just got to know. He will surely take some time to be back. And it's just a matter of two days.'

'Besides, there will be too many people there. I don't want people to be talking about it.'

'They won't. I will wrap up everything before you arrive. And I promise you no one will get to know about it.'

'Then, why can't we do here after you return.'

'Because Manali is a lovely place! And I want the mountains as a backdrop. Why limit ourselves to a studio when the nature is so bounteous?'

Reva finally gave in. A part of the reason for her agreeing to his request was the place. She had always heard about Manali's beauty, and the shoot was giving her opportunity to see things for herself. So, that weekend, she flew off to New Delhi. As promised, Siddharth Kashyap picked her incognito from the Indira Gandhi Airport and drove her all the way to the valley. It was almost a nine hour journey. But once they crossed Chandigarh and got on to NH 21, things seemed to get better. She loved every bit of the view outside.

But the photographer sitting next to her couldn't make out what was more beautiful - the inky sky dotted with stars which had never looked closer, framed by the looming hills on a side and the murmuring Beas on the other, or the freckled face resting on the window framed by the black mass of tousled hair, with just the slight hint of a smile. He wished he could stop right there, take out his camera and take her pictures. But Siddharth knew he couldn't do that, so he decided to wait until the next morning.

They reached the hotel around half past nine in the night. By the time the car pulled in, Reva was already yawning. Her eyes were red, and he realised that she had tried very hard to stay awake and keep him company during the journey.

'You can order dinner from your room,' he said, 'or if you are not sleepy, we can meet in the dining hall.'

She looked sheepishly. 'You won't really mind if I have it in the room, would you?' the question was rhetorical. 'I just want to have a bath and relax.'

'I understand,' he walked her to her room. 'Good night.'

'See you tomorrow morning,' she smiled.

'Yup,' he nodded.

She turned the key and went in. He saw her enter and walked towards his room. She turned the lights on, and peeped out to catch a glimpse of him as he traipsed slowly, clearly disappointed. She shook her head and went back in. When he turned back to look at her room, the door was already shut. He sighed and went off to order some food for himself.

*

The next day started with a light breakfast before they left for the photo shoot. The town cradled by the Himalayas, with a river in its bosom, nurtures animated apple orchards in its vicinity, houses a temple for an unheralded character from a Mahabharatian myth, treasures its reserves of secret "springs" that miraculously spew hot elixir from the recesses of the earth, provides many a jaundiced eye its first view of fresh, virgin snow, prides itself of a spooky old world charm, and attaches itself to a pass to Afghanistan through a perilous stretch of flimsy road.

They roamed around, looking for the ideal backdrop for their pictures. Finally, when they realised that the light was fading, Siddharth decided to call it a day.

'There is so much in this town to see, and yet that will make you pause by the river, sit next to it, make you hear it gurgle and talk and make it so singularly unnecessary to see anything else but the river,' he said as they sat next to the river. 'The town and your heart will resonate in harmony.'

'Wow!' she exclaimed in surprise. 'I didn't know the photographer is a poet as well.'

'The man who takes pictures,' he smiled, 'can write verses too, ma'am.'

'Ah ha,' she poured coffee from the flask and handed him a cup, 'so how come a romantic and famous man like you doesn't have a girlfriend?'

'Well,' he sipped the hot brewing Nescafe, 'I had one.'

'Really?' she was suddenly curious about the photographer's love-life. 'When was it?'

'College!' he smiled. 'The ideal time for love!'

'What happened then?'

'Life!'

For a moment, they both sat silently, watching the river flow mellifluously. There was a sudden pang of awkwardness between them, impregnated by the first rays of friendship seeping through the door of formality.

'Nothing to be so gloomy about,' he joked to break the ice. 'It happens so often with college goers. I was from a small city, Ajmer. But I never wanted to stay in that city. For me, Mumbai was the ultimate destination. She hailed from a local family and you know girls in our community get married quite early. It was not possible for her to wait till I found a foothold in Mumbai.'

Reva listened to him with rapt attention, surprised that the guy whom she had taken for a frivolous charmer had a vulnerable side as well.

'You know the kind of mentality we have back in small towns. Mumbai is a dream city but a dreaded one at the same time. The idea that an average Ajmerite who is neither an engineer nor a doctor can make a mark there seemed next to impossible. But I couldn't afford to give up my dreams.'

'What did she say?' she looked at him misty eyed.

'Nothing,' he replied. 'She just rested her head on my chest and cried. I held on to her for some time before realising that I had to let go of her before it got tough for either of us. So, I kissed her for the first and last time and asked her to be happy.' He rubbed his eyes and tried to put on a brave smile, 'She is happily married now and the mother of a cute son.'

'That's nice,' she could manage to say.

**

That night, she knocked on the door of his room to call him for dinner.

'Come in,' he said unaware that it was not a porter but Reva herself. She walked in and caught him by surprise, adorned in a pair of track pants and a vest, reading his diary.

'Hey,' she said and he jumped up in surprise.

'Oh hi,' he rushed to put on a shirt. 'Come in.'

'What are you reading?' she sat on the bed and tugged at the diary.

'Nothing,' he tried to take it away but by then she had already opened a page.

'A poem?' she said in surprise. '*A Red House,* you wrote it?'

'Yeah,' he pulled it from her hands in embarrassment, 'a long time ago.'

'Let me read it...' she insisted. 'What is it about?'

'It's nothing great,' he dismissed the request. 'So, what brings you here?'

'Let me read the poem,' she stretched out her hand. 'Or you read it out to me. Whom is it for?'

'My ex,' he said a bit clumsily. 'I kind of wrote in her memory.'

'Oh!' she withdrew her hand. 'Is it that personal?'

'Not quite,' he replied with a shy smile, 'just that I haven't read it out to anyone.'

'So can I read it?' she gave her hand again.

This time, he passed the diary to her.

'Go and get dressed while I read it,' she signalled.

'For what?'

'For dinner!'

'Oh! Okay.'

Siddharth entered the washroom to change for the dining hall, as she leafed through the book until her eyes again caught the title "A Red House". She read it silently and carefully.

A Red House

With curtains in yellow
Contrasting with the blue divan
A dog called Buddy
Sticking his neck
Out of our blue sedan
Two tykes rummaging around
One a Sachin in the making
The other a Shaan to be
With eyes like yours
And voice like me

Your pile of clothes
Fighting for space
With my pile of snaps
Your bangles and make up box
Propping against my new camera

One weather-beaten remote
That flits between
TLC and ZEE
One blackened kitchen
Bearing testimony

To attempts at cooking
Gone wrong

A red house walled by
Stained glass windows
That frame the rain...
We love watching the drops
Cuddled together…

I stand beside
Another stained glass
As I take in the scene
Of memories forlorn
Of love left unseen
Of words unspoken
That never said what they mean
Of a wrecked red house
A red house...
That could've been.....

Reva read it again, this time even slower and in greater detail. Tears filled her eyes. The pain in the concluding lines overwhelmed her. It exuded the same pathos as the one she had read in Chand's room. She waited for Siddharth to come out of the washroom.

'Did you write the poem I saw on Chand's studio wall?' she asked all of a sudden.

He waited for a while before nodding.

She closed the diary and put it back on the bed. For a moment, she felt betrayed that he didn't divulge the fact when she had heaped praises on Chand for the verse. *Maybe I wasn't privy to that side of his,* she told herself. *Maybe I don't know him yet.* But then, she had ignored the possibility when he thanked for her appreciation of the poem. She wanted to say something but the feeling was too ineffable to be put into words.

'Let's go,' was all she managed to say.

**

The dinner was quiet – both of them ate less and spoke even lesser. Occasionally, they stole shy smiles. Neither of them had envisaged that all of a sudden, their acquaintance would pass through an altogether new phase.

'So, you will be back to your normal life tomorrow?' he said while they walked back to their rooms.

'You are not leaving tomorrow?' she looked surprised at him.

'No,' he replied. 'I'll go day after. You didn't want to be seen with me, remember?'

'We can meet on the flight, can't we?' she nodded suggestively.

'Aha,' he exclaimed in surprise. 'So, you don't mind?'

'Not if you can adjust your tickets,' she smiled.

'That I don't think will be a problem,' he smiled.

'Good night, then,' she bade an abrupt farewell as they reached her room. 'See you tomorrow morning.'

'How about a glass of white wine in the memory of our first photo shoot?' he mustered the courage to ask her.

For a moment she hesitated. Then, a smile left him besotted.

'Okay.'

**

She watched eagerly as he loaded the photos on his laptop and edited them one by one.

'Why do you guys always edit the pictures?' she complained. 'It kills the originality of the pictures!'

'It doesn't kill anything, Ma'am,' he looked up. 'It just enhances a few things.'

'But that's fake,' she said and immediately it struck her how the word has permeated into her vocabulary from Anshuman's.

'Nothing is fake until you morph it altogether. I am not making major changes in these photographs. Little bit of fine tuning doesn't do any harm.'

'What about other portfolios?'

'Those require more editing. They determine whether the models will get a job or not. I get paid to produce the best possible output.'

He minimised the page and showed the other portfolios he had done – some for new and upcoming models, and some for popular celebrities.

'People often determine whether to buy a magazine or not, purely based on the cover page,' he analysed. 'So, we can't compromise on that. It's all business. And I am sure you know that as much as I do'

Reva nodded. Indeed, even her profession demanded slight modifications in content to suit the palate of the readers and raise eyebrows. There had been more than one occasion when Dipanwita called Reva and recommended changes in the articles or stories the latter had submitted. The clock ticked by as they sat in Siddharth's room. It was almost a re-enactment of their first night out at the Andheri West studio. They chatted endlessly about many things varying from their backgrounds to their hobbies, from their romantic lives to future family planning. The only difference was the bottle of Moscato which had replaced the cups of coffee. She sat on the sofa with her legs stretched out on a small table, while he lay on the bed. A sudden gust of informality breezed through the alley of their relationship. As Siddharth spoke, he realised that it was a pure turn of events that the same woman who had declined his offer for a photo shoot was then sharing an amiable conversation, away from the prying eyes of not only society but also her own family.

*

There was a faint light outside when Siddharth woke up with a start. His head was rested on the laptop. The timer on the screen showed 04:55. *Shit! I fell asleep!* He cursed softly, only to realise that Reva was possibly in the same room, or at least that was the last thing he remembered. He looked up towards the sofa, and found her still sitting there. Only this time, she was immersed in a world beyond the realms of consciousness.

For a moment, Siddharth thought he should wake her up but then decided against it. Reva looked serene as she lay somnolent, her head slanted sideward while her legs crouched under her. A faint smile outlined the pink lips. *She must be dreaming,* Siddharth told himself as he walked up and covered her with a blanket. She held it tightly and turned as her hand fell on his. *He* feared she'd wake up but she didn't. He slowly pulled out his fingers from underneath hers. He wanted to take a picture but his mother never liked him taking people's pictures in their sleep. So, he decided to capture the moment and the frame it in his mind.

Siddharth didn't realise how much time had passed as he sat there watching her breathe, move at times, scratch her cheek and then fall asleep. He had never seen a woman as perfect in her sleep as Reva. *People do so much to look good while they are awake,* he told himself, *and she is perfect even when she is asleep.*

The first rays of the sun shone in soon after and by then both of them were awake and ready to leave. They conveniently avoided any topic pertaining to the previous night. Thankfully for Siddharth, no discomfort crept in to wane their friendship, which had blossomed over the past couple of days. They went for a long walk and had tea at a small store before making their way back to the hotel. As the car made its way back to Delhi, Reva reclined on the back seat and pored over an old Jackie Collins, and Siddharth sat on the front seat, next to the driver, and looked out at the Beas. As the car meandered through the road next to the river, it spoke to him, as it always had. It murmured into his ears. *See...I told you... every single time you questioned me I'd told you...you'll find love...love will find you... See.*

Fourteen

Present Time

DAY 1
10:25 p.m.

Chand was on his way back to the waiting lounge when he saw Anshuman Mehra strolling outside and talking on the phone.

'Thanks, Banerjee,' Anshuman said, 'that's really great news.'

Chand waited as his mentor kept talking.

'I wouldn't have been able to manage all by myself. Handling police cases is not my forte. And Reva's state requires my presence all the time.'

'I know,' Shubhanshu Banerjee spoke on the other end. 'Don't worry. Kabir is a friend. He throws airs but is essentially a nice guy.'

'You don't foresee a problem?' Anshuman asked fearfully. Shubhanshu was the only one he had confided the entire matter to. And his best friend had stood by him, pretty much as Anshuman had expected.

'Don't worry,' Shubhanshu consoled his mate. 'I have told him everything. Kabir will take care of the matter now. He might give that chap a tough time though.'

'I don't want him to do that,' Anshuman spoke alarmed. He knew Reva would never like it if she got to know that Anshuman had taken advantage of the situation to trouble the man who had not only been a part of her life but had also been burdened with a lot of pain and guilt for the past twenty hours. After all, Siddharth was also the reason Reva was still alive. 'I just want him to issue a clearance. There is no point harassing a man who can't even get up from the bed without aid. I owe this much to him for saving Reva's life.'

'Fair enough,' Shubhanshu exhaled. 'Tell Kabir when he comes over. He should be there soon.'

'Okay,' Anshuman said.

'Is Dipa there?' Shubhanshu asked and diverted the topic.

'No,' Anshuman recollected the message she had sent some time ago. 'She said she was in some conference at Taj. I asked her to wind it up and then come. Anyway, there's no point hurrying.'

'Okay,' Shubhanshu said. 'Ask her to call me after she gets home at night.'

'I will,' Anshuman smiled feebly, realising how the Banerjees had grown closer while Reva and he had become estranged.

'You take care, AM,' Shubhanshu concluded the conversation. 'Let me know if you need anything. I feel so guilty that I can't be with you through this crisis.'

'What you are doing for me, Banerjee, is something I can't ever pay back.'

'You don't realise, young man, I owed you this,' Shubhanshu replied. 'I am repaying you for all my midnight intrusions into your house.'

Both the men chuckled as they bade goodbye. Anshuman had often heard people say that a professional relation could never lead to friendship. Moreover, his friends would also opine that friendship starts losing its essence beyond a certain age; and only your childhood buddies stand by your side. He had seen the same being largely corroborated by real life examples. But his rapport with Shubhanshu belied the inductive generalisation of the theory;

testifying the fact that one never runs out of age to make a new friend. At the juncture of life where he stood, Anshuman couldn't envisage himself calling up anyone else but the man older to him by a decade and also a professional associate.

Anshuman turned around to see Chand standing by him, trying to look poised but lost in a sudden vortex of thoughts.

'Is anything the matter?' Anshuman asked worried. 'Is Mr Kashyap alright?'

'He is,' Chand nodded. 'It's just that he thinks he is always right.'

'Well, so do I,' Anshuman realised that Chand's change in mood was due to the altercation with his friend, '*Sorry* is a word that doesn't come naturally to me.'

'But he is getting too obstinate about this entire thing!'

'Don't drive him up the wall. He will have no option but to retaliate.'

'He doesn't realise he is wrong.'

'How would you react if people tried to convince you that you are wrong about something you so special in your life? Would you accept what others tell you?'

Chand looked at Anshuman, wondering how the man could see the situation so objectively even when his own life was so intricately linked to it.

'You guys should leave now,' Anshuman suggested. 'You have important work to do.'

'Don't worry, Mr Mehra,' Chand assured him. 'I will be here till the cop issues a clearance.'

'That won't be necessary.'

'Perhaps. I would still like to do it.'

The ad-wizard patted the younger musician's shoulder and walked past him.

**

Dipanwita Banerjee arrived at quarter to eleven. She wore one of her traditional embroidered cotton saris, matched with a pearl set and a watch. The firmly knit bun was circled with a string of jasmine, while a bag hung from her right shoulder. *Reva had always been a huge admirer of her dressing sense*, Anshuman thought. *And had she been well, she would have appreciated her senior's attire for the conference.* Dipanwita was well aware of the entire scenario. Shubhanshu had apprised her in vivid details and she had messaged Anshuman informing him about the conference. The latter had suggested that she should come once all her work was done.

'How is she?' Dipanwita asked.

'Still unconscious, but better,' Anshuman reported. 'Out of danger and is expected to regain consciousness soon.'

'That's good news.'

'Yeah,' Anshuman sighed with a faint smile.

'What about the cop?' Dipanwita looked at her watch. 'When are you going?'

'No. Banerjee said he is going to come over himself.'

'Who? The cop?'

'Yes.'

'Now, that's something,' Dipanwita smiled surprised. 'When did Shubho make friends with cops?'

Anshuman chuckled at the sarcastic tone of the question.

'Let's go and sit somewhere,' he proposed seeing the exhaustion on the guest's face. 'You look very tired.'

'Yeah, it's been a very long day. And trust me, driving from Apollo Bunder to Bandra is even more tiring, especially with the crowd out on the streets now.'

'It is.'

They walked down to the cafeteria. It was scantily occupied now. As they sat at one of the corner tables and ordered for coffee, Anshuman realised that he had forgotten to inform Chand and

Sophie. He called up Chand's number but the latter's number was engaged. Almost immediately after he cancelled the call, his phone began ringing. It was Sophie.

'Sir, were you trying to call him? He is talking to his mixing engineer.'

'I just wanted to inform you guys that I am at the cafeteria with Reva's boss.'

'Oh, Mrs Banerjee has arrived?'

'Yes.'

'Fair enough. You talk to her. We are here upstairs. If the nurse comes here, I will let her know.'

'Thank you so much.'

The two cafe lattes arrived as he put the phone down on the table.

'Quick service!' Dipanwita smiled.

'Yeah!'

'Is someone else upstairs?'

'Sophie, my....'

'Your oh-so-able junior!'

'Yes,' Anshuman nodded and then wondered how Dipa knew about her and did not seem to have a favourable opinion about her too. Surely it must have been Reva who conveyed such an idea. 'How do you know her? Has Reva told you anything about her?'

'Nothing as such,' Dipanwita said cautiously, not wanting to reveal what Reva thought about her. 'At times she felt the girl intruded too much into your private space.'

'Sophie is just an able employee.'

'Reva didn't harbour any doubts about you. It's just that she detested the amount of attention the girl gained at times.'

'She earned it, Dipanwita. She is the most promising employee at Genesis.'

'Never mind,' the senior journalist brushed aside any further argument. 'Had you met the guy earlier?'

'Never,' Anshuman shook his head and sighed. 'Heard about him from Chand Pias, that's all.'

'How do they know each other?' Dipanwita questioned.

'They were flatmates earlier.'

'I see. Reva never spoke about him, even vaguely?'

'I never doubted the fact that she was smart.'

'Then, why did you doubt her decision to get into Crime?'

'It wasn't that I doubted she would succeed,' Anshuman held the cup in his palms. 'I know she would have done that equally well. It was just too risky.'

'Do you think there is a chance Reva might refute everything the man said?' Dipanwita hardly expected Anshuman to be optimistic about it.

'Frankly,' Anshuman took a deep breath, 'no. He seems pretty honest.'

'Then?'

'Are you interviewing me?'

Dipanwita looked startled. Then, she broke out in a giggle. 'Did I sound like that?'

'Perhaps,' Anshuman sipped the coffee, 'but these are questions everyone's going to ask me. So, I should better be prepared to answer them. I have already lied once today, but it can't go on for long.'

'To whom?'

'What?'

'You lied.'

'My boss.'

'K. Balasubramaniam?'

'Yeah. And don't tell me Reva had something to say about him as well!'

'No, no,' Dipanwita laughed. 'Reva is not a sceptical person, Anshuman.'

'She was not in a position to be, Dipa,' Anshuman wanted to bite back the caustic retort but couldn't. 'I should have been one. But I trusted her too much.'

'You can't possibly forgive her, can you?'

Anshuman sighed. He wondered if there could be an apposite answer, but his silence conveyed everything to the middle-aged woman who had been through a turbulent marriage herself.

'Then what are you holding on to, Anshuman?' Dipanwita quizzed.

'I am holding on to my marriage. As backward as I might sound, there are aged people who wouldn't like to find out this about the girl they thought was perfect.'

'Is it only about them?'

'Do you blame me for being bitter?'

'Absolutely not!' Dipanwita spoke in an assuring tone. 'I have been through a rough patch myself, Anshuman, and I know how tough it is trying to stick to your marriage.'

'Neither Shubho nor you were cheating on each other,' Anshuman said, his eyes filling up with tears again.

'That's true,' Dipanwita paused and sipped her coffee. 'But we couldn't recover from our crisis, could we?'

'You know what, Dipa, as angry as I am now, I love Reva too much to let her go.'

'I know,' Dipanwita leaned forward and held his hands. 'I have seen both of you in love. And no one knows more than me how much she means to you.'

'How would you have reacted had you been in my position?' Anshuman could almost feel himself deprived of any strength to fight this battle any longer.

'You know, Anshuman, both Shubho and I have been through a stage when all we lacked was mutual faith.'

'Banerjee had told me about it,' Anshuman exhaled realising that his was not the only marriage in trouble, 'though I never knew the details.'

'We lost the thing we both valued beyond anything.'

'How did you lose it?'

'I guess we were destined to,' Dipanwita promptly took a tissue paper and wiped a tear.

Dipanwita Banerjee was four months pregnant when "Lagaan" made it to the top five in the Best Foreign Film Category for Academy Awards 2002. After a long time, since Mira Nair's critically acclaimed "Salaam Bombay", an Indian film was getting its due at the world's biggest award ceremony. This time, everything seemed to go in favour of the Aamir Khan starrer that had deftly mixed patriotism, romance and the nation's favourite game – cricket. It seemed that the versatile actor would get the award home, which only the maestro Satyajit Ray had been able to do so far.

'*You are pregnant,*' *Shubhanshu had argued.* '*What makes you think you can go on such a long journey?*'

The 9/11 attacks on the Twin Towers had already spread panic all across the world. The American aviation industry was already under threat. Amidst this, Dipanwita was risking not only her own life but also her child's. The Banerjees had long planned for a child. After years of failed attempts and medical check-ups, much to the delight of the couple, Dipanwita had finally conceived a child. This was a risk Shubhanshu Banerjee was not ready to take.

'*This is once in a lifetime opportunity,*' *she argued.* '*I am going to take care of myself.*' *She came ahead and gave him a hug.* '*Baby, I'll manage. I have already spoken to the concerned people and they are going to ensure both your child and wife are safe.*'

'*I won't be there with you.*'

'*Are you there with me at office? If things have to go wrong, they will.*'

'*Don't say such things.*'

'And you don't be superstitious.'

Shubhanshu didn't relent. Dipanwita kissed him.

'I will be waiting for you at the airport when you come back,'
Shubhanshu sighed.

Contrary to all hopes, Lagaan failed to make it to the big stage.
Dipanwita was the first one to interview the team and listen to its
views after it came out of the Los Angeles auditorium.

After the four-day tour, the Daily Times team commenced their
journey back to Mumbai. Dipanwita knew that Shubhanshu would
mock the futility of her entire journey. She had already planned what
to tell him at the airport.

The British Airways connecting flight from Heathrow landed at
the Mumbai International Airport on a warm Tuesday afternoon.
Dipanwita took her luggage and proceeded towards the exit gate.
While her other colleagues departed one by one, she stood at the
arrival gate waiting for Shubho to turn up. After almost an hour, she
took out her mobile phone and dialled his number. It went on ringing
without any response, before getting disconnected automatically. 'He
must be driving,' she told herself and waited for some more time,
before calling him again. This time, he answered promptly.

'Hi, I was about to call you only,' Shubho sounded exuberant at
the prospect of meeting his wife after the hazardous journey. 'Where
have you reached?'

'What is that supposed to mean, Shubho? I am waiting at the
airport,' Dipa spoke agitated. 'Why aren't you here?'

'You are still standing there?' the surprise was evident in his voice.
'Hasn't anyone come to pick you up?'

'What?'

'I got busy at office,' he sounded alarmed. 'So, I sent a driver to
pick you up. He must be carrying a placard with your name!'

Dipanwita hadn't thought of looking for someone with a placard.
She looked around hastily, but there was not one board with her
name on it.

'There is no driver, Shubho,' she said vexed. 'Had I known this is going to happen, I would have asked any of my colleagues to drop me home.'

'Sweetheart, he left two hours ago. He should have been there by now.'

'I don't care, I am leaving.'

'Wait, wait… don't do that. I will see what I can do.'

'I can't stand here any longer, Shubho,' she pushed the trolley and started moving forward. 'I feel extremely tired in this heat.'

'Will you be able to take a cab?'

'Do I have any other way out?' she blurted.

'I am really sorry, honey. The driver should have been there long ago.'

'He is not here, Shubho,' she walked towards the cab lane. 'And that's the fact.'

'I know…'

Shubhanshu had hardly spoken when it all happened.

'Shubho,' there was a sudden panic in Dipanwita's voice which shocked her husband.

'What?' Shubhanshu cried. 'What happened, Dipa? Are you there? Dipa? What happened?'

Dipanwita was in no state to answer. She let go of the mobile and held the handle of the trolley tightly with both her hands, as blood started streaming down her legs. There was an excruciating pain as her stomach contracted and her muscles seemed to give in to the sudden attack. Within no time, her white salwar was doused in red as she bent down on her knees, clutching on to her abdomen. She knew what was happening and realised what repercussions this would lead to.

'This can't be happening to me, God!' she murmured as her strength drained out.

When Shubhanshu ran into Nanavati hospital, his wife lay unconscious under the effect of sedatives. The doctor informed him about the entire incident that had led to the miscarriage.

'*She conceived after a lot of complications,*' Shubhanshu tried not to weep.

'*I would advise her not to get pregnant again,*' the doctor said. '*It can be very risky.*'

That one remark seemed to dash all their hopes. It had been their last wish, which had been granted after years of dedication.

'*She won't,*' Shubhanshu nodded in agreement but a part of him also resolved that he couldn't forgive her for this. How many times had he expressed his fear? He never consented to the long journey and stress she took for one goddamn event. It was her adamant attitude that cost them their child.

When Dipanwita woke up, she had all her anger pent up for her husband. In her condition, she had been asked to strictly avoid two things – extreme climate and exertion. And after the climate in the US and moderate temperature in the flight, she had been kept waiting on the warm street for more than an hour. He knew she was coming. How could he possibly be so callous so as to send an irresponsible driver instead of coming down himself?

Their complaints remained unspoken. But the years of togetherness didn't leave any requirement for words to express their feelings. Their anguish soon turned into an ego-tussle, where neither of the contending parties agreed to concede. The fracture soon turned into a crevasse that parted the couple forever.

'Shubho blamed me for going to the US,' she said as Anshuman paid the bill. 'I accused him for the mess at the airport. But somehow, we both knew it was just not in our hands. Neither of the reasons should have caused a miscarriage. It happened because it had to happen. People do lose their kids. Ours wasn't an exceptional case. Women earlier have also lost their babies in the womb due to stress, and my experience was hardly traumatic to take a life. But what could we have done?'

'Things are getting better,' Anshuman looked at her, 'aren't they?'

'I guess,' she nodded. 'But it's still a long way to go before it's what it used to be in the beginning.'

'Do you think someday Reva and I will be able to realise that the entry of this man happened because it had to? Will we be able to drop all charges and move on?'

'It would be best if you could,' Dipanwita replied. It was the most cogent advice she could provide the younger couple at that point of time.

Anshuman leaned on the backrest of the chair and bent his head backwards when his mobile rang. It was the ACP. Anshuman had noted down the number from Shubhanshu and had saved it in the contacts. *He would call you up before he drops in,* Banerjee had said over the phone, *you don't call him out of impatience.*

'Hello,' Anshuman got up from the chair and walked out of the cafeteria.

'Mr Mehra,' the cop spoke pragmatically. 'I have reached Apollo. Where will you be able to meet me?'

'Sir, right now I am on the second floor,' Anshuman hurried towards the staircase as Dipanwita gathered her belongings and followed him, 'I will meet you at the reception.'

'Okay!'

'You wait for us on the fourth floor,' Anshuman cancelled the call and turned to Dipanwita, 'I will bring him up.'

**

The man was stout and dark, his thick moustache and overgrown stubble lending firmness to his square jaws. The white chequered shirt was neatly tucked into the black trousers and the folded sleeves revealed the thick hair on his hands and a sparkling silver watch on his left wrist.

The cop had noticed Anshuman as the latter ran all the way to the reception.

'Thank you so much for coming,' the ad-man gave his hand. 'Anshuman Mehra.'

The cop nodded without any acknowledgment, and shook hands uninterestedly. 'Let's go,' he said, 'which floor?'

'Fourth!'

**

Dipanwita stood in the corridor with Mrs Gaitonde when Anshuman walked out of the elevator followed by the ACP. The journalist had quickly found the nurse herself and asked the latter to get Reva's police report ready. Swarnalata, by now aware of the entire proceedings in this complicated case, readied the file in no time.

'This is Mrs Banerjee,' Anshuman introduced the cop to Dipanwita, 'Shubhanshu's wife.'

'Oh!' Kabir looked curious. 'Are you family friends?'

'Yes,' Dipanwita smiled, 'and Reva also works with me at *Daily Times*.'

'Aha! So, may I see the report?'

Swarnalata Gaitonde quickly handed over the file to the cop. He scanned through it perfunctorily and looked at the nurse.

'Where can I find this *S. Kashyap*?'

'305,' Swarnalata replied obediently.

Suddenly, it struck Anshuman that the cop was predetermined to give Siddharth a tough time. That was not something he wanted to happen. 'Sir, he is badly hurt,' he spoke up. 'Is it necessary to bother him now?'

'I need his statement, Mr Mehra,' the cop looked straight at Anshuman. The stolidity in his eyes was unnerving.

'Just his statement?'

'Don't worry, Mr Mehra,' Kabir patted his shoulder. 'He won't get anything he doesn't deserve.'

**

Siddharth Kashyap was half-asleep when the nurse rushed into the room. He looked up at the sound of the door opening. The nurse looked perplexed as she panted and rolled up his bed.

'What happened, Sister?'

'There is a police officer who wants to meet you.'

For a moment, Siddharth felt a shiver running down his entire body.

'Can you tell me if the woman who was admitted with me is alright?'

'She is, Sir,' the nurse seemed to be in a hurry. 'The officer wants to meet you for some kind of statement.'

'Oh!'

Siddharth realised it must be the police verification to change Reva's identity in the police report. *Anshuman Mehra was surely desperate to reclaim his wife,* Siddharth smirked. *All I need to do is explain the circumstances under which I had to change her surname.* As much as he tried to console himself, the entire idea of a police interrogation was unnerving. However desperately he wanted, things were not under his control that night.

'Send them in.'

**

Chand and Sophie were walking through the third floor corridor when they saw Anshuman straight ahead. A middle-aged man, unknown to them, walked along with him while the two women tried their best to keep up with the men.

'This must be the cop,' Chand told Sophie.

'Cop?' Sophie sounded petrified.

'To change the police report'

'Okay,' Sophie exhaled. *What a mess we are all in,* she wanted to say.

As Anshuman and the others drew closer, the man unknown to them looked up at Chand.

'This is Chand Pias,' Anshuman said. 'He is Mr Kashyap's friend.'

Chand noticed the way he was introduced to the officer, but didn't make a remark. As much as he would have loved to point out the insult, he didn't want to stir things up further.

Kabir nodded, as if it hardly mattered to him. 'Are you a musician by the way?' he spoke as Chand shook his hand.

'Yes,' Anshuman interrupted and said.

'Fashion, media, music and nuisance – they are all so intricately related, aren't they?' the cop smiled haughtily and walked past him. Anshuman pursed his lips to express that nothing could be done about the arrogance of the cop.

'I really don't care if he just does what he is here for,' Chand said softly and Anshuman smiled at him.

**

Siddharth waited for the police officer when Anshuman pushed open the door and came in.

'Are you in a state to talk?' Anshuman enquired, 'Shall I...'

'Bring him in,' Siddharth said. 'You are an impatient man, Mr Mehra.'

'I didn't want to disturb you.'

'Never mind, ask him to come in.'

Anshuman opened the door and the man entered. There was a look of contempt in those eyes which signalled that the conversation wouldn't be an easy one.

'Mr S. Kashyap?' the officer walked up to his bed.

'Siddharth.'

'ACP Kabir.'

Anshuman Mehra had brought an IAS officer to officialise the matter, he thought. Siddharth cordially gave his hand but the cop preferred to ask the next question. The nurse who had intimated Siddharth about the cop's arrival rushed in with a chair. Kabir snatched it thanklessly and sat on it.

'Is this your signature?' he showed the police report produced by the nurse.

'Yes,' Siddharth replied with as much temerity as he could muster.

'So, you agree that Ms Reva, admitted to Apollo at roughly four in the morning today, is not related to you and is Mr Anshuman Mehra's wife?'

'Yes.'

'Not that you had any other choice, did you?'

'I think…' Anshuman was about to intervene but was brusquely cut short by the cop.

'May I know why you signed her in as your wife?'

'I needed to be a relative to sign the bond.'

'And you had no way to contact Mr Mehra? I assume you knew who he was!'

'Yes, but I didn't have his number.'

'Does Mrs Mehra own a gadget called a mobile phone?'

'She does.'

'Didn't it have his number? I am sure it does.'

'It didn't strike me at that point of time.'

'Would it have come to your mind had he not appeared here himself?'

Anshuman wanted this thing to end at the earliest. 'I believe,' he interrupted the conversation, 'we should let him relax now. He has been through a tough time since last night.'

'You know I can arrest you, Mr Kashyap,' Kabir went on, 'if either Mr Mehra or the hospital decides to press charges against you for registering a fraudulent identity of the victim.'

'I did what was the best for Reva,' Siddharth knew he had far too many contacts to save him from such a charge. 'If Mr Mehra feels I should be charged for registering his wife on time, so be it.'

'So, you are now calling her his wife when you find yourself in danger,' the ACP smirked.

'I have said all that I needed to,' Siddharth looked at him. 'I want you to excuse me now.'

For a moment, the ACP looked stunned by the audacity in the man's voice.

'We need to let him rest,' Anshuman mediated again.

'You are very lucky, Kashyap, that you have someone like this man in his position to help you,' the cop spoke and got up. 'Someone like me would have proved a lot worse.'

'Thanks for your concern, officer,' Siddharth smiled dryly. 'I will keep that in mind.'

**

Chand and Sophie were waiting along with others outside Siddharth's room when Anshuman reappeared.

'Is everything sorted?' Dipanwita asked them.

'Yes,' the ACP responded. 'But the man doesn't know the mess he's got himself in. It is the pride in his contacts that reflected every time he spoke. What he doesn't know that daily I meet people who have more contacts!' He looked at Anshuman, 'Let him come around, we'll take care of him.'

Sophie held Chand's arm realising how the latter felt every time someone insulted his friend. As bitter an argument as they might have, Chand could never take anyone bad mouthing the guy he shared the most important years of his life with. Sophie knew that Siddharth was the first person Chand had come out to, and that their friendship was extremely special to him.

'I don't intend to do any such thing officer,' Anshuman shook his head. 'I will do anything to make this case less bitter.'

'Of course,' Kabir looked at him. 'Who wants people to know that his wife was cheating on him? I think what you said sounds smart. By the way, who is the doctor in charge?'

Everyone stood around, appalled at the behaviour of the man.

'Sure,' Anshuman paid as less heed as he could, 'I can introduce you to her now if you want.' He looked at Sister Gaitonde who nodded in agreement. 'I think...'

Before he could finish, Kabir's phone started ringing. He answered the call and signalled to Anshuman to lead the way.

'Yes, Deshmukh,' Anshuman could hear Kabir say over the phone as they strode towards the fourth floor office of Dr Ahmed, 'I am at Apollo. Yeah, some accident case of a woman... obviously yaar, normal people anyways don't get admitted here... this one's a pretty high-profile case as well... not celebs but pretty renowned people.'

'Your daughter's favourite singer is also here,' the cop joked as they walked up the stairs. 'He's not directly related but one of the parties' friend. Yeah, there are two parties. One is her husband, and the other who claimed to be her husband.'

Anshuman could feel his fist tightening at the tone of the officer. This was the first time he heard their situation being mocked at and it quickly became clear that such tones would be common once they got out of the hospital. Things were bound to get murkier. Perhaps he was as agitated as Siddharth, but he had more at stake than the photographer. He had to keep his cool. *I don't need to see this cop after he issues a clearance,* Anshuman pacified himself.

'By the way, who won the Man of the Match? Dhoni? Gambhir is today's Dravid I tell you. I pretty much knew that Dhoni would take away the trophy for winning the match with a six. And... Yuvraj? Man of the Series? Really? Wasn't he supposed to be dropped from the team? Getting away from Kim Sharma is doing him good, isn't it? Hahaha...'

Anshuman knocked on the doctor's door and pushed it open to seek her permission. Dr Ahmed, engrossed in the papers lying on the table, asked him to bring the police officer in. Kabir was still on the phone and didn't notice the name on the board hanging outside. But the moment he stepped in, his voice seemed to crack up in surprise. Dr Ahmed looked straight at him, though her dilated look showed equal astonishment.

'I will... umm... I will call you... later,' Kabir stuttered. 'Yeah, yeah, I'll be there in some time.'

'You wanted to see me, officer?' Fariza Ahmed's voice was stern.

'Ye... yes,' Kabir was still groping for words, making it apparent to Anshuman that they knew each other, 'I wanted to see you before issuing the clearance.'

'Anything I can help you with?'

'I just wanted to ensure you knew everything.'

'I do.'

'That will be it, doctor.'

'Thanks. Let me know if you need anything else.'

'No,' he looked at Anshuman. 'Let's go.'

Anshuman looked at them, trying to gauge the reason behind this sudden turn of events. He thanked Dr Ahmed and followed Kabir, who seemed to be in a sudden hurry to leave. Kabir didn't utter another word till they reached the reception. He signed at the places ticked by the receptionist. Then, he brought out a folded envelope from his trouser side-pocket and handed it over to Anshuman.

'This has the version of police report you want, along with my signature,' he said and handed it over.

'Thank you, officer,' Anshuman realised that the man had prepared the report even without inquiring into the matter, 'I really appreciate your help.'

'Since when has Fariza Ahmed been practising in this hospital?' Kabir asked abruptly. 'When did she leave her previous hospital?'

Anshuman was right. They knew each other. 'I have no idea,' he shrugged, 'I have met her just today.'

'Okay,' Kabir nodded. 'Call me up if you need any other help.'

'Thanks again,' Anshuman gave his hand.

This time, the grip was gentler and the shake humbler than the last time. Kabir turned and rushed out of the hospital. Anshuman Mehra looked on as the cop walked out towards his jeep, while the sky above was engulfed in a deluge of fireworks. Everyone, save him, seemed to be joyous, cheering for the victorious Indian team, Dhoni and Sachin Tendulkar. They had won the World Cup. But not he; Anshuman Mehra had lost the most crucial match of his life.

Fifteen

Some Relations Change

The idea of keeping the portfolio a secret from Anshuman burdened Reva with guilt. *There is no logical reason behind it,* she told herself, *he might very well take it positively.* Anshuman often behaved unpredictably. So, she could never be certain how he would react to the pictures. *The pictures are pretty decent,* she justified herself. *But he would surely not like the fact that I went off to Manali without informing him. Shit!* Ever since she returned from the valley, she had thought of sharing the truth but couldn't muster the courage. *This is bad,* she cursed herself, *and I feel like a criminal.* Reva had never felt so troubled coming clean about something.

Reva sat at her dressing table, moisturising her arms. Her white noodle-strapped nighty flowed over her body, while the table lamp illuminated her face. She had bought the lamp shade from the streets of Cambodia and painted it herself. It was one of her prized possessions.

That trip had been one of their unplanned escapades. She still admired that part of Anshuman, but the feeling was not the same. Had he changed over the years? Or was it a change in her approach towards the same man? She wasn't perfect herself, then why was she craving for Anshuman to be perfect. After all, it was she who believed that the imperfections in men make them more relatable than God. Her trance was suddenly broken as a hand stroked her shoulder. She looked up and saw Anshuman. He knew she was lost in her thoughts.

'Pass me that,' he pointed at the moisturiser.

She handed it over to him.

'So, what were you thinking?' he poured the lotion on her shoulder, and it slowly rolled down her body.

'Nothing,' she said.

'Well, I can always say that there is something on your mind when you look blankly at the mirror,' Anshuman massaged her shoulder. 'Two and a half years of togetherness taught me this much, hasn't it?'

'I was just thinking about Siem Reap,' she sighed. 'I still cherish those days.'

'I know,' he slipped his hand into her dress and massaged her back. 'You liked the place a lot.'

He moved his hand from her shoulder to her waist as it casually rubbed against the side of her breasts.

'I still think it was just okay,' he went on. 'Frankfurt was much more gorgeous.'

'Frankfurt was surely the most luxurious trip I have ever had,' her feet moved from the sensation of his hands on her body. 'But there was something special about Cambodia.'

Anshuman ran his fingers over her shoulders and removed the straps of her dress from the shoulders. He pulled off his shirt and sat on the stool behind his wife. Carefully, he placed his hands on the anterior part of her body, and tipped her breasts with his moist hand. Her pink tits hardened at his touch, as her bun loosened, letting her hair cascade down her body. He parted it into two divisions and pushed them over her shoulder to the front. Numbed by the arousal, Reva didn't refuse to anything that Anshuman did. He kissed her back and slid his hand through her dress between her legs. She closed her eyes tightly and suppressed a moan. Letting his right hand roll along her thigh to the butt, he brought out his left hand. Holding her shoulder with the hair wrapped around his fingers, he turned her lips towards his mouth and kissed them. Slowly she responded and opened her mouth as he kissed her again, this time with more passion.

*

'Let's go to Angkor again,' Reva said as he lay naked beside her on the bed. Anshuman had put on a bit of weight in the past five years of their acquaintance.

'Again?' his voice came unclear as his mouth lay perpendicularly on the pillow. 'Why do you want to go there again?'

'Because I love it,' she said.

'But you have seen it already,' he tried to dissuade her. 'There's nothing new in that city to see. You will get bored.'

'You see me every day,' she got up. 'Do you feel bored?'

Anshuman sat up and looked at his wife. 'There is no logical connection between the two,' he protested.

'Surely,' she wrapped the bed-sheet around herself and rose to her feet. 'Only what *you* say is logical.'

'I didn't mean that,' Anshuman sounded like a court-martialled soldier.

'I know very well what you meant,' she stared at him. 'Two and a half years of togetherness taught me this much, hasn't it?'

And before he could say anything further, Reva had walked out of the bedroom.

She was casually draped in the sheet, sitting on the swinging cane chair in the balcony when he arrived in his boxers.

'Okay,' he knelt down. 'When do you want to go there?'

'I don't want to go,' she looked out. 'And even if I do, I won't tell you.'

'Okay baba, I lose,' he stood on his knees and held her face in his hands. 'When was the last time I won an argument with you anyways?'

'But you still keep trying,' her smirk expressed the joy of a winner.

'It gives me a kick to think that my wife is smarter than I am,' he went on buttering her. 'Who would not like that?'

'Yeah right,' she got up and walked back towards the bedroom. 'It's the only thing about me that interests you.'

'Who said that?' he got up and followed her. 'I adore a lot of things about you.'

'Really?' she turned to charge, 'And what are they?'

'I respect you for being candid in what you say,' he explained, 'and what you write.'

'I don't want you to respect me,' she blurted out. 'I am not a saint. I am your wife and I want you to love me.'

'Oh come on,' he moved forward and tried to hold her but she shrugged him off. 'What crap is that? You think I don't love you?' He waited for a response. 'I mean...' he groped for words, '...we just made love. You can't say I don't love you.'

'Loving is not just making love,' she said exasperated.

'That's not what I meant,' he went on rambling.

'Then think and tell me,' she walked towards him, 'when was the last time you told me how much you love me.'

'Reva...'

'When was the last time you came up to me and said "Baby, you look great", when, Anshuman?'

'Oh come on, you really need me to tell you that I find you beautiful and that I love you.'

'You would have said it had you really felt it. The only time you feel that your wife is pretty is when you want to have sex.'

'Rubbish!' Anshuman threw up his hands in exasperation. 'I don't believe in redundant comments. I don't expect you to tell that you love me because I know that. We have passed that stage, Reva.'

'You never do that,' she looked straight into his eyes. 'No one does. Love needs much more than hormones and money to stay alive.'

Reva hurried back to her room, while Anshuman stood in the drawing room. She slumped back on the bed and was about to switch off the lamp when her phone started ringing. It was Lata Mangeshkar's voice singing "Jaane Kya Baat Hai"! She rolled over and picked the phone from the bedside table. The display flashed "Dipanwita" and the timer showed 11:30 p.m.

'Hi Dipa,' she said. 'Is everything alright?'

'Yes,' the senior correspondent said hesitantly. 'Were you guys asleep?'

'No,' Reva looked at Anshuman who had walked into the room. 'We were pretty much awake. Tell me.'

'Actually, we wanted to know what you guys are planning to do this Saturday night.'

'Who wanted to know?'

'We – Shubho and I.'

'Okay.' It took Reva a moment to let the words sink in. 'Well, we haven't planned anything yet. Why?'

'Actually, it's our fifteenth wedding anniversary this Friday,' Dipanwita spoke with a palpable sense of embarrassment. 'Since all of us will be busy during the week, we thought Saturday would be a good day to celebrate.'

'Wow! That's awesome.' Reva was jubilant.

'You will be there, right?' Dipanwita said coyly.

'Absolutely!'

'Great. By the way, is Anshuman there?'

'Yeah, he is.'

Anshuman looked on curiously, still clueless about the news which changed his wife's mood instantaneously. He wondered who could possibly be calling, refuting chances of it being either of their families purely based on the time of the call. The only option left seemed to be Dipanwita. But what could she possibly say to make Reva so happy?

'Please pass the phone to him. Shubho wants to have a word with him.'

'Sure!'

Reva handed over the phone to Anshuman, while he looked at her quizzically.

'The Banerjees are having their fifteenth anniversary party this Saturday. Shubhanshu wants to talk to you.'

Anshuman pursed his lips in surprise. That was the last thing he could have anticipated. After deciding to stay away from each other, the Banerjees had decided to throw a party to mark the beginning of the sixteenth year of their conjugal life.

'Old man,' he spoke over the line. 'So you are finally doing something good in life!'

Shubhanshu laughed. 'So you guys are coming, right?'

'Not if you expect us to bring gifts,' Anshuman walked over to the bedside table and lit a cigarette.

This time Banerjee laughed even louder. 'Only four of us, dude. It's just dinner, not some lavish celebration. So, just bring yourself. That will be good enough.'

'And my wife?'

'She doesn't depend on you. She can come on her own. So, don't act smart anymore. Just come over.'

'Okay.'

'Bye.'

'Bye.'

Anshuman cancelled the call and looked at Reva. He felt that the conversation would have lightened her mood. But it didn't. She turned over and switched off the lights, leaving him in darkness.

**

After much deliberation, the Banerjees finally agreed on the restaurant "Blue Frog" as the venue for the dinner. Dipanwita hated the venue. *It's stingingly expensive,* she argued against the Lower Parel restaurant. *The ambience more than makes up for that*, Shubhanshu argued. *It will also be easier for you to return to Chembur at night.* Dipanwita relented.

When Reva walked into the restaurant, the Banerjees were already seated at a corner table. Dipanwita waved at her as she looked around trying to spot her hosts. Surprisingly, both of them looked younger and rejuvenated than they used to some time ago. The gradual development of camaraderie was doing them some good and it showed on their faces.

'Congratulations' Reva handed over the bouquet to the Banerjees. 'You both are looking great.'

'Thank you,' Dipanwita smelled the orchids, 'this is so nice.'

'Where is the young man?' Shubhanshu asked as Reva sat down.

'He will be a tad late,' she smiled dryly. 'He's got a meeting with Bala Sir.'

'Oh God,' Shubhanshu exclaimed. 'I think we should order the drinks in that case. Balasubramaniam thinks even slower than he talks. Your husband will get late.'

'Tell me about it,' she rearranged her dupatta. 'When is he not late?'

Shubhanshu didn't notice but Dipanwita could always make out when her junior's tone showed disapproval.

'I'll have a Margarita,' Dipanwita looked at both of them. 'What will you guys have?'

The drinks and appetisers arrived soon after. Dipanwita couldn't help crib about the premium price the restaurant charged, while Shubhanshu poured praises for the live performance going on. Like any other couple arguing over a trivial matter, they also asked Reva to referee their debate. She looked sheepishly at both of them and decided the best way out of this was to take the middle path.

'It's costly,' she agreed with her boss and looked at her husband to say. 'But I must say the ambience is good.'

Dipanwita was about to counter the second part of her statement when all of a sudden Chand arrived at their table.

'Hello, everyone,' he greeted. The Banerjees greeted him in return.

Reva looked at him and was appalled at his clothes. He wore something that looked like an undersized kaftan with jeans, paired with flip-flops and a hat. Though she had been angry with Sophie in the past, the girl had an impeccable dressing sense. Reva wondered how the two could possibly be dating each other; rather how could Sophie go around with a guy who dressed like this. *But then again,* she consoled herself, *Chand's fashion sense had never gone so wrong in the past.*

The musician could read the expression on Reva's face. 'I know this has gone terribly wrong,' he looked at his outfit and joked. 'One of my designer friends experimented on me, and has come out with disastrous results.'

Reva felt embarrassed that her face had given away what she felt but she couldn't help chuckling at Chand's acceptance of the same.

'Where are you sitting?' Shubhanshu asked, 'Why don't you come and join us?'

'Thank you so much,' Chand smiled back. 'I just came over to say *hello*. Actually I am here with a friend of mine. He is waiting outside. I came in to check whether there is a seat. But I guess we will have to move to HRC.'

'Why don't you two join us?' Dipanwita reaffirmed her husband's suggestion.

'Actually, ma'am…' Chand had just started on his answer when it struck Reva that the friend could be Siddharth. 'I would love to but we have a few more friends joining us.'

'Excuse me,' she took out her phone and got up. 'I need to make a call. I'll just be back.'

Everyone nodded and she quickly made her way out of the restaurant. There was no one at the main door, as Reva looked around to see if she could spot Siddharth. *It's ridiculous of you, Reva,* she chided herself for hurrying out to meet the photographer. It was the first time she had felt so immature, almost reacting like a college girl to catch a glimpse of the cutest boy in college. *What the hell are you doing?* Despite the self-deprecation, Reva found it hard to resist walking further ahead in search of the photographer. She walked on for a few minutes and found him standing at the entry of the mill compound, almost on the main street.

As she walked ahead towards the gate, Siddharth turned and seemed pleasantly surprised to see her. He had wanted to meet her again after their Manali jaunt but could not muster the courage to call. *She is a married woman,* he restrained the numerous impulses to take up the phone and dial her number or send an sms. *There is no future to your desires. Forget her!* How he wished they would meet inadvertently and hit it off again. But his busy schedule restricted him from visiting parties where he might have bumped into her again. As she walked ahead, wearing the red Anarkali suit, Siddharth felt that their relationship hadn't yet seen its inception.

'Hi,' Reva smiled at him. 'What are you doing here?'

'Actually,' Siddharth took his right hand out of the pocket and briefly waved at Reva. 'Chand has gone in to check if they have vacant seats.'

'They don't. I met Chand.'

'Oh. Where is he?'

'Inside,' Reva walked on until she almost reached the spot where Siddharth stood. 'He's talking to my boss and her husband.'

'Okay. And you guys have a table?'

'Yes. Do you want to join us?' Reva successfully hid the enthusiasm in her voice. In a tinier part of her heart, she preferred to keep her acquaintance with Siddharth as obscure as possible. *I don't want him to meet Anshuman,* she had instructed herself, *I don't want them to start talking about my photo-shoots or the trip to Manali.*

'No, thanks. We have a few other friends coming.'

'Okay,' she was relieved but her heart sank momentarily, 'so, how is your work going?'

His mind rushed through questions he could ask to continue this conversation. They had not run short of words in their previous couple of meetings, but things seemed different that night. They were handicapped by a sudden blaze of formality.

'Good.'

'I saw those pictures,' she seemed flustered at having to mention them voluntarily. 'I couldn't believe it was me.'

'Were they that bad?' he winked.

'No,' Reva laughed. 'They were great. I loved them.'

'Thanks.' Siddharth couldn't control the tinge of red on his cheeks.

'So, what else is happening in your life?'

'You don't wear western clothes, do you?'

The question was as random as it could get. It was so out of the line of their discussion that it completely caught the journalist off guard, leaving her groping for words. She looked baffled.

'Not much,' Reva had never even thought of preparing an answer to a question like this, 'why?'

'I am sure you'll look good in them,' Siddharth looked so nonchalant that one wouldn't guess how awkward he felt himself at the question. 'Why don't you try them?'

'Never been in the habit actually,' she flushed. 'Don't I look good in Indian wear?'

'You look excellent,' he clarified, 'but then, there's no harm in experimenting.'

'Hmm... I will think about it.' She pursed her lips and nodded, and both of them started laughing.

'Perhaps we need to do another shoot and make you realise that you won't look bad in westerns just the way you didn't look bad in my pictures.'

'Not a bad idea.'

Reva realised she had reacted too fast to the proposal. Was she so eager to spend time with him? She had never thought about it until this point. *What's wrong with me,* she scolded herself. *First I hurried out to meet him and then agreed to the shoot even before he could ask.* Even Siddharth couldn't believe she had said yes so swiftly. Was she undergoing the same emotions as him? He couldn't let this moment go away.

'Next week,' he said without wasting another moment. 'In my studio. I will call you.'

Chand was on his way out. Siddharth could see his friend walking towards the main gate.

'Keep yourself free on any one of the weekdays,' he spoke softly enough to avoid Chand eavesdropping on the conversation. 'We will co-ordinate it. Chand is here. Laugh.'

Reva didn't turn around to see Chand; she just started laughing. Siddharth joined her. *What am I doing,* she could feel her toes tingle with fear. *Why was I talking to him for so long when I knew Chand would be coming out?*

'You guys know each other?' the musician interrupted the laughter.

'Obviously,' Siddharth looked at him. 'Wasn't she there at the DFW?'

'Oh yes!' Chand recollected the finale where Reva had dropped in to cover the event. 'So what's the big joke?'

'About a common friend,' Reva covered up this time. 'You won't know her.'

'Okay!' Chand nodded dubiously and looked at his friend. 'Shall we go?'

'Sure,' Siddharth nodded. 'See you around, Mrs Mehra.'

'Bye, ma'am,' Chand waved.

Reva smiled and waved at both of them. She stood there as the guys walked off. A minute later, as she turned to walk in someone called out her name.

'Reva.'

She thought Siddharth had come back to finalise the shoot. She smiled and turned to look at him, only to be caught on the wrong foot again. It was not Siddharth. How could she have not recognised the voice? It was Anshuman. It was her husband. He stared curiously at her, taken aback by the way she smiled and turned towards him, after the past few days of coldness that had pervaded their relationship. For a moment, Reva didn't realise how to react to his expression – she knew the reason behind it and she knew what he wondered. The glow in his eyes exuded a hope that she had dropped all the anger and accusations she had been brooding over. She knew he was wrong, but proving him wrong was not the best option. Any such clarification would usher in a lot of questions, none of which she was in a position to answer.

'Hi,' she smiled at him, this time with more conviction to prove his doubts wrong.

'You look nice,' he complimented.

'Please,' she shrugged. 'Don't say it after I have asked you to.'

'At least I'm saying it after you asked me to.'

'God, Anshu,' she looked at him. 'You always have a point to prove. Why are you behaving so strangely these days?'

'I was always like this,' the faint smile was accompanied by a sigh. 'You have started disliking it recently. Or I guess you didn't notice it earlier.'

Reva didn't expect such vulnerability in the answer. Anshuman had never been susceptible earlier. Was he right? Had Anshuman really turned insouciant? Or had she started looking at him differently as he pointed out? Reva had never thought of it that way. Was it possible that Anshuman was brooding with similar complaints as hers? She looked down, unable to speak, when he came forward and put his arm around her.

'The Banerjees are waiting,' he rubbed her upper arm. 'Let's go in.'

Reva nodded and the Mehras entered the restaurant to the teasing sounds of the elder couple.

**

The live band performed to a collection of memorable English tracks and latest chartbusters. When the singer crooned to Justin Bieber's "Baby", the entire young crowd seemed to come alive.

The pasta was delicious, but Reva found herself the only one at the table not having non-vegetarian food; everyone else seemed to be savouring the taste of chicken. With years of staying with Anshuman, she had started eating without heeding for the smell which used to make her want to throw up earlier. For a long time, he had never brought non-vegetarian food into the house. Even when they went out, his choice of food complied with her preferences. But, gradually she realised that he yearned for his earlier tastes which he had given up. So, one day, she voluntarily took up the phone and ordered his favourite Mixed Noodles to usher non-veg food into her house. Anshuman had made it clear that she didn't need to cook meat; he would order it as and when he wanted it. She was happy with the arrangement. But, his desire for the same grew more frequent by the day and after a point of time the appointed shop started delivering some chicken dish or the other every night. So, finally she put her foot down and decided that a cook be appointed who would cook both varieties for them.

'Why is this Bieber so famous?' Shubhanshu sipped his whisky. 'This media doesn't stop from over-hyping people!'

'He is a sensation at the age of sixteen!' Dipanwita looked at him angrily. 'He deserves all the praise he is getting.'

'Girls all over the world are going gaga over him,' Reva supported her boss. 'You can't but admire him for all that he has achieved so quickly.'

'I know many guys who sing equally well at his age,' Anshuman joined the men's team. 'They just don't get a chance.'

'So give them a chance,' Reva countered. 'We are there to highlight that.'

'How much did you write about Chand before he sang for that movie?' Anshuman turned around to look at her. 'Forget that, how much have you hyped him after he won a National Award? You publicise faces that come in front of the camera. Our media only sensitises the heroes and heroines, not the ones who work behind it.'

'Because the public are fascinated about them,' Reva defended her stance.

'Come on guys,' Shubhanshu interrupted before the argument could heat up further. 'This is just a casual discussion. Why are you guys fighting over it? Who cares for what happens to Justin Bieber or Pamela Anderson?'

The Mehras subsided as everyone at the table broke out chuckling.

'Well,' Shubhanshu guzzled down the remaining Black Label in his glass and waved at the waiter. 'I might still care for the latter but not Bieber for sure.'

Dipanwita looked shyly at her colleague's expression as the younger couple decided to look into their food and avoid the comment.

'You speak nonsense after the drinks,' Dipa looked furiously at her husband. 'Look they are reddening with embarrassment. You can't ever hold yourself after the whiskies. That's why I absolutely hate it.'

'Now what's wrong with whisky?' Shubhanshu looked naughtily at his wife, 'I agree it has taken a few lives but a lot more have born because of it.'

There was a sudden roar of laughter as the men high fived each other and Reva covered her mouth to suppress herself from cracking up. Finally, even the ladies decided to break the restraint and broke out into guffaws.

**

Shubhanshu had his arm around Anshuman's shoulder as all of them walked back to their cars.

'Why do you do this to yourself?' Dipa sounded frustrated. 'How are you going to drive back in this state?'

'You can drive me home, can't you?' Shubhanshu looked at her. 'You can stay at Santacruz for one night. It's your home after all!'

It was their anniversary, and they were going to drive away to their respective homes. The Banerjees had pondered over the thought throughout the past week. But it was the destiny they had mutually chosen, they consoled themselves, and it had worked favourably for them. The sparkle of tears in his eyes seemed to defy the Jericho's wall of logic they had build up with remarkable pragmatism.

'And what will happen to my car?' Dipanwita gathered herself. 'You want the police to tow it away?'

'How do you win such arguments, AM?' the senior guy looked at Anshuman.

'Explain how you are correct,' the ad-man assured his friend.

'You always explain how you are right in an argument?' Dipanwita looked complainingly at the younger man. 'How convenient is that, Anshuman!'

'What else do you expect?' Reva frowned at them. 'There is always a justification ready.'

'Whenever I am right,' Anshuman seemed trapped by the women.

'And when are you not right?' Reva looked at him with a smirk.

'Can we please come back to my predicament here?' Shubhanshu shouted loud enough to make everyone smile. 'I need my wife to drop me home.'

'I'll take care of your car,' Reva giggled and held her senior's arm. 'You carry on.'

'Thanks,' Dipanwita finally gave in and pretended to glare at Shubho. 'Come on.'

Reva drove her senior's car to the latter's apartment. Anshuman followed her all the way to pick her up from the Chembur building. She parked the car and sat on the front seat of her husband's vehicle as the Mehras drove back to Lokhandwala.

Anshuman still remembered the day he had picked Reva from Dipanwita's apartment and drove her to their flat for the first time. It was a surprise for her and she had badgered him all the way to know what was in store. The thrill, love and exuberance were apparent on that journey. She knew something big was going to happen, yet unsure how big it could possibly be. This time, they sat sordidly, hardly engaging in a conversation. Today, there was neither joy nor hope. Somewhere down the line, oblivious to both of them, routine and conventions had peeped in through the door and superseded the zest and yearning. Both of them sat in the car, each wanting the other to start a conversation. And neither of them relented to utter the first word as expectations kept fluctuating between indifference and anguish. Time, they both thought, hadn't spun the most fairytale romance for them.

**

Reva poured the first cup of black tea for herself and rolled out on the white futon. Sunday morning was always the favourite part of her week. That was the only day when Anshuman woke up after her. So, she could afford the luxury of a peaceful cup of tea lying down on the sofa with the newspaper spread across the table for her to throw cursory glances. After a long time, thanks to the Banerjees' anniversary, she had spent a Saturday evening away from the cacophony of parties. The life-sized Shakuntala painting hung on the wall behind, while the noodle strap nighty flowed over her body as she sipped the tea. The brass clock showed 9:15. Anshuman would get up only an hour later and ask for breakfast.

Anshuman liked having tea in the morning without sugar. *Milk,* he said, *not only kills the benefits but also the aroma.* She agreed and the beverage made its way into her daily life just like other things Anshuman had introduced. He would blow air into the cup and soak the vapour in his face and eyes. It was hilarious, she had tried pointing it out to him once but he seemed rather offended. Hence, she never broached the topic in the future.

Though her eyes skimmed perfunctorily through the headlines, Reva was afloat in a wave of retrospection. There were things going amiss, she knew, and she knew she had to fix it soon. Suddenly, her phone beeped. *Who's messaging on a Sunday morning* – she wondered and picked it up reluctantly.

'How due Tuesday after luk 2 u?' the question was as abrupt as its sender. *Siddharth Kashyap doesn't know how to start a conversation conventionally,* she thought and typed the response.

'Cnt say. Seems tuf!'

She was hardly back to her tea when he messaged again.

'Evnin?'

'Need 2 get hme by 8! :-)'

'Tek a day off!'

How audacious, she thought to herself. *Did I give him any hint by running out of the restaurant yesterday?*

'Lemme see!' she had barely replied when the phone started ringing. For a second, it shocked her. But she realised it was the landline and it couldn't be Siddharth.

'Mesg me... I m off 2 sleep!'

Off to sleep, she read it with a frown and walked up to pick the cordless receiver, one of their more utilitarian wedding presents.

'May I speak to Anshuman?' the caller asked.

It was a deep-throated resonant voice. *Who could possibly be calling Anshuman on a Sunday morning, that too on the landline?* Reva thought. She was sure she had heard the voice somewhere, but couldn't pinpoint who it was.

'Actually he is sleeping,' she replied while her memory hurried to match it with the correct face. 'May I know who is calling?'

**

Anshuman was partially awake. He was lying with his face pressed to the pillow, struggling through a barrage of thoughts. *What is going wrong?* He was still lost in the last night's thoughts. *We need to talk about it. How could we possibly let our relation succumb to such silly arguments?* And then she shook him. He looked up, his eyes wincing at the sudden light filtering through the Venetian blinds.

'Papa,' Reva passed the phone.

'Talk to him, na?' he said. 'I will brush my teeth and will then speak to him.'

'Papa,' she repeated. 'Your dad.'

Then it struck him. She used to call her father "Baba". It was his father calling him. Did his mother finally succeed in convincing him? Knowing him, it couldn't have been that easy.

'Tell me,' Anshuman quickly grabbed the receiver and spoke.

'Anshuman?' Akashdeep Mehra asked.

'How come you called me?'

Reva gave him a stern look; it was one of those "be polite" expressions. Now-a-days, she hardly cared how he spoke. But she always thought it was wrong.

'Can you come over, beta?'

Beta! Anshuman couldn't recollect the last time his father had called him that.

206 An Unequal Harmony...

'Why? What happened?'

'How soon can you come?'

'What's wrong? Where's Maa?'

Anshuman could suddenly feel himself trembling in fear. Why was his father asking him to come over without stating a reason? And, moreover, why was the caller his father and not his mother?

'When is the earliest you can get to Lucknow?'

'Can you please tell me what happened?' this time Anshuman cried out. 'Where is she?'

'Anshu…' Akashdeep Mehra swallowed. 'Gayatri is not with us anymore.'

'What?' Anshuman wasn't aware he was already crying. Reva knelt on the ground in front of him and held his left arm.

'She didn't wake up today morning,' the reply came. 'She passed away in her sleep. I am calling from the hospital.'

'I am going to kill you, Akashdeep Mehra,' Anshuman had never referred to him by the first name. 'I am going to kill you if this is true.'

Reva had realised what the discussion was about. She shook her head signalling him not to be rude but she knew what Anshuman was going through.

'You need to perform the last rites,' for the first time his father didn't react. 'Your mother needs you here. See her off before she's gone forever.'

The phone dropped from his hand as the usually stoic advertisement wizard burst out howling. Reva tried to hug him but he was inconsolable. Not once in their five years, had she seen him breaking down to that extent. In fact, she always complained about his lack of emotions.

'He killed her…. He killed her,' Anshuman sobbed. 'That sonovabitch killed my mother.'

'Anshu!' Reva cried out.

'She died,' Anshuman shouted at the top of his voice and kept oscillating back and forth. 'My mother didn't wake up today morning. He never made her happy. She always kept imagining a perfect life. But it couldn't last beyond a point. He killed her.'

'Control yourself, Anshu,' Reva tried to hold him tightly. 'We have to get there.'

'I've lost my mother,' he collapsed on the floor. 'I've lost my mother.'

Reva caught him and put in all her strength to hold Anshuman. She was crying herself but at that point of time, it was more important to console him. She had always loved and admired her mother-in-law and her sudden loss came as a huge blow. After all, if there was anyone with whom she could discuss Anshuman, it was only that woman. She was always fair and had never taken sides with Anshu. Despite the few days they had spent together, Reva had come to respect Gayatri Mehra like her own mother. And though she knew that Anshu was attached to his mom, she could never fathom the insurmountable pain he would suffer upon this loss. Reva realised that, for once, her mother-in-law was wrong. Gayatri Mehra was irreplaceable in Anshuman's life – Reva would never be able to take that position.

**

It was the first time Reva was visiting her in-laws' house. The bitterness between Anshu and his father had severed all possibilities of them ever visiting. Even in the three years after becoming a part of the Mehra family, the only contact she had were the telephonic conversations with her mother-in-law. It was almost certain that after her demise, there would hardly be any further interaction. Anshuman had few cousins, but none of them stayed in touch, not that Anshuman himself had ever expressed a desire to keep any association with them.

When Anshuman and Reva entered the Mehras' Manak Nagar residence, almost all his relatives had gathered there, waiting for him to arrive. Reva had met many of them during their wedding but failed to recollect the relations. Some of them smiled half-heartedly while others looked teary eyed. Anshuman had barely spoken in the past few hours, but had largely regained his composure. Reva tried to nod at them as Anshuman's eldest uncle's son ushered them into the room where Gayatri Mehra's body was kept.

Anshuman was unprepared for the sight. Gayatri looked ethereal in her radiant bridal wear. She was dressed up like a newlywed, draped in a red sari and a shawl, the partition of her hair smeared with vermillion, a big red bindi on her forehead and bangles on her two arms. Her face had lost its colour but it was compensated by the extravagant effort to make her look colourful. A single-wick oil lamp and an incense stick were kept lit while a photograph of Guru Nanak was placed at the head side.

Reva noticed her father-in-law sitting on the floor, in one corner of the room, surrounded by other men whom she assumed to be their relatives. Akashdeep Mehra looked up with a start as his son came in. However Anshuman had noticed none of it. He traipsed into the room and knelt in front of his mother. Reva expected him to react; she had seen the surprise in his eyes when they had entered the room. But Anshu was unusually phlegmatic. One of his relatives went over and rubbed his back. It didn't work. The apathy seemed unassailable. No one had expected him to react that way; it could do him worse, they thought. Some of them sitting in the room signalled at Akashdeep to come over. *It is not a wise move,* Reva thought but hesitated to intervene.

The senior Mehra walked up to his son and tried to hold him. Anshuman immediately shrugged him off. Akashdeep tried again but it fetched a similar response. Though there was not a word spoken, Anshuman made his intentions very clear. Reva looked at his father-in-law who looked shyly at her and then moved away. She came forward and placed her hand on his shoulder. Anshuman turned towards her, his eyes cold like a vampire's.

'Let's get her going,' he said.

Anshuman's maternal grandmother was brought in earlier that day to bless her daughter before the latter could be cremated. And though the old lady didn't understand much of what was going on, she did exactly as she was asked to do. As two middle-aged women clutched her arms, the nonagenarian slowly sat on the floor and kissed her late daughter's forehead without realising who the woman was or why she was doing so.

'Say "M*ay God keep you happy*",' one of the relatives said and the old lady repeated the same.

The ladies pulled her up again and took her out of the room. She walked back, claiming to be hungry.

'Can I have those spicy chips that Manu's son got for me that day?'

'You just had a bowl of *kheer*,' one of Anshuman's aunts explained to the old woman. 'You can't have chips now.'

'Okay,' she resigned. 'Can I have some more *kheer* then?'

**

When the men returned late at night, Reva was sitting by her grandmother-in-law's side on the bed. A few other female relatives sat in the room, talking to her, while the old lady lay fast asleep.

'Good that she doesn't understand anything,' one of them told Reva. 'At least she has been spared of the realisation. Who wants to see her child being carried off to the crematorium while she is still alive?'

'Seriously,' Reva replied. 'It was so sudden. Maa had no problems. She was absolutely healthy.'

'Jiji always showed that she was happy,' Gayatri's younger sister spoke up. 'But all her life she kept on struggling to make peace between Anshuman and Jijaji.'

'I know,' Reva had seen this herself and admired the woman for her perseverance. 'Sadly, neither of the men realised that she was being made the scapegoat for no fault of hers.'

The women nodded and sighed.

'But Bhaiya will be very lonely now,' Anshuman's paternal aunt lamented. 'He doesn't have a clue about his own life. Bhabhi used to look after every aspect of the house. He was totally dependent on her.'

'Maa had told me that once,' Reva agreed. 'That's why she could never come over and stay with us. She said that Papa wouldn't be able to manage by himself, but asked me not to cite this reason to Anshuman.'

'See,' Anshuman's maternal aunt said almost spontaneously while others nodded in agreement with Reva, 'she always wanted to keep both of them happy. And they didn't realise that. Men, I tell you.'

A young girl rushed in to inform them that the men had returned from the crematorium. The women got up and walked into the drawing room.

When Anshuman's grandmother woke up later that evening, for some inexplicable reason, she asked whether the men were given neem leaves to chew upon their return.

**

Anshuman decided to stay in a hotel till the last rites were over. Though few of his relatives tried to dissuade him from doing so and some even invited him to stay at their place, he resolved that it was best to avoid undue complexities of staying with a family. Reva initially insisted that they stay at the Mehra residence but in the end she gave up.

'If you have any urgency,' he said one night after dinner, 'you can go back to Mumbai.'

'Did I say I have any urgency?' she retorted.

'No, but I just don't want you to get tied down in case…'

'In case I want to free myself from anything, Anshu, I won't wait for you to tell me. I can't be Maa.'

'What do you mean?' Anshuman sounded surprised. He didn't expect her to make such a statement.

'Don't you know what I mean?' she looked straight at him. 'All her life, she was tied down working and pleasing you and your dad. I won't do that to myself.'

'You think I didn't care for her?' he sounded incriminated for being indifferent towards the person he loved the most.

'You did?' she spoke with an overt expression of astonishment. 'Were you not aware of what she really wanted?'

'Dad walked out on my wedding day…'

'And you wanted him to take the first step towards reconciliation?'

'Shouldn't he have done that?'

'Then, why did you push him away that day?'

'I wasn't….'

'You want everyone to massage your ego,' she cut him off emphatically. 'You want to have the centre stage and the last word.'

'That's not true,' Anshuman began breathing heavily. 'He took the first step after Maa died.'

'He came forward but you walked away.'

'After Maa died!' he blurted.

'If you lost your mother, he has lost his wife,' Reva spoke louder than him. She knew it was required to make him understand. 'She was his life-partner, his other half.'

'Really? Then, why didn't he ever try to make her happy?'

'Oh really? And who did? You? Were you there with her? You were not, Anshuman Mehra. You came to Lucknow after six years to inform your parents about our wedding. Six years! And what did you do for the last three years? Did you ever try to talk to your dad and persuade them to come and stay with you? His anger might be misplaced but your indifference was no less selfish. You were okay not meeting your mother, provided you didn't have to talk to your father. Did you notice how Maa silently accepted all of this? Yet, through everything, it was Papa who stayed with her. Maa was a far more important part of his life than yours. What part of your present existence had Maa in it? For him, it was everything.'

Anshuman listened to Reva. He wanted to argue but this time she was correct. She had never spoken to him that way about the issue. Neither had Maa ever made it so evident. Anshuman stiffened his jaws and held back his tears.

'His loss is greater,' Reva went on, 'and he has no one else now but you. Do what Maa had always wanted to. Make her happy now at least.'

Anshuman looked at her. He wondered if he really had that courage or honesty of intent.

'Go and talk to him,' Reva held his face in her hands. 'It's your responsibility to bring the family together. Bury your anger, Anshu. Don't continue this fight any longer. Maa had seen enough of it when she was alive. Don't make her go through it now.'

**

Parminder was cleaning the house when Anshuman and Reva entered through the main door. She was a married woman now, but still working in the Mehra household. She looked jubilant upon seeing the most anticipated guests, and asked whether they would like to have tea. Reva asked her to continue her work and took upon the responsibility of making tea for everyone.

'You go and talk to him,' she told Anshuman. 'I will make tea for both of you.'

As Anshuman turned sceptically towards his father's room, she held his arm. He turned to face her. 'Do it for Maa.' Anshuman nodded and walked off.

Akashdeep Mehra was lying on the bed, half asleep, when Anshuman walked in. The sixty something man who had maintained a reputation of being an authoritarian, suddenly appeared so frail and shaken. The blow that had hit his world a few days ago had left him defenceless and exposed. He looked up at the sound of the footsteps, and seemed startled seeing his son at the door.

'Anshu…'

'Are you tired?' Anshuman spoke. 'Should I come later?'

'No, no,' Akashdeep tried to get up hastily. 'Come in. Sit.'

Anshuman stepped in and sat next to his father on the bed. For some time, both men looked down, unsure how to continue the discussion.

'You have been through a huge crisis all alone,' Anshuman said finally. 'I can't even fathom how you must have felt.'

'Trust me I couldn't feel anything,' Akashdeep smiled self-deprecatively. 'It just didn't sink in.'

Anshuman gently held his father's hand.

'She was absolutely fine the previous night. I listened to her as she read the Granth. She didn't forget anything. She had even immersed the fennel and candy in water because I wanted to have it in the morning. When I got up, she was still asleep. That didn't happen often. I thought she was tired and went away for my walk. When I came back, she was still asleep. I thought it was better not to wake her up. I read the newspaper and made my tea. All this while, she was lying there, dead, and I didn't even feel something was terribly amiss. How could I be so ignorant? When the radio news ended at eight, I called her. She had never slept beyond seven. But there was no response. I called her even louder but she didn't reply. When I finally walked up to the bed and pushed her arm, it was ice-cold. My entire body started shivering as I held my fingers under her nose and realised she was not breathing. I called Bunty. He came in immediately and we took her to hospital but, as we travelled in the ambulance, both of us knew we had lost her. The doctor hardly took time to confirm the same. It still has not sunk in that Gayatri is dead. When the clock strikes eleven, I still feel she will come out of the bathroom wearing her kaftan, with the towel wrapped around her wet hair. I am yet to get used to her absence.'

Akashdeep Mehra was gradually breaking down into tears. Never before had he shared the day in such vivid details with anyone.

'Will you like to come to Mumbai?' Anshuman held his father's hands in his. 'Come and stay with us.'

Akashdeep Mehra looked up, his eyes swollen with tears. He couldn't believe Anshuman had asked him to stay at his place. Neither could he recollect the last time the two of them had sat together and spoken heart to heart. The last time they talked, it had been a heated discussion on the morning of Anshuman's wedding.

'You really want me to,' he said finally, 'stay in your house?'

'Yes,' Anshuman nodded. 'I don't want you to be alone here now.'

'I can't. My entire world is here,' Akashdeep shook his head incredulously. 'How can I possibly stay somewhere else?'

'What world?' Anshuman spoke authoritatively. 'How will you take care of yourself? It was always Maa who managed the chores. Do you even realise when your monthly medicines run out? You can't expect others to leave their homes and come running every time you want something. Your daughter-in-law and I can mind the things you would need. At least you have a family there. You won't have any problem.'

'Not that, Anshu,' Akashdeep still seemed surprised that how earnestly his son wanted to take him along. 'I know I won't have a problem.'

'Maa would love to see both of us together,' Anshuman's eyes filled up with tears again. 'I also want to have my father with me.

For all the anger that we possibly had against each other, nothing takes away the relation we share.'

Akashdeep wiped a tear that rolled down his son's cheek and impulsively both the men hugged each other tightly and wept.

Somewhere high above Maa must be very happy, Reva thought as she stood by the door and saw her husband and father-in-law. She carried the tray and looked at them teary eyed.

She herself had been sharing a strained relation with Anshuman for the past few days. There had been times when she got angry, when she failed to understand, when she felt hurt at his unapologetic behaviour. Despite all those moments of anguish, she deeply revered his sense of commitment towards anything he attached himself to. And by burying the hatchet with his father that day and asking the latter to come and stay with them, he enamoured her once again. She was still very much in love with him. It was for her to find out where all the excitement of earlier years had hibernated and bring it back to their home.

Sixteen

Present Time

DAY 1
11:40 p.m.

Chand and Sophie readied to leave after the cop departed. Anshuman saw them off as they got into the elevator.

'Thanks for waiting,' Anshuman looked at them. 'I wasted your entire evening.'

'Please don't say that, Mr Mehra,' Chand replied while Sophie nodded in agreement with her beau. 'I had two special friends here. I had to come. After all, I share a connection with both Siddharth and you.'

Anshuman didn't realise the pun in the musician's word. He sighed and looked at them with a feeble smile. After all the insults he had hurled at Chand upon the latter's entry, it was humbling to see his graciousness.

'You know I'm just a call away whenever you need me,' Chand looked at him.

'Always,' Anshuman agreed.

The elevator closed and moved down. Sophie looked at Chand and held his hand.

'You are still offended by the way he introduced you to the ACP,' she looked at him.

'He still doesn't consider me his friend.'

'It's not that, baby,' Sophie held his face in her palms. 'He just wanted you to testify as Siddharth's friend.'

'A common friend wouldn't have done any harm,' Chand could feel his jaws stiffen.

'Come on, Chand.'

'Do you really think I can prove to be a good friend?' he looked at her.

'What do you mean?'

The elevator stopped and the door opened as Sophie spoke.

'Let's go,' Chand stepped out of the lift and walked towards his car.

'Chand,' she moved behind with quick steps. 'Tell me what's the matter.'

Till then, Sophie had surmised that the pain in Chand's eyes was only due to the manner in which Anshuman had introduced him to ACP Kabir. But, there was certainly something else. She knew Chand wasn't a guy to express his pain so easily, neither could he bring himself to complain about others.

'Leave it, Sophie,' Chand walked ahead and pressed the unlock button on the key ring. The red hatchback SUV beeped with a single tone. 'I'll drop you home,' he walked ahead.

'Then why the hell did you bring it up?' she shouted angrily.

'I didn't bring up anything,' he looked back calmly at her.

'Tell me, Chand,' Sophie controlled her temper and looked at him with stubborn eyes. 'Did Siddharth say something when he called you in?'

Chand looked silently at her. She had hit the right chord. He looked away, unable to find a suitable explanation to ward off the answer.

'What did he say?' she insisted.

'Let's not get into that,' Chand scrambled for the perfect reply though he knew nothing that he said would suffice. 'Nothing as such! It's already quite late.'

He got into the car and sat in the driver's seat.

'So, you are upset for no reason?'

'Sophie!' Chand looked exasperated at the thought of another argument that night. He could see her through the windshield, standing on the driveway. She showed no intention of getting into the car before getting the clarification.

'If you don't tell me, he will.' Sophie turned to walk towards the elevator.

'Sophie...' he came out of the car and shouted.

Chand called her a couple of times but she quickly trotted back to the elevator.

'Listen to me,' he said as she moved ahead.

Sophie was far more adamant than he was, and far more implacable when angry. There was not even a hint of slowing down as he continued calling her. Chand knew he would have to come out with the truth.

'He thinks I will never be loyal to you,' Chand finally said as she pressed the *Up* arrow beside the elevator door. 'He thinks I have kept you under an illusion.'

Sophie turned to face him. She seemed livid but there was no tinge of disbelief in her eyes. Somewhere within her, she expected Siddharth Kashyap to make such a comment sooner or later. She had thought of talking about this to Chand but never did as she had witnessed how much Chand trusted his best friend. And she had never disregarded Siddharth herself. On the contrary, she had only admired the support Siddharth had extended to Chand. But there was a tinge of arrogance about that man which had always been annoying. Though he was more good looking than Chand, she always found Siddharth to be high-headed – a quality in stark contrast to Chand's humility. And this showed even today as Chand weakened at his friend's remark, but declined to talk about it.

'What did you tell him?' she walked towards him.

'You really trust me, don't you?' Chand's moist eyes conveyed the pain he had been trying to subside.

'Would I have agreed to this marriage if I didn't?' the anger in her eyes expressed empathy for and faith in her fiancé.

'That's what I told him,' the urgency in his voice conveyed the belief she reinstated by saying exactly what he had told Siddharth. 'You wouldn't have married me had you feared of losing me to someone else.'

'Did you ask him on what basis can he give someone advice on his married life?' Sophie hated the thought that Siddharth had made Chand cry. 'He's the one who has trespassed into someone's marriage.'

'Talking to him is of no good,' Chand shook his head. 'He is undergoing a lot himself. There is no point driving him up the wall.' Chand could recall exactly what Anshuman had said when he expressed his frustration over Siddharth's behaviour.

'That doesn't allow him to judge others,' Sophie protested. 'I will talk to him.'

Somewhere within her, she had wanted to confront Siddharth ever since she arrived at the hospital, but thought that it was none of her business. This time, she didn't want to let it go because the man had directly attacked her personal life.

'Don't,' Chand held her hand, 'we'll wait for a better time.'

'I would have, had he not made you cry,' Sophie could feel her face tightening in disgust for Siddharth.

'He is my best friend, Sophie,' Chand said calmly. 'I can let it go if he behaves badly one day.'

'But I can't,' she put her foot down. 'If you are not coming, I'll go alone.'

'Sophie,' he cried out but she had already stepped into the elevator.

**

Sophie was called into the cabin by Anshuman Mehra to discuss a client meeting she had attended the previous evening. She was ready with her points and had even made a document with a prospective plan of action, including the client's renewed Business and Media Objective. She carried a stapled bunch of the printouts, with fluorescent highlights over the major points. Anshuman listened with rapt attention as she ran him through the entire discussion and the suggestions she had thought out.

'That's great,' Anshuman said in the end. 'I can now abscond whenever I want, relying on you to do everything right.'

Sophie laughed. 'But everything I do still needs your finishing touch.'

'Thank God it needs that. Or else I will be out of work.'

She laughed again.

'By the way, Sophie,' Anshuman cleared his throat, 'I need to talk to you about something personal. I hope you don't mind.'

'No, no,' Sophie was evidently surprised. Anshuman had never discussed his personal life with her. What was it that he wanted to say?

'You know Chand, right?' Anshuman spoke cautiously.

'Yeah,' she nodded, unable to grasp what this could possibly be about.

'He wants to take you out,' Anshuman broke the news.

'What?' she sounded alarmed. 'You mean Chand Pias, right?'

'Yes.'

'Oh!'

'Give it a thought,' he leaned ahead on the table. 'Let me know if I shall ask him to call you.'

'Ok,' she got up. She had never expected such a thing to happen.

'He's a nice guy, don't worry,' Anshuman smiled.

She smiled and moved out.

The following Friday Chand invited her out for dinner. She reluctantly agreed. Though she liked him, she wondered what could be Chand's objective behind asking her out. After all, popular musicians were known for their philandering habits. But Chand proved delightfully different – he was still a middle-class Panjim-bred Konkani at heart, who loved his music, beer, sea fish and austerity of life.

Though he lacked the savoir faire of her mentor, Chand came to occupy a special place in her life. She could always feel happy whenever he was around, and none of the attention came with any charade. Moreover, Chand had deftly kept the media glare away from their relationship. Despite the journalists vying for the information on the girl their heartthrob was dating, he did not disclose her identity and vouched to keep it a secret till she felt comfortable.

Finally, when he called her to discuss "something important", she knew he would propose marriage. But that evening, a much bigger revelation awaited her. Chand disclosed the biggest secret of his life.

'Not many know about this,' he said. 'After Siddharth and Rohit, you are the only one I am telling this to.'

'Why didn't you tell me this before?' Sophie looked straight at him. The pain and anger in her eyes were palpable. She felt betrayed for being kept in the dark for so long.

'I didn't want you to hate me before knowing me.' He knew she had every right to feel hurt.

'I wouldn't have hated you then,' her eyes were red. 'But I might hate you now.'

'I will still be able to live with the love you have given me.'

'Don't throw these filmy lines at me.' Sophie said in disgust. Chand chuckled.

'Seriously,' he passed her a glass of water. 'I will bear no hard feelings even if you decide to leave me and hate me all my life.'

'What does Rahul have to say, or whatever his name is?' she rubbed her eyes and looked at him.

'Rohit…' Chand corrected. 'He knows about it. He is okay. He supposedly expected it to happen earlier.'

'What if someday you feel that you want to go back to him or, for that matter, any other guy?' she knew she could have framed the

question better but at that moment, she couldn't care less. She was cross and her tongue was apt to be sharp.

'Had that been a possibility, I would have never approached you.' There was a spark of honesty in his eyes, which didn't let her probe into the matter further.

'Don't you think I can go out and tell the media about your secret?' she wanted to test his reaction.

'I know you won't,' he smiled. 'I have more faith in you than I have in myself.'

'And what if that Rahul tells everyone that you were in a relation with him?'

'Rohit,' Chand said. 'He won't do so as he loves me.'

'Were you seeing both of us at the same time?' Sophie sounded surprised.

'For a very short time,' Chand confessed, his eyes and shoulders drooping in shame.

'This is disgusting,' Sophie blurted. 'You think I wouldn't feel I was being cheated?'

'Obviously you would. That's why I said I won't have hard feelings even if you leave me today.'

'Are you saying this now because you know that you have gained a special place in my life?'

'No...' he held her hands gently. 'I guess you are so special to me now that I have moved beyond the fear of losing you.'

'Would I ever be as special as Rahul?' she knew that breeding the insecurity in her heart would ruin the very foundation of their relationship. 'Didn't his unconventionality make him more desirable? I can't take that position.'

'Rohit...' Chand paused and continued. 'Don't ask me to compare the two of you, Sophie. I was in love with him. But I have always loved you as much.'

'Can someone love two people at the same with the same intentions and intensity?'

'I don't think that's impossible.'

Sophie looked down for a moment, wondering what to say.

'I guess every wife fears losing her husband to another woman. But I never thought I would have to fear losing mine to another man.'

Chand chuckled and waited for her reaction. Her stolid face gradually broke into a smile and when he laughed, she eventually joined him, before she relapsed into tears and he held her tightly in his arms.

**

Chand waited and pondered over his action as he walked back towards his car. He didn't want to referee another argument but he knew he needed to intervene in this one. The door of his car was still wide open. Chand pushed the door close, only to realise that the keys were still inside. He opened the door and scanned for the keys. For a moment, the keys on the passenger seat eluded his sight. Then he saw them. He hurriedly picked them up and closed the door. He locked the car and ran back to the elevator. The elevator was stagnated at the fourth floor.

'Shit,' he kept slapping his trouser pocket. 'Who the hell has kept the lift stuck there?'

Chand knew he was already late. He pressed the button with all his force but the lift hardly showed any signs of movement. Chand kicked the door and decided to rush up the stairs. He himself was unsure why he was suddenly hurrying so much. But something in him said that things could possibly get uglier as the night progressed. And the last quarrel he wanted was between the two people who mattered the most to him.

Chand was running up the stairs up when his eyes caught the arrow on the wall saying "Fourth Floor". Immersed in his thoughts, he had crossed his destination. Chand quickly controlled himself, took a deep breath and made his way to room number 305.

The door was partially open and he could hear their voices as he slipped in. Sophie turned to leave the room and stopped for a moment at the sight of her fiancé. Chand looked at Siddharth who stared back at him.

'You have no idea how much I trust him,' Sophie turned towards Siddharth to make her concluding remark, 'even if that comes as a token of compromise for something else. Lay down your shield and look beyond your ego. You will realise where you lose out.'

Siddharth didn't reply. Sophie walked out of the room. Chand stood there, wondering which would be a better option – walking out with Sophie or staying back to have a word with Siddharth. He had not accounted for this situation when he walked into Apollo, but this was even more awkward than being the middleman between Siddharth and Anshuman Mehra.

'So from now onwards your wife will talk to me on your behalf?' Siddharth said. 'That's what our friendship has boiled down to!'

'She was just hurt, man,' Chand tried his best to sound convincing. 'You are my best friend and nothing's ever going to change that.'

Siddharth nodded, tightening his jaws as if trying to control an outburst.

'Give me a hug man before you leave,' he said. 'I need one.'

Chand quickly stepped forward and held his friend tightly in his arms. In his grip, he could feel Siddharth's body tremble. His best friend needed to be comforted – fighting this long battle had shattered the staunch warrior in him.

'How do I look now?' Siddharth said as Chand held him. 'As handsome as you always said I looked?'

'You do,' Chand patted his back. 'But you still don't turn me on.'

They both laughed.

'Do you want me to stay back tonight?' Chand said as he stood up. 'I can drop Sophie home and come back in an hour.'

'No, man,' Siddharth turned down the idea. 'But I want you to do something else.'

'What?'

'Tell Sophie she was right. You are indeed a better person than I am.'

'Siddha...'

'Go!'

Chand lifted his friend's hand and kissed it.

'I'll come back tomorrow morning.'

Siddharth nodded. Chand turned and quickly wiped his tears before walking out of the room.

**

'How are you planning to go?' Anshuman asked as Dipanwita and they walked alongside in the car park. It was well past midnight and Anshuman had to literally coerce Dipanwita to return home as the latter insisted on staying back. Somewhere in her heart, Dipanwita felt it was her duty to fill in for Shubhanshu's absence as well. In the end, she just relented to Anshuman's insistence. As they walked towards her car, Anshuman could see her limp worsening. He had noticed her limping around an hour ago, but the middle-aged senior correspondent ascribed the same to the heels she wore for the conference. *All I need to do is soak my feet in hot water,* Dipanwita assured Anshuman. *I will get better in no time.* Anshuman wondered how he would have fought the battle without the Banerjees by his side.

'I mean, which route are you planning to take?' he asked.

'I think I will go through Sion,' Dipanwita pushed the key inside and turned to unlock the door, 'I don't trust the Kurla traffic even at this time, especially with this victory and all...'

'How come you are so indifferent?' Anshuman smiled. 'This should be big news for you. Actually, it's great news for everyone.'

'It is actually,' Dipanwita held the door and turned to look at Anshuman. 'But there are others covering it. By the way, when is your father-in-law arriving?'

'Tomorrow afternoon,' Anshuman sighed wondering how he would react to the same.

'I'll send someone from office to pick him up. Message me his flight details once you know.'

'Thank you.' Anshuman exhaled.

'And don't stress yourself,' she patted his arm, 'Reva will be fine.'

Anshuman wanted to smile convincingly. He thought of making an attempt but gave up.

'If you don't mind,' Dipanwita treaded cautiously, 'shall I tell you something?'

Anshuman nodded, almost anticipating what Dipanwita would suggest.

'Keep this Kashyap thing to yourself,' she spoke like an elder sister advising her sibling. 'Her father might not be able to take it. So, let's wait till Reva gets up.'

'That's my plan as well.'

'Good.' Dipanwita smiled. Her respect for Anshuman had gone notches up at his display of maturity even in a crisis. She just wanted to see Reva and him happy, just the way she had thought of them till then. The pain of marital discord was not unknown to her, and she didn't want the young couple to go through the same.

Anshuman lit a cigarette as the car zoomed off. He had been a non-smoker when he arrived at Mumbai years ago. He had confidently said in his interview that he didn't need creativity inducers. But with the mounting work pressure, he had gradually succumbed to nicotine to clear his mind of a thought and relieve tension. Reva used to always disapprove of this habit of his.

'It's all in the mind,' she used to argue. 'It helps in nothing.'

'It's not a thriving industry for nothing,' he would reply.

'It's the world's biggest fad,' she would dismiss him.

He exhaled the smoke when his phone started ringing. He took it out.

'Papa,' the display flashed again.

He had abruptly cancelled the call earlier and hadn't called back. It was but natural for the old man to call again, after anxiously awaiting his son to respond. For a moment, Anshuman toyed with the idea of cancelling the call but eventually he slid the green bar. He knew the questions he would be asked. He owed an explanation for his behaviour, and sooner or later, he would have to reveal the truth.

Akashdeep Mehra was in Lucknow for a month. He was looking for a suitable buyer to sell off their house. His son's lifestyle in Mumbai didn't indicate they would ever go back and settle in the smaller town. Neither did they want him to stay in Lucknow alone. On top of that, maintaining an old building from a different city was getting more cumbersome by the day. Hence, the best option was to put it up for sale. Almost immediately, offers started pouring in to buy the corner plot ancestral bungalow – larger than all the houses in its vicinity.

'Papa,' Anshuman answered.

'Don't you think you ought to call back a person after you cancel his call without saying anything?' Akashdeep was justifiably angry.

'I know…' Anshuman winced.

'Don't do this to me at this age, Anshu,' the old man went on. 'I can't bear such tension these days.'

'I know…' Anshuman exhaled a puff of smoke.

'Where is Bahurani?'

Akashdeep had given this name to Reva not only out of tradition, but also out of fondness for his daughter-in-law. She was his queen. Ever since Akashdeep arrived at Mumbai, Reva had taken utmost care of him and ensured that he never felt out of place. Though the topic was never hatched, Akashdeep knew that his Bahurani had also orchestrated the union of his family.

'Reva is not here,' Anshuman said knowing what the next question would be.

'Where is she?' Akashdeep sounded worried. 'Her phone is also switched off.'

'Yeah, she is a bit ill...'

Anshuman walked around the car park, smoking inconspicuously lest his dad heard the sound of his heavy breathing.

'What happened to her? Is she alright?' Akashdeep sounded paranoid.

'Papa...' Anshuman spoke aloud and then promptly softened his voice. 'I'll ask her to call you when she gets up. You relax, alright?'

'Oh! She is asleep? Did you two have a fight?'

Akashdeep had seen them quarrel during his stay at Mumbai. At times, they remained aloof of each other for weeks. Anshuman's frequent trips away had only worsened the situation. Though they maintained an imperturbable maturity, the old man's experience could see through the veil of their civility.

'No dad... she is just ill.' Anshuman sighed when someone's shout caught his attention.

'I hope you are telling me is true and there is nothing to be worried about,' Akashdeep didn't believe his son completely. Reva wasn't someone to keep her phone switched off because of a minor illness. 'Why don't you stop your tours for some time? Give her company. She feels very lonely at times, managing the house all by herself.'

Anshuman walked along the basement to the place from where the voices came. There were two people involved. The male voice was loud and threatening while the female one seemed mellow and sombre. The conversation was in Marathi and Anshuman could barely make out what they said. As he moved closer, Anshuman could hear the man spout expletives while the woman appeared to be breaking into sobs. When he finally caught a glimpse of them, Anshuman saw a man standing in one of the dark corners. He was dark, stout, with a thick moustache and appeared to be in his mid 30s. His shirt was open, just partly tucked inside the crumpled trousers. Even from a distance, Anshuman could make out that the man was intoxicated and asking for money. The woman's back was towards Anshuman. It took him a moment to realise that it was the same nurse who was attending to Reva – Sister Gaitonde. For a moment, Anshuman hesitated and thought that he should walk away and not embroil himself in someone else's family dispute. Akashdeep was still talking on the phone.

'Are you listening to me, Anshu?'

'Yes,' he spoke softly.

'When are you going out of Mumbai again?' his father questioned.

'Not soon,' Anshuman turned when he heard a loud sound. This time it wasn't a voice but that of someone being hit. The man had slapped Mrs Gaitonde tightly and started calling her profane names again.

'Good,' Akashdeep Mehra spoke.

'Papa, I'll call you tomorrow morning.'

'Okay.'

Akashdeep didn't notice the sudden urgency in his son's voice. Anshuman quickly cancelled the call, stuffed the phone in his pocket and walked to the spot. The man hit her yet again. This time, the blow was louder. Swarnalata cried out in pain as she fell on her knees. Her sobbing grew louder as the man charged in to kick her. Anshuman intervened just in time.

'Hey,' he called out aloud. He threw his cigarette away and began to walk towards the two.

The couple looked up at him with a start. Evidently, they didn't expect to see him there at that moment. The air was filled with the pungent smell of liquor as Anshuman moved towards them while the man, evidently inebriated, shifted his weight between his legs for support.

'Who are you?' the man's voice trembled seeing the formally dressed man coming towards him. 'This is our personal matter.' He was still speaking in Marathi.

'If you don't leave right now,' Anshuman spoke in Hindi as he walked forward, 'it won't be your personal matter anymore. It will barely take me a moment to get the guards here and kick you out of the hospital.'

The man seemed befuddled, searching for an answer, as he looked towards his wife to speak in his favour. Whenever he looked up at the stranger, the latter kept staring straight at him, scaring him.

'Excuse us, sir,' Swarnalata spoke all of a sudden.

Anshuman felt stumped for a moment. He didn't expect her to cut him short. After all, he was only speaking in her favour. She should have been thankful to him for stopping the monster. But she wanted him to go away?

'What?' Anshuman looked at her in surprise.

'This is between my husband and me,' she got up gradually. 'Please don't say anything to him.'

Anshuman stood there startled as she turned towards her husband.

'Go home,' she said calmly to her husband. 'This is my work place and I am new here. Any trouble might cost me my job.'

Swarnalata took out a couple of hundred rupee notes from her wallet and handed them over to her husband. The man looked at Anshuman with a sardonic smile of achievement. Anshuman could feel all the blood in his body drain to his feet as the man arrogantly walked past him. He looked at Swarnalata, who stole a glance at him and quickly brushed her uniform with her hands. She removed the hair that had stuck to the tears on her face and pinned them in place with the clip. As Anshuman turned towards the elevator, Swarnalata took out her handkerchief and tried her best to cover the bruises on her face.

Seventeen

Love, revisited

She couldn't believe she was actually doing this. But she had to admit that she was secretly thrilled. The only man she had ever sat with in the front seat with was Anshuman. And now, in what could easily be perceived as a romantic escapade, she was with Siddharth as the car cruised all the way to Ghatkopar from his Andheri studio.

He wanted to watch a movie.

She was reluctant.

He insisted.

She gave in.

Why the hell am I doing this? Yes, I had agreed to the shoot when we had met at "Blue Frog" and he waited till I could resolve all the rituals after Maa's death. So what? I am not obligated to do the photo shoot with him. He has been a good guy, compassionate, expressed his condolences, didn't even badger me once for the shoot – but so what? What if someone sees us at the mall?

Yet, she loved the excitement. It was unnatural, unexpected, and perhaps unreasonable.

'We are here!' Siddharth announced.

She looked at him. In a loose yellow t-shirt with a red downward pointing arrow painted on it, ending with the caption "I am Available", navy blue track pants and chappals which could pass off as bathroom slippers, Siddharth was Anshuman's antithesis in every way. And look at her – in a white top, denim skirt and a jacket – her mother would have had a heart-attack if she had seen her daughter in these clothes. Not that Reva had anything specific against western outfits, but she had naturally stayed away from them all her life. Reva couldn't even recollect the last time she had worn a skirt. And there she was, literally dragged to the theatre to watch "Band Baaja Baraat", a film she had already watched on its release.

'But I haven't seen it yet,' Siddharth insisted. 'And I can't watch it alone or with Chand. So, you've got to give me company.'

'Why don't you get some other girl?' she had reasoned. 'I am sure you'll get some model who would die for this opportunity.'

'I don't want someone to die,' he rebuffed. 'I just want to watch a fucking movie. Sorry…'

She laughed and hit him on the arm.

'Get out and run,' he declared.

'Excuse me,' she looked appalled. Siddharth never stopped surprising her.

'We have five minutes before the movie starts,' he handed over his credit card. 'Get the tickets.'

'Are you crazy?' she looked at him angrily.

*

She was actually running. In skirts and heels! *What the f… I am actually scampering across the mall. But for whom? And why?* She panted as she reached the counter.

'Two tickets for "Band Baaja Baraat",' she handed over the credit card. 'Has the show started?'

'No, ma'am,' the counter executive said. 'It will start in half an hour.'

Reva looked baffled. She was about to call Siddharth when she felt a tap on her shoulder. Siddharth was smiling gleefully. He had done it intentionally, just to make her run. And now, he was laughing at the idea of conning her.

'You knew it, didn't you?' she was livid.

'I thought it might help you reduce weight before the next shoot,' he was still chuckling.

'Yeah right,' she threw the credit card at him. 'I am going. Watch your movie alone.'

'Gosh, you are angry,' Siddharth ran behind her. 'I am sorry, baba.'

Reva darted towards the gate. She was in no mood to relent. Siddharth caught her hand but she shrugged him off with force. He had made her run all the way from the ground floor. She must have looked really odd, and some people have surely been amused at the sight. He had made her a laughing stock. She was fuming with anger. Anshuman would have never done the same to her. He treated her like a woman.

'A hundred sit ups in front of the entire crowd?' the voice came from behind.

She turned around. He had folded his track pants and removed the slippers, standing there, with a fair number of people looking on.

'What are you doing?' she demanded.

'A hundred sit ups or perching like a cock for five minutes,' he looked unencumbered by the sudden attention they were grabbing, 'whichever you prefer.'

He is pretending to be cool, she was certain. *The best way to get him is to play along.* She resolved to keep a sombre face.

'A hundred sit ups,' she said.

For a moment, he looked shocked. But, of course, Siddharth knew how to conceal the amazement. He pushed up his sleeves and started almost immediately.

'One… Two…' he went on as Reva kept staring at him.

Siddharth looked at her and went on squatting, sans the weights. Damn, she looked cute with her cheeks scarlet in anger.

He had this feeling growing within him for the past few weeks. Reva's overpowering presence loomed over everything he did. Every time they chatted over phone, he would ponder about their discussion and play her voice in his mind over and over again. Almost everything about her was unabatedly attractive. Her beauty, her charm, they way she smiled, they way she would say "Yeah right!" every time he teased her – Siddharth couldn't stop himself from falling madly in love with her. *But she is a married woman,* he would slap his own forehead, *aarghh...*

It had taken some time to develop this friendship and even more persistence to make Reva drop her guard. Now, he couldn't besmirch all that effort by crossing the line. He felt he could go on looking at her forever, and something in his heart told him that it was possible, only if he could muster the courage to confess it. But he wanted to take his time, not rush things in desperation.

'60, 61, 62...' he went on counting and by now, there were certainly more than sixty-two people standing around and giggling.

Reva's face was softening. Siddharth could see a smile outlining her lips.

'Can I skip a few numbers to reach 100?' he said. 'Or else the movie will start.'

'Do up to 95,' she said nonchalantly.

'God,' he went on with his punishment. 'I thought you would smile and ask me to stop.'

This time, Reva gave in. She started smiling.

Wow! He was willing to do 70 more sit ups to make her smile all over again.

**

"Band Baaja Baraat" was a delightful watch even the second time. They sat on the top row – laughing and munching popcorn. She was enjoying the company and basking in the attention. It had been a long time since Anshuman and she had gone out on a fun trip, made any impromptu plans or indulged in juvenile mischief. Why was she getting drawn into this friendship? Her father-in-law had been staying with them for over a month now, and she knew she should return by 10 p.m. There were too many thoughts lingering in her mind. She just didn't want to think about them. All she wanted was to cherish the movie and go home. The first half ended on a high note as the two protagonists made love followed by the hero feeling overcome by guilt.

'The music is good, right?' Siddharth asked.

'Yeah,' she smiled. 'Pretty good!'

'You want something to eat?' he said and got up without awaiting her response. 'Let's go out and grab something.'

She indeed felt hungry. There was barely any time to eat when they had wrapped up the second portfolio shoot and decided to watch the movie.

'What will you have?' he looked vaguely at the menu board above the food counter.

'Not much,' she was equally confused. 'A veg sandwich I guess. Excuse me. I'll be back from the restroom.'

He nodded, still pondering over his options. Their confusions were different. He was whacking his brains over what to eat while sshe was confounded by her own behaviour. However hard she tried, the thoughts would never escape her. Was she suffering from a similar guilty conscience like the hero in the film? But she had not been physical with Siddharth. How could she? She loved Anshuman. Then, why was this happening to her? She had seen the movie once and watched how the girl falls for the guy – who is by no means the archetypal prince charming. To an extent, he was so not the right guy – uncouth, vernacular and a blabbermouth. Why was she herself getting drawn to the wrong guy? Siddharth was never the kind of guy she wanted to be with. He was too immature at times, impulsive and nut-headed. Anshuman was always the ideal guy. Was it because of Siddharth's fallibility that she started liking him? What if Anshuman had been a photographer who took pictures of skimpily dressed models? Her family would have cringed. And she herself believed that such love partners work only in fairytales and Bollywood movies – where reality and rationality are not essential aspects.

As she was about to push open the restroom door, she felt a tap on her shoulder. She turned around, without even having the time to think who it could be. But the moment she saw the person standing behind her, she froze.

Samaira Khan stood there, giggling at her. Wearing a deep purple salwar suit, Sam looked gorgeous as she sized up Reva.

'My my, someone's looking different,' Samaira seemed delighted to see Reva in a skirt. 'You seem to have taken Siddharth's suggestion quite seriously.'

Reva knew Samaira must have met Siddharth.

'I know it's a bit odd,' Reva tried hard to conceal her shock.

'Are you kidding me? You look ravishing!'

'Sam…'

'No, seriously,' Samaira gushed. 'You should wear these more often.'

'Which movie are you watching?' Reva tried to evade the discussion.

'Don't change the topic, girl,' Samaira giggled seeing the journalist turn scarlet in embarrassment. 'Okay, never mind. I am here to see Woody Allen's latest film, the "Tall Dark Stranger" one. Who are you here with?'

In a moment, it struck Reva that Samaira had not met Siddharth. It was a relief.

'With a friend,' she mumbled. 'If you don't mind, I just want to change and get back to the theatre. The movie might start.'

'Sure,' Samaira knew something was amiss. 'Go ahead. We'll catch up some other time.'

'Yeah,' Reva nodded and entered the washroom. She kept her bag on the commode and pulled out her dhoti and jacket. Within a moment, she had changed into her new set of clothes. Suddenly her phone started ringing.

'Where have you been?' Siddharth asked.

'Let's go,' she said, pushing her skirt into the bag.

'Why?' he was palpably surprised. 'The second half has just started and I am inside.'

'Sam is here,' she asserted.

'Samaira?'

'Yeah... and I don't want her to see us together.'

Siddharth somehow liked the way Reva said "us together". But, for a moment, he was as nervous as her, at the thought of being seen by Samaira. Of all people, Sam was the last person he could have expected to see in Ghatkopar. She hardly got out of Bandra, and when she did, it had to be the southwards.

When Siddharth reached the parking lot, Reva was already there, waiting. He realised that she had already changed into her pre-shoot clothes. The indication was clear. He didn't want to talk about the incident further and make her feel uncomfortable. Throughout the journey, she stayed quiet. Siddharth's mind raced thinking of possible things he could say to break the silence. But every time an idea came up, he decided against it. After an hour's drive, they finally stopped near Juhu circle.

'I might have over-reacted a bit,' she bent down and looked at him through the window. 'Sorry for making you feel awkward.'

'It's alright,' Siddharth smiled. 'I thought you were comfortable being friends with me.'

'I am,' she sounded a bit sceptical. 'I was plain nervous.'

'Then, shall I drop you home?' he teased.

Reva was stumped. She looked so sheepish that he couldn't resist laughing out loud.

'Bye, Siddharth.'

Siddharth looked on as she walked across the road and waited for a while before finally getting an auto-rickshaw. She knew that Siddharth was keeping a watch from the other end of the street. She thought of waving at him after getting the auto-rickshaw, but something within her told her that it was inapt to do so. Why? She had no clue.

Anshuman was in New Delhi for a pan-India meeting of Genesis. He was scheduled to arrive the following morning. His absence from home had increased over the past few months and at times, she felt excruciatingly lonely. But she tried to hide it as much as possible. She couldn't let her father-in-law feel the tension in her life. The man had shifted base and was acclimatising to life in Mumbai. After all the loss and changes he had been through, the last thing Reva wanted Akashdeep Mehra to go through was the crisis between his son and daughter-in-law. Contrary to the image she had of him, Akashdeep was not finicky about anything and accommodated with the lifestyles of the younger Mehras.

The phone rang in her bag. Reva opened the zip and took it out. The display flashed "Jaan".

'Hey.'

'How are you, baby?' Anshuman sounded jubilant.

'I am fine. I will reach home in some time. You sound excited!'

Reva looked out of the auto-rickshaw. The vehicle was crossing Adarsh Nagar, cruising through the moderately congested New Link Road.

'I do,' he was obviously surprised how she could read his voice. 'There's good news.'

'Really?' she wondered what it could be.

'Yes... I am finally writing the lyrics for Tahir Khan's next film.'

'Wow! That's great.'

She had forgotten all about it. Anshuman had been part of discussions about the possibility of writing the songs for a film that Tahir Khan was supposed to produce and act in. Anshuman had been extremely upbeat about it. Who wouldn't be? After all, Tahir Khan was one of the most sought after actors of the nation – known for his experimental yet commercially successful work. He had epitomised quality and most people in the industry would give an arm to work with him. The discussion had started when Anshuman worked on an advertisement that starred the superstar. They two had hit it off really well and Tahir, who was impressed by Anshuman's writing prowess, asked him to write the lyrics for his film.

'Yeah,' Anshuman turned a bit cautious. 'But there is a small issue.'

'What is it?' she could decipher the sudden sombreness in his voice.

'It means it will take me one more week to return home,' he revealed.

'Why? They are working in Delhi?'

'No. The music-director is from Chennai. Shashikanth Pillai…'

Reva knew Anshuman was working with two stalwarts at the same time. The South Indian maestro was a phenomenon in the music industry. Though he had a prodigious body of work in Tamil and Telugu films, his compositions for Bollywood were few and far between. But whenever there was a Shashikanth Pillai album, the entire nation went berserk about it. He was incomparable when it came to melody, perhaps second to someone as magical as a Sachin Dev Burman.

'Wow, that's great!' she exclaimed.

'And Tahir wants me to be with the entire music team in Chennai and write the lyrics as a collaborative process with Pillai.' Anshuman's voice was filled with an amalgamation of joy and turpitude.

'I see…' Reva sighed.

'Are you mad at me?' Anshuman sounded penitent.

'No, baby,' Reva was hardly sincere in her reply. 'How can I be? You are doing so well. What else do I need?'

'Reva...' As much as he knew the reason behind her anger, he hoped to get a better response from her. She was privy to his dreams, and none could fathom his joy of achievement as dearly as she could.

'I am sorry,' she realised she was overly sarcastic in her last statement. She was indeed happy but her insecurity made her selfish. 'It was just that...'

'Any problem at office?' he sounded sincere.

'I guess you can say...' *Could she ever tell him that she was angry with herself for being caught off guard by Samaira, while watching a movie with Siddharth?*

'I can postpone this thing by a couple of days.' There was a mark of genuine concern. It was not often that he found her carrying professional woes home. *There must be something else,* he was sure. *She'll never tell me on the phone.*

'Absolutely not,' she felt ashamed of her behaviour. 'It's a very big thing. And I want you to be fully devoted to it. Did you have a word with Papa?'

'Not yet. You can tell him, right?'

'No, Anshu... you should tell him this,' she reprimanded, forgetting her grief. 'He deserves to know about his son's achievement directly from him.'

'Okay, I will call him.' He complied like a child.

'I will talk to you tomorrow.' Reva looked out again and realised she was about to reach their building.

'Love you, baby.'

'Thanks,' she was looking at the fare-meter.

'Thanks?'

'I mean I love you too...'

'I know you do,' he chuckled. 'Good night.'

'Good night.'

Reva exhaled and looked outside. Another week! She tried not to think of it. *It's wicked of me to think that way,* she chided herself. *I should be celebrating his success.*

***

A few days had gone by. She had strictly avoided contact with Siddharth but didn't seem to get him out of her mind. His presence was suddenly overpowering in her life. There was a palpable attraction and she knew it was bad. She couldn't afford to get involved with a man. After all, she was married.

Anshuman had not returned from Chennai. The stay had got extended due to the music director's demand. And given Shashikanth Pillai's busy schedule, it would be too risky to take a chance. They had talked over the phone and she had extended her support and encouragement. But how long could she live with this dilemma, she wondered?

She lay on the bed, the peacock blue chiffon sari flowing loosely on her body. Akashdeep Mehra had gone to meet a relative in Bhopal, and was scheduled to return in a few days' time. Somewhere in her heart, Reva felt guilty of embroiling the man into her troubles. Though Anshuman and she had barely fought in front of him, her father-in-law was just too experienced to not feel what was going on in the house. He had tried to be accommodating but like his son, Akashdeep was too polite to directly ask questions – something her mother-in-law could have. Surprisingly, Anshuman never realised the awkwardness his father felt at his absence. She had alluded to the idea but he rubbished it every time, complimenting her that she was a great daughter-in-law.

The phone beeped and she bent over the bed to pick the set from the stool adjacent to the bed. It was a BBM from Siddharth. Around two week had gone by after the unceremonious ending to their previous meeting. But there was no dearth of silliness in Siddharth's behaviour...

'Can I disturb you?' the message read.

She held the phone and turned on her back. Reva was thinking of a suitable reply when another message popped up.

'Do you feel awkward being with me?'

Before she could think of a suitable reply, another one came in.

'I was wondering if you would go clubbing with me.'

She was irked. He was not only childish but also annoying in his audacity at times.

'No,' she typed and sent.

'As in you don't feel awkward being with me?'

She wanted to hit him. She was sure he knew what the *no* was for. But like his inane questions, her own daft temper finally made her laugh.

'No,' she wrote again.

'Means you feel or you don't feel?'

She giggled. He always made her smile. How did he succeed in doing that every time?

The bell rang. She kept the phone down and walked over to the door. She hated opening the door when she didn't expect anyone, especially after a long day at office. The bell rang again. Who could have come at ten in the night and disturbing her like that?

She pulled open the door. For a moment, she was dumbstruck. Anshuman was standing at the door, carrying a grand bouquet of flowers for her. Her heart pounded in excitement. It was possibly the best surprise she could have ever expected. She jumped forward and hugged him. Anshuman held her tightly.

'Happy Birthday, my love!'

'It's my birthday?' Reva was evidently surprised. 'What's the date?'

'Today is 22nd September,' he said. 'Aren't you celebrating your birthday tomorrow?'

'It absolutely skipped my mind,' she was ecstatic that Anshuman had remembered it and had flown all the way to celebrate her birthday. No one could possibly love her that much.

'I don't believe this. You forgot your birthday?'

Anshuman walked inside, pulling in his suitcase.

'It happens,' she mocked and closed the door, 'when you spend your life alone.'

'Very funny,' Anshuman kept the flowers on the table and pushed the bag towards the wall. 'I took my day off just because I wanted to be with you on this special day.'

'Especially for this?' she tried to conceal her joy. She had to pretend a bit offended so that Anshu would put in more effort to please her.

'Of course,' Anshuman came up and put his arms around her waist. 'I was asked to fly to the Genesis London office for a month. I postponed it for one day just because it was your birthday. Can you believe this? The International Headquarters wants me to handle a crucial project for them!'

Reva looked blankly at him. She was appalled. Anshuman knew how sorely she missed him at home. They were in their fourth year of marriage and for the previous eight months, they had hardly spent time together. And now, he was going away for another month. But he seemed absolutely casual about it. She could feel all the excitement drain away, and replaced with a sudden rush of anger. How insensitive could he be?

'One month?' she pushed his hands away. 'If you are going away again for a month, then why did you come down and have this farce?'

Anshuman was caught on the wrong foot. He had gauged she would be upset but didn't expect such a remark.

'Don't say that, jaan,' he tried to hold her hands. 'A month's time is nothing. It will pass off in a whisker. And today is *your* birthday,' he emphasised. 'How could I have missed it?'

'The way you have missed so many other important things,' she replied coldly.

'I have not missed out on anything,' Anshuman was offended and as usual he could not digest an accusation. 'Don't blame me for any random thing you feel like.'

'I feel suffocated in this house, Anshuman,' Reva blurted in exasperation, 'I can't live here alone anymore.'

Anshuman softened immediately. He knew that her pain was true and justified.

'There are certain things that I want from my husband, certain desires like all other women,' she looked at him with moist eyes. 'And I find it tough to swallow them as my husband is always somewhere else.'

Anshuman moved forward to touch her. But she immediately moved back and pushed him away.

'I know, baby,' Anshuman sounded apologetic. 'Don't you know that I miss you too? I feel terrible without you around me.'

'Then, why are you going away, Anshu?'

'Reva, we are mature people,' he tried to reason. 'How can you say this? We are already into our thirties. I can work this hard only now; I won't have this stamina for long. We need to know and understand that at this stage of our lives, nothing can be more important than our careers.'

'Not even our marriage?' her eyes were red now, revolting against him and the tears that were gradually welling up in them.

'Obviously not,' Anshuman stated ambiguously and immediately groped to rectify himself. 'To me, my relation with you is the most important thing in this world. Otherwise, I wouldn't have wasted my day here…'

'So, you know that you are wasting it?' she was stoic all of a sudden. The last few words had left her livid.

'I didn't mean that,' Anshuman had made a blunder again. 'You are putting words in my mouth.'

'You know what you meant and so do I. After all, we are mature people, aren't we?' she shot back sardonically. 'Don't you ever feel that you are wasting your entire life with someone who doesn't deserve you? I'm sure you do. You need to give that a more serious thought.'

Reva stormed into the bedroom and banged the door. Anshuman walked up and knocked on it. He waited for fifteen minutes, calling her but there was no response. He could hear her weeping but she didn't respond to his calls.

Reva sat on the bed, crying profusely. She felt terrible. How could Anshuman do this to her? She gritted her teeth; she wanted to take something and destroy everything in the house. What was the purpose of all this? Her head was spinning in fury. Why did this have to happen? That too, on the eve of her birthday! She had forgotten all about it, no doubt, but why did it need to get spoiled like that. Why couldn't Anshuman and she be happy like they were earlier? He still loved her… She still loved him… Then, why?

A part of her said she was over-reacting. After all, he was only doing his work. He had always been like this. She knew it. At least, unlike his nonchalant "less expressive" self, Anshuman had travelled all the way to celebrate her birthday. He had started expressing himself more often now. Yet, he barely seemed to realise her solitude. But she wasn't fully justified in her demands, was she? She dropped her head and held it in her hands, trying to stop the throbbing with all her force. She stopped crying. She was still hiccupping though. She took the bottle from the bed side table and guzzled the water. As the liquid drained into her system, the anguish in her mind seemed to gradually alleviate. With the end of her sari, she wiped the tears off her eyes. The smudged kohl stained the cloth.

As she controlled her breathing, Reva walked up and opened the door. She needed to apologise. She had been too selfish. He was right. They should behave maturely. He was touching 35, there were not many years left for such hard work.

As she looked out, the drawing room was empty. She looked around. The suitcase wasn't there. It sank in painfully. Anshuman was gone. She strolled around the house to ensure she was not wrong. The bouquet was lying on the floor of the kitchen, bearing testimony to the fact that someone had thrown it there, mercilessly. Reva tried to rest her balance on the door. But even the support could not keep her standing. How could he do it? Just because she was angry, he left even without trying to ameliorate the entire situation. She had come out to apologise, but wasn't he repentant so as to be patient with his wife. Couldn't he show this much magnanimity? Was this the depth of his love? The veins in her forehead were throbbing again. She held her head tightly between her two hands but the pain didn't relent – She was not going to take this insult. The tears were streaming torrentially down her eyes while her breathing inflated as she rushed back to her room. The phone was still lying on the bed. She took it up hastily and typed the message.

'Which club do you want to go to?'

**

An hour later, Reva found herself dancing fanatically on the second floor of Hawaiian Shack – a small congested club in Bandra West. She hated the closed space but loved the music. It was not anytime in the near past that she had danced so much. The white spaghetti top was wet with sweat as she moved to the beats in a tight fitting pair of jeans. She used to hate high heels but tonight she loved them. As she moved her lips in sync to a JLo song and grooved with it, she could feel a host of male eyes staring at her. She had always gained attention from guys but had never imagined them ogling at her while she danced. She chuckled arrogantly to herself.

All of a sudden the music went off and everyone in the club sighed in disappointment. But someone spoke on the mike and all voices were hushed.

'I am sorry,' someone said. 'The music will resume in a minute.'

It took Reva a moment to realise that the voice was familiar. It was Siddharth. She looked around. *What is he doing in the DJ's box?*

'My dear friend out there,' Siddharth pointed at Reva. 'Yes, the lady in the jeans at whom most of the guys are staring. I don't blame you. She is gorgeous. Well, it's her birthday today.'

Reva immediately looked at her watch. Both the hands were together at the 12 mark.

'I want you all to help me in wishing her a very happy birthday. And yes, in return, one beer for everyone in the house – on me!'

The entire crowd erupted in a thundering applause. For the first time in her life, Reva heard a chorus of more than hundred people singing "Happy Birthday" for her as Siddharth waved his hands like a Mozart directing his musicians.

Siddharth never revealed if he had actually paid for the beer or how he came to know of her birthday. But she was happy. She felt special. Though dancing in a club on birthday was never on her wish list, it was worth the experience. She had let herself go totally. Siddharth was now a friend she cherished.

**

He had finally convinced her about the third photo shoot. 'This is the last one,' she insisted at the end of the *"please- no- it would be great- I feel uncomfortable- please yaar"* back and forth volley.

'Done deal,' he confirmed. He just had a way of coaxing her into agreement.

Third time around, they were back to the traditional outfit. Siddharth wanted to give her the rural Bengali Bahu look – simple yet exotic. *'Bengali bahus don't wear saris without blouses any longer,' she said. 'But that's the way they would look best,'* he shot back and winced as she hit his arm. *'Come on'* he cajoled, *'it's a period setting. And artistic liberty...'* She had raised her hand and said, *'Get on with it.'* He smiled.

The sari fell over her bare shoulder, as she looked sideward with a full moon of vermillion smeared on her forehead.

'Adjust your sari,' Siddharth shouted, as he stood behind the camera.

The off-white sari with red border had moved from its original position, revealing the blouse that was camouflaged to look non-existent. Reva pulled the sari to its former position. Her hair was neatly tied into a bun, with a silver key ring attached to function like a clip.

'Here we go,' Siddharth switched on the lights. 'Chin up, and look here with a smile.' He pointed his finger at a point on the wall.

Reva lifted her chin and looked at the wall, her eyes highlighted with deep lines of kohl. This was her third photo shoot with Siddharth. So, by now she knew what her photographer friend wanted. She could just escape the worries of home and the trivialities of the Page 3 parties, and just concentrate on herself for a change. There was a friend who understood her and made her look good. The flash struck her face and her job was done. She looked at Siddharth and heaved a smile of relief. Absent minded, she ran her fingers through the clip. And before Siddharth could say anything, she had plucked the clip out and her hair had flown down.

'Shit, no,' Siddharth almost shrieked in alarm. 'I told you I want to take another shot from the other angle.'

'Oh, I am so sorry,' Reva bit her tongue. She realised she had just spoilt a lot of hard work. In none of her previous shoots, had she been absent minded. But there was something that had kept her preoccupied that day. Was it just the photography, the feeling of being special in those few hours or her growing friendship with Siddharth?

Siddharth was everything Anshuman was not. He was not elegant; neither did he have the aura Anshu did. Siddharth's beauty lay in his irreverence and in his espousal of the idea of frivolity. He was gorgeous, and though he knew it, he barely took it with gravity. *'You should rather have been a model,'* she had commented more than once, *'you would have done well.'* He had no idea who Kafka was, neither was he interested in Martin Luther King's speeches. Siddharth just knew his photography, and he knew it well.

But then, she didn't need to care whether she sounded stupid while having a discussion with him. How many times had Anshuman's knowledge and precision made her suffer from inferiority complex! But Siddharth was careless about such things. He had a child-like immaturity and was obsessed with his passion. And the fact that Siddharth was five years younger to her also gave her a sense of upper hand in the relation.

'Hello,' Siddharth clicked his fingers and broke her reverie. 'You just spoilt the hair.'

Reva looked up, back to her senses. 'I am sorry,' she spoke hurriedly. 'I shall just pin it back again.'

'Don't,' Siddharth instructed. 'It would be very tough to make it the same.' He sighed and looked at his model. 'We will do it with your hair open.'

She sighed as there was nothing she could say to rectify her mistake. Siddharth hastily grabbed a comb and ran it through her hair, before pushing the tresses down over her right shoulder. With his finger running softly under her eyes, he smudged the kohl and rubbed the vermillion partially, to give her a dishevelled look.

'This is perfect,' Siddharth explained, as they gaped into each other's eyes. For a moment, they didn't say anything. He bent closer to rub his fingers on her lips to smudge the scarlet lipstick.

The red paint smudged around her lips as if someone had kissed them passionately. The smudged kohl felt like someone had held her face in his hands and fondled it with utmost care. And the moment of growing intimacy snatched the shields of resistance from their armour. Their breaths grew faster and heavier as their faces came closer, the noses rubbing softly. Siddharth didn't smell of cigarettes and there was freshness in his breath, while her fragrance reminded him of fresh morning flowers that his mother used for the puja. There was such serenity in that moment that neither could feel themselves getting drawn into something that could ruin the friendship they had nurtured over the previous few months. Their lips touched when she withdrew herself and broke the building proximity. Looking around, perplexed, she dragged the sari around herself and stood up, ready to leave.

'I should go now,' she bent her hand backwards and knotted the blouse. 'It's pretty late.'

'Reva,' Siddharth threw his hands in awkward helplessness. 'It's alright. It was just a moment.'

'It shouldn't have been,' Reva gathered herself. 'It was my mistake. And we are overdoing this photo-shoot thing.'

'Stop blaming yourself,' Siddharth attempted to reconcile. 'Our relation isn't just that of a photographer and a model. Above everything, we are friends.'

'I don't need a friend,' Reva picked up her purse. 'I am not supposed to. I am married to a guy who gives me everything.'

'Between us, it's not about giving or taking,' Siddharth refuted, 'it's just about being together. You don't need to pretend to be someone else when you are with me.'

'You can't tell me what's wrong with my marriage,' Reva looked at him, her eyes as red as the vermillion smudged on her forehead. 'I should have never let you into my world.'

Grabbing her mobile phone, she pushed the door open and darted out.

'You did that because you trust me,' Siddharth spoke as she rushed down the stairs. 'Because you know I would never do any harm.'

Reva rubbed the tears betraying her restraint, and ran down.

'Because I love you,' he shouted, 'and you love me as well.'

For a moment, he felt her legs tremble to a halt, but she regained her strength and walked away. Almost a minute after she was out of sight, he closed the door. He had never predicted such a brusque ending to their relation. They both knew the truth, but the sudden realisation and the repercussions were too difficult to deal with.

He switched off the sun guns and shut the lid of his camera. The key ring used as a hair clip was lying on the floor. A little spray of vermillion was scattered around the stool and the smell of her perfume was still in the air – Reva was all around. He opened the door leading from his studio to the drawing room, when a knock on the door stopped him.

With hasty yet hesitant steps, Siddharth walked back to the door and opened it. She was back. Slowly, she slid past him and passed through the studio to the drawing room.

**

She felt like a bitch. But it didn't matter. She might be a slut. It didn't matter either. She was not having sex for the sake of it. It was with a man who sincerely loved her, cared for her and accepted her the way she was. Making love to Siddharth was very different from what it was like with Anshuman. The younger guy was much more agile and adventurous than her husband. Siddharth moved and guided her with so much ease that it took her by surprise. It was not rash or wild. He was affectionate, tender yet erotic.

He gently fondled her breasts, softly pressing them and running his tongue over them. She moaned as her nipples tightened. Siddharth slid his hands along her thighs and through her pantyhose. She rose up and started kissing his neck as her fingernails clasped on to the smooth skin of his back. Siddharth slowly looked up and holding her face with his right hand, he kissed her. It was a long and passionate kiss as their lips and tongues erupted into action. The slow initial process gradually picked up speed. He pulled open his t-shirt as she unbuttoned his jeans and pushed them down his legs. Caressing, fondling and kissing later, they lay on each other, naked. Finally when he realised that she was willing, he went in.

**

Reva was engrossed in the file she was carrying as she entered her cabin. She was expected to write a story on the collaboration between a leading TV channel and a giant production house. One of India's top film production and distribution house was entering television, and people had anticipated that a revolution was on its way. The house was supposedly shooting on high-end digital cameras which were till then used only for movies. Their production values were supposed to be way better than the existing ones, and their content was projected as path-breaking and progressive – targeting the youth who were habituated to American television on Star World, HBO and internet downloads.

'Platonic,' Reva muttered under her breath as she sat on her chair, shaking her head at the over-ambitious proposal by the channel's programming head.

'What's platonic?' someone said and Reva jumped in surprise. The file dropped from her hand.

Samaira Khan was sitting across the table, dressed in a garish violet sari paired with a shocking pink halter necked blouse, along with hanging diamond earrings.

'What the...' Reva controlled her breathing, and stared at her friend's dress, 'and what...'

'How do you like my dress?' Samaira said as if reading Reva's thought.

'Why are you wearing such a thing in the middle of the day?' Reva looked at Sam.

'Do I look like someone's wife?' Samaira slurred.

Reva was slowly making sense of it all. Her own state of shock and astonishment had made her overlook the fact that Samaira was drunk – her eyes were bloodshot and her speech convoluted in inebriation. Reva had never seen Samaira like that before, and was surprised that the latter was let into the office premises in such a condition. On the top of everything, no one had even informed her about Samaira's presence in her office. Reva cursed the security for being irresponsible.

'Sam...' Reva picked up the file and walked across to her. 'Are you alright?'

'You didn't tell me,' Samaira looked back at her, straining her eyes to keep them open. 'Do I look like someone's wife?'

'What kind of a question is that?' Reva sat on the chair next to Samaira and kept the file on the table.

'Or do I look like a whore?'

'Sam...' Reva said, 'you should go home. You are not well.'

'Of course I am not,' Samaira shrugged off the suggestion. 'I am a slut. That's what I get to know after serving someone for almost a decade?

'Bhalla told you something?' Reva looked concerned.

'He asked me to get lost...' Samaira sneered, a bitter feeling of despondency marking her expression of self deprecation.

'You guys keep having fights...' Reva tried to appease her, though in her heart she knew how futile it was. A part of her heart, however, did not want to deal with it.

'No, baby,' Sam referred to her as baby only when she was down and out. 'He fights with his wife and I face the consequences. I am just a mistress you see.'

Reva took Samaira's hand in hers and rubbed them to comfort her.

'Don't worry,' Reva looked straight into her friend's eyes. 'Everything will be alright.'

'I doubt that,' Sam couldn't fight her tears. 'My life is beyond repair, sweetheart. And I am the only one to blame. I fell for Raj knowing well that he was married and would never break up with his wife to be with me. After all, everything he has today is his in-laws'. I told myself, *Sam, he is the man you love. So what if you can't get married? You can be with him... So, be his mistress...*

Reva looked at Samaira. She knew the woman well. She was always boisterous, full of life, enjoying every moment of life and even cracking jokes on herself. Samaira was hardly a woman Reva could envisage getting so vulnerable for a man. Reva had never approved of the relation Sam shared with Rajvardhan Bhalla, but then she never overtly spoke about it.

'And look what I have made out of myself today!' Samaira went on. 'As cheesy as it sounds, there's no substitute for a happy marriage.'

'True,' Reva nodded. 'You should get married... it's not...'

'Me?' Samaira burst out in a full throated laugh. 'Who will marry a 40 year old chick who has been sleeping with the country's biggest businessman cum philanderer?' Before Reva could say anything, Samaira answered her own question which was in any case a rhetoric one, 'No one.'

'Sam...'

'Baby,' Samaira sat up. 'Forget about me. I am used to this life. I might be drunk today but I will be sober tomorrow, tipsy day after and happy again...But I need you to take care.'

'What's wrong with me?' Reva sounded cautious.

'You are married to a great guy,' Samaira bent forward and cupped her friend's face in her hands. 'Never think of throwing it away.'

'Why would I do that?' Reva gaped into Sam's eyes.

'I know you won't,' Sam leaned back on the chair. 'I just wanted to be sure you don't. If there's anything going on, it's better to make your priorities clear before it's too late.'

'What do you mean?' Reva could feel her limbs freeze while a host of questions raced through her mind. Did Sam know anything? Did Siddharth tell her about their relation? Was it all a ploy to set her up? Did the others know about it? No, it cannot be. Siddharth couldn't do this to her. Reva could feel her breathing quicken while Samaira mumbled an answer.

'I just felt something amiss when I met you that day,' Samaira pointed out. 'At the theatre...'

At that moment, Jennifer pushed open the door and barged into the cabin.

'We have a meeting in ten minutes,' Jenny said. 'Dipa wants to freeze this channel thingy...'

'I will be there,' Reva looked at Jenny and sighed. She could feel herself thanking God for sending Jenny and stopping this discussion.

Samaira, though seemingly sloshed beyond her senses, took the cue and got up to leave.

'I will let you work in peace,' she laughed as she held the arm rest of her chair tightly and pushed herself up. 'I have troubled you enough.'

'You don't trouble me, Sam,' Reva walked towards the door. 'You are a great friend. And I am humbled that you found me worthy of a discussion. I am sorry I've got a meeting lined up now.'

'Oh, no worries, baby,' Samaira patted Reva's cheek, 'but keep my words in mind.'

Jenny looked at the two of them, surprise palpable in her eyes.

'Sure,' Reva held the door as Samaira walked out.

Jenny looked at Samaira and then turned towards Reva with a smirk. 'In high spirits!' she winked.

'I will be there in ten,' Reva released the door as it automatically sprang to a close.

Eighteen

Present Time

DAY 2
1:35 a.m.

Anshuman stood in the lobby, looking at Sister Gaitonde through the venetian blinds, as she walked through the corridor towards the waiting room, presumably to meet him. He had just witnessed an ugly side of the male-dominated Indian society. *Such things are surely rampant among the poorer sections*, he surmised, *where the women never have their say despite their selfless contributions to the family*. Her silent surrender to the assault despite his presence could only imply the amount of torture she went through at home. Why did she refuse to take his help? She must surely envisage a life emancipated from the clutches of a man who treated her like shit.

Pretty much as Anshuman had predicted, Swarnalata entered the waiting room and looked at him. Her face looked stolid as if nothing had happened. Anshuman wondered how could women shake off everything and pretend to be normal.

'Dr Ahmed wants to see you before she leaves,' she said.

'Sure,' Anshuman couldn't conceal the surprise in his eyes as he looked at the nurse.

'Your intrusion wouldn't have helped anything,' Swarnalata displayed an impregnable poise, untouched by the malice of the event that happened an hour ago. 'Things would have only become worse for me at home. I won't have anyone there for support.'

'So, it's better to surrender?' Anshuman looked surprised.

'It's better to know where you stand...' Swarnalata smiled feebly. 'Dr Ahmed is waiting for you.'

**

Fariza Ahmed was comfortably seated in her cabin when Anshuman stepped in. Despite the radiant face which Anshuman had noticed the first time he had met her, she looked tired. It had been a long day and Reva's double operation had taken a toll on her. In his heart, Anshuman knew that the woman sitting in front of him was responsible for the fact that his wife was still alive. And never in his life could he thank her enough.

'I'll be leaving in some time,' Dr Ahmed spoke. 'There will be a doctor around whom I will brief about the case.'

'Fine,' Anshuman spoke appreciatively.

'We do not expect any emergency to arise,' Fariza cleared her throat. 'Sorry... yeah... we do not expect any crisis. In case there is any, I will come immediately. Or else I will be here by 12 tomorrow. I believe she should get back to senses before that. If she does, I have given instructions to the nurses to let you meet her.'

'Perfect,' Anshuman nodded. 'I owe you for everything you did. Thanks a million.'

'What do your clients owe you when you make a successful campaign for them?' Fariza picked up her planner and looked at him.

Anshuman laughed. 'None of the campaigns I make saves lives.'

Fariza Ahmed smiled, humbled by the comment. 'Mr Mehra,' she sighed, 'there is something I want to talk to you about.'

'About ACP Kabir?' Anshuman guessed.

'So, you know?' Dr Ahmed looked surprised. 'He told you about it?'

'Actually, no,' Anshuman wondered if he had taken an unwarranted step. 'He asked me when you had left your previous workplace and joined Apollo. So, I assumed that the two of you are acquainted.'

'I see,' Fariza swallowed. 'Well, he was my husband, Mr Mehra.'

Anshuman was not surprised. Perhaps he had seen too much over the course of the day to be taken aback any further. He might not have expected them to be ex-spouses but surely he hadn't eliminated the possibility altogether. For a moment, he pondered what to say. In the end, he decided it was best to nod and say nothing.

'I have been through this myself,' she rubbed her nose hesitantly. 'I have experienced what you have faced tonight. It might not be the identical scenario but something on those lines.'

'Oh...'

'Perhaps that's why I couldn't bring myself to talk to Mr Kashyap,' she went on. 'I know exactly how it feels to meet the other person in your spouse's life.'

Anshuman looked at her in surprise. He recollected the events throughout the night. She was right. She had deliberately refrained from talking to Siddharth. Even when she had met both the men, she avoided any interaction with the younger guy.

'Thankfully, in my case, there were no cops involved,' Fariza Ahmed said and corrected herself, 'though Kabir is a cop himself.'

Anshuman looked on as Dr Ahmed smiled at the irony of her last statement.

'He was being rather harsh with Siddharth,' Anshuman said.

'That's expected, Fariza replied. 'He is usually harsh to people. That's how he is. On the top of that, it was something he had been through before. A guilty conscience also manipulates our behaviour, doesn't it?'

Anshuman nodded. He wanted to know the details but couldn't bring himself to ask any questions. Rekindling someone else's pain was hardly the way of placating his own.

'So, what should I do?' Anshuman smiled half hearted.

'I got divorced,' Dr Ahmed declared. 'I didn't even talk to him after that incident, but then what I did is hardly the ideal solution.'

'You repent the divorce?' Anshuman looked anxiously for a response.

'I don't know,' Fariza Ahmed pursed her lips to express the doubt that still lingered in her mind. 'But I feel bad that I never asked for any clarification from my husband. I should have done that.'

'Just took a hasty decision?'

'Yeah... It's not that I repent not having him with me or not being married. I just regret not even trying to fix a part of my life which was so precious to me.'

Anshuman sighed and nodded his head.

'Did you ever blame yourself?' Despite Dr Ahmed's disclaimer, Anshuman knew that her life might possibly be the guideline for him to follow.

'For not asking?' Fariza lifted the glass of water and sipped from it.

'No...' He shook his head.

'For his adultery?'

Anshuman nodded and left out a sigh. "*Am I to be blamed?*" was a question he had asked himself many a time throughout the day.

'Not always,' Fariza clarified. 'But yes, may be somewhere in my heart, I do hold myself partly responsible for what he did. I was married to him after all.'

'So, do you think I am to be blamed?' Anshuman looked straight into the doctor's eyes. He wanted to see the reaction. He needed to know the truth from someone who could be objective about the scenario. And for a moment, he caught the hesitation on the doctor's face.

'Who am I to comment on your relation, Mr Mehra?' she replied. 'All I can say that we can't clap with one hand, can we?'

Anshuman had got his answer.

'Moreover, there's a difference in the way a woman shapes her relation and a man his,' Dr Ahmed sighed.

'Is it?' Anshuman smiled.

'Yes,' Dr Ahmed nodded with a smile and added after a pause. 'All I can advise you, if *advise* is the word, please have a word with your wife before you take a call.'

'I haven't taken any call,' Anshuman looked back, his firm voice reassuring of his intention. 'At this point of time, all I want is to see her recover.'

'That's good,' the doctor smiled. 'I think I can leave now.'

'Thanks,' Anshuman stood up, 'not for just doing your job, but for talking to me as well. This is something you didn't have to do.'

Fariza Ahmed didn't say anything. As Anshuman walked towards the door, she called him again.

'Do you want to sit beside her for some time?'

**

The teacher was beaming and showering her son with praises. In her heart she felt so proud but she couldn't show it. She only smiled. Her nine year old son sitting next to her was solving the Rubik's Cube, oblivious to the pride he had brought to his mother.

'Farhan,' the principal said and the little boy looked up from the game. 'You have to promise that you will keep on working hard.'

'Yes, ma'am,' Farhan nodded and looked down at the game in hand. He was too close to solving it.

'Dr Ali,' the principal said, 'he is little genius. We are all very proud of him. Of course, he is born to talented parents and he has it in his genes.'

Fariza smiled and touched her son's head affectionately. The little boy shrugged her hand off. He hated any distraction when he was so close to achieving his objective.

'All I can complain about is that he is too reclusive at times,' the principal went on. 'It can happen to kids whose parents are in such jobs. I understand the gravity of your profession as well as his father's, but it would be great if you both could find more time to spend with him.'

Fariza nodded. Her job was overpoweringly hectic at times. And her husband, ACP Kabir Ali, was mostly preoccupied with his cases. Farhan suffered from their lack of attention, they both knew, but the child never complained. It was a guilt that had kept pinching her conscience.

'I will try my best,' Fariza replied when her phone started ringing. 'I am sorry,' she looked at the principal who smiled. 'It must be an emergency or else they wouldn't have called me.'

'Please go ahead,' the principal permitted.

*

As Fariza darted into Fortis, she could see the nurse carrying the case file running towards her. It was a criminal case. The victim had been shot on the temple and was critical. Only an immediate surgery could save her from further peril.

'Why was she shot?' Fariza exclaimed as they walked hastily towards the OT.

'She is a gangster's girlfriend,' the nurse responded, quite excitedly.

'My goodness!' Fariza was shocked. 'So, a rival party shot her?'

'Not really,' the nurse informed her. 'She was shot by the gangster himself.'

'Why?' Fariza looked at the 3-D CT scan and then at the nurse.

'She was cheating on him with some police officer,' the nurse said. 'At least that's what the rumour is.'

Fariza walked into the OT, with the apron and gloves on and the mask still loose and dangling around her chest. Her assistants were ready, and everybody seemed anxious. Not only was the injury serious, the backdrop itself was equally unnerving for everyone. None of them had ever dreamt of treating a woman shot by a gangster.

Fariza looked at the woman's face. She lived in a city where news about gangsters and their love lives were not uncommon. The men in crime were reputed for their fascination for pretty women, and the patient lying in front of her only reinstated that popular belief. Tabassum was beautiful and looked gorgeous even in the state she was lying in. She had the most perfect features with large eyes outlined by long curved eye-lashes, a pointed nose, perfect lips and flawless skin that could make top actresses shrink with inferiority complex. No wonder the gangster had fallen obsessively in love with her. And it was no surprise either that the woman had another admirer, that too from the gangster's nemesis – the police.

It was the first time Fariza was dealing with such a severe case of traumatic brain injury. Fariza was desperate to save Tabassum. Besides her profession, she could also feel a selfish motive creeping up in her heart. She wanted to hear the story of Tabassum. The blood loss seemed negligible compared to other damages done. Tabassum was on a Glasgow Coma Scale of five and it was almost certain she'd slip into a coma, provided they succeeded in saving her. The entire team rallied on to make sure that Tabassum survived the operation. Yet, they succumbed to the inevitable at the end of it as Tabassum sank into hibernation. Fariza could feel her entire body turn cold in disappointment over the failure. She could barely rejoice the fact that Tabassum had not died during the operation, which going by the *severity of the injury, had been a very high possibility. They shifted the patient to the ICU. If things were to turn worse, Fariza knew they would have no option but to put Tabassum on a ventilator.*

*

It was around eight in the evening when Kabir walked into the hospital. He wore a black t-shirt teamed with denims and boots, as he unabashedly opened the door of his wife's cabin and entered her room. Fariza, still perturbed by the partial success of the surgery, was immersed in the post surgery reports when Kabir came in. They had never visited each other's workplaces in the past few years and the sudden unsolicited appearance was rather startling.

'Kabir?' Fariza looked up in surprise.

'I heard you were dealing with a serious case,' Kabir pulled a chair and sat down.

'So, have you come to inquire?' Fariza asked her husband. 'Or do you want me to give a statement or something?'

'You can say so,' Kabir nodded. 'I want to know how Tabassum is. Your authorities are not revealing anything to the media.'

It was a strict instruction from the hospital board to not disclose the facts of the case to anyone, definitely not the media.

'Have you been appointed on this case?' Fariza eyed him inquisitively.

'Save her, Fariza,' Kabir answered brusquely. 'She should not die.'

'I am trying my best,' Fariza suddenly turned defensive at the request. 'But the injury was severe.' For a moment, she pondered before asking, 'Do you know Tabassum?'

'She was my...' Kabir groped for an answer, 'in... umm... informer.'

'Oh,' Fariza sighed.

Kabir had never discussed his work with her. And she respected the professional secrecy he maintained at home. After all, his job demanded some kind of shut lip policy and he couldn't compromise it.

But almost immediately, another thought struck Fariza. Like a bolt of lightning, the thought almost crippled her. She remembered the nurse explaining how Tabassum was shot due to her alleged affair with a cop. And of all days, Kabir had walked into her office requesting her to save the gangster's moll.

'What?' Kabir could see his wife frown.

'Is she just an informer?' Fariza wanted to kill herself for asking the question. How could she possibly rely on rumours to insinuate what she did?

'What else?'

'Swear on Farhan that there is nothing else to it.' Fariza felt her toes curl within the shoes.

'What crap, Fariza!' Kabir banged his fist on the table. 'Are you trying to…'

'I just want you to confirm there is nothing else…' Fariza replied as calmly as she could.

'So, now you are going to ask me random questions just because the media houses are running around with false stories?' Kabir seethed in anger.

'Just swear on Farhan once that Tabassum is only an informer,' Fariza was unsettled by the anger in Kabir's voice, 'I won't ask you again.'

'I am not doing any such thing,' Kabir stood up. 'Believe what you want to.'

Fariza could feel her eyes well up with tears as Kabir darted out of the room. He had pulled the door so hard that it shook for a moment before it closed.

*

A week later, despite the best efforts from the team, Tabassum succumbed to her injuries. Kabir earned praises for heroically arresting the gangster but he ended up confessing his affair to Fariza. She cried for a couple of days but didn't delve into the matter. She even refused to listen to any kind of explanation. While Kabir was away at work, she packed Farhan's belongings and her stuff and walked out of the house. Months passed filled with requests, marriage counselling sessions, family discussions and court cases before an eventual non-amicable split.

***

Fariza looked through the glass as Anshuman sat in the ICU, next to Reva's bed. It was not a favour she did for everyone. But somewhere in her heart, she felt connected to the man sitting inside. He had brought back a chapter of her life and the penitence that she had long effaced from her life came creeping in. She had strictly instructed him not to touch Reva or any of the equipments. And she knew he wouldn't. It was just a formal instruction from a doctor, just because she had to say something.

Anshuman sat hesitantly on the stool next to Reva's bed. He had sceptically accepted the offer, remembering how he had freaked out the last time he saw her in the ICU. But he wanted to talk to her, even if she couldn't listen. He wanted to see her, even if she couldn't see. He wanted to feel her presence even if she couldn't realise it. Tonight, he wanted to be with her without anyone intruding. It was long overdue.

Anshuman looked at the heart beat rate. It was steady, hovering around sixty. The saline was flowing into her body. The silence in the room was awkward. Anshuman could clearly hear the sound of saline dripping into the tube.

'Why did you do this to me, Reva?' Anshuman said aloud. 'Why did you do this to me?'

Reva looked unusually calm, breathing slowly, her face covered by the oxygen mask.

'You knew how I much loved you,' Anshuman went on. 'You knew it, didn't you? Then, what went wrong? What went so terribly wrong that made you fall in love with another man?'

Anshuman could feel his eyes moisten. He fought hard to hold back the tears. Tonight, he wanted to speak to her, undisturbed. Not even his tears could come in the way.

'Yes, we had our share of problems. But who does not? Which couple is absolutely perfect?' Anshuman rubbed the tears trickling down his cheeks. 'You knew I was chasing my long-standing dream. And you supported me. You had stood by me whenever I had spoken about pursuing these goals and fulfilling them. You knew me more than anyone did. Then why, baby? Why did you hold it against me when I was desperately trying to grasp what I wanted so badly? I promised I would give more time to our home, to our relation, to us. And you knew I meant it. All I needed was time. Couldn't you give me that much?'

Anshuman could feel his jaws tighten. He wondered if he would be able to muster courage and ask her these questions when she woke up.

'If things were that bad, why didn't you tell me about it? Why did you manage my home and pretend everything was alright? Why did we need a Siddharth Kashyap to tell us where we went wrong?'

A strange feeling of surprise, hope and despair rushed through his veins as Anshuman volleyed his next set of questions into nothingness.

'Will you really wake up and tell me he is lying? Will that really happen? I want it to, but I don't think that will happen. The man seems honest. Why didn't you tell me the truth? If you were happier with someone else than you were with me, couldn't you say that? Why did I have to know it from him? Didn't you ever think how would I feel when I would eventually discover this?'

Anshuman knew all his questions were going unheard. He cursed himself for being so desperate, so melodramatic for no reason. Still, he wanted to get the questions out of his system.

Would she give him the chance to ask the questions when she woke up? Or would she walk out on him with Siddharth? No, his heart thumped ferociously, she couldn't do that to him. After four years of staying together, how could she possibly do that to him? Had she really wanted to desert him, couldn't she have easily done so when he had been away? But she didn't. A part of Anshuman's heart convinced him that Reva wanted to stay back.

'What do you want to do now?' he spoke. 'I want you to be back with me. I want you to be with me. After all, we love each other, don't we? We were happy. Even if there were minor issues, we came out of those. We can fight this together.'

As he spoke, an overwhelming urge to cry seemed to get the better of him. Anshuman, despite all his efforts to combat the grief, succumbed to the same. He breathed heavily, trying desperately to fend off the moments of weakness. He was alone with Reva, and even if she wasn't listening to him, he could not afford to cry.

'Forget everyone else. It's just about us. What others think or opine doesn't matter. What we think about us is important. This one day will soon be forgotten. People will stop talking about it. Anyway, not many people know about this. Dipa, Shubho, Sophie, Chand – they are all friends. I have not even told our families about it. They don't need to know – they won't be able to handle it. We are their ideal kids. Milind looks up to us. Why should we spoil it? Get up baby, get well... we need to amend many a thing.'

Anshuman wanted to stretch out to hold her hand. But he was strictly instructed not to touch her. He needed to curb himself. It was extremely kind of Dr Ahmed to let him sit in the room in the first place. Anshuman wondered if he could bend over and kiss Reva's forehead once. It had been some time since they shared their last moment of affection. The last time they warmed up to each other he had felt things would look up, but they had only gone downhill. If this was the last chance, he was willing to give everything to make his marriage work.

'For every instance I made you angry, for every time I acted irresponsibly, for every promise I left unfulfilled, for every mistake that took you away from me,' Anshuman could feel a huge lump in his throat, 'I am sorry, baby. I am very very sorry. You are the world to me. I cannot imagine this life without you. I cannot imagine myself without you. Please wake up and help me put every misplaced thing back in its place.'

***

A floor below, Siddharth Kashyap looked aimlessly outside the window in his room. He wished he could walk out and see Reva once. His head was still aching. The right arm felt heavy. There was no way he could climb the stairs stealthily. Almost inevitably he would get caught. But the desire to see her was growing every moment. There was no one else who would know what he felt. Even if she didn't open her eyes and comfort him, the very sight of her would alleviate his tension.

In the last one day, no one had been kind to him. He didn't fail to observe that. Though inconspicuously, Dr Ahmed had stopped speaking to him. All her instructions were to the man legally attached to Reva. It seemed as if she didn't care for the fact that he was the one who brought Reva to the hospital in the middle of the night, bleeding profusely himself. As soon as Anshuman arrived, he was sidelined in any discussion pertaining to Reva.

Anshuman himself had not left any stone unturned to humiliate him. If getting a cop was the last resort, the man had done even that. As if it was all pre-planned, the cop tried to pin him down. He had to bear the insult just because he had registered her with his surname to avoid complications or any delay in the treatment. At four in the morning, with things seemingly getting out of hand, how could he have called Anshuman and waited for the latter to arrive till things got rolling? But no one seemed to even bother.

Sophie had barged into his room to add exacerbate the pain. Like everyone else, she had only reinstated that at the root of all problems was *he* – a selfish guy who prioritised himself above everything else. According to her, he was neither a good friend nor possibly a good lover. Wasn't *he* the one who had accepted Chand without any hesitation? He had held Chand's secret close to his heart, supporting and comforting his friend whenever the latter required. But tonight she didn't bother that no one else had cared for her fiancé as much as he did.

Siddharth had loved Reva – a love that never asked her to prioritise her aspects in life. He gave her space and understood her even when she darted out of his house, accusing him of trying to ambush her. He had waited for her to choose the man she loved. It was tougher for him to know that Reva would go back every night to the man she was married to and any day she might decide to call off their relation and stay with her family. But he hung on, because he had an unflinching belief that whatever she did would be the best for them. And Chand said *he* didn't know what faith was.

Why was his love not important – just because he was not married to her? How could a ceremony or the lack of it possibly make him any less important? He loved her no less. But no one was willing to try and be in his position and realise what he was going through. He was just a target for ridicule and no one had any clue about the relation he shared with Reva. This had to end. Reva had to wake up and tell the world that he meant as much to her as she meant to him. She had to wake up. Till then, he only wanted to walk up and see her face once, and reassure himself that things would be alright.

Siddharth pushed his left arm on the bed and slowly got up. The crutch was beside the bed. Yet, it seemed too far as he tried to roll sideward and drag his feet to the floor. The right foot was bandaged with thick cotton and wouldn't get into the slipper. He tried to stretch and wear the white slipper but it only moved further away. Siddharth felt his breathing become heavy even from this minor movement. The doctor had strictly advised not to budge, but he couldn't keep lying down. Siddharth took a couple of deep breaths and slowly got up. As his left foot touched the floor, the cold from it seemed to send a shiver through his body. He held the bed with his unhurt arm and wore the slipper. Managing his weight on the same, he ambled inconveniently and grasped the crutch.

As he peeped out of the door, a nurse walked past. She immediately saw him and rushed in.

'What are you doing, sir?' she sounded paranoid.

'I want to go upstairs,' he said brazenly walking outside.

'But you cannot do that,' she chided. 'You are not supposed to walk out of room now. It's 3:30 in the morning.'

'Obviously I can,' Siddharth pressed the crutch with his underarm and moved towards the elevator. 'I want to go to the ICU to meet Reva. And don't tell me about timetables and routines. I am not a visitor here. I am...'

'I know,' she strictly replied. 'But I can't allow a patient to walk out of his room.'

'You are not helping me or yourself us by arguing, sister,' Siddharth held the wall and looked at the nurse. 'I am going upstairs. If you can think of any way to make it easier for me, you should do that instead.'

The nurse looked at him in despair. She realised that the obstinate patient in front of her would not listen.

'Wait,' she looked at him. 'Don't walk in this condition. Let me get you a wheelchair.'

Nineteen

Anshuman-Reva-Siddharth

Akashdeep Mehra sat across him at the table. He looked at his father with penitent eyes. It had become usual of him to forget promises. And with his additional job of writing lyrics, it had almost become habitual. Reva had stopped complaining, though her nonchalance was conspicuous in every reaction. Akashdeep, a constant witness to the growing apathy between her son and daughter-in-law, had only his son to blame for spoiling what seemed to be a perfect family.

'This is not the first time,' Akashdeep said as the maid served dinner.

'I know, Papa,' Anshuman turned his plate and looked back at his father. 'You know the reason as well.'

'How old are you right now?' Akashdeep didn't wait for the answer, 'A few months from now, and you will be midway through your 30s. You need to start a family now and not run after money like a maniac.'

'It's not just about money,' Anshuman took a spoonful of vegetables from the bowl and served himself. 'It's something I always wanted to do.'

'First you wanted to do advertising,' his father went on, 'and you left your parents. Now, you want to write lyrics and you don't spend time with your wife. In the first case you found a woman to stand by you. Whom will you find this time?'

'I am not as selfish as you might think,' Anshuman looked at his father. 'I love Reva as much as I have loved Maa and you.'

'In that case, Anshu,' Akashdeep looked fondly at his son, 'you have to make her feel that.'

Anshuman didn't reply.

'I am going to Lucknow for some time,' Akashdeep Mehra said. 'By the time I come back, I hope you will make things better.'

**

Reva sat on the bed working on her laptop. She wore a white night-suit that fitted her frame perfectly, with her loose bun kissing the shoulders. She looked up once as he walked across the room and entered the washroom.

'Why didn't you eat anything?' he asked.

'I told you,' she looked up briefly, 'I had a heavy snack in the evening.'

He brushed his teeth while she kept scrutinising her reports.

'Anything urgent?' he wiped his face. 'You look grave!'

'Nothing as such,' this time she didn't even look up, 'just checking some reports before they are finalised for print.'

Their conversation had been this formal ever since he returned from London, though neither of them brought up the argument that had marred their relation on the day he left. It was the first time since their first meeting that they had spent a birthday separately. Every year, they ensured that the other's birthday was always celebrated. A couple of days after reaching London, Anshuman had sent a mail and she had replied with a "Thanks", but both of them knew how insincere it was. Anshuman had made some efforts to warm up their relation but more than a month had passed and nothing really seemed to work.

'What time is it?' he asked.

'Quarter to ten,' she replied, 'and the date is 27th February 2011.'

'Why are you talking like that?'

'How come you are wearing a watch and asking me the time?' she pointed at his arm.

'No,' he chuckled and walked up to the bed. 'I was just wondering, why don't we go out for a while, have a coffee or something? Carter Road or Versova maybe?'

'I said I am checking some reports for print,' she replied brusquely.

'I know,' he sat next to her. 'But you can always finish these once you are back, can't you? It won't take long.'

'How come you think my work can wait when yours can never?' she looked straight into his eyes.

'Baby, come on,' he held her hand. 'Let's not argue. I can't recall the last time we sat together and had a pleasant talk over coffee or anything for that matter.'

'If you really need to talk to you wife, Anshu,' she briskly removed her hand from underneath his, 'you need to be with her.'

'I am trying to be with you,' he spoke earnestly.

'Like, right now?' the disgust was overt in the way she spoke. 'A relationship is not a one-way street, Anshuman Mehra, that you cajole me into a talk when you want to and just pack your bags when you don't want to.'

'I shouldn't have gone like that, I know...' Anshuman looked sincere but not remorseful.

'And you didn't even call me after that,' she said roughly. 'It was my birthday. You sent a mail as if I should be satisfied with just that.'

'I want to make up for that.'

'By giving me the pleasure of your company over a cup of coffee?' She could not believe that Anshuman could take things for granted.

'This is not done. I am trying to mend things.'

'How? How do you think we should mend things?'

He reached out for her hands again and held them gently.

'I think we should start a family,' he smiled. 'Maybe a child would do wonders to our home.'

'Or maybe the child would bear the brunt of its parents' relationship,' she shot back.

'What?' He looked nonplussed.

'No, Anshu...' she shut her laptop and kept it aside. 'I don't want my child to come into this world as a solution to our problems. Trust me, for a quandary between two adults, a child is neither the cause nor the solution. We haven't successfully dealt with our issues. Why should be presume that the child would come and take care of everything? What if we still can't? The child will grow up in an unhappy home. And I, of all people, don't want that to happen to my kid.'

'For god's sake, Reva,' Anshuman got up. 'You think I want a child because I can't find a solution to our problems? Really? I felt it's time that we take our relation to the next stage. Having a child is just a gradual progression. I don't need the child to bear the brunt, but want him to grow up with parents who are still young and capable of taking care of him. I don't know about other stuff but blaming each other is surely not a solution to our problems.'

He stood at the window and lit a cigarette, fuming and emitting his smoke intermittently. Reva sat on the bed, running her fingers through her hair and clasping it to control the pain that throbbed in her head. She had avoided any discussion till now for she was sure any such attempt would culminate into another argument. She was tired of the rift.

For a long while, the two remained silent. When Reva eventually looked up, Anshuman was still at the window, breathing heavily, the second cigarette burnt through midway. She rubbed her eyes slowly got up and walked over to Anshuman.

'Anshu...' he kept her hand on his shoulder.

Anshuman turned to look at her.

'I am sorry,' she said. Somewhere in her heart, a feeling haunted her – it was she and not him who was still apologising. She smiled, 'And I thought it's the husbands who always say *sorry*. Not in my case at least.'

'Reva...'

She cut his explanation short and went on. 'Let it be. Shall we go get some coffee?'

*

That night, Anshuman and Reva made love again. It was not as heartfelt as it used to be earlier. It took time for Reva to respond to his touch, to his fondling but her body gradually reciprocated. Anshuman seemed a tad desperate, something that didn't go well with his stoic personality. But then in the end, they just did it.

***

The strum of guitar chords filled the air. Siddharth lay on his couch, dressed in three quarter cargos and a purple t-shirt, listening to his friend sing as the latter crooned an old Goanese folk number. Chand sat across the room, deeply immersed in the song while his curly locks hid his face. In the black kurta and jeans, Chand seemed to have evolved from his unkempt days of Mira Road. It was after a long time that the two friends had planned the night-out at their Andheri apartment. Despite being neighbours, their personal lives and professional schedules had forced them to put off the get-together. So, they decided to revisit their early days of professional strife and spend quality time, away from mobile phones, in the flat that saw them rise to excellence.

'So, when are you getting married?' Siddharth asked when Chand finished his song.

'17th April,' the musician took a gulp from his bottle of beer. 'I told you. It's a Sunday.'

'Yeah, I remember it's a Sunday,' Siddharth nodded. 'Any pre-wedding jitters?'

'What jitters?' Chand chuckled as he turned the pages of his diary. 'Sophie is a great girl. And she is taking care of everything.'

'What are you going to do then, asshole?' Siddharth kept his beer on the floor. 'Sing at your own wedding?'

Chand laughed out aloud.

'My parents will arrive a week before the date,' he clarified. 'They will oversee all the last moment preparations.'

'They must be really happy,' Siddharth remarked.

'You bet,' Chand adjusted his guitar for the next song. 'Well, not that they ever knew I could also settle with a man.'

'Thank god for that,' Siddharth winked, 'or else they would have thought I was that man.'

Both of them laughed at the last remark.

Siddharth clumsily sang along with his friend as he began the next song. It was Pink Floyd's "Comfortably Numb", one of the all time classics and their mutual favourite. Chand didn't mind when his friend sang with him, mostly off-key. Their jamming after all was never really synchronised.

'Well, what about you, Mr Kashyap?' Chand said as Siddharth took out two bottles of Corona for Chand and himself. 'My bachelorhood expires soon. How long will your innings last?'

'No clue,' Siddharth handed over the beer to Chand. 'Let's see.'

For someone who always said, *I am happily single... don't talk about marriage... I am not husband material...* the reply was a marked change. And for someone who had known him for so long, the answer was bound to come as a surprise.

'Excuse me, what did you just say?' Chand looked at his friend, 'No clue! That means you are trying to find a clue, Sid?'

'Could be,' Siddharth smiled.

'Are you seeing someone?' Chand's curiosity was now increasing with every passing moment.

'You can say so,' Siddharth replied sheepishly, correctly anticipating the response.

'Fuck, man,' Chand got up. 'And when were you going to tell me this? I mean, had I not taken up the topic now, you would have just evaded it altogether.'

'Oh I was so sure you would take it up some time during the night,' Siddharth winked. 'You are just too inquisitive.'

'Don't be a smartass, Sid,' Chand wanted to walk over and smack his friend's nose. 'Who is she?'

'There's a girl...' Siddharth played on.

'Of course it's a girl and a pretty one,' Chand stared at his friend. 'But who is she?'

'How do you know she is pretty?' Siddharth was taken aback by the usage of the adjective, and by the conviction with which his friend used it.

'Oh, your machismo won't allow you to settle down with someone not pretty...'

Siddharth wondered if Chand's observation was right. Of course, Reva was pretty, but was it a coincidence or natural consequence. Was he so obsessed with looks? *Well,* he comforted himself, *which man doesn't want his girl to look great.*

'Someone I know?' Chand asked.

'Perhaps!'

'What perhaps?' Chand couldn't hide his excitement.

'Yes,' Siddharth appeased, knowing pretty well that the affirmation will only stimulate his friend's excitement.

'Shit!' Chand couldn't believe his best friend was dating a girl he knew. 'Dude, don't tell me it's Maya Bose. I mean she is single now.' Chand felt his feet go numb at the thought of how to react if Sid said yes. 'But are you dating her?'

'Maya Bose?' Siddharth guffawed. 'Dude, you've totally lost it.'

'Who is it then?' Chand blurted out. 'Come on, man. Why are you acting so pricey?'

'Nothing, dude,' Siddharth placated his friend. 'I will tell you when the time is right.'

'What's wrong with now?' Chand persisted.

'Dude,' Siddharth got up from his couch and walked towards the window. 'She is married.'

It took him a moment, but Chand collected himself promptly.

'No shit,' Chand grasped the bottle which was slipping from his hand. 'You are dating a married woman?'

'Why?' Siddharth looked back at his friend who stood a few feet behind him.

'Come on, there are plenty of single girls who have an eye on you,' Chand drank his beer. 'Why get into someone's happy married life?'

'Why would she be with me if her marriage was happy?' Siddharth replied defensively.

'Still...' Chand pursed his lips. 'Are you really serious about this?'

'Let's see...' Siddharth smiled and turned to face outside.

'You are an ass....' Chand laughed. He was certain it was a casual fling; Siddharth couldn't really have played his cards that badly. He moved back to the bean bag and picked up his guitar.

Siddharth stared outside blankly. Was this relation really going in an untoward direction? *Certainly not*, he assured himself, *Reva and I are madly in love. But I can't tell Chand how serious it is.* Chand revered Anshuman Mehra way too much to stand by him in this. Possibly when the opportune moment arose, he would tell him everything. His parents were supposed to arrive in a week. He wanted them to meet Reva. He was sure they would love her. But would they have similar reservations as Chand? Siddharth was sure his parents would never approve of the relationship if they knew Reva was married – they were too conservative. Divorce for them was blasphemy. But he could still convince them. If they had supported him all throughout his career, then it should not be a big deal. The toughest question, however, was whether Reva would leave Anshuman Mehra to be with him.

***

'You cannot take out your personal vengeance in an interview,' Dipanwita spoke aloud. 'For all I know, Rajvardhan Bhalla might sue us for defamation. And I don't want that to happen.'

Reva stared at her boss, unabashed but quiet. She had just returned after an interview with Rajvardhan Bhalla. She was supposed to enquire about his company's newly acquired stake in an EPL football team. The country was rejoicing with their celebrity industrialist now becoming a known face in an arena, which they had only seen on TV. And Bhalla was basking in the glory, much of what could be attributed to the earnings of his father-in-law's parent company. While it was expected of Reva to be in awe of the man and come out fawning on him, her questions were non-adulatory, to say the least. She had questioned him about his personal life, the source of his investment in the club, his failed investments in hotels, his equation with wife and his alleged affairs with other women. While Bhalla tried to reply to the other questions with a straight face, it was the last one that had left him incensed. He brusquely ended the interview, and presumably called Dipanwita right after it.

'Are you getting what I am trying to say?' Dipanwita leaned on the table and looked at her junior. 'We cannot make him uncomfortable, no matter what he does to your friend.'

Reva looked at her boss, startled by the harshness of the statement.

'Samaira Khan chose to be what she is,' Dipanwita went on. 'That's not my problem, not yours, and definitely not this company's.'

Reva had rarely heard her boss being so blatant about anything. Dipanwita was never one of those to behave unctuously for rich and powerful men. Of all people they knew, Rajvardhan Bhalla was surely not one of her favourites. Thus, the sudden change in her stance came as a surprise.

'What's wrong with you Reva?' Dipanwita spoke, her voice suddenly calmer.

'I shouldn't have asked him about his personal life,' Reva said, not looking into her senior's eyes.

'Exactly,' Dipanwita replied. She paused for a moment, studying Reva's reaction. 'You have never done such a thing before.' She leaned back into her seat. 'Personally, I don't expect this from you. If Bhalla's company stops its advertisements in our paper, how are we going to explain this to the business development team?'

Reva nodded. From a practical point of view, Dipanwita's stand was right; there was no ambivalence in it.

'Look at me, Reva,' Dipanwita spoke calmly.

Reva looked up to find her boss staring at her, as if reading every thought that crossed her mind. She had unknowingly intertwined herself with Sam's life, and the fact that Dipanwita might just discover it was unsettling.

'Why are you so bothered about what's happening between Bhalla and Samaira?'

For a moment, Reva could feel her limbs tremble in the anxiety of responding to the question. What could she possibly say – because her own life was getting as uncertain as Samaira's? She might not be Siddharth's mistress but there was no name that could possibly define what they shared. She was sleeping with two men, unable to forgo either. She had no clue why she was doing so. She was not in a perfectly happy marriage, but then who really has one of those. Then, why was she holding on to Siddharth Kashyap? Was it purely because he made her feel better? Or was it his randomness that brought about a change in Anshuman's button-down way of looking at everything? Yet, it was the same quality that made Anshu a more reliable husband, didn't it?

'Reva,' Dipanwita spoke and broke her reverie.

Reva looked up startled, her eyes still unsure of the reality that so starkly lay ahead.

'What happened?' Dipa asked. 'What's bothering you?'

'Samaira,' Reva was perplexed by the way she answered straight-faced to this question.

'I've known her much longer than you do,' Dipanwita leaned ahead and held her junior's hand. 'She will be alright. She learns her lessons pretty well.'

Reva looked quizzically at her boss. Dipanwita leaned back on her chair and sighed.

'Once you sell your soul to the devil, it never lets you go.'

**

Reva stepped out of her boss' cabin. She was reeling under a sudden sense of guilt. Were people going to talk about her the same way they were talking about Samaira? She looked ahead but suddenly everything started spinning. Reva stretched out her hand for support but there was nothing to grip. A sudden sense of helplessness seemed to debilitate her body. Jennifer saw her from the other end of the room, and rushed towards her.

'Are you alright?' Jenny held Reva's arm. 'What happened?'

'Just been over-working,' Reva breathed heavily as she spoke. 'I am fine. Need to go to the washroom.'

'Shall I take you?' Jenny looked concerned.

'No,' Reva shook her head. 'It's okay.'

Only she knew how much strength it took to drag herself down the corridor, yet pretend to be fine. There was a swarm of eyes staring at her, each intending to help. Almost as she entered the toilet, her entire body convulsed and she bent over to puke into the commode.

The water was still dripping from her face, as she stood in the washroom, looking at herself in the mirror. She knew what it was. It was not the consequence of hard work. It had first struck her when the menstrual cycle hadn't started at the scheduled time. She thought it was just getting delayed. But now, she was almost certain what it was. The implication shook the ground beneath her feet. She needed to meet a gynaecologist and confirm her suspicion. She knew any hope of finding a contrary result would be futile. She knew who the father was, but it was the thought of intimating the other that killed her. How could she possibly tell the other man about it? She was a bitch. She was the one they both would blame. And rightfully so! It was her indecisiveness that had brought everyone to this juncture. She picked up her mobile phone which was lying beside the washbasin and dialled Siddharth's number.

***

The taxi meandered through the Four Bungalows traffic, making its way towards Versova. The smell of incense sticks kept before the picture of Sai Baba permeated through the stench of gutkha that the driver was chewing. Reva looked outside vaguely, her mind wandering into a state of chaos, yet unable to solve that one question – 'How will the other man deal with it?'

'Can you please hurry up?' she said as the driver's mobile phone rang again. Thankfully, her tone worked and this time, the driver didn't answer the phone.

March had just started and it was slowly starting to get warm. She could see the frowns on people's faces as they made their way in the heat. Though the denizens never experienced winter, the heat was not something they ever got accustomed to. As her mother would say, *You might compromise with something you don't like, but you never get used to it.* Irony, of course, is the bitterest truth of life.

Even when her mind raced with anticipations of multiple reactions from everyone, an unusual thought struck her, bringing a sudden lining of a smile on her lips. *By the end of the year, I will be a mother.* Amidst all her anxieties, she hadn't cherished the biggest gift of her life - she was rearing a child in her womb, her own child. Nothing was more precious than that. What Anshuman would feel and how Siddharth would react – nothing mattered more than the fact that it was her baby growing within. A scooter stopped right next to her cab. A young woman sat ahead with a young boy clenching her waist tightly from behind. The boy looked at Reva. She winked playfully at him. The toddler responded with a wide grin. The lady's glance fell on Reva. She turned back and saw her son. The women exchanged smiles.

***

The signal showed the gradual descent of the elevator from the 17th floor. Reva took her phone out and dialled Siddharth's number. Somehow, she had anticipated he would call her on the way and pester to come quickly, just the way he did every time. After all, it was his juvenile spirit which enamoured her the most. But there had been no call that day. As happy as he seemed on getting a call from her, he hadn't called back even once to ask how far she had reached. That was pretty unlikely of him. The phone kept ringing for half a minute before he finally picked it up.

'Hey,' he sounded cheerful, yet exhausted.

'What happened?' Reva said anxiously.

'What?' she could feel his smile. 'Tell me, where you have reached?'

'I am downstairs,' she replied. 'Why are you panting?'

'Nothing as such,' he ignored the question. 'Come up.'

The elevator stealthily moved up the eight floors as Reva wondered how to hatch the topic of the child in front of Siddharth. As the elevator doors finally parted and she stepped out, she saw him standing there, dressed in a casual pair of t-shirt and jeans, sweating profusely yet smiling merrily at her.

'Hi,' Reva smiled as they stepped forward and hugged each other.

'Why are you sweating so much?' Reva said as they parted. 'I mean, I know it's getting warm and all, but not so much…'

Siddharth grinned at the remark. 'It's just the travelling,' he held her hand. 'Good that you came today. I was going to call you up.'

'Why are you beating around the bush?' Reva said as they moved towards his flat, 'I can't make out anything.'

'Oh! I didn't tell you, did I?' Siddharth bit his tongue. 'My parents have come over from Ajmer. I want you to meet them.'

'What?' Reva almost jolted to a halt.

'I want you to meet my parents.'

'Why would you want to do that?' Reva looked alarmed, 'And why didn't you tell me that your parents are here?'

'I forgot, yaar,' Siddharth said apologetically. 'But what's the harm in it. We are in love. My parents have come. I want you guys to know each other.'

'Siddharth, you know I am married,' Reva spoke hastily. 'You cannot ask your parents to meet a married woman. As what? Why would they want to meet me? And forget them, why do you think I would want to meet them?'

'Baby,' Siddharth came closer, 'I thought we would talk about a relation sooner or later. Meeting my parents would give you a clearer picture about my background.'

'Listen, Siddharth,' Reva raised her hand and forbade him from coming forward. 'We haven't talked about a relation. You cannot ambush me like this by introducing me to your parents.'

'I am not trying to ambush you,' Siddharth defended his stand. 'I just wanted to get things on track. They keep telling me that I should get married but am not committed to anyone. So, I wanted to let them know why I haven't talked about marriage – that I have chosen someone and want to spend my life with her.'

'Yeah right! And what do you think will this impromptu meeting achieve?' Reva looked straight at him. 'How do you think they will react when they come to know that you are dating someone not only elder to you but also married to someone else?'

'Of course it isn't something they see every day or consider as a part of their culture,' Siddharth replied aloud. 'But they have always stood by me in all my decisions. And I am sure they will do so even this time around.'

'You know what, Siddharth,' Reva spoke exasperated by his explanation. 'You need to grow up. Just because you felt your parents are accommodating enough to accept a married woman as their son's bride, you had no right to trap me here like this. You had no right to deceive me by concealing the presence of your parents.'

'That's not fair Reva,' Siddharth spoke a little hurt. 'I have put up with everything in your life without complaining. This is the first time I am asking you to be a part of mine. Is it such an impossible thing to do?'

'Not when you ask after putting me in a spot,' Reva shook her head. 'I am not going in there, look like a fool, bear their disapproving nods and shocked reactions. No!'

With those last words, Reva turned around and hurried towards the lift. This time, Siddharth didn't call her from behind. Neither did he make an attempt to stop her. As he looked on quietly, Reva got into the elevator and disappeared without turning back even once.

***

It was a late Thursday evening as she looked up from the pages of "The Little Red Book" and stared blankly at him. He stood in the balcony, his body barely visible in whatever little light the table lamp threw. The shamrock green sari was draped over her body, as she rolled on the bed with the book in her hand. His white kurta fell unabashedly over his bare legs as he stood there, smoking. She hadn't disclosed it to him yet. All she could say to console herself was that the right moment would come soon. However, the dilemma made Reva restive as she deliberately attempted to divert her mind by doing multiple things at the same time, purely in an effort to keep her mind of the anxiety.

'It's tough to agree to all of it,' she volleyed from bed.

'You don't need to agree,' he replied without looking back. 'It's about his perception and ideologies.'

She pursed her lips. 'Hmmm... true.'

'And in any case,' he turned to look at her. 'He is long dead to argue with you.'

Was he joking or was he being sarcastic? As he turned away again, she realised she had failed to understand him. Perhaps the same way, he had failed to interpret her over and over again. But, whom had she really decoded? The man she legally stayed with or the man who accompanied her illicitly. Neither. Pretty much like they never managed to know her fully! Yet, she loved them. Both of them, each for his own reasons! And they loved her back in return – possibly more than she loved them. Yet, as much as they loved her, they hardly seemed to observe the recent change in her. She looked frailer, got exhausted and stayed away from everything she had gorged on earlier. Nothing, absolutely nothing seemed amiss to them.

Anshuman had noticed none of it. Like most other things in life besides work, he was blissfully oblivious. And thanks to the increasing lyric writing assignments, he stayed even more aloof. On the other hand, Siddharth was so ecstatic when she spoke to him three days after their argument that he found everything normal. Even when they met, he was so enthusiastic talking about his new assignment for a series of commercials, that he overlooked the fact that she had abruptly left the table twice. *Men*, she smirked to herself.

The landline started ringing in the drawing room. She got up from the bed clumsily and walked out into the drawing room. Barely ten minutes were left to strike ten as she lifted the receiver, her eyes glancing over the framed photographs hanging on the wall.

'Hello,' Reva said.

'Reva?' Krutika Gokhale spoke from the other end of the phone. Reva should have guessed it. Her mother was the only one who spared the phone from disuse.

'Aai,' Reva. 'How are you?'

'I am not fine,' the reply surprised Reva.

'Why? What happened?' she asked anxiously. 'Is Papa alright?'

'How can he be alright?' Krutika lamented.

'Can you be specific about what you want to say?' Reva sounded irritated.

'Your brother has made our lives miserable,' Krutika grumbled.

'Now what did he do?' Reva unplugged the portable handset and walked into the bedroom. 'In any case, you don't miss an opportunity to blame him.'

'He has failed in his exams,' Krutika cried. 'Can you believe that?'

'He failed?' Reva sounded surprised.

Anshuman turned to look at his wife.

'Just imagine,' Krutika Gokhale complained. 'His father is a principal and he fails in his college exams. Who fails in engineering? You tell me. People study for a fortnight before an exam and still score good marks... And this scoundrel... I can't make him study for even an hour a day.'

Anshuman could see his wife wince as the voice of his mother-in-law emanated from the receiver at a volume audible to him. He smiled and pointed at her to put the phone on loudspeaker.

'Your father has given up hope,' the voice was feebler due to the loudspeaker. 'And so have I. In any case, he has never listened to me. Maybe you can drill some sense into him.'

Anshuman signalled at his wife to maintain her cool over the phone.

'Give the phone to him,' Reva sat on the bed. 'I will talk to Milind.'

Anshuman smoked with an air of purported nonchalance as his brother-in-law haplessly took over the receiver from his mother and heard, for what Anshuman was sure, the third bashing of the day. He was only surprised to think why the young boy was being made a scapegoat when the entire engineering exercise had been imposed on him against his will. The guy was passionate about music, and though his parents had trained him in the same, they never allowed him to pursue it as earnestly as he wanted to. Pretty much as Anshuman anticipated, Milind fared poorly in the course. After struggling for two years in subjects he hated, the chap flunked in the fifth semester. Somewhere down the line, Anshuman could relate Milind's struggle to his own, and how he could never convince his father that he was meant for creative arts. When Anshuman finally took over the phone from his wife, the first question he asked surprised Reva and his parents-in-law.

'What do you really want to do, Milind?'

Someone had finally said something he wanted to hear, and Milind burst out crying. Anshuman nodded at his wife to indicate that this was what Reva needed to do as the senior sibling.

'Stop crying,' Anshuman spoke as a doting elder brother, 'and think what you would like to see yourself doing five years from now.'

'Jiju,' Milind sobbed, 'I hate engineering.'

'I know,' Anshuman said calmly. 'But that's not the point. The question is what do you love? What do you want to do?'

'Music,' Milind replied promptly. The answer was to the surprise of none.

'We all know that, I assume,' Anshuman replied. 'Now tell me... what you want to do with music. Play music with bands? There are far too many music bands in the country. How are you going to differentiate yourself?'

'Are you counselling him now?' Reva asked agitated. 'Haven't we been through this before?'

Instead of responding to his wife, Anshuman promptly cancelled the loudspeaker and picked up the receiver.

'You all have spoken to him,' Anshuman held the mouth of the phone with his hand, 'only to shout at him. Is that going to yield a result?'

Reva looked away in disgust.

'I was thinking I could do sound engineering from somewhere like FTII,' Milind replied timidly.

'Now, that's a plan,' Anshuman sounded upbeat. 'Awesome. But even they need graduates, right?'

'Yes,' Milind accepted, 'with physics at the 10+2 level.'

'So, you tell me now,' Anshuman lit another cigarette. 'Is doing another graduation look better on your CV or finishing this engineering?'

'This course,' Milind said the inevitable.

'So, take it up just like another stupid chore,' Anshuman puffed out the smoke, 'something that you will have to complete for a greater goal. No one expects you to top the class - neither your parents nor Taai. But at least finish the course so that you can do what you want to. Even when I had to shift from engineering to advertising, I knew I had to finish my course and prepare for my dream at the same time. And I did. My engineering was also a compromise but it surely fetched me some distinction in my batch. Your engineering might just do the same.'

'You are right,' Milind had controlled his sobs by now. 'What should I do now?'

'Take a re-test,' Anshuman smiled. 'Clear it and move ahead. The solution is right before us. All we need to do is to think peacefully and implement what's best for all of us.'

Anshuman won over his brother-in-law, who was already a devoted fan. However, the same appreciation didn't go down well with his wife, for whom the entire intervention came as unwelcome misguidance to a guy who had already been negligent towards his studies. She listened to their conversation without interrupting. However, the best thing to do at that point of time was to avoid it.

'There's no point talking about it now,' she told herself. *'Bring it up tomorrow morning.'*

***

Anshuman sat at the dining table, looking into his laptop and carelessly eating the parantha. He had a crucial presentation due the following day. Though he was not one to fret over presentations anymore, it was one of the special cases. Suraksha, one of the leading FMCG companies of India, was breaking its long-standing alliance with its ad-agency and looking for new partners to execute their marketing campaign. For Genesis, getting the contract would mean not only be an extra feather in its cap, but also one-upmanship over the market and crores of additional revenues. There were plenty of other players who were vying for the same account, and the entire Genesis team was looking up to Anshuman Mehra to get them this new client. What new concept could he propose to Suraksha which none of the other ad-agencies could? Sophie and he had worked for weeks over finalising every aspect of the offering – detailing the new brand positioning, segmenting the customers, determining the self-image and reflection of the TG, to even shooting a sample ad to provide Suraksha a fair idea to what they can expect in an association with Genesis. It was going to be a tough day ahead.

The following day was a Saturday and with the World Cup final, the meeting was in the first half. This meant that he needed to finish everything by the end of day. He had to oversee every detail and ensure there was nothing amiss. Bala Sir was well informed about every move, and though he planned to attend the meeting, he never thought of interfering in Anshuman's preparation. However, Anshuman planned to discuss the entire presentation with his mentor before they met their clients the following day.

'What time will you be back today?' Reva walked out of the room, dressed in a dark purple georgette sari complementing the black sleeveless blouse with purple hemlines. For a moment, Anshuman forgot that his wife had asked him a question. He kept staring at her. Still adjusting her bun, Reva had not noticed her husband's reaction.

'When will you be back?' she said again and looked at Anshuman.

'Not sure,' Anshuman responded. 'Why?'

'I need to talk to you,' she said curtly. 'When will you have time?'

'Umm… you can tell me now,' he said sceptically. 'Is there anything urgent?'

'About last night,' Reva sat down at the table and poured herself a cup of tea.

'What about last night?' Anshuman saved his presentation and closed the file.

'All the suggestions you had for Milind,' Reva looked at Anshuman.

'Yeah, go on…' Anshuman shut his laptop and lifted his bag to put in the computer.

'Why did you tell him that?' Reva asked.

'Huh?' Anshuman frowned and looked at his wife.

'About the entire sound engineering stuff and all,' Reva sipped the tea. 'Why are you adding fuel to that fire?'

'What's wrong with that?' Anshuman zipped the bag and looked at is wife. 'We all knew that he doesn't want to get technical. Still, we coerced him to do engineering. Now that he has failed, how come he is the only one to blame?'

'You mean we are responsible for his flunking the class?' Reva looked amazed at Anshuman's interpretation of the scenario.

'Of course you are,' Anshuman asserted. 'Had he been studying something he liked, maybe he would have done really well. But he was forced to do what others wanted.'

'Yeah right. You don't know Milind,' Reva raised her hand. 'You have absolutely no clue what the guy is capable of doing and not doing. You think he is going to excel in music? Just hanging headphones around your neck all day long doesn't make you a musician.'

'Of course not…'

'Baba got him enrolled into music when he was seven. I left my dance so that he could learn singing. But he has never done something great.'

'At least give him the chance to do so…'

'Anshu… how many good singers and instrumentalists do we have in India?'

'If every musician thought so, we would have had none.'

'Fair enough! But have you seen him doing something exceptionally well in music? Because I haven't….'

'Listen, there's no point discussing this. I know what it feels like when your parents impose something on you. I was someone who could stand up, be rude, rebel and get my things done. Milind is not like me. So, I will stand by him.'

'How come you are equating both the scenarios?' as much as Reva liked the way Anshuman empathised with Milind, she couldn't help but censure the naivety of the analogy. 'You were a brilliant student. You cracked the exam to get into your communications institute. You deserved to be there. Milind is not you.'

'You are assuming that he will not clear the tests for sound engineering?' Anshuman hated the tone for he had heard his father speak in the very same way, many a time.

'Yes, I am assuming that,' Reva stated firmly. 'Because there are about 13 seats and he will be competing with students far better than he is. What if he doesn't get through? How is "just passing" as you said going to help him get a job?'

'So, it's eventually about getting a job?'

'Of course it is. What else is he studying for?'

'I didn't think that you, of all people, would give more emphasis to a job instead of someone's passion.' Anshuman shook his head in despair.

'I wouldn't have if he were so meritorious that I could be certain he would crack any goddamn exam he appears for. But I know he isn't. And nobody knows him more than I do. If he can do anything with his career, it has to be on the beaten path.'

'Well, I don't support that. And if you think the way to get someone to perform is by underrating and demoralising him, then awesome. You guys know best.'

Anshuman pushed his chair back, taking Reva by surprise.

'What do you mean by you guys?'

'Don't you know what I mean by you guys?' Anshuman stared lividly at his wife. 'When you scream in front of your son as if he had killed someone "we have lost all hopes" blah blah – is that the way to talk about your son?'

'You don't need to teach anyone how to raise a kid,' Reva couldn't believe that Anshuman had just dragged in her mother into their argument. How could he possibly insult her mother? What does he know about her mother's contribution and sacrifices for them? Anshuman had never done such a thing before, but today he had crossed the line.

'I am not saying anything about how to raise a child. I am saying how you should react in front of your son. If you dramatise something and exaggerate your emotions, it doesn't help.'

'Oh really? So basically my mother was creating a scene there. Of all people, Anshuman Mehra, you are the last person to tell me about family dynamics. You called your father *"son of a bitch"* because your mother died. Your father walked out on your wedding because you had met your in-laws before introducing your girlfriend to him. I remember everything vividly.'

'You know what, of all things my family shared, they didn't raise a child who fails in college. Their son got admitted to the best institute even without guidance.'

Like many previous arguments, this one got worse as they hurled accusations at each other. There was no conclusion and neither of them made an attempt to put things aside. It only got uglier till Reva went into the bedroom and slammed the door. Within a minute, Anshuman Mehra walked out of the house with his bag, banging the main door even harder.

Twenty

Present Time

DAY 2
4:00 a.m.

The elevator door parted and the nurse pushed Siddharth Kashyap's wheelchair out. She seemed agitated with the patient who was being so troublesome at such an unexpected hour. The patient, however, looked calm and in control of the entire scene.

'None of the doctors will appreciate my bringing you here,' the nurse said angrily, 'especially at this hour.'

'But I do,' Siddharth said as they moved from the elevator towards the ICU. 'I really appreciate your cooperation.'

The nurse didn't respond. She was too flummoxed by the behaviour of the man to say anything.

'Can you open the door for me?' Siddharth asked unabashedly as they reached the entrance of the Intensive Care Unit.

'Sir, you can't go within the unit on a wheelchair,' she argued. 'All you can do is watch from here.'

'Well, I didn't come all the way just to stay outside,' Siddharth replied calmly, showing no signs of agitation.

'Listen to me, sir,' the nurse was agitated, 'It is…'

She was about to continue when the door of the ICU opened and a man in the blue kurta and jeans appeared in front of them. Siddharth seemed confounded seeing Anshuman Mehra standing in front of him though, somewhere in his heart, he had known that the latter might be present in the unit. Anshuman Mehra looked equally surprised to see Siddharth Kashyap – partly because of the wheelchair, but mostly because he didn't expect to see the man whom he wanted to push away from his life.

'How is she?' Siddharth asked.

'Better,' Anshuman replied softly. 'The doctor hopes she will recover soon.'

'Good,' Siddharth nodded.

'You can leave,' Anshuman looked at the nurse. 'I will take care of him.'

'Please ensure he doesn't enter the ICU,' the nurse seemed blessed by the intervention of this man. 'Not only do we need permission, we can't let him in because he is in a wheelchair.'

Anshuman looked at Siddharth without responding. The photographer didn't protest this time. He nodded calmly to the surprise of the nurse who thanked Anshuman and left with a smile. It was the way the nurse fled from the scene that bore testimony to the fact that she was relieved to be off her duty. Both men looked at the nurse hurrying towards the staircase.

'I assume you gave her a tough time,' Anshuman smirked at Siddharth.

'I am pretty capable of it, isn't it?' Siddharth replied dryly.

Anshuman couldn't help but smile at the instant remark.

'I am not in a mood to disagree,' he said straight-faced.

Siddharth looked up at the unexpected response and started smiling. They hated each other, but at this point of time, smiling was something they could afford to do.

'How come you don't feel sleepy even after all the painkillers?' the ad-wizard folded his hands and looked at the person he should have been so angry with.

'Well, I have cops waking me up,' Siddharth volleyed back promptly, 'don't I?'

Anshuman was still repentant about ACP Kabir's behaviour towards Siddharth Kashyap. Though it was evident that he hadn't intended that to happen, it happened as a consequence of him telling the cop. For a moment, he couldn't figure out an appropriate reply to the statement. He loosened his hands and looked apologetically at Siddharth.

'See, I really didn't want that to happen,' Anshuman scratched his left palm with his right thumb. 'I just wanted to ease out the insurance thing.'

'I know, Mr Mehra,' Siddharth blinked. 'I also saw your face when the man was interrogating me. Though I was angry with you, somewhere in my heart, I knew that you didn't want the questioning to turn out like that.'

'Thanks,' Anshuman nodded, putting his hands on his back for support, wondering what else to say.

Siddharth could feel his legs getting heavier. He had been instructed complete bed rest to ensure that his injured leg would heal quickly. But he knew that passing the night lying on a bed was just not going to happen. Yet, the swelling in the shin was invigorating every moment, along with the accompanying pain.

'I don't find these walls very interesting,' he flinched as he tried to move his right leg. 'Shall we go somewhere? Now that they won't allow me inside on this wheelchair...'

'Sure, where do you want to go?'

'I thought a cup of coffee would do me some good,' Siddharth smiled, 'since sleep won't be coming anywhere near us tonight.'

'I would love some masala tea as well,' Anshuman walked behind the wheelchair and began pushing it towards the elevator. 'I am sure you won't fall over another chair this time.'

'Yeah,' Siddharth leaned back. 'This one's already pretty big for me.'

***

He was still asleep when the bell rang twice. He had just returned from Colva the previous night after shooting a print ad commercial. He rolled over the bed and picked his watch lying on the stool. It was 11:15 a.m. Damn it. Whoever it was could wait till he got up. He adjusted his eye-cover and rolled over. Almost instantly, his phone rang with the automated heavily American accented voice saying "Reva". Siddharth scouted for the set on the bed before locating it underneath his pillow. He pressed the answer button.

'Hey, baby,' he said, his voice still somniferous.

'Where are you?' Reva said abruptly.

'I am at home,' he said, trying to stop yawning. 'Why?'

'Because I have been standing outside your door for the last 15 minutes...' she said.

'Oh,' Siddharth promptly answered, 'you should have called me earlier. I was asleep. So, I guess couldn't hear the bell.' Siddharth bit his tongue and hurried to open the door.

With the sunglasses on her temple, she was standing at the door, looking livid. For a moment, he failed to notice how gorgeous she looked in the purple sari. She darted past him into the house, threw her bag on the sofa and grabbed the water bottle from the dining table.

'How come you are here at this time?' Siddharth shut the door as she drank the water thirstily.

'You mind my being here?' Reva looked at him. Without waiting for his response, she walked to the sofa, picked up her bag and rushed towards the door.

'Relax,' Siddharth stood up alarmed and his drowsiness instantly vanished. 'Why are you so pissed off? I just asked you a simple question.'

'I am sure it's a trivial question,' Reva stopped short, breathing heavily. 'Whatever you guys say is minor, only I do all the wrong things.'

Siddharth was still clueless about the reason behind her anger. He had never seen her so furious, not even the day when she left, unwilling to meet his parents. However, he realised that she had a bitter argument with Anshuman Mehra.

'Okay,' *he walked cautiously and held her arms.* 'Let's sit down and have a cup of coffee.'

'I don't want to have coffee,' *Reva threw her bag across the room.* 'I just want to sit in peace. Can I?'

'Of course,' *Siddharth was more than happy to oblige.* 'Just sit in peace.'

She walked back towards the sofa and collapsed on it.

'You want me to turn on the music,' *Siddharth wondered what would calm her down,* 'maybe something soft.'

'No,' *she didn't even look at him. She just stared outside the window.*

'Okay,' *Siddharth sighed.* 'Can I have a quick wash and come back in five?'

Reva nodded, looking vaguely at the open space outside.

Siddharth paced into the washroom and brushed his teeth as quickly as he could. He carelessly splashed water on his face and ran his fingers through his hair. When he finally wiped his face with the towel, he was almost out of breath. Shit! He had never thought a girl's temper would make his hands tremble. And Reva... She wasn't the kind to get mad so easily.

Siddharth changed his t-shirt and walked out into the hall, hoping in his heart that her anger had subsided. But when he finally walked past the wall that curtained the drawing room from the bedroom corridor, Reva was no longer sitting on the sofa. For a split second Siddharth thought that Reva had left. However, she appeared from the kitchen carrying a tray with two cups of coffee. She looked calmer, with a palpable ease on her face.

Siddharth knew it would be wiser not to hatch the topic of her anger.

**

'How much love does it need to be satisfied?' Reva sat on a chair, overlooking the setting sun, with the fading glow illuminating her skin.

Siddharth walked across the room and sat in front of her. 'As much devotion as it needs to set yourself free.'

Reva didn't reply.

'Just be with me on this road,' he held her hand gently. 'Everything else will fall by the side.'

Reva leaned forward and touched his cheek. 'If only holding hands could take us across the street.'

Siddharth looked at her as she turned her glance at the restful sun, slowing sinking into a lull. The orange looked so pristine on her skin – as if it had diffused into her body. Siddharth could go on looking at her tirelessly. Endlessly. He could vividly recall the early morning in Manali, when he woke up to find Reva sleeping on the sofa, her locks of hair caressing her face. He could wake up every morning with her face in front of him.

'I am just too unsure of myself,' she looked at the horizon.

'Aren't we all?' He looked at her.

**

At eight, they left the house. The Friday evening streets were surprisingly empty as they drove to the Sahara Star. As they entered hand in hand through the door, they could hear Enrique's "Tonight I'm loving you" playing in The High Lounge while the crowd crooned along with it. Siddharth held her arm and took her to the middle of the club, as she giggled and pirouetted to take her position. The last time they had danced together at Hawaiian Shack, her agility on the floor had taken him by surprise. He was not a bad dancer either, but she was something else altogether. He held her waist and dragged her closer as the DJ changed the track and Britney Spears sang "Hold it against me".

The High Lounge is known for its exquisite crowd and that night was no exception. The gorgeous club boasted some of the prettiest *female faces in the city, but none equalled her beauty. Even in the all-covering sari, she looked so much more gorgeous than the fair damsels who flaunted their shapely bodies in knee length dresses or hot pants. 'Marry me,' he wanted to say. 'Leave everything else and just be with me all your life.' He really wanted to say it, but it wasn't the right time. He convinced himself that the apt moment would come soon. He had seen her throughout that day, fighting against her own conflicting emotions. Finally, she had decided to keep the troubles aside and come to the club with him. He didn't want to put her back in the same spot. She looked at him quizzically and smiled. She knew he was lost in his thoughts.*

'What are you thinking?' she said.

'Should I have a beer or stick to white rum,' he joked.

'Tough question,' she knew he was lying. 'That needs a serious thought.'

'What will you have?' Siddharth held her tighter.

'Can we eat something?' she said. 'I am really hungry.'

**

Anshuman Mehra sat in his office, going through the Suraksha presentation due for the next day. They had everything in place. He knew there was nothing wrong with what they had prepared. Even Bala Sir had approved of it. But there was something still missing. That one line, that one word – which would "wow" his clients! He sipped from the cup of ginger tea and pondered when his phone started ringing. "Reva" he immediately thought. Throughout the day, he had been wondering how to call her. What should he say if she called? But like most times, he hadn't succeeded in being the first one to call up and apologise. He picked up the phone and saw the display.

"Tahir Khan" the name flashed.

For a moment, Anshuman was startled. He didn't expect the superstar to call him up at this hour. He exhaled and answered the call.

'Hi, Tahir.'

'Good time to talk?' the actor spoke exuberantly on the other side of the connection.

'Sure, tell me.'

'I have something important to discuss,' Anshuman could hear Tahir take a drag of his cigarette. 'I am planning to make a movie to launch my elder brother's son – Shaukat.'

'Oh cool,' Anshuman sipped his tea.

'Yeah,' Tahir spoke. 'It's a great script – though a bit tricky to execute.'

'Okay,' Anshuman was clueless where the discussion was heading.

'See, the guy is taking his first step,' Tahir went on. 'It's very crucial that I give him a good start. A lot of what he does later will depend on this.'

'True.'

'He is a young chap and the script I have chosen is quirky in its own ways.'

'Okay.'

'I want someone with a mature head to take charge of the film.'

'Right.'

'You are not getting what I am saying, are you?' Tahir laughed.

'What?' Anshuman sounded confused.

'I want you to direct the film,' Tahir stopped and waited for Anshuman to react.

'What?' for a brief period, Anshuman was clueless about how to react. 'Are you serious? But I am not a filmmaker.'

'Come on,' Tahir coaxed. 'You have been through so many advertisements. You are brilliant at conceptualisation. And you will have technicians helping you out with the nitty-gritties.'

'Hmmm…' Anshuman wondered how to react. He knew there would be thousands who would give their lives to be on his end of the conversation. It wasn't that he had never contemplated directing *films, but it was all too sudden. On the other hand, this was too tempting an offer to turn down. And given Tahir Khan's reputation, Anshuman was sure that the man would have neither locked the script had he not found it excellent nor would he have approached Anshuman had he not found the latter worthy enough.*

'Sleep over it,' Tahir said with his usual equanimity. 'We can talk about it on Sunday.'

'Sure,' Anshuman smiled.

'So, are you watching the match tomorrow?'

**

Siddharth was three beers high when they finally left The High Lounge. She sat on the driver's seat while he settled next to her.

'Where shall we go?' she said as they drove out.

'How about away from everyone?' he looked at her.

Reva burst out laughing.

'That's the cheesiest thing you have said today,' she looked at him.

'Cheesiest thing I said today?' he feigned anger. 'That means I keep saying cheesy things every day, is it?'

'Well,' she lingered, 'almost.'

'What crap,' he turned childishly and looked out of the window.

'Shall I drive to your home?'

'How about,' Siddharth turned and looked longingly at her, 'away from everyone?'

This time, Reva didn't giggle. She stared at him for some time with a faint smile on her lips. She knew what he meant. She knew what he wanted to say when he was immersed in thoughts on the dance floor. Yet, she was thankful that he didn't say what he felt. It was good for them that way. It was better for everyone else that way.

'The Sea Link?'

**

She released the brake and gently pressed her stiletto on the accelerator. The speedometer moved from the 55 kmph mark to that of 70 as she firmly steered the black sedan through the dimly lit Worli Sea Face. The watch on her right arm showed the minute hand just overtaking the hour hand and moving towards four. The radio channel was playing one of her all time favourite songs – "Meri jaan... mujhe jaan na kaho meri jaan" – the legendary Geeta Dutt's last recorded song, picturised beautifully on the ethereal Tanuja and her father's favourite actor Sanjeev Kumar. The purple sari rolled down her arms as she pulled it over her shoulder, around the black blouse. Through the windshield, her eyes caught the deserted stretch of the Rajiv Gandhi Sea Link – lit up by fluorescent cable wires.

He was in the next seat, wearing a crimson shirt teamed with black trousers and black boots. There was something impregnable about the silence that had ruled their conversation through the last twelve hours, with unspoken pangs of grief relegated behind the facade of smiles. If only he didn't love her so much, maybe things would have been much simpler.

She downed the windows and a sudden gust of breeze filled the car. The day had been warm and the nation had been praying that, contrary to certain predictions, it wouldn't rain at the big event scheduled in a few hours' time.

'Eight years later, we are at the same spot,' one of the RJs said, 'will we repeat what we did eighteen years ago? Will Dhoni be the one to realise Sachin's incomplete dream?'

She turned the headlights on full blast and ran her fingers fondly through his curly hair. Such a baby, she wanted to say but decided against it. He looked up, smiled affectionately, held her arm and turned around.

'Leave my hand,' she giggled like a teenager. He always brought out this aspect of hers. 'I am driving, sweetheart.'

'You can drive with one hand,' Siddharth cajoled, 'this is my side pillow now.'

She laughed out, when a sudden shriek caught them by surprise. Almost in a flash, four cars zoomed past them. Filled with youngsters hooting and cat-calling at the other cars, they relentlessly chased each other, neglectful of the speed limit.

'Bastards,' Siddharth spoke from the adjacent seat.

'Come on,' Reva hated curse words, 'they are young guys. They are entitled to this much fun.'

He shook his head and looked outside the window. Reva held the steering wheel and took a left turn as the car cruised up the incline of the Sea Link. The three and a half mile bridge looked resplendent in the series of lights as Siddharth gazed at the serene Arabian Sea, with its faint ripples illuminated by streaks of golden and blue. It knows everything, he felt, the sea knows everything about all of us yet it is quiet. Is it a confidant or a secretive old man who doesn't share secrets with others? But then there are people who say that the sea returns everything – is it because the sea is vindictive or is it too generous to appropriate without donating in return?

'Hey,' she looked at him, 'what are you thinking?' Reva softly touched his cheek.

She knew what he had been pondering over – for not just that day, but the previous few weeks as well. Both of them knew what his reply would be. In a way, it was good that she had broached the topic. Some things have to come to an end, he thought, and maybe we should have thought of it earlier. Maybe they had; maybe they were just too naive to prognosticate the implications of the very feeling that they had sequestered behind the walls of formalities and conventions; or maybe they had just feigned ignorance of the same, expecting the reality to never beckon them out of their reverie. He was about to respond when a crashing sound alarmed them.

Reva promptly grabbed the steering wheel – her fists clenching into the cover, her eyes dilating in shock. Trying to overtake a rival, one of the cars carrying the youngsters banged into the divider. The driver seemed desperately attempting to rein his car but the SUV spun at an indomitable speed across the lane, and suddenly a young girl was thrown out of the right rear door.

'Look out,' he shrieked.

But it was too late. Their car was barely 200 metres away and the girl was scarily close to the wheels. Reva knew that even if she were to pull the brakes, the car would stop only after running over the girl. With all her might, she swerved the car. Siddharth shot up and held the wheels with her, as the SX4 screeched across the breadth of the bridge and crashed into the left railing; not being able to control the motion, it toppled rightwards.

Reva's head struck the horn and the sound permeated through the silence of the night as Siddharth struggled to open the seat-belt and put his hand under her blood-soaked eyes.

***

'I am sorry,' Anshuman finally brought himself to apologise. 'I shouldn't have behaved like that.'

Siddharth carried a plastic glass of cold coffee while Anshuman held a paper cup of masala tea. They had picked up the beverages and went out of the cafeteria. Anshuman casually leaned on the bonnet of his car while Siddharth sat on his wheelchair, as the two men conversed in the desolate car park.

'I can understand what you must be going through,' Siddharth replied, 'and to be frank, you had controlled yourself far more than I had expected you to. Maybe I would have reacted much more had I been in your place.'

Anshuman smiled.

'You know I felt afraid when I saw you in my room yesterday,' Siddharth confided. 'All the arrogance and sarcasm was only a projection to protect myself from your incisive sight and maybe your contempt. I knew that the only way I could fight it was to be strong, or at least pretend to be so.'

'You did a good job then,' Anshuman chuckled. 'Come to think of it, even my anger stemmed from my own sense of despondency rather than hatred for you. Making you feel guilty was just a way to salvage my own fractured ego that couldn't stomach the fact that Reva loves you.' Anshuman lit a cigarette and offered one to Sid. 'It took me some time to realize that there is no point getting angry with you. You got in because we had opened the door for you. I can't blame you to cover my faults.'

'So, you think you can forgive us?' Siddharth refused the cigarette.

'I don't know,' Anshuman recollected what the doctor had said. 'I need to give that a thought.'

**

The two men sat quietly in the driveway. Reva had been recovering but there was still no news as to how long it would take before she would regain consciousness. Dr Ahmed had given special instructions to allow Anshuman meet Reva as soon as she returned to senses. The last time Anshuman had checked it was five in the morning. Her health had stabilised and the nurses hoped that Reva would wake up pretty soon. It was an exceptionally quick recovery, one of the senior nurses said, especially after such a serious surgery.

'I can't compare my love to yours,' Siddharth felt unnerved by the renewed strength in Anshuman. 'But I do love her a lot.'

'I am sure,' Anshuman smiled. 'If Reva stepped out of her home for your love, then you must have loved her a lot. And it's better not to compare yours and mine. When you get married, a lot of things come into play besides the love factor. I know it from my experience.'

'She needs to take a call,' Siddharth gritted. 'She should be ready to make her decision.'

'Yeah,' Anshuman sighed, 'the sooner the better.'

'Doesn't that scare you?' Siddharth looked at Anshuman sceptically.

'I just don't feel I can lose anything anymore,' Anshuman shook his head. 'So, the sensation of fear has gone down. I don't know if I would be sad even if she decides to stay with you.' After a pause, he added, 'Are you?'

'Perhaps,' Siddharth inflated his eyes and controlled his tears. 'I am slowly failing to conceal the fear that has been creeping within me ever since I saw you yesterday.'

Anshuman sighed and walked up to the young man. As he patted Siddharth's shoulder, the photographer found himself clinging on to the arm. As Anshuman stood there silently, his nemesis cum closest empathiser burst into tears. Anshuman kept his other hand on Siddharth's head to comfort him. As much as he would hate to be in Siddharth's position, Anshuman knew that the man sitting on the wheelchair was someone who could easily give his own life for Reva. It took for a while for Siddharth to regain himself.

'You know what Reva would have said had you told her that she needs to take a call?' Anshuman joked.

'She would have said *yeah right*,' Siddharth smiled. Anshuman waited for a moment and then started laughing. Siddharth joined him in it.

*

'It's still dark,' Siddharth looked at the sky, 'almost six now!'

'The Mumbai sun is a late riser,' Anshuman winked. 'It loves the nightlife as much as the Mumbaikars do.'

'Perhaps that's what helps keeping their secrets in dark,' Siddharth smiled half-hearted.

Anshuman pursed his lips, 'No one knows this better than me.'

'You know wherein lies my biggest defeat,' Siddharth exhaled.

Anshuman looked at him.

'People will never try to put themselves in my shoes,' Siddharth looked at the sky blankly. 'I will always be on the wrong side. You will be justified if you get a divorce and hailed if you stay with her. But I will always be the unwelcome intruder. My love will never be legitimate, and I will be blamed for all that has gone wrong.'

'I don't blame you,' Anshuman crushed the cigarette butt under his shoe. 'Trust me.'

'You will, one day or the other,' Siddharth wiped his tears. 'You would think I am a keep or a parasite that ate into your marriage.'

'It doesn't make sense trying to think of all this right now,' Anshuman placed his hand on Siddharth's shoulder. 'We need to sit together and find a way out for all of us.'

'There can't be one way good for all three of us,' Siddharth looked back.

'I don't know about the good part,' Anshuman chuckled. 'I just know that there will be a way out.' He looked up and said. 'See, even the late rising sun agrees.'

Siddharth looked up at the sky. The sun was slowly glowing on them. Their night was slowly coming to an end. He looked at Anshuman and was about to say something when a nurse walked up to them and interrupted their conversation.

'Are you related to Ms Reva?' she looked at both of them.

'Yes,' Anshuman said anxiously as Siddharth turned the wheelchair to look at the nurse.

'Your wife is back to her senses,' she beamed. 'You can go and meet her now.'

Both men looked at each other...